THE
BLOOD
FLAG

HUS

Printed in the United States of America

First Printing, 2015

ISBN: 978-1-5046-6962-7

Blackstone Publishing
31 Mistletoe Rd.
Ashland, OR 97520

www.Downpour.com

For Colleen

The heart is deceitful above all

things, and desperately wicked:

who can know it?

—Jeremiah 17:9

PROLOGUE

I turned our rented Mercedes down Kunibertistraße in Recklinghausen and scanned the dimly lit buildings for numbers. There was no moon, and no traffic. The deserted one-way street had barely enough room to pass a parked car. It ran through the historic center of the city, between buildings that were hundreds of years old. My teenage children were growing restless when something caught my eye. A large group of people huddled directly ahead of us in the darkness fifty yards away. I slowed almost to a stop and looked in my rear-view mirror. Others were behind us. They walked up the street toward our car. People swarmed around our car heading toward the others. They wore black hoods, some in long cloaks, like monks; they passed us on both sides, blocking any escape.

Suddenly those in front of us were illuminated by fire. Torches. There were fifty, then a hundred, then two hundred or more carrying lit torches. We were the only car on the street. I put the Mercedes in reverse, waiting for a chance to slowly back out of whatever was developing. Michelle put her hand on my arm. "Look."

They started a slow ominous march. Their faces had caught her attention. They were pure white. Not skin white, mask white. White masks covered their faces with a small mouth forming not quite an "o" but not truly open. A look of menacing anonymity.

They marched straight toward us with a long sign held by those in front. The lettering looked like Old English but was German. On they came. They spread across the street. Their torches threw over-sized shadows on the ancient buildings.

They drew even with our car. My son leaned forward in the back seat to take a picture with his new digital camera I'd bought him for the trip. It was set to eliminate redeye, which resulted in a multi-flash picture of the front of the march.

They stopped. One pointed at me. I hesitated. I put the car in park. They came at us in complete silence. One ran directly at our car. I moved my hand to the door to make sure they were locked. He ran up to our car with his torch and put his gloved hand on the back window where Christopher was sitting.

"Dad," Chris said in a shaky voice.

"Don't look at him."

The man put his masked face a few inches from Chris's window and looked at all of us. He moved his hissing torch to the window and touched it against the glass. It blackened a spot on the glass. Two others moved toward our car.

He dragged the burning end of his torch to my window and waited for me to look at him. I wouldn't. He tapped the burning torch against my window, slowly. It was louder than I expected. I kept my hands on the steering wheel.

He suddenly struck the butt of his torch loudly on my window. I still wouldn't look at him, which angered him. He struck the window harder and harder with his torch, which threw sparks over the car. The window shattered. I covered my face with my arms as glass pieces covered my head. He punched the rest of the window in with his gloved fist and said something in a whisper in German. I didn't understand what he wanted, and then he turned his fingers, like starting a car. I took the keys out of the ignition and handed them to him.

"Kyle, no!" Michelle protested.

"We have no choice," I said.

He pressed the button on the remote to unlock the car. I jumped as the locks flew up on the doors, and he grabbed Chris's door and threw it open. "No way," I said, as I opened my door to climb out. He slammed my door against me and held it closed. Another man ran over and held my door shut. Two others on the sidewalk held the doors of my wife and daughter.

The first man opened Chris's door again, leaned in and stuck out his hand. "Camera," he said in English.

"Dad?"

"Give it to him!" Michelle responded.

I turned to see what was happening. He stared at Chris with the torch almost in the car. Emily, sitting on the other side of Chris, was crying. She slumped down in her seat.

Chris gave his camera to the man who took it and dropped it onto the pavement. He then stomped on it with his boot. He slammed Chris's door closed, pressed the door lock button on the keys, then flung the keys on top of the building next to our car. He turned and joined the march. As he turned away, I saw the Nazi swastika armband over the sleeve of his long black cloak.

CHAPTER ONE

I grew up in a house with a Nazi flag hanging in the basement. It had been there since before I could walk, in my father's den, a book-lined room with a dehumidifier running all summer. My father was an intellectual, a history professor at a large state university in the Midwest. But he had also been an army infantry officer in World War II. He went ashore at Normandy in July of 1944, and fought through the Battle of the Bulge to Germany and to the end of the war.

One day it occurred to me to ask him where he'd gotten the flag. He said a sergeant in his battalion pulled it down from the city hall when they took a German town in the war. April 1, 1945. Recklinghausen, Germany.

My father learned he had been selected to receive the *Légion d'Honneur,* the Legion of Honor, and they wanted him to come to France to receive the award and attend the anniversary of D-Day. I knew I had to go with him. Seeing him receive the award in the American cemetery on the cliffs of Normandy was humbling.

World War II had been a constant presence in my youth, from watching the *Combat* TV series to war movies like *Sink the Bismark, Patton,* and *The Dirty Dozen.* They all helped confirm the story I knew, that it was the good guys against evil, and the good guys won. It was the perfect story that you could hear a hundred times, because you knew it would always turn out right. No matter what part of it you read about or examined, no matter how dark or twisted a particular part of the story was, no matter how haunting or scary, it all came out right in the end. And the present given to my generation from my father's was the gift of defeating the evil of Nazism.

After the celebration in Normandy, I took my family on a short driving tour of Europe, and the one place I insisted on seeing was Recklinghausen. I had to see where my father's flag had come from.

It was there we had encountered the neo-Nazis with their masks and torches. We went to a few other places in Germany, but I didn't enjoy the trip after Recklinghausen. On the flight back, chasing the sun westward and never seeing darkness or sleeping, I had a lot of time to think. I thought about the flag in my father's den flying over the city hall at Recklinghausen. I thought about the men who had defeated Nazism in the forties. And I thought again of my father.

His division was made up mostly of Midwesterners from Kansas and Missouri, with a few others like him thrown in from Indiana. When my father got to France in July of 1944, the battle line in Normandy was a few miles inland. His division was sent to take a city in Normandy called St. Lô. It was a terrible, bloody battle; and there began the massive casualties that decimated his battalion. They fought the Germans hammer and tong. From village to village and town to town, across rivers all the way to the Elbe River and to the end of the war. Of all of the officers in his battalion who went ashore at Normandy and fought to the end of the war, he was the only one who wasn't killed or wounded.

But as I sat on the airplane on the way home, I was hit by the stark awareness that the poisonous philosophy that had grown to full bloom under Hitler's Third Reich still lived. Some of its original advocates were still living, and now there were new advocates in Germany and elsewhere. I lay my head back on my seat and looked at my sleeping family.

They were exhausted from the trip and the way it had ended. They hadn't recovered, and truthfully neither had I. Unable to sleep, the images of those neo-Nazis in Recklinghausen haunted me. I decided to make some discrete inquiries when I went back to work at my job as a special agent of the FBI in the J. Edgar Hoover building in Washington, D.C.

CHAPTER TWO

Ever since 9/11, I'd been tracking terrorists. Recently I'd been transferred to headquarters at the J. Edgar Hoover building in D.C.; I was a fish out of water. The bureau had only recently started bringing special agents into headquarters and assigning us to various groups or taskforces. Until recently, and still primarily, those groups were populated with analysts. They didn't know what to do with us. We weren't assigned any specific roles, so we created our own jobs. But in doing my self-created job I'd seen how terrorists work, and how they measure their success by how dramatic and violent their actions are. And I longed to smash them.

I booted up my computer in my windowless office where I could access intelligence files on various people who were intent on destroying America. While I waited to start analyzing all the intelligence that had come in in my absence, my mind drifted to Recklinghausen again.

I had known there were neo-Nazi groups in various places. But I'd always thought they were part of the lunatic fringe. But now it was different. I started to take them seriously.

I searched the Internet for Nazis known to be operating in Germany, as well as those elsewhere of the same mind but trying to avoid the stigma of "Nazism" by calling themselves skinheads or something else. I found articles about a march in Dresden. Ten thousand skinheads turned out to protest the anniversary of the allied fire-bombing of Dresden. The numbers had grown every year and now they topped ten thousand people. Neo-Nazis, skinheads, whatever they called themselves, were alive and well, and the racism and anti-Semitism and hate and poison that colored the river in which they stood was still a force. I found neo-Nazi groups in other countries, like the Golden Dawn in Greece, or the *Bloed, Bodem, Eer en Trouw*—Blood, Soil, Honor, and Loyalty—in Belgium.

I got up to get more coffee. As I finished pouring, Alex Walsh came in. Her actual name was Alexandra, but everyone called her Alex. I worked closely with her in counterterrorism. She was a pistol. She livened up whatever room she was in. She was full of spunk and humor. She was in her thirties and had come to the FBI because of her degree in International Affairs and her fluent Arabic. She had her usual eager look as she reached for her cup. "Morning, Kyle." She wore black slacks, a tan sweater with a large drooping neck, and shoes with two-inch heels. She kept her hair fairly short.

"Morning. How's it going?"

"Excellent. How was your trip?"

I paused for a minute. "The ceremony was unbelievable. Absolutely spectacular. I got to meet Tom Hanks—you get that picture I sent?"

"I thought it was a joke."

"That was right after the ceremony in a garden just behind *Les Invalides*. Talked to him for quite a while. Nicest guy you can imagine."

"Why was he there?"

"Bunch of his guys from *Band of Brothers* got the Legion of Honor along with my father. The real guys, not the actors."

"That's just unbelievable. Was he proud?"

"My dad?"

"Yeah."

"Yeah. He bought a brand new army colonel's uniform, which was his rank when he retired in the reserves. It fit him like a glove, and he looked like he was still on active duty. What a stud."

She stirred milk into her coffee. "I want to see more pictures when you have a chance."

"Absolutely."

"How was the rest of your trip?"

"Paris was great. And it was truly unbelievable to show my kids a couple of places where my father fought, like Belgium where the Battle of the Bulge was. Then we went to Germany. We ended up in a town called Recklinghausen."

"How was it?"

"The city was great, but it left me with a bad taste in my mouth."

She stopped stirring and turned to look at my face. "What happened?"

I told her the whole story.

"Wow. You just don't think things like that are still possible."

"Of course in my obsessive way I've been reading up on neo-Nazism ever since. That's all I've done this morning."

She frowned. "You're *supposed* to be tracing that cell in New York."

"Can't."

"Have to. Refocus."

I shook my head as I started to leave the coffee room. "Can't. I sat there in that American cemetery at Normandy, with thousands and thousands of dead Americans lying in the ground next to me, listening to President Obama talking about the sacrifices made to defeat Nazism. But it's still alive. There's unfinished business out there."

"Well, there's nothing you can do about it."

"Maybe."

She studied me, clearly wondering whether I was going to be able to move on. "Well," she said as an afterthought. "You could talk to Karl."

"Karl who?"

"Matthews. Up on the sixth floor. Domestic terrorism. See if he has any thoughts."

"You know him?"

"Met him a couple of times. He's kind of odd—like that distinguishes him in this building—but he seems to know what he's talking about."

I poured my coffee into the sink, put my mug in the cupboard, and said, "I think I'll go see him right now."

* * *

It took me a few minutes, but I finally found Karl. He had a fairly roomy but windowless office. His door was open. I knocked on it. He looked up from his desk. "Yeah?"

"Hey, do you have a minute?"

"What for?"

"I wanted to talk to you about what you do."

He seemed annoyed, looked at his computer, looked back at the materials on his desk, looked at the clock, and finally said in a tone that sounded like capitulation, "I don't get many visitors. What do you do?"

I stepped inside his office and sat in the office chair across from him. "Counterterrorism." I extended my hand. "Kyle Morrissey."

"Oh yeah. I've heard of you. The *Top Gun* guy. Tom Cruise."

"Well more like Goose, but yeah, that's me."

"You're the ones who get the visitors. I just sit up here reading about idiots."

"Oh I get to read a lot about idiots too."

"Yeah, but your idiots are international idiots, the targets in the continuing war on terror."

He had put his hands up to put quotations around the "continuing war on terror." As if it didn't really exist, or was imaginary, or was overblown. Not my feeling at all, but I didn't want to start on that topic. "So, Alex Walsh told me that you keep track of neo-Nazis."

"Yup. Them and all the other self-appointed ethnic cleansers of our great country."

"Skinheads?"

"Sure."

"Klan?"

"Yeah, but they're not much of a player right now. They're sort of peripheral. Still out there, just not very engaged. The white sheet thing is sort of old news. But why do you care? You can read about most of this online."

I nodded slowly, not sure how to broach the subject with him. "I just got back from Europe. After . . . well, I took my family on vacation to Germany. Something happened that really pissed me off." I told him the whole story about the march. "What do you make of that?"

He shrugged. "That surprises you? That there are still Nazis in Germany?"

"Yeah. It did. I thought we defeated Nazism."

"We did, but we didn't kill them *all*. The only ones who got put on trial were the ones who committed war crimes, and not even all of them, just the ones involved in the Holocaust, the really bad guys. And most of them only served a few years jail time and were released back into Germany. There were millions of others, some were true believers then and I'm sure still are. Doesn't surprise me at all that there are still some guys out there."

"You think they're mostly just old guys from World War II?"

"Not at all. Those guys have continued to peddle their Kool-Aid. They'll tell anybody who will listen that Germany has never been as organized and running as well as it did during Hitler's years before the war. That's what they claim to want to return to. Hitlerism without the war."

"Isn't that illegal in Germany?"

He chuckled and shook his head, "Sure, if they call themselves Nazis or start throwing around the swastika. They're usually smart enough not to do that. They call themselves something else; but when they get into the room where no one is there other than those they've known for twenty years, then the real stuff comes out. No, they're still there they're still active. It's real."

"The marchers wore swastikas."

"Pretty bold for Germany. That's why they wore masks, no doubt."

I picked up the small blue stress ball that was sitting on his desk and began playing with it. It was from a local pizza restaurant and had their phone number on it. I squeezed it a few times as I thought about what he had said. I didn't say anything.

He finally asked. "Is that it?"

"No," I answered. "Tell me whether this is a big problem or just a side show we don't have to worry about."

"In Germany?"

"No, everywhere. In the U.S., Germany, wherever."

He sat forward and leaned his elbows on the desk. "It's a big problem and it's getting bigger. Here and elsewhere. It's like a poison. It infects almost every society that it touches."

"And that's what you're working on? That's what you're doing?"

"Here in the U.S. Yeah. I'm trying. It's a tough nut."

"What's so tough about it?"

"Well, mostly the First Amendment. In the U.S. these assholes can say anything they want as long as it doesn't call for the violent overthrow of the United States, or incite riots or conspire to commit crimes. But what's it to you? Just because you encountered these guys in Germany, now it's your thing?"

I stood up to leave. I shrugged. "It just got to me."

He sat back and scratched his gray hair. "We can do some things about it, but we can't make them think differently."

"But you said it's getting worse."

"It is."

I looked out into the hallway and thought. I looked back at him. "Then we've got to do more. This is bullshit."

He stood and tucked his shirt into his overly tight belt. "If you're that interested, then you better come with me."

"For what?"

"There's somebody I want you to meet."

* * *

We pulled out of the parking garage in his Honda Accord. "Where we going?"

"To meet somebody."

"Who?"

"You wondered what we were doing about all these neo-Nazis. Well, maybe you should meet one. He's one of our best CIs."

This was unusual, to say the least. We didn't get to meet other agents' confidential informants unless we were working the program. But if he was going to let me meet him, I wasn't about to let the opportunity pass.

We drove away from D.C. down State Route 29 into rural Virginia and finally entered Warrenton. We parked on Main Street and went into the Southern Café. Karl picked a booth toward the back. He glanced at his watch and said, "He won't be here for another fifteen minutes."

The waitress came over and brought us coffee, even though we hadn't asked for any.

"Who are we waiting for?"

"You'll know as soon as he steps into the restaurant. I promise," he said cryptically as he sipped his black coffee.

I took in everything in the café. It was right out of an *American History* magazine: red vinyl booths with hard white tables, and a long counter flanked by silver pedestal stools with red vinyl seats. It was mostly clean, but I noticed some dead flies in the corners of the large front windows. It was eleven o'clock. The place smelled of bacon and toast. We sat awkwardly on the same side of the booth facing the front door. The diner held about sixty people, but there were no more than fifteen people there at the time. The coffee was good and fresh. The waitress was quick to recognize we didn't seem particularly hungry, but felt obligated to give us menus. We likewise felt obligated to order, but told her we would wait until our other friend arrived.

Finally the door opened and a man walked in slowly. I felt Karl's elbow touch mine as he looked at his coffee.

I looked up and tried not to show my surprise. I'm not sure what I expected, but this wasn't it. He was about my height, five foot ten inches, but had to outweigh me by fifty pounds. He was maybe two thirty or two forty. I'm told I can look intimidating. But this guy was in a different league.

He was built like a weight lifter with the neck of a bull. His buzzed head accentuated his muscular build and ferocious look; yet nothing about his appearance had the impact of his tattoos: an iron cross on his throat and two tilted swastikas on either side of his neck. He was wearing a white T-shirt, just a plain white T-shirt with a round neck. The tattoos were dark and bold and incredibly aggressive. His shoulders had tattoos that you could see through the white material of his T-shirt but not enough to identify them.

The tattoos extended down his arms, outside the sleeve of his T-shirt down to his wrists. As he walked with his hands in his pockets I couldn't make out what the tattoos were on his arms. I tried not to stare. He was looking me right in the eye, which made it difficult to do much more surveying of him. He was the most intimidating person I had ever seen, and I've seen a lot of intimidating people. He looked like he could kill you in one motion and would be more than happy to if you gave him a reason.

He slid into the booth across from me. He glanced at Karl, and then looked back at me. The waitress put a mug of coffee in front of him, which he took in his hand. I noticed that there were letters tattooed on the knuckles of his right hand. On the third knuckle of his ring finger was the capital letter *H*, and on his middle finger knuckle was the letter *I*, and on his first finger was the letter *T*. When he made a fist you could see *HIT* on his right hand. Nice. It's probably what people saw right before he smashed them in the face.

He continued to look at me as I stared at his knuckles. "Who the hell are you?"

Karl intervened. "This is Kyle Morrissey. He's with the Bureau."

He nodded and said intensely, "I told you. I don't want to talk to anybody except you."

"Anything you can say to me you can say to him."

The man looked at Karl. "Why him?"

"He had a recent experience that was unsettling. He wants to know what can be done."

He looked back at me, bored. "What experience?"

I extended my hand to shake his. "It's nice to meet you."

He looked at my hand and did not shake it. "What experience?"

I lowered my hand. "What's your name?"

He stared at me like he was trying to bore a hole through me. He had very dark blue eyes, the color of an ocean. His eyebrows were blonde. Finally, he said, "Jedediah."

"Nice to meet you, Jedediah. What's your last name?"

"What's it to you?"

"I just think it's polite."

"What makes you think I'm polite?"

I leaned forward slightly. "Nothing."

"Thom. And that's spelled *T-h-o-m*. Pronounced 'Tom.'"

"Interesting. Where are you from, Jedediah?"

"You've got a lot of questions. Where are you from?"

"Midwest, originally."

"So. You're a Yankee?" His southern accent was very noticeable. He truly seemed offended that I was from the North.

"That bother you?"

"Just means you couldn't be a member."

"Of what?"

"Don't worry about it."

"I still would love to know where you're from."

"Irmo."

"Where's that?"

"South Carolina."

He pronounced it *Sath Kaylina*. "What part of the state?"

"Near Columbia." *Klumbya* with a barely perceptible "ah" at the end of it. More implicit than overt. *Klumb*. He went on, "So what's your story?"

I began telling him about my experience in Recklinghausen. He watched me carefully, holding me in his stare. I told him about Normandy, about the Legion of Honor, and my father's flag in the basement. And I told him about the neo-Nazi group marching in black hoods with white masks and Nazi armbands.

He asked, "That bothered you?"

"Yeah. Having just been to Normandy it stunned me that there are still neo-Nazis around ready to cause more problems."

He leaned back slightly and played with his coffee cup. I then could see the tattoo marks on his first, second, and third knuckles of his left hand. *L-E-R*. Ah. When he put his two fists out together his hands spelled *HITLER*. He looked at me with a look that I couldn't quite identify. Something between pity and disgust. He said, "So this was news to you? That there were still Nazis around?"

"I was surprised that they were so overt about it."

He nodded slowly and stared down at his cup.

I looked at him and looked back at Karl, then looked at him again. "So what can we do about it?"

"Do about what?"

"Nazism. Neo-Nazis. How do we shut them down?"

Jedediah sat up taller and rested his massive arms on the table. He looked like an MMA fighter. I found myself studying the tattoos to try to make sense of them. I looked back at his face. He finally said, "You can't. There are a million neo-Nazi groups in this country alone. Some of them are run by idiots. Some of them are run by men who are smarter than you are. I know you don't think that's true, but it is. Smart in a twisted genius sort of way. They don't talk to each other that much, sometimes they hate each other, and there are rivalries, conflicts, and attempts to undermine each other. They think a lot of the same things, but they aren't united. So even if you took out two or three groups, it wouldn't have any effect on the others. They'd probably be glad. Like rival gangs. Everybody wants to be the big-ass neo-Nazi group in the country with a hundred thousand followers; the group that marches right down on the capital one day wearing black shirts and swastikas. But until somebody gets those numbers, until they can dwarf all the others, you can't take them all out at once. You have to do it one at a time. And it's not easy. You have to catch them committing a crime. First Amendment protects almost everything they say in the U.S., so it turns into criminal investigations, which is pretty tough because they don't act like most gangs. They don't sell crack or run prostitutes. They think that's all evil. They are all about being tough, wearing steel-toe boots, strutting around, spouting slogans, and attacking people of other races and religions. And waiting for the great race war that is always in the future."

"We've got to be able to do something."

"We are doing something. That's why I'm here. What I don't get is why *you're* here."

"Because I want to be a part of it. I want to help. I want to take them down."

"Who?"

Karl interjected, "Look Kyle, Jedediah and I are here to talk about what he has learned. This is what we're trying to do. We're trying to take down some organizations inside the U.S., and he's helping us. So why don't we start talking about that and then maybe we can get back to some other ideas. Okay?"

I nodded, sat back, and then drank my cooling coffee. I looked for the waitress to refill it. She saw me looking and came over with the pot.

Karl said to Jedediah, "Tell Kyle about your group."

He nodded. "I am the Vice President of the Southern Volk. Spelled V-o-l-k, but pronounced "folk," of course, because it's a German word. So the Southern Volk is an openly neo-Nazi organization. We're sort of new, but we're trying to unify as many of the other neo-Nazi groups as we can in the South. We're not just in the South, but we have Southern roots, and play on the Confederacy. A lot of Southern boys who spout phrases like, "The South shall rise again!" are pretty easy prey. It's not hard to pull them over. They all want to belong to something. They all want to defend some right that they think is being trampled on by somebody. Then, once you get them in, getting them to buy off on even some of our crazier stuff isn't that tough. A lot of them aren't very well educated, and they want to be in a gang without being in a gang. They're not intellectuals. They want to be tough guys, and be feared. And that requires a group."

"You're pretty intimidating yourself."

"True."

"I wouldn't want to mess with you, even if I had a gun."

"You do have a gun. And you still don't want to mess with me. I can see it in your eyes."

"You sound like you still buy this stuff."

He looked at me with a gaze I hadn't seen and said nothing.

I continued. "Tell me how you got here today."

Karl intervened, "Another time. Jedediah has something he wants to tell me."

I nodded, sat back, and remained quiet.

Karl said to Jedediah, "So what's up?"

Jedediah got an animated look on his face. He lowered his voice. "I still don't know this guy," he said pointing at me. "You I trust. Him, I don't."

"Well, he can wait in the car if you want."

Jedediah considered.

I didn't want to miss this. I said, "I've run dozens of CIs. Never had a problem with any of them. You have my word I won't do anything without Karl's approval and involvement."

He sat silently, drank his coffee, and looked at Karl. "We got a visit."

Karl asked, "From who?"

He moved his eyes from Karl to me and back. "We don't want anything to do with other groups. You know that. If they screw up, we don't want them to tar us. Nobody's as pure as we are. But there's been a movement over the past couple of years to unify. The world-wide black shirts of the twenty-first century."

"You mean brown shirts?" I said.

Jedediah regarded me with disdain. "Not the SA, the *SS*." He looked toward Karl, "Last week we got a visit from a German. Says he's only visiting three groups. The Aryan Nation, the Southern Volk, and the National Socialist Movement."

Karl asked, "What did he want?"

Jedediah shook his head. "One of the most amazing guys I've ever met. Speaks English perfectly, slight German accent, not the usual type. More like a politician. But man is he a true believer. And rich. Apparently, he's well known in Germany. But this guy—"

"Got a name?" Karl asked.

"Yeah. Rolf Eidhalt. Says he owns a castle. And has one goal, the unification of all the neo-Nazi movements in the entire *world*. Not just about Germany, it's about all of Western Europe and the British Commonwealth, Canada, Australia, New Zealand, Russia, everywhere the population is predominantly white. And establishing the Aryan world against the rise of Islam, brown people, immigrants, and Jews. This guy is as serious as a heart attack, but the thing is, he's no muscle head. He's not a stick swinging kind of a guy. He's not out there just to break windows. He's out there to make political change using *us*. He wants to unify us, get us all to sign off on his manifesto, all wearing the same things . . . and when the day comes, then the day *really* comes."

I sat forward slightly, fascinated. "Who is he? How does he have any authority to meet with groups in the United States? How does anybody know about him?"

"Oh everybody knows about him in my world. Two years ago he bought that castle in southern Germany and had it refurbished. Been using it as a training base for neo-Nazi groups. Physical training, sure, but he's really talking about dogma, getting people on the same page about what we think and what we want. And if he gets everybody to agree, he can theoretically unite all the neo-Nazi groups in the world under his direction. And he's only talking to long-established people. Nobody who could rat him out."

I said, "Except for you."

"Except for me."

Karl asked, "How does he propose to do this? How does he propose to unite everybody?"

Jedediah took a deep drink from his water glass. "First, he said 'read *Mein Kampf*.' Second, we have to read and agree to the manifesto. It's—"

Karl interjected, "Do you have a copy of the manifesto?"

"No, not yet. He's going to email it to us."

I was surprised. "Email? That's pretty traceable."

"Not the way he does it."

"Go on," I said.

"Okay, read *Mein Kampf*, sign off on the manifesto, and last is we have to authenticate."

"What does that mean?"

He had a German word for it. I can't remember what it was. I wrote it down because I'd never heard it before."

"Do you speak German?"

"Self-taught."

"How?"

"When I first joined the Southern Volk, the leader said that the people who would rise to the top would be those who could read *Mein Kampf* in German. The hardest part of that is finding a copy in German. It has been illegal in Germany for decades. It's difficult to find, but it can be done. Everything's on the Internet, just a little pricey sometimes. Then you have to learn enough German to read it. The two of us who actually tried it, and found copies, basically just read through it with a German dictionary. And, of course, I had an English copy right next to it that I read at the same time so it wasn't that tough. And copies in English are easy to come by. You can find them in any used bookstore for about two bucks."

Karl pushed, "So what was the German word?"

"Can't remember. I just remember that it basically meant we had to authenticate."

"What did he mean by it?"

"Prove ourselves."

"How?"

"He didn't say."

"Well, what did you take it to mean?"

"Something big, something dramatic. Something that will show him that *we* are the future of the movement in the United States."

Karl looked at me and thought for a moment. "So he wants you to do something that will show your movement is one of the future leaders."

"Yeah. And it's not just do it 'someday.' Has to be before November. That's when he's having his meeting of all the world's Nazi leaders. And those who are chosen, that have authenticated, will be there. In Germany, at his castle."

Karl and I noted the date and thought nothing of it. Karl asked, "So what's your plan?"

"Don't know. That's one of the reasons I wanted to talk to you. We're not going to blow up a Federal building or anything. We're not ready to go to prison for something stupid."

"That what he wants? Some dramatic violent event?"

"No. He said that would be the worst thing we could do. He doesn't want us killing a bunch of people. He wants creativity. Something that will 'demonstrate our validity.' And if we don't get it done in time, we won't get invited."

Karl asked, "So what's your plan?"

He shrugged his massive shoulders. "Don't know. Thought maybe y'all could help me. But I'll get there one way or another. At the beginning of the Fourth Reich, according to him."

"What does that mean?" I asked.

"White countries unite, throw out the non-white occupants, stop color and Jew and Muslim immigration, and finish the job that was started in the forties."

I couldn't believe my ears. "All this turns on the neo-Nazi groups 'authenticating' and then meeting with him?"

"Yes."

Not only was this movement bigger than I thought, it was the opportunity I wanted. "When do you have to let him know?" I asked.

"We show him by doing."

He handed Karl a flash drive. "You want to see him? Here he is. We record everything."

CHAPTER THREE

As Karl and I drove back to D.C. my mind turned in a thousand directions. As we crossed the river I said, "You going to help Jedediah come up with something?"

He thought for a minute, perturbed. "First we have to figure out who this Eidhalt guy is. I have to talk to our friends over at the BKA." The Bundeskriminalamt.

I asked, "Think anything will come of it?"

"If this German guy is serious, could be a big problem."

"You haven't heard of him before?"

Karl got the implication. He pretended to watch the traffic before responding. "We've got the number two guy in the whole Southern Volk, the second largest neo-Nazi group in the country, so I guess we're making some progress. But if you mean do we have a plan on how to take advantage of this, not yet. I just heard about it when you did, so give me some time."

"I've got some extra time. My counterterrorism stuff takes up most of my day, but I could dedicate a few hours to this, after hours."

"You don't know anything about it. It'd be like me coming to work for you—you'd spend all your time telling me what was what. I wouldn't contribute."

"That a no?"

"I don't need your help."

"What if I get permission?"

"From your boss? I don't care what he says. We've got enough people. What we don't have is a plan. And that's my job. If you come up with something brilliant though, let me know."

I thought for a minute. "Can I contact Jedediah directly?"

"Hell no. Stay out of it. Just keep on protecting us from the terrorists."

I almost said lots of things but held my tongue. "Interesting guy, Jedediah."

Karl relaxed. "One of a kind."

We pulled into the parking garage and got out of the car. "He's the key to the whole Germany thing," I said.

Karl started walking, then turned. "You want to help? Here. Check out the German guy." He tossed me the flash drive and walked away.

* * *

When I got back to my office I put the flash drive in my USB port. There were several video files, not just one. They were in chronological order.

I clicked on the first file and it opened in a video window. It was from a camera attached to someone, like a GoPro on a helmet or a chest strap. The video was crystal clear even though it had been shot at night. The only light was from the rear of a store where a single glass door opened onto a parking lot in the back of a strip mall. There were several men behind the camera talking in low, bored tones, as if waiting for something.

One asked, "What the hell is halal anyway?"

"It's like kosher, but for ragheads."

The others snickered. "Figures," one said. "You got this guy's picture?"

"Yeah, but don't need it. He's the only one left in the store."

Another added, "Anyone in there is fair game."

"Shit yeah," one replied laughing. "You sure he won't have a gun?"

"Let him pull a damned gun. He'll yell and scream and then I'll just shoot him in the face. You think he's ever shot anyone? He'll wet his pants. He won't have the balls to shoot first."

The lights of the store went out. "Here he comes!" one whispered.

The camera moved, and I could see several men. At least six, probably eight, all dressed in black, with gloves and cotton masks made of Confederate flags. They moved toward the lone car behind the store. The young man headed toward the car had his head down and was unaware of the approaching men.

The camera was pointed directly at him. He put the store keys in his pocket and searched for his car keys. He found them and took them out.

Just as he reached to open the door one of the men to the left of the camera spoke. "Hey, raghead!" he said.

The man turned and his face blanched. He said nothing.

"What the hell are you doing out here?"

"Nothing. Going home," he said, his voice quavering. He spoke with a slight accent.

"You're not American. Where are you from?"

"I am a citizen. I got citizenship last year."

They laughed. "I don't care what our corrupt multicultural shithead government says. You're not from here! I asked you a *question*! Where are you from?"

"Iraq. I was born in Iraq."

"Well you should go back there, raghead," he said closing the distance. "Take all your Muslim shit and go back there. We don't need your bullshit Arab kosher grocery stores. We're going to burn it down."

His back was to his old Honda Civic. The men formed a semi-circle in front of him. The camera was in the middle. They moved slowly toward him. "No! Please. It is my business. It supports my family!" he begged, near panic.

"That's the whole point, asshole! We don't *want* your family to be supported. We want you to die of starvation! We want you to leave and go home!"

"Please," he pleaded, "let me go home. I don't want any trouble."

"Well you've already got it." One of the men punched him in the mouth with surprising force. His head jerked back as his front teeth broke and his lips split. He put his hand up to block further punches but it was of no use. Another struck him in the nose, breaking it. Blood gushed over his mouth and onto his shirt. Another blow, then another, as the men closed in on him, swinging madly, waiting their turns, reaching over others to hit him. "No! Stop!" he cried, covering his face with his arms, trying to think of any way to make it stop.

A hand flashed in from off screen and went by his head. A blackjack. He slumped against the door of the car and slid to the ground, nearly unconscious. The men started kicking him with their boots. Some kicked him in the head, but most kicked him in his ribs and his back. One was intent on stomping on his feet and ankles, then kicking the end of his shoes, trying to break his toes. The man made no protests as he was kicked again and again. Blood ran down his face onto the pavement and he went still.

"Enough! Get the bottles!"

Two of them ran to the bushes and retrieved Molotov cocktails. They inverted them to moisten the rag stoppers, then lit them with a Zippo lighter that had a skull and crossbones on it. They ran over to the glass door of the halal grocery, and threw two bottles through the glass. The alarm went off as the bottles smashed onto the floor spilling their gasoline and setting the small grocery store on fire.

"Let's get out of here!" the primary voice yelled. They all ran, and the video went dead.

I sat back. My heart was pounding. Holy shit. Sometimes I'd see a security footage that had recorded a crime, but never a high-quality video by the perpetrator. I took a deep breath. Multiple felonies right on the video. Jedediah gave us enough to convict all of the men on the video. All he needed to do was identify who was there.

I clicked on the rest of the videos in sequence. One was a nighttime attack on an Islamic charity office, also in a strip mall. I couldn't tell where it was. Numerous men broke through the glass door, and while the alarm howled, they took all the computers and all the papers from the office. They were out and gone in less than three minutes. Long before any law enforcement could possibly get there. In another they sprayed graffiti on a mosque and removed the doors by force. They took the doors with them and left the building open. Then another halal grocer, and the last was an immigrant camp. They ran through the tents and small buildings in the middle of the night, dropping road flairs and pulling everything down as they terrorized the people by firing handguns into the air.

Finally, I opened the file with Eidhalt. It contained their entire meeting. I studied him, his posture, his voice, his presence, everything. He wore a black sport coat with a white dress shirt and dark pants. His hair was combed perfectly, and he gave the impression of someone who was in complete control and got what he wanted. He spoke excellent English, and told Jedediah and Brunnig, the president of the Southern Volk, about the meeting in Germany. He made very clear that their invitation to the meeting was conditional. They had to distinguish themselves from the other neo-Nazi groups to make it to Germany. They declared their understanding and enthusiasm. Eidhalt had their undivided attention. He was clearly accustomed to this reaction. Jedediah and Brunnig were not accustomed to yielding. But yielding they were. And then Eidhalt described his plan for Germany.

* * *

The next Monday I went to see Karl again. "Let's go see your boss," I said. "I've decided to work with Jedediah."

"Just like that?" He took off his reading glasses. Did you not hear what I said last time you were here? I don't need your help."

"I understand that. I'll stay out of your way. I want to do something on my own."

"Like what?" he asked sharply.

"Not sure. I want to work with him and see where it goes."

"You can't have two agents handling the same CI. He'll get confused."

"No confusion," I promised. "I'll check everything with you."

"Not interested."

"It could take some of the burden off you. If I come up with a plan to get them 'authenticated' with Eidhalt, you could direct your attention to other things." That got his attention.

"You'd have to run everything by me."

"Guaranteed."

"What was on that drive?"

"Multiple felonies, assaults, robbery, arson, you name it. And the meeting with Eidhalt. Just like he said." I stood. "Can we go see your boss now?"

He got up reluctantly and followed me. On the way he muttered that Murphy wasn't a confrontation kind of guy, that I should have submitted an EC, an electronic communication, that I should have made an appointment, that this put Karl in an awkward position, and that he didn't even know what my plan was. I said nothing.

We got out of the elevator and walked down the dingy hallway to Ralph Murphy's office. I looked up to see the familiar water stains on the ceiling. I should have gone to my boss first, but at this point I just wanted to get this done. We turned into Murphy's office and spoke with his secretary.

Karl said, "Is he available?"

She looked up at him with puzzlement. "Is he expecting you?"

"No. A proposal. Short fuse."

"He's meeting with Debra Turner right now. They'll be done in a minute though, and then he's heading off to lunch. Maybe you can catch him right before he leaves."

Karl nodded and put his hands in his pockets. "We'll just wait here."

Karl and I stood awkwardly by the secretary's desk as we waited for the door to open. I looked at my watch. It was already twelve thirty. After ten more minutes, the door opened.

Turner walked out, and Murphy looked at Karl with some surprise. "What's this?"

"Sorry, Special Agent Morrissey here wanted to talk to you about something. About joining our group temporarily."

Murphy looked at me with surprise. "What? A transfer? Where are you now?"

"Counterterrorism."

"Why would you want to transfer?"

"It's a bit of a long story. And it's not really a transfer."

"I don't have time for a long story. Have you talked to your boss about it?"

"No, I came straight to you."

"That's not the proper chain of command."

"I know, I wanted to see if you thought it might work, then if so, I'd go ask her. I didn't want to raise it if there was no chance of actually doing it."

"That's bass-ackwards."

"Probably right. I'd like a temporary transfer. There's going to be a meeting in Germany of all the neo-Nazi groups around the world."

"What? What are you talking about?"

Karl intervened. "We met with our CI last week. There's a lot that's starting to happen. This could be a show."

"How could he help?" he asked indicating me.

"He thinks he has an idea. The Southern Volk have to show this rich German guy that they're the real players, the ones that need to be dealt with in the United States."

"I'm not following this." He looked at me. "You go talk to your boss. See if she's willing to let you go for a couple months. If she says yes, we'll talk." Being done with me, he said to his secretary, "I'll be at lunch."

He walked out and left us standing in his entry area.

Karl still had his hands in his pockets. "Hope that's what you wanted. Wasn't a no."

"Let's go see Young."

Karl rolled his eyes. "You're just determined, aren't you?"

"Yes."

"Let me know how it goes. I sure don't need to see her."

"Nope. You come with me. I need you to endorse it." He sighed and fell in behind me.

* * *

One of the reasons I didn't want to put this in front of our "bosses" was because I didn't like Carol Young, my boss. A classic bureaucrat. She had never served in the field, had never been a special agent, and was from the world of intelligence. I don't have anything against intelligence. A lot more of us would be dead or in trouble if it weren't for intelligence. But there are different kinds of people who deal with intelligence. There are the active ones, the ones who really wish they were spies and had joined the CIA, there are those who are brilliant and can see connections and see things that I would never get, and then there are those who are born bureaucrats who have simply settled into the intelligence field as their power base. She was one of those. A supervisory intelligence analyst, or SIA. A lifetime bureaucrat who had repeatedly been promoted through the Peter Principle.

Her office was less impressive than Murphy's. Her door was open. I knocked on the open door and she looked up. She was perturbed. "What?"

"You got a second?" I asked.

She glanced at Karl over my shoulder, wondering what he was doing there. "Not really."

"Only take a second."

"What is it?"

"I'll cut to the chase. I want a temporary transfer to Karl's group at Domestic Terrorism."

She frowned, "What for?"

"Well there's a long story behind it. But the short story is I think I can take down a growing worldwide neo-Nazi movement. It's building. It's a real problem. There's going to be a meeting in Germany and I want to stop them."

"Why you?"

I inched inside her doorway and said, "I was just in Europe. I went to Germany on vacation, and ran into a neo-Nazi group. They threatened my family as they marched with their masks and Nazi armbands. I want to help snuff it out."

"How do you plan on doing that?"

"Karl has a CI. I want to work with him to get him there and turn it."

"How do you plan on doing that?"

"I haven't made a final decision on which way to go yet, but the key is to get invited. To show them something that will get their attention. I'm finalizing it now." Of course, I didn't know what I was going to do yet.

"And what you're doing here is so unimportant you can just walk away from it."

"No. And I don't plan on walking away from it at all. I'll keep monitoring everything and doing my job probably at about a two-thirds rate. And Alex said she can cover for me, even work extra hours." I hesitated. "I need to do this. Just give me sixty days."

She exhaled heavily. "Have you even looked in your inbox? Did you open the high-priority email I sent you an hour ago?"

I hadn't looked at my email since nine thirty. "I haven't been in my office."

"I noticed. You didn't respond. Mohammed al-Hadi is on the move. Heading for Europe. Germany, we think. And since that's directly in the area that you have been working on, you have more work, not less. I can't spare you, particularly now."

"Understood." I paused. "Can I at least talk to Karl? Can I help him out on the side? Not to interfere with what I'm doing?"

"Al-Hadi needs your full attention. How are you going to have extra time to help out Karl?"

"I'll cut back on my sleep."

"You should have already cut back on your sleep."

"Just give me a little room."

She was done with me. She dismissed us with a wave of her hand. "Just get your job done."

"Guaranteed."

I turned quickly and walked down the hall with Karl following. I didn't want her to say anything else. As we waited for the elevator I said to Karl, "I'm going to need Jedediah's number."

"You took what she said as a 'yes'?"

"Absolutely."

Karl shook his head. We clearly weren't of the same mind. Karl finally responded, "He doesn't have a number. We don't call him."

"How do you contact him?"

"Untraceable Gmail account. His email address is nonsensical. It's just letters and numbers about twenty-six characters long. It's one that you could never remember; you've got to have it written down. And he will only respond to another Gmail account. I've set up an account that I talk to him through. He only accesses it—"

The elevator arrived and the door opened. Karl watched to see who was getting off. He waited till they got off, we got on, and the doors closed in front of us.

"He only accesses it from computers at Internet cafés and the like. Nothing in his house, nothing traceable."

"What is his email?"

He pulled out his wallet and showed it to me. "Here."

It made no sense and was just as Karl described. "Do you have this in your computer? Can you email it to me?"

"Sure. You should make an account to contact him. Something completely random. You should know that Jedediah is very careful. Don't let his looks fool you. He's actually incredibly bright. He looks like a thug, which throws everybody. They expect nothing but grunts and stupidity. And then when you throw in a southern accent, two-thirds of the country assumes he's retarded. But this is a guy you want on your side. He's courageous, bright, and the best chance we have to do anything with these guys, if he's legit, about which I still have my doubts. So I'll let you talk to him, but you've got to do it right, and you've got to run everything by me."

The doors opened and we stepped out. He continued, "But, I guess it all depends on you coming up with some brilliant idea. Anything occur to you?"

I shook my head. "I need to talk to him first. I've got to understand what drives them."

"Pretty simple. Racial purity. But their big play right now is illegal immigration, particularly those identified with Islam. We've handed them the best issue they've ever had on a platter. We continue to pretend we have immigration policies, and continue to do nothing about them. So, as they see it, they have Mexicans and Ecuadorians and Iraqis invading South Carolina with the endorsement of the federal government. Once you get into the anti-immigration world, it's broad and deep across the country. Something like ninety percent of Americans disagree with the way the federal government is handling immigration. When you've got unemployment and a lot of jobs in the heart of the south taken by Spanish-speaking people, you've got a formula for trouble. They capitalize on that. They soft pedal the anti-Semitism and white supremacy but it's there. They suck people in with the anti-immigrant bit, how the country's been overrun by immigrants, then they start on the Muslims, with the Jews thrown in for good measure. There are still a lot of people out there who sign off on this rubbish. A lot. Never ceases to amaze me."

"I'm going to contact him right away. You okay with that?"

He paused, then said, "Sure. Keep me posted."

* * *

I went back to my office. I logged onto Gmail and created a new account. I copied Jedediah's address into the "to" line and left the subject line blank. I typed, "I am the other one from Virginia. We need to meet." I didn't put any signature or name to it. I didn't really have a good sense of how secure this type of communication was. I knew it wouldn't be very secure from the NSA if they chose to monitor it, but I thought it was probably secure against the people he'd be concerned were watching him. Others like him. If he never accessed his email from any known computer, I couldn't imagine how they'd ever know about it. Still, it paid to be as cautious as possible.

As I was about to log off I was surprised to see the first email pop up in my inbox. It was from Jedediah. It contained one word. "Why?"

I typed quickly, "To help with your idea."

"Have one?"

"Not yet."

"Email me when you do."

"I need to talk through this. To find out what would work."

Nothing happened. There was no response. I stared at my inbox and hit send/receive ten times. Nothing. Then suddenly an email. "Asheville, N.C., next Tuesday 10:00 a.m."

I replied immediately, "Sure. Where exactly? What's your cell?" There was no reply.

CHAPTER FOUR

I flew to Charlotte Monday night, then got up early and drove my Toyota rental car to Asheville. I pulled into town about nine thirty, wondering how I was supposed to find him. It was a beautiful day in the quaint, artsy mountain town, but it wasn't a town of a thousand people with one street. It was bigger than I expected. I drove around the city for a while, mostly downtown, and then to the older section. I didn't see him. I found myself driving slow and being obvious, something I didn't usually do. I passed used bookstores, quilt stores, hand-made furniture stores, and art galleries. I lowered my window and inhaled the fresh air.

I found a public parking lot, which had clearly been constructed for all the tourists. I parked, locked the car, and walked toward the center of town. It was exactly ten o'clock. I had no idea where to go. My cell phone buzzed in the inside pocket of my sport coat and I pulled it out. I didn't recognize the number.

"Yes?"

"You here?"

"Yes. How'd you get my cell number?"

"Your friend. Where are you?"

"Walking toward the center of town."

"There's an art museum, the Rafferty. It's in an old house. Pay your admission and check out the art."

I put my cell phone back in my pocket and headed toward the main street to see if I could find the museum. I didn't really know which way to go. There was a café at the corner where I stood. I walked in and spoke to the man standing behind the cash register. "Excuse me, can you tell me where the Rafferty Museum is?"

He was looking at several bills that were stacked in front of him. He replied without looking up. "Down the street to the left, by the church on the left side. Big white house."

"Thanks."

After three blocks I saw the large, beautifully restored Victorian house. I walked up the steps onto the broad front porch and opened the screen door. I pushed the glass door open and stepped into the entryway. A woman sat behind a desk reading an art magazine. She looked up at me and smiled. "Good morning."

"Morning. One, please."

"Yes, ten dollars."

I gave her the money. "Which way should I go?"

She smiled. "Most people like to go with the flow of the house, so you could just go that way," she said pointing to my left, away from her into what was the drawing room. "That would be the best place to start. Then just follow the rooms around the ground floor of the house and then you can go upstairs. There's more art on the second floor, but you should start on the first."

I nodded. "Anyone else here?"

"Yes. A couple people."

"Should be pretty quiet."

"Oh, it's always quiet," she said smiling. "It's *important* that one be able to look at art in quiet. It allows you to *engage* with the artists."

"No doubt." I gave her a polite smile and walked into the first room, feigning interest. It was all attractive, mostly landscapes and probably painted by local artists. I tried to linger long enough in the first room to appear to study the paintings, then moved quickly to the next room where she couldn't see me. I still hadn't seen anyone. I went to the next room, then into what must have been the kitchen when the house operated as a house, and then to the dining room and living room. Still no one. I came back around to the front of the house where the receptionist was still sitting.

"You're quick," she said.

"Yeah, I ah, I just like certain things. I guess I'll go upstairs."

"Help yourself."

I walked up the polished wooden stairs, turned at the landing, and went to the second floor. The house was completely quiet. I picked a direction once I got to the top of the stairs and went into the first room on the right.

It probably used to be a bedroom or sitting room, but now was a beautifully lighted room with eight or ten paintings. I walked through the first three rooms and then found him in the fourth. He was standing in front of a watercolor scene of a house with the sun setting behind a mountain. He was wearing a long-sleeve high-neck fleece and a baby-blue baseball hat.

"Morning," I said. He didn't respond.

I stood next to him, looking at the art. "You're a little less intimidating when your tattoos don't show."

"If I walked down the street of this artsy town in a wife-beater, I'd get some serious attention." He almost smiled. "Maybe I will one day."

"I'm not sure this is really the best place to talk."

He looked away from the painting and turned directly toward me. "This isn't where we talk. This is where we find out if anybody followed us. I've been looking out the window since long before you got here."

"You think I need help figuring out whether I'm being followed?"

"Yes." He glanced at me for the first time. "There's a path that leads off this street. Let's go."

He headed toward the stairs. I followed. We walked half a block, turned on a side street, and went to the end of the street, where there was an entrance to a city park and a nature walk. No one was around. It was beautiful, flower filled and inviting. The air was cool.

After we had walked fifty or so yards in silence, he asked, "So what do you want?"

"I've asked for temporary assignment to Karl's unit. I want to help you take down these Nazis."

"I don't even know you."

"No, but you know I'm serious or I wouldn't be here."

"So how do I get to Germany?"

"Do you have a date? When's the actual meeting?"

"I told you."

"I don't remember. I know it's a couple of months."

"November 9th, of course."

"Why of course?"

"The anniversary."

"Of what?"

"You don't know?"

"Remind me."

"The beer hall *putsch*. When Hitler marched with his followers—two thousand of them—from the Bürgerbräukeller to the Odeonsplatz to take Munich. November 9th, 1923. The beginning of Nazism."

"Of course." I said. I had read about it while I was in Germany, but didn't remember that much about it. "But the reason I'm here is I want to hear from you. About the Southern Volk, and other neo-Nazis. What makes them tick. And what you think this guy from Germany is looking for."

He turned. He looked back down the path from where we'd come. We were alone in the woods. I was acutely aware of his strength. I could handle myself in a fight but this wouldn't be close. I was aware of the weight of the gun in my shoulder holster, and knew that since I was within an arm's length of him, I'd have no chance of getting it out if he decided to do me harm. He was staring at me with his usual intimidating intensity.

He spoke with an aggressive but soft tone. "So you asked me to have a meeting, to meet with an FBI agent which I *hate* doing, so you could tell me you have no idea what we should do."

"No. I'm here to listen. I want to hear how you guys think. What gets your people stirred up? I'm going to get you there, Jedediah. You can take that to the bank. And no, I don't have the idea yet. It takes time. I have to have the background, the understanding."

He looked down at the trail and moved a twig around with his foot as he pondered. "What do you want to know?"

"What's your primary motivator? What do you use to motivate and recruit people?"

He contemplated, then said, "The two I's: Islam and immigration. We've got beaners in the Carolinas now, and we've got the federal government looking the other way while people pour over the borders every day. They seem to think it's a joke. Immigrants coming in here taking up welfare, taking up jobs—pisses people off. People act like they don't mind immigrants, but they hate *illegal* immigration. You want to change how many people can immigrate here? Fine, change the laws. Let's vote on it. 'Cause what the feds are doing would lose any vote. And the government doesn't seem to get that. Or they do, and don't care. It's insulting. So we get a two for one. We get people to hate immigrants, and hate the federal government. That's our number one issue. We count on it, we rely on it, we bang on it, and we get people riled up.

"Once they're riled up about immigration and they think that we're one of the few groups that will do something about it, they start thinking about joining. That's when we start talking about the Muslims trying to kill us all over the world and how we need to get them out of America before we're under sharia law. That's an easy one too.

"Then we talk about the moral decline of the country, and how that's the fault of the Jews. But we don't spend too much time on Jews. That's old stuff. We'll get around to them, but the hot issues are Islam and immigration. Like taking candy from a baby."

"Jews still? Really? What do you say about them?"

"How long do you have? It's an easy sell. Most people these days aren't sensitive to how Jews wreak havoc on a country. They don't get how our country's moral decline—its feminization, its lack of moral clarity—is because of the Jews. It's an active, intentional determination by the Jews to ruin our country. But the funny thing is, it's not just us. It's every country. Wherever they show up in numbers, they ruin the country. That's why you've got to read *Mein Kampf*. It's the same story over and over again. The Jews own or control all the levers of the culture. Newspapers, movie studios, art, music—all Jews.

"I don't think it's hard at all to say that the film industry undermines the morals of the country. Easy to prove, I think. They don't make pro-family movies. They never portray a father as a strong character. All fathers are dumbasses. Abortion's good. Kids need independence. Adultery is good. Fine. Easy to make the case, I think. So of the eight major movie studios in Hollywood, how many are run by Jews? Any guesses?"

"I don't know."

"All of them. And television networks? All of them. Maybe you say, *So what.* But it's pretty easy to make a case they have destroyed the moral fabric of the country. Torn apart the family. Promoted an anti-family pro-gay agenda.

"Oh, and print? *New York Times? Washington Post?* All started by gentiles, now all Jew run.

"And they always push for no accountability for moral conduct. It's the Jewish lawyers who tear down our structures and try to eliminate religion from our society. They're the ones suing everybody over praying at football games or putting up the Ten Commandments in the city square or singing Christmas carols in schools. It's not called the ACL Jew for nothing."

I was stunned. I'd been around a long time, been in a lot of locker rooms. I'd been in a lot of military settings. I'd been around a lot of guys who'd felt free to say whatever they wanted. But I'd never heard anybody talk like this in my life. It was chilling. "You sound like you believe this shit, Jedediah."

"Don't even get me started. Not only are the Jews trying to tear apart the moral structure, they're the assholes who gave us Communism. Who the hell did you think Karl Marx was? A Jew, and the founder of Communism. They're the ones who said religion is the opiate of the masses. They're the ones who gave us atheistic godless Communism, which nearly took over the world and ruined it forever. They're the ones who gave us the great Bolshevik Revolution in Russia, run by Jews, like Trotsky. Do your research. The Bolsheviks were thick with Jews. And even here. They're the ones who have given us the wonderful pornography industry . . ."

"Come on . . . "

"Check it out. Check out Sturman, and Hirsch. Not only have Jews made the vast majority of porn flicks in America, they've starred in them. The vast majority of men in porn movies are Jews. Go look at the guys out in the San Fernando Valley in California who started it all. And you know what some of them have even said? Been quoted? That they do porn as a middle finger to puritan, Christian America. They are *fighters* in the spiritual battle between Christian America and secular humanism! Believe that shit? It's not us saying it, it's *them*. They're trying to 'destroy the puritanical beast.' *They're* talking about the moral fiber of the country. And I read about it in a *Jewish* magazine! We pull this stuff out and people go ape-shit."

"But the Jews aren't your focus," I said, still shocked by his outburst.

"No, they're not. But it's always there if you want to bring it out. Talk about how our country is in moral decline, then show them why—the Jews—and people get it."

"What about Islam?"

"They've been trying to kill us all since 9/11. When our president says our issue isn't with 'Islam, which is a religion of peace,' we vomit. What a bunch of bullshit. Islam hates us, and everything we stand for. Show me a country where the majority of the people are Muslims and there is *any* freedom. Nowhere. And absolutely no religious freedom. They demand it, but don't give it. Just look around. If they're less than ten percent of the population, they demand fairness, and respect, and committees. But when they get over ten percent? They want control. Watch France. They're past ten percent. Go talk to their police and local politicians confidentially. They'll tell you the true story. And you know what? When we went to Saudi Arabia to defend those ragheads in Desert Storm? They told us we couldn't celebrate

Christmas! They made our chaplains take off their insignia, no crosses or Stars of David on uniforms allowed in Saudi Arabia! No, sir. We could die to defend them, we just couldn't *mention* our religion in the process. And the U.S. government went along with that bullshit. Again, I talk about this stuff and people go nuts."

"Frankly, you sound a little crazy too."

"Have to. If I'm going to sell that I'm still a big-shot neo-Nazi I've got to talk the talk."

"It's hard to listen to."

"You're just not used to people speaking their minds. In the PC world nobody says what they think anymore. Which we love. Because then when we do, people eat it up. It's what they've been secretly thinking. Nowadays we have to pretend like all people are the same even when it's obvious to everybody who walks on the earth that that's just not true. So you have this tension out there. The politically correct bullshit says, we're all the same, and if we're not it's because of 'discrimination,' and its complete crap. It makes people not trust the media, not trust the politicians, not trust anybody, except the neos, once we get a hold of them. They trust us, they hang on every word, because it feels *true* to them."

"So you used to believe all this stuff."

"Absolutely."

"What happened?"

"Don't worry about it."

"How do I know you're different?" I moved slightly closer to him and gave him my own hard look. "How do I know you're not just trying to figure out what the FBI is doing? Spying on us for the Southern Volk, a sort of double agent?"

Jedediah turned and walked back down the path. I called after him. "Hey!"

He kept walking, shoulders hunched. He walked faster. I hurried after him. "What's up?"

"I don't need this, and I don't need you. I don't really give a shit if you understand. And your big plan to come up with some genius idea to make us all look good is just smoke. You've got nothing. Then you accuse me of infiltrating the FBI. You're unbelievable."

He turned to go again.

"Wait. Just tell me one thing."

He stopped and looked over his shoulder without turning his body. It was a very sinister look. I could feel the tattoos burning through his pull-over, like they were already imprinted on my mind and went with him in my head wherever he went.

"Pick one thing, pick the most impressive thing that you have ever heard of or seen in any neo meeting or conversation. What has gotten the most comments, the most excitement?"

"Like where?"

"Anywhere. Any neo meeting you've ever been to, some indoctrination, some . . . whatever. What has gotten everybody's attention the fastest."

"Somebody with authority. Somebody who goes way back."

"Like somebody from World War II?"

"Not really a person, but something he has. People love having Lugers, or old German rifles."

I thought for a minute, and he turned to face me as I pondered. He put his hands on his hips, growing impatient. I said, "What if we brought your guy a whole cache of World War II German weapons. Machine guns, Lugers, bayonets with swastikas on them. The whole bit. All authentic."

He thought for a minute. "I don't know. Maybe. That would be hard as hell to get into Germany."

"I could do it."

"Yeah, but the fact that you could do it would make them suspicious. They'd think you had German government help and that it's a setup."

"What about an original signed copy of *Mein Kampf*?"

"That might get you somewhere. But you can just buy it on the Internet. Not that creative to get it."

"You think he's thinking of something like that? You said you weren't go-ing to blow up a federal building or anything."

He turned back around, more calm. "He left it wide open. We just have to impress him. I'm sure he'd love something big and violent. But he also might think that is exactly the wrong idea. Draws too much attention. Now is not the time to go blowing shit up, as much fun as that is."

"Alright. Give me some time, let me think about it."

Jedediah didn't seem impressed. "Yeah, you think about it. You come up with something brilliant, you let me know. Otherwise, I'm going to have to come up with something on my own." He walked ahead of me out of the woods. I waited until he was out of sight then headed to my car.

* * *

When I returned to D.C. I turned back to tracking terrorists. But I found myself drifting back to my conversation with Jedediah and what I'd heard. Right before lunch Alex burst into my office. "Go to CNN."

"What's up?"

"Bombings in Germany."

"What?" I said, sitting up. "Where?"

I went to the streaming video of CNN and put it on full screen. Alex watched over my shoulder.

I ignored the reporters and focused on the images. The screen was split. The images on the left were from Munich and on the right from Berlin. People staggered out of a subway entrance with blood streaming down their faces. Some fell to the ground. The cameraman in Munich moved against the flow, down into the subway, the U-Bahn. People pushed past him, fighting for air. Police and medical teams rushed by, heading down toward the subway trains.

"What happened?"

"Bombs on the subway in Munich and Berlin. Went off at exactly the same time, 5:00 p.m."

"Anybody take credit?"

"Not yet."

"Coordinated attacks sounds like al Qaeda."

"They haven't said yet."

I looked at the images from Berlin. The graphic on the bottom of the screen said forty-five dead, at least ninety more injured. I listened to the reporter. " . . . a few minutes ago. The bomb went off at a station where many people change trains. Five lines come together at this stop," she said, indicating over her shoulder, "Alexanderplatz, and apparently a bomb went off on one of the trains, and at multiple locations in the station itself, all at exactly the same time. It has completely shut down the U-Bahn."

They switched the audio to the reporter in Munich. "Yes, thank you. Here in Munich the bombs were the same. In the station and on one of the trains. Simultaneous, and apparently set to go off at the same time as in Berlin. Here the bombs went off at Marienplatz, where ten lines pass near to each other. The entire system is shut down, the city is frozen, and many are dead with dozens more injured. We will get casualty figures as soon as they are available. The blast in the station was so strong the ceiling of one of the platforms caved in and the train that passed overhead fell down into the lower area. The explosion was devastating. It is unknown how someone got a bomb with such force into the station, let alone onto a train."

The reporter held her hand to her ear and said, "We now have images from the subway tunnel." The view switched from outside to the underground platform by the damaged train. The video zoomed in. The front of the train was blown off like an exploding cigarette. The second car was heavily damaged and the entire train was off its tracks. Dead and injured lay all around the platform as emergency personnel attended to the injured. You could hear the crying and screaming of those suffering. A police officer turned and saw the cameraman and immediately ordered him to turn off the camera. He grabbed it and forced the lens to the ground. CNN switched back to the reporter outside the subway entrance. "As you can see, the damage to the train is shocking. This was clearly a powerful bomb, as were the other two that went off inside the subway station at the height of rush hour, with people of Munich returning to their homes . . . "

I looked at Alex. I was about to speak when my phone rang. I picked up the receiver. "Morrissey."

"Kyle. You watching this?" It was Rebecca Anderson. CIA. My counterpart at the Agency who tracked international terrorism and finance.

I answered, "Unbelievable. Who's behind this?"

"Not sure yet. But there are some who think it's your boy, the one you told us to pay attention to."

"Al-Hadi?"

"They think he's moved up, from pure finance to running operations. They think this is his first."

"Damn. What a way to start, if it's him. He's sure painting a target on his chest."

"I'll give you updates as soon as I can, but you might check any sources you have that I don't."

"Will do." I hung up.

I talked to Alex while I watched the images on my screen. "They think it may be al-Hadi."

She frowned. "He's too smart to go at it directly."

"That's my thinking. We follow him, trace him. But we don't send a predator to put a hellfire through his bathroom window. But if he did this, we sure as hell will. Or Germany will."

* * *

A few days after I got back to D.C., while researching everything I could on al-Hadi, I began my baptism into Nazism. I finished *Mein Kampf* then stayed up past midnight for several nights as I read Ian Kershaw's massive two-volume biography of Hitler. Then I watched films on the Nazis from Netflix and Time Life, and one in particular, *Nazism in America*. Finally I watched *Triumph of the Will*, the 1934 film by Leni Riefenstahl. I started to get it. Hitler's core belief was that Germany was being ruined. Morally and politically ruined. And he knew who was doing it. He fomented hatred against them for what they were doing to Germany. He called for hatred of those who would destroy his great country. It was the Jews, the Communists, the immigrants, and they all deserved hatred. He called on Germans to hate those causing the moral and political decline of the German people. But that was only half of the story. The other half was his *message* to his followers on who *they* were. He persuaded his downtrodden followers that they were *not* worthless people from a bankrupt country; they were *proud Aryans*, the greatest people ever, from a country which would rise again from the ashes if they would trust him! They belonged to a great nation that would be great again under National Socialism and its mesmerizing symbol—the swastika. My wife thought I was going over the edge. My children said I was neglecting them. But I had to understand Nazism under Hitler, and I had to understand neo-Nazism now.

I went to see Karl again. I had mostly stayed out of his way after I had come back, other than telling him about my Asheville meeting. I said, "I need to get over to Germany."

"Germany? Not on our nickel."

"On my own. On vacation."

"Got to give you credit for determination."

"But I need a contact. Who do you deal with at the BKA?"

Karl seemed to be thinking about whether to tell me the man's name. "Why do you need him?"

"I've got to understand what's going on in Germany. What do they know about Eidhalt? And to help me figure out what will make him interested in the Southern Volk."

He took a deep breath and finally said, "The BKA guy I know spends a lot of his time in Munich. He gets all over Germany, especially Dresden, where a lot of the stuff is happening. His name is Florian Köhler."

"Do you have his email?"

He turned toward his computer, looked up his contacts, and forwarded his contact to me. I looked at my BlackBerry and saw that it had arrived. "Thanks. Does he know about Jedediah?"

"Just that we've got a guy."

"You got any problem if I call Florian today?"

"Go ahead."

I nodded, gave him a wave of thanks, and returned to my office. I didn't want to waste any time at all. I picked up my phone and dialed.

* * *

Germany was six hours ahead. The phone rang three times and an energetic voice answered in German.

"I'm Kyle Morrissey. I'm with the FBI. Trying to reach Florian Köhler."

"Yes," he said switching to English. "This is Florian Köhler."

"Sorry to bother you. You're probably pretty tied up with the bombings."

"No, that's another department. I'm not involved."

"Okay. Then let me tell you what I'm doing. I'm working with Karl Matthews, developing something that I think I need your help with. I'd like to come over and meet with you."

"What is it you're working on?"

"I'd rather not discuss it on the phone. It'd be better in person. I can come to Berlin, or Munich, or wherever you'd like to meet."

"Why here?"

"To learn from you, and to discuss what I am trying to accomplish." He was skeptical. "And exactly what is it you are trying to accomplish?"

"Well that's what I want to talk to you about. I think at this point, you're just going to have to trust me."

He sounded annoyed. "It is a very busy time, even without the bomb-ings." He hesitated. "If Karl sends me an email, I will meet with you for an hour or so. In Wiesbaden."

"Yes, that's fine. I appreciate it."

I made a reservation to Wiesbaden for later that night. I sent a request for three days of vacation and didn't even wait for the response. I rushed home, packed a bag, and headed for Dulles.

CHAPTER FIVE

I had never been to Wiesbaden. The hotel was beautiful and old, and it had clearly been restored at great expense. I attempted to check into my room, but was told that check-in time was three o'clock. If I wanted to check in now I'd have to pay for another night. I needed to shower and change so I found the fitness center and changed in the shower room. I asked them to press my shirt, and I hung my suit in the bathroom while I showered to let the steam move through it and relax the wrinkles from being triple folded into my roll-aboard. I turned on the television and watched CNN International in English.

I grabbed a cab and asked him to take me directly to Thaerstraße, the headquarters of the Bundeskriminalamt.

We pulled up in front of the imposing white building and I climbed out. It wasn't quite as ominous as the J. Edgar Hoover building, but it had its own impressiveness. The BKA's reputation was excellent. They were serious, diligent, trustworthy, and clever. Their opinion of us was slightly less elevated.

I approached the man behind the counter and asked for Florian Köhler. He typed in his computer, looked up the extension, and called. He looked up at me and said in English, "Mr. Köhler said he was not expecting you yet and that you did not have an appointment."

"I came as soon as I could. I'll wait until he's available."

He tried not to show that he thought that was a bad idea. He spoke again to Florian. "He said he can come get you in a half hour."

I nodded. "Perfect."

The large sterile lobby had a modern chrome couch with black leather seats. I sat down on the supple leather and opened my briefcase on the glass coffee table. I pulled out a binder into which I had put articles and information about various neo-Nazi groups around the world. They were large, growing, ambitious, and dangerous. I turned to the German neo-Nazis. They had become increasingly bold. And the rate of increase, both in size and number of groups, was increasing at an exponential rate. They were drawing in the disaffected German youth. Unemployment was the starter fuel, Europeanization was the kindling, and Islam was the firewood. There had even been a series of murders of Turks by German neo-Nazis. The murders had a name—the Doner Kebob killings—because many of the murdered men ran small kebob shops or carts. Innocent men going about their lives trying to carve out a living in a country where they felt like outcasts and strangers, cooking their kebobs on the vertical spits common to Doner cooking, and now exposed to vicious murder.

I was reading about the marches in Dresden when I realized there was someone standing right next to me. I looked up from my notebook and he said, "I am Florian Köhler. Welcome to Wiesbaden."

I stood and put the notebook on the coffee table and extended my hand. We shook hands and I evaluated him. He was at least two inches taller than me. He was very athletic, had spiky blonde hair and stylish glasses. He was smiling, which surprised me. He actually seemed pleased to see me. A very different tone than in our phone call. What surprised me the most was his age. He was perhaps thirty-five; very young for the responsibility he had in the BKA.

He said, "I hope your flight was uneventful."

"Lufthansa. Nonstop to Frankfurt."

"An excellent flight. I have taken it many times. I hope you flew business class."

"That would be the day."

"Ah. Too bad!" He smiled even more broadly. "Please come, let's go to the café and have an espresso."

He motioned me in a direction away from the reception desk and through security. We passed through two automatic glass doors into a gleaming new, mostly white modern café. It was set up for the purpose of receiving guests and having casual conversations over coffee.

"Espresso?" He asked as he walked toward the counter area. "Americano?"

There was an attendant there but also a fancy coffee machine for self-service.

"Sure. Americano, please."

He took two white cups with saucers from the stack and pressed a single button on the face of the machine. It hummed and hissed. Florian handed me mine then poured cream in his own. He pointed to a table toward the window and said, "Let's sit over here."

The coffee had a slight brown foam on the top. Florian took a sip and said, "So. What is this that you wanted to talk about?" Florian spoke excellent English, with a slight trace of an accent.

"It's sort of a long story." I hesitated. I'd never had a conversation about World War II with a German. Ever. I had no idea what he thought about the war, or what they were taught in school. I told him the story of my father's division and the anniversary celebration of D-Day at Normandy. Then I told him about Recklinghausen. He listened carefully. Then I told him about the coming meeting in Germany with Eidhalt. That got his attention.

"He is the one who bought that castle to train skinheads. Not 'Nazis,' of course, because they can't say that. We would put them in jail. So they find other ways. It's all the same."

"In a few weeks he's going to have a meeting of all the, as he calls them, uber-leaders from the strongest neo-Nazi movements all over the world. He said the reason they have not had the worldwide impact they deserve is that they have lacked unity. Instead, they compete. He says they need a unified vision, a unifying leader, and the finances to make this real. The time is nearing when they will come out into the open. They will be overt, uniformed, and aggressive. They will have public meetings and marches and openly recruit people. They will have enough numbers that no one will *dare* challenge them, just like the SA in the twenties and thirties. They will live inside the laws mostly, especially inside the United States, where as long as they don't call for the violent overthrow of the government, they can say whatever the hell they want. They can publish the most scurrilous rubbish, and nobody can touch them. And what they know, is that people buy it. They believe it. He wants everybody wearing the same uniform, publishing the same documents, and calling for the same result: The racial purification of each country; and then his ultimate objective, the violent overthrow of each country's government."

Florian shook his head. "Violent overthrow would never work here."

"I think it's more likely they would try and do it like Hitler did. Get elected or appointed, then take over. Hitler's party joined the Reichstag with thirty-five percent of the vote."

"You know a lot about Hitler."

"Been reading a lot lately. And frankly, probably like a lot of others, I'd always taken him lightly. I dismissed him as a lunatic. Now I sort of get it. How he convinced so many people that his ideas were good for Germany. He wasn't the only strident Jew-hater in Germany. Everyone in politics was at the time."

Köhler looked out the window pensively. He looked back at me, adjusted his glasses, and said, "Many people here don't take Eidhalt seriously. Of course, this is how people initially regarded Hitler, the stupid corporal, the uneducated painter. But of course the fact that Hitler was uneducated does not mean that any other uneducated man can do what Hitler did. Each circumstance is unique. But this man, I have been watching. I have followed him very closely."

"Do you have anyone inside his organization?"

Köhler went on pretending I had not asked a question. "Eidhalt is not very well educated and is from what was formerly Eastern Germany. Dresden. He enlisted in the German Army. He was trained as a solider. He stayed in the army for six years and became a sergeant. His record is not distinguished. He was an adequate solider, and was good at marksmanship, but was a troublemaker. He had anti-immigrant beliefs, and was disciplined for fighting with a solider of Turkish descent in his unit. He was demoted, though he was promoted again. He got out of the army as a sergeant. And, of course, Rolf Eidhalt isn't his real name."

"What is his real name?"

"Herman Dieckhoff."

"Why Rolf Eidhalt?"

"We don't know. He started calling himself that when he started going public with his nonsense." Florian moved a little closer. "One interesting thing. They give soldiers tests to find out how intelligent they are. To find out if they can do some of the more sophisticated training, like electronics or radar maintenance. He scored at the highest of his class, but wanted nothing to do with radars or electronics. He said he wanted to be a solider. He said he had joined the army to be a soldier and to carry a rifle. His commanding officers thought he was humorless and intense, and believed he was forming an underground group—like a club. Men who thought alike. He did form this underground club, but we, well, army intelligence, could never break into it. It seemed to be anti-immigrant—and there were only white Germans—but no one would talk about it. To this day, they don't know what he did inside the army."

"How's that possible?"

"Like I said, it was not possible to break into his circle. He was not considered a significant threat, and he left the army."

"What about now? How did he get to the point where he could buy a castle?"

Köhler smiled, "Ah. That's where the story really gets interesting. It turns out he has quite the business sense. Just as he got out of the army his father died, leaving him a money-losing auto maintenance shop in the center of Dresden. He tried to run it for a while. He was trained as a mechanic by his father. He wasn't very good at it, and he didn't enjoy it. He continued to lose money and finally gave up. But what he apparently didn't realize at first was that the property on which the shop sat was also owned by his father. So when he finally gave up on the shop, he put the property on the market and found out that the property was worth more than a million euros. He sold it, and began his new life."

"What did he do?"

"Well, he disappeared off the radar for a bit. Have you heard of the marches in Dresden?"

"Yes."

"You know about the Dresden bombing."

"In World War II?"

"Yes. It is one of the things that is not talked about very much in the United States, I suspect. But it is still talked about quite a bit in Germany, if anything is talked about." He smiled ironically.

"The Allies killed more than twenty-five thousand people in Dresden. By fire bomb. Dresden used to be called The Florence of the Elbe . . . it was so beautiful. Your American writer, Kurt Vonnegut, was a prisoner of war in Dresden and was there when the bombing happened. Did you know that?"

"No, I didn't."

"He had to collect the bodies. They were later burned. Too many of them. He was in a prison they called Schlachthof Fünf. Do you know what that means?"

"No."

"Slaughterhouse Five, the name of his famous novel. In any case, in 1990 or so, the neo-Nazis—or skinheads—decided to use the anniversary of that bombing to demonstrate. They have marched there every year since. This year, there were ten thousand of them. So for those that think Nazism is still not alive and well in Germany, they need only go to Dresden on February 13th."

"What does that have to do with Eidhalt?"

"He's from Dresden. Ever since he made his money, he's been involved in the march. We know he has helped fund it. He doesn't march, but he sends people to it. And pays for people to travel."

"He stays behind the scenes."

"He was playing a very clever game. He didn't join any organization. He would monitor them all and help them all. Waiting for the best to rise to the surface. Those that were led by stupid men, he would ignore. Those that were led by smarter men, with better connections and better financing, he would help. He has been waiting for ten years to seize the moment, and now is that time."

"Why do you say that?"

"Because in taking that one million euros he has now converted it over the last twenty years to fifty million euros. He purchased property all over the former East Germany. When companies were motivated by the government to move into Eastern Europe and therefore needed land or buildings, he would sell to them. And when the government needed a new headquarters for their agency, he would sell it to them. As I said, he is now worth a lot. Maybe more than fifty million. And much of it is liquid. We know where all his accounts are, at least we think we do, but we also believe he has some accounts in Switzerland now. And maybe even in the United States. He has a very clever accountant. We think some of the money has moved without us knowing where it went."

He shifted. "And now there is money coming into his accounts—a new account that he thinks he has hidden—that we can't trace back. But we know it isn't from Europe. We think it's a secondary source of funding. Someone who is supporting him or funding him."

"So," he said, sighing. "We have a man who is Nazi to the core, rich, clever, and now believes it is time to stand on top of what he sees as a rising tide of nationalism, anti-Semitism, anti-immigration and anti-Muslim sentiments, and economic fear. Things aren't as bad as they were in the twenties and thirties, but there are enough young men who are unemployed and enough who think all of Europe is about to be destroyed by immigration that Eidhalt has many followers. And they see Turks as the cause of their unemployment. Turks and other immigrants. They, of course, also blame Jews for the decline of social morals and standards, and *hate* the European

Union for—they say—taking away Germany's identity. It doesn't have to make sense. It just has to work. And people follow it."

"He sounds dangerous."

"He is. Even the press is noticing. There were many reports of his buying this castle. It dates back to the 1400s in Bavaria. One of the few available to the public, and it was in some disrepair. He bought it two years ago and put it in workable order. He installed the most modern security, power everywhere, air conditioning, and comfort. So instead of a drafty old stone castle, he finished the stone walls to modern standards with structural steel and electronics. And he will not let anybody in. There are no photographs of the inside of the castle since the completion. Only rumors from workers and employees, but not much of that. They are all very loyal and quiet."

I asked, "So what is it he's doing with this castle?"

"Would you like some more coffee? I'm going to get an espresso."

"That sounds good."

We both stood then walked over to the gleaming white machine. Köhler pressed the button for the small espresso cup and then did one for me. He put sugar in his and offered me some, which I declined. We took our cups to the table and pushed our larger coffee cups aside. He drank half his espresso in his first sip.

"Okay. That's the question. He is much more difficult to observe now that he is in his castle. And he has put up such security that we can't even get close to observe. We are left to watch the people going in and out of one of the three gates. Often times, they come in black-windowed cars, which we trace. But they are almost always cars for hire. Sometimes people arrive on motorcycles with fraudulent license plates, or even buses. But we understand he is establishing a headquarters for a new movement, which some call the Azi Party. Legal, but so close as to be an insult. Likewise, he has apparently devised a symbol. He has taken what is missing from the Azi party, the *N*s and put two of them, one across each other in the middle of a red and black flag. It is not a swastika, but it is remarkably close. Everyone immediately recognizes it, I am told. I have not seen one of his flags yet. Apparently, all of this is being formed in secret. We can only guess that he intends to reveal this at some point."

"And when is that to be?"

"We think soon. That is why your visit is of note. What is it that you have learned?"

"We have a confidential informant in the Southern Volk."

Köhler nodded. "I have heard this. You know what the word Volk means?"

"Sure. Folk. People."

"Yes. But it is a little more than that. It is the common man. The everyday person. You may not know for example that the car, the Volkswagen, was given its name by Hitler himself. That was called the people's wagon. The Volkswagen."

"Seriously?"

"It is not commonly spoken of, but it is true. It was started in World War II, at the direction of Hitler himself, to produce a cheap car for the common person. But go on."

"Well, after I had my little experience in Recklinghausen, I had decided to try to do something about this growing neo-Nazi movement. I don't really know if I'll be able to do anything, but I am sure as hell determined to try. I met with Karl, who you have been working with in Washington."

Köhler nodded.

"I met this CI with him. Eidhalt actually went to visit his organization in South Carolina. In person. He said it is time for unification. All to wear the same uniforms, to have the same philosophy, and to achieve the same objective—to take over their country's governments, peaceably if possible, and through violence if not. But here is the key. He said there would be a meeting here in Germany on November 9th, and he would only invite those who had done something to show they were deserving. He has promised that those who are invited will be part of the new movement. The leaders."

"We have not heard this." He looked around like he was expecting someone else. He turned back. "What do they have to do to get invited?"

"Eidhalt didn't say. They have to show they *deserve* it. He left it up to them. Our CI thinks some other groups may try something really dramatic, like blowing up a federal building or having an anti-immigration raid in a worker's camp in California or Arizona. But I think he's looking for something smarter. In any case, I told our informant that I would come up with something that would get him invited."

"How do you propose to do that?"

"I don't know. First, I have to come up with the idea. Then I have to see how I fit. Because together, you and me, we're going to bring all these men down."

Köhler's eyes widened. "How? And if they're doing nothing illegal?"

"Oh, they'll be doing something illegal. I promise you. At the very least, it will be an international conspiracy to undermine foreign governments. It may also be a conspiracy to undermine the German government itself."

Köhler nodded as he considered what I'd said. "You may be right. What is it you propose to do?"

"I hadn't thought about the castle very much. You say it's located outside of Munich?"

"Yes."

Thoughts flooded into my head as something occurred to me. "After Recklinghausen, I took my family to Munich because I'd heard it was a beautiful city. We stayed in a wonderful hotel, and when we asked the concierge where we should go to dinner, she recommended that we go to the Hofbräuhaus am Platzl. She said it was a wonderful place with traditional German food, great beer. It was great. The place is huge. Great oompah band, men in lederhosen, women in those dresses—"

"Derndls."

"Right. All very cheerful and upbeat. But when I got back to our hotel room—did I tell you that my father was a military historian?"

Köhler shook his head.

"Quite the expert on World War II history and American diplomatic history. Maybe that is why I knew, but I remembered that Hitler started his whole movement at a beer hall in Munich. I had to look it up to find out if I had just had dinner where Hitler marched. So, I looked it up, and that's when I read about the beer hall *putsch*."

Köhler nodded. "It's very famous."

"It's not widely known in the States. So the beer hall where the *putsch* occurred is gone. I guess that gave me a little bit of comfort, but I read on, trying to remember exactly what it was about. They stormed out of the beer hall, armed, and headed toward the center of the city. So Hitler's gang and the hundreds of men—armed with guns and sticks and wearing swastikas and carrying a big Nazi flag—stormed toward the city hall. But somebody warned the authorities, and before they got there the police stopped them.

They told the Nazis to stop advancing or they would be fired on. Hitler ordered them forward and the state police fired. I think sixteen were killed. The first Nazi martyrs, as Hitler called them. Hitler was arrested, thrown in prison, and that's where he wrote *Mein Kampf*."

"Exactly."

"So this castle being in Bavaria is not coincidental. He's starting where Hitler started."

"I agree."

I sat back, suddenly struck with an idea that made me start. It sent a chill through me. I said, "I may have just thought of the idea I was looking for."

"What is it?" Köhler asked.

"One of the men in front was carrying that large Nazi flag. He was shot and fell, and the flag fell to the ground. Other Nazis who were shot fell on top of the flag and bled to death on it. That flag became famous. It became known as the Blood Flag."

"It is very famous. In German it is *die Blutfahne*."

I sat forward. "After the battle, somebody took the flag. They hid it until Hitler got out of prison. And when he began his public life again, he used the Blood Flag like it had magical powers. Any big ceremony or swearing in was always in front of the Blood Flag. He would have them touch it, to show respect to the original Nazi martyrs. In that movie, *Triumph of the Will*, the flag was right there, leading the parade. It was everywhere; it was Hitler's favorite symbol. He touched it to other unit flags, passing on the strength of the Nazi martyrs."

Köhler nodded again. "All true. But so?"

I spoke a little more quietly. "The flag disappeared in 1944 and has never been found. Most people think it's still out there, in some basement, or in storage. Maybe in a safe deposit box in Switzerland. What if I tracked it down and used *die Blutfahne* to help the Southern Volk?"

"He would think it is fake."

I sat back. My mind was spinning. "Well, we are members of two of the organizations that have the best forensic teams in the world. If we can't prove it's real, nobody can."

Köhler smiled. "I don't think that Herr Eidhalt would want authenticity from the FBI or the BKA."

"Obviously. But we can help find the way to do it. And maybe you can help me. We know the names of the men who died on that flag. Their DNA has to be on the flag. All we need to do is find the flag, then find a family member of one of the dead men."

He nodded, considering. "What makes you think you can find the flag?"

"We'll have to do it as if I'm a private citizen. If anybody smells the FBI coming, everything will blow up. But I need to know what Germany believes happened to that flag. What's the official German version?"

Köhler looked at his watch, "I need to go get a few things done in my office. But I think I know the person who might be able to best answer your question. A good friend here at the BKA. Patrick Sonnenstrahl. He's spent a long time studying German World War II history. He'll be very interested in your question. His grandfather was an American GI." He looked at his watch. "I propose the three of us go out to lunch."

I smiled. "Shall I wait in the lobby?"

"I have your cell phone number—I assume it works here?"

"Yes."

"I will call you."

CHAPTER SIX

If I could produce that piece of Nazi history we were guaranteed to get to the meeting. I walked out of the BKA headquarters and strolled around a nearby park. I checked my BlackBerry. Nothing. It occurred to me that I might need some help. I texted Alex. "Want to help on my special project?" My phone rang. It was her. She was in her car. "Can't text while I drive," she said. "Might kill somebody, including me. What's up?"

"Want to help with my project?"

"Where are you?"

"Germany."

"What are you doing there?"

"Meeting with our counterparts."

"About the project?"

"Yes."

"Anything interesting?"

"Very. Want to help?"

"Don't know," she said, thinking. "I have this job and all. Working for the FBI. And covering your ass."

"Yeah. I heard."

"How could I help?"

"On the side. Like I'm doing."

"This is on the side? Being in Germany?"

"It's pretty this time of year."

"You're insane. Send me an email and I'll read it when I get to work." She hung up.

I sat on a bench by a bus stop and typed her an email. I told her about the Blood Flag, and the Southern Volk. I asked her to put them both under a microscope. I knew she wouldn't be able to resist. I finished then wandered around the park waiting for Florian's call, wondering how to find a flag that disappeared sixty-five years ago.

Finally Florian called. He told me the name of the restaurant and the street it was on. As I walked toward the restaurant, I thought of one of the other men I'd met in Paris at the ceremony. A tough old bird with the nose of a hawk. He stood erect in a brand new crisp khaki uniform with a Screaming Eagle patch on the shoulder. He stood at attention like a twenty-year-old, with a barrel chest and an invincible face. He wore a black beret just like he had on D-Day, when he was six foot two, two twenty-five. He had jumped into France the night before the landing and was captured. They took him to a POW camp. They forced him to fight in bare-knuckle boxing matches against bigger Russian opponents until one of them broke his jaw. The Germans refused to set it, and he couldn't eat. By the end of the war, he was a hundred and twenty-five pounds. And yet, there he stood at eighty-nine, tall, strong, and victorious over the Nazis.

I reached the restaurant before Florian. He walked in with another man, and introduced him to me. "Kyle, this is Patrick Sonnenstrahl."

He was huge. Maybe six feet four inches tall, two hundred fifty pounds. He had a warm smile on his face and extended his hand. "Nice to meet you. Florian has told me about you."

"Thanks for coming. I hope you don't mind helping."

Florian spoke with the hostess and she escorted us through the restaurant, across hardwood floors and past red and white tablecloths. After we sat down, I scanned the menu. The waiter came just as we were ready to order.

I drank from the bottled water on the table and Patrick asked me, "So your father was in the army?"

"Yes. He came ashore after D-Day and fought all the way to the Elbe." I paused, then said, "I've never actually discussed the war with anyone from Germany before."

Patrick nodded. "We have no problem talking about it. Some of us have family members who were in the German Army. But others of us had family members who were true Nazis. True believers. Some just pretend like they don't know about it, others truly don't know. Those who do know about this have the most difficult time. It is as hard for us to understand as it is for Americans."

"Florian tells me that your grandfather was American."

"Yes. He lives in Memphis. He was stationed in Germany after the war. During the occupation. He met my grandmother who was German and they were married. I go to Memphis every year to see them, which gives me no excuse that my English is not good."

"Your English is excellent."

"It's not as good as Florian's. I have some difficulty reading long English books."

"So do I."

Patrick was engaging and enthusiastic. He was the kind of person you'd want on your side in any project, particularly a fight.

As our food arrived, Patrick couldn't wait anymore. "So, I understand you are going to look for *die Blutfahne.*"

I looked around to make sure we weren't being overheard. "That wasn't why I came, but that's what has occurred to me now. Did Florian explain it all?"

Patrick nodded. "He said you want to know what the German belief is about it."

"I don't want to chase a myth. No wild goose chase. You know what a wild goose chase is?"

Patrick laughed. "Of course."

"So what can you tell me?"

Patrick swallowed his steak and said, "I've studied this era in Germany. I am fascinated by it, and like you have wondered how it could have happened. I know all about *die Blutfahne*, and wondered what happened to it. As you said, there are different theories. Most historians believe in the early part of 1945 when it was becoming clear that Germany would lose, the Nazis tried to hide certain things. Some were given to people Hitler trusted to keep them secure until Nazism could be restored.

"One of the things was *die Blutfahne*. It was his number one symbol. It had to be preserved at all costs. He knew that millions who fought for him would survive. And from that group someone would rise up and reestablish what he had put in place. And they could use the flag to do it. So how did he do it? No one knows for sure. Some say it is in a basement somewhere in Berlin, or Munich. Some say it is in a Swiss bank. Some say it has left the country. Some say it is lost forever. Some say it was burned after Hitler committed suicide. So where is it?" He shrugged. "No one knows."

Most of the possibilities held that the flag still existed. I asked both of them, "Do most people think it still exists?"

Patrick nodded vigorously. "Yes. The Nazis believed in their cause so strongly that they thought it would survive Hitler's death. I don't think the public thinks about it much, though. To them, this is just another relic of a time they want to forget."

"Who do they think probably has it?"

"That's where the trail becomes interesting," Patrick replied. He drank deeply from his beer and took a deep breath. "It would have to be someone Hitler trusted. But not someone who would be arrested and executed. It would also have to be someone who could preserve something in secrecy, possibly for decades."

"And who would that be?"

"Many possibilities. Many left the country, some to Switzerland, some are still here."

"How many Germans are still alive who fought in the German Army in World War II?"

"The number is not exact, but there are still thousands," he glanced at Florian for confirmation. "There were about eighteen million who served in the war. There have to be a hundred thousand still alive. They're all in their eighties and nineties now, but some are still in very good health and would love nothing more than the resurrection of Nazism."

I asked, "You ever heard them talk about the *Blutfahne*?"

"No. Not a single time."

"What if they thought it existed?"

"It would be, I don't know the right word, maybe like an earthquake. But if it was kept private, if it was just known among the Nazis and they knew who had it, it would be a big tool for power. It would be the most sought-after thing in all of their wild imaginations."

I turned back to Patrick. "What do you think happened to it?"

"I always thought it would be found with the family of the man responsible for the flag. Hessler. Hitler entrusted it to him. Every place it showed up, he is the one with the flag."

I was interested. "What do you know about him?"

"A very a faithful member of the Nazi party. Part of the *putsch*. Commissioned into the Sturmabteilung, the SA, then the Schutzstaffel, the SS. He kept the flag in the Braunes Haus in Munich, the headquarters of the Nazi Party. That's where it was taken after it was last seen publicly. I thought maybe he had hidden it there, or gave it to someone in his family. I just can't imagine him letting it out of his sight. Maybe he hid it in the German Alps, or buried it in a secret cave. I don't know."

"Are members of his family still alive?"

"His children are alive."

"Where was this Braunes Haus? Does that mean Brown House?"

"Yes, Brown House, which was not brown," Patrick said smiling. "It was named after the SA men who were always there, in their brown shirts. It was at 45 Brienner Straße in Munich."

"Is it still there?"

"No, it was damaged in the war, and then torn down."

I sat silently for a while as I finished my lunch. "We've got to find the Blood Flag and use it to trap Eidhalt. When he brings all of the leaders of these neo-Nazi movements together, I need to use it to get in, and then we have to stop them."

Florian and Patrick looked at each other, and then Florian said, "How do you plan on stopping them?"

"By doing whatever it takes."

"Within the law," Florian said with raised eyebrows.

"Of course."

"Good."

"But I need to know if you're willing to help. Florian?"

"Yes, if I can."

"Patrick? Can you give any time to this?"

"I will make time. I will do it on my own time. I will do whatever I can."

"Can you use the agency's tools—or access, to help?"

"I will do whatever I am permitted to do and will tell you if there is something I would like to do but cannot. If that is the case, and it is critical, we may be able to get permission. But we will deal with these things as they come."

"Let me tell you about our confidential informant. I can't tell you his name. But, he's the key to this entire plan."

I told them what I knew about Jedediah. They were amazed, not only about him, but about the Southern Volk.

Florian said, "We will help." He glanced at Patrick who gave him a very subtle nod of agreement. "But we have something to tell you about. You told me of your experience in Recklinghausen. The thing that made you start thinking about these neo-Nazis."

I nodded.

"The group you encountered. We know them. They call themselves die Eternals. The Eternals. They say they are already dead. That the government has already killed them. That the only people Germany cares about are foreigners, immigrants, Turks, Muslims. They are neo-Nazis and are becoming more dangerous. But they are sophisticated. Most of them are young; they arrange their marches by a private Twitter-like thing. Encrypted. They send out the location the day of the march and everyone goes there and knows what to do. It is like a flash mob, I think you call them. Unless you catch them in their masks, you have nothing."

"Not very surprising. Makes sense," I said.

Florian almost smiled. "Ah, but we have broken their encryption. Their next march is tonight. And we will be there."

"Truly?"

"Yes, in Koblenz. Would you like to come?"

* * *

We met at 10:00 p.m. The march was to be at midnight, and Florian and the others wanted to be in place and out of sight long before then. There were many BKA involved, as well as other police. I gathered with a group of them who went over their plan before dispersing in numerous cars and vans to carry the arrested.

I climbed into the back seat of Florian's car. Another BKA agent was with him. He said over his shoulder as he started the car, "We have been waiting for this evening. We have been monitoring your friends for quite a while, but never knew where they were coming from or where they were going until it was already over. Then they would post another video on YouTube, which made things worse. Their movement continues to grow. Tonight, maybe it shrinks a little. They may think we have infiltrated them." We drove away, got on the highway, and finally arrived in Koblenz.

Florian drove slowly around the city, which was dark and still. There were few cars on the streets and no pedestrians. The large church was lighted. The few city lights reflected peacefully on the Rhine and Mosel rivers.

"What's the plan?" I asked.

"We know where they will start, and we will close the street behind them—they won't know. Then, as they march our men will be waiting for them; and as they approach the end, we will prepare a trap to round them up. They often wear swastikas, which is illegal; in addition, the march does not have permission. They are not large offenses, but we will put them in jail. We will then have their names . . . and they'll know we will be watching them from now on."

"How many do you think will be here?"

"The last one had almost four hundred. Maybe that number, or close."

"That's a lot of people to arrest."

"Yes, we won't get them all, but the leaders, the ones in the front carrying banners. Those we will get."

I couldn't tell what was being said on the radios, but the preparation seemed unhurried and sure. After a half hour we pulled into a field where there were numerous BKA agents in marked and unmarked cars. Local police hurried around excitedly. They checked their watches.

Coffee appeared, and Florian and others drank while we waited. "Won't they see us all here?" I asked, looking at the assembly.

Florian shook his head. The march begins on the other side of town. We will go to our places in a few minutes and prepare to greet them."

"How long do the marches last?"

"Generally less than fifteen minutes. Sometimes thirty, but they want to be fairly quick so they can avoid arrest."

I nodded and waited. Finally midnight approached. Florian and I got into his car with his other partner and headed toward our position. We were to be at the end of the march with the others. There were at least fifty police and BKA waiting, most behind buildings or in alcoves. Twenty of them had assembled riot fences, which were to be pulled into the street to block it and prevent anyone passing. There were others on side streets with the same fences, ready to make the primary street into a large corral where the marchers would be trapped.

Midnight came. I could hear the quiet crackle of radios as the marchers assembled right where they were supposed to, in the old part of town surrounded by shops and low buildings hundreds of years old. Just like Recklinghausen, I thought. They always started with Old Germany, the old traditions and history. The way things used to be.

Florian looked at me. "They're on their way. Masks, torches, the usual things."

I strained to see them as they approached down the main street. I couldn't yet see anyone around the curve, but I could hear singing. In Recklinghausen they had been silent. But tonight they were singing. They kept their voices very low, just above a whisper. But enough to be heard before they were seen.

I could now see shadows dancing on the sides of the buildings as the marchers approached the curve. The light from the torches illuminated everything around as the singers came closer. Finally the leaders turned the curve and I could see them. My heart jumped at the sight of the line of masked people in black capes carrying a large banner in the front of hundreds of marchers, all singing their soft dirge, with a lone cameraman filming the entire procession.

The march slowed as the leaders looked around. Florian watched them. They seemed to be on guard. The marchers stopped dead in the middle of the street a quarter mile away, close enough that I could hear their torches hissing; the same kind of torch that broke the window on my rental car in Recklinghausen.

Suddenly they laid their banner down on the street. They all turned their backs toward us, facing the way they had come. Before I could figure out what they were doing, they turned back toward us and threw Molotov cocktails into the street toward us. Each of them had been carrying a gasoline-filled bottle inside their cape or coat. They crashed into the street, creating a wall of flames between them and us. They began running back the other way with their torches, as others tossed firebombs down the side streets.

This wasn't just a retreat; this had been planned. There was no panic, no screaming, no sound at all. Even the dirge had stopped. As they rounded the curve in a trot they began removing their capes and masks, leaving them in the street. The flames rose to six or eight feet, too much for anyone to run after them without the risk of setting himself on fire.

Florian's radio cracked as the police tried to decide what to do. All the side streets were blocked by fire as was the main street. The marchers now were unmasked, but couldn't be seen. Their capes lay on the road behind the fire wall, with the white masks and the burning torches next to them. We could see the marchers running fast now, breaking away from the main body and heading for their escape routes—to their cars or bicycles or however they had planned to get out of Koblenz.

Before any backup plan could be put into place they were gone. Florian listened to his radio. "They have captured one of them. Not a marcher . . ." he paused. "Someone on a roof." He looked up but didn't say anything. "He had night vision binoculars and has been there for hours, they think. Long before we got here."

"They knew we were coming," I remarked.

Florian nodded. "These are different Nazis. Perhaps we underestimated them."

We walked forward to inspect their masks and capes as the flames began to die.

I looked down at the banner in the street that the leaders of the march had been carrying. It was on a pole, and was written in that same old English font I had seen weeks ago. "*Dein kurzes Leben, mach es eternal.*" I asked Florian, "What does that say?"

"Your short life, make it eternal."

"Meaning?"

"They are trying to say that the way to become eternal is to recognize you're already dead. The German government has killed you. Emasculated you. You are nothing to them, only others matter. It is what we discussed before."

I watched diminishing flames around us from the discarded torches and the gasoline. "They are going to attract a lot more people with this."

He nodded. "That is what we are afraid of."

* * *

As the next day came to a close and I was back in D.C., my BlackBerry rang. "Yes?"

"What are you doing tonight?" Jedediah.

"What do you have in mind?" I asked.

"You know Lady Bird Johnson Park?"

"Sure."

"There's a trail, right by the river. Be there, east side. Nine o'clock. I'll pick you up."

"I'll be there."

The connection broke. I went home, had dinner with my family, and then headed to the Potomac River.

I wore jeans and a black North Face fleece, and as usual, carried my Glock nine millimeter.

I arrived fifteen minutes early. It was dark, and traffic rushed by in front of me. I waited. At exactly nine my phone rang again. A different number.

"Yes?"

"Can you get to the river?"

"What for?"

"That's where I am." He hung up.

I shook my head and headed across the grass and through the trees until I was at the bank of the river. As I stepped close to the water, the lights of a boat came on directly in front of me. It had been there, moving very slowly against the flow of the river to hold its position without its lights. The boat moved sideways against the current and turned upstream as it nudged into the bank. As I jumped on board, the motor roared and we turned away and headed downstream. It looked to be about twenty-two feet long with a small covered cabin. I stood next to Jedediah, who was wearing jeans and a long-sleeve white T-shirt. He was barefoot. He looked at me, unsmiling. There was an awkward tension.

"You finally got a cell phone?"

"Thanks for the reminder," he said as he reached up on the panel next to him and tossed it into the river.

"That's expensive."

"Not really. One-time use. You can learn a lot from the people who run drugs. Half the people I know in the mountains of South Carolina run meth. Those boys know all the tricks."

"You can never be too safe," I said.

"I would assume you'd know that."

"That's why I said it."

He motored downstream around the point of Fort McNair, and headed up toward the Frederick Douglas Bridge. He passed under the bridge and turned to the bank on the right, across from the Navy yard. We approached a soft bank that was marshy and hidden by trees. He drifted between two overhanging trees and stopped. He turned off the lights of the boat and put the engine into idle. He dropped the anchor over the side and let the rope feed out until it touched the bottom. He let it play out a little more, and then tied it to the cleat. He sat in the padded seat in the back of the boat, and pointed at a folding captain's chair for me to sit in front of him. I did.

I said, "So what's going on? I've got a lot to talk to you about, but first tell me what you're doing in D.C."

He stared at me in the dark. What little light there was reflected off the river onto his face in an uneven way, like a candle through a piece of silk. Somehow it made him look even more dangerous.

"Business. A national chain of body shops is trying to buy me. They flew me up here to persuade me what a good idea it would be to sell my shop to them."

"You interested?"

"No. But I like free food and drink."

"So what's going on?"

"Well you failed—thanks for nothing—but our head guy came up with an idea. I thought I should tell you what it is. It's going to be pretty damned dramatic."

"No, don't! I just got back from Germany, and have the perfect idea. If we pull it off, you'll be the biggest player in Germany!"

"Too late. He's said what we're going to do."

"*Can't* be too late. This is huge. You've got to give me some time."

"I'm not in charge. He is. And he's determined. Once he sets his mind to something, just clear out. That's what's going to happen."

"What does he want to do?"

"He's sort of a World War II history buff and thinks one of the ways to get back to what Hitler had going was to get some things that were important back then."

"Go on."

"There's a display going around the country. *World War II through Russia's Eyes.*"

"And?"

"Hitler killed himself in a bunker in Berlin. The Americans let the Russians take Berlin. We figured why take all those casualties ourselves. Let the Russians die. And die they did, but they took Berlin with a vengeance. And they found Hitler's bunker intact. They pulled all the stuff out of that bunker that was there when Hitler died and kept it. The stuff that was in that bunker, Hitler's personal stuff, is what's on this tour."

"Wow. So what's the plan?"

"One of the stops is in Atlanta. He's going to break in and take all of Hitler's shit. Shoes, uniform hanging on the coat rack when he shot himself, his riding crop, and his hat. This is the real stuff. It's what Hitler had when he died. And we're going to go get it."

"Has to be a lot of security."

"A ton. He doesn't care. He's got a line on some C4, and he's going to do it full on. Get as much of the stuff as he can. We're going to hit it on the last day. We're going to have guys go through with hidden video cameras every day to check out the security, the timing, everything. And then we're going to take it down on the last day."

"Don't do it. And if they insist on doing it, I don't want you involved."

"May have to be. I do what he says, or he gets suspicious. He's suspicious anyway. Every time I leave town he's suspicious. He suspects his *wife*. He suspects *everybody* is ratting on him. He's paranoid. So we do what he tells us. Plain as that."

"Tell me about him."

"Don't you have a file on him?" I nodded.

Jedediah waited, then said, "His name is Greg Brunnig. He's extremely smart. College educated. Been in some trouble, but nothing serious. He could pass for a banker."

"It's like stealing a Picasso. People don't get away with that."

"Oh, he'll figure it out. He's that smart. And nobody's going to be looking for somebody to steal any of that stuff."

I doubted it. "You think the Russians haven't thought about somebody grabbing this stuff?"

"Well, we're going to. Or at least we're going to try."

I listened to the dissipated wake of a passing ship slapping against the side of the boat. "Seems like a really bad idea. And I think I've got something better."

"Yeah, *now* you do. We have our marching orders. It's set. It's going down next week."

"Next week? How are you going to get a plan together in a week?"

Jedediah thought he heard something in the marsh and waited.

I looked out over the marsh with him. "What are you listening to? How could anybody be out here? There's no place to *be*."

"I don't take chances."

"So how does he plan on pulling this off?"

"Even if it's really a sophisticated thing. Even if we have to hack our way in with axes and blowtorches, it's not a problem."

I was perplexed. "How is that not a problem?"

"Because we have a couple of guys who will take the fall. They've been unofficial parts of our group for years, but they're always in and out of prison. They're fully criminals. They *like* being criminals, and they don't care if they go back to the house. It'd be like a family reunion. They're big-shit Nazis with tattoos they got in prison. They protect each other and nobody messes with them. They've already committed a couple of felonies and the cops are right on their tails. So, they know they're headed back to the slammer anyway. They say they'll sacrifice themselves for the cause. It will be glorious."

"That's the plan? To get caught?"

"If necessary. We won't know the exact plan until we see the layout. But this thing is on. You should know that." His eyes narrowed. "And you'd better not tell your police friends what's coming. They don't need any help in catching us."

I rubbed my fingers through my hair, frustrated not only at this ridiculous plan but at the possibility of a lost opportunity. "You've got to call it off. You've got to get to Brunnig. Not only will they catch your pre-qualified felons, they'll catch all of you."

"They'll never prove it."

"Of course they will. You think the police are stupid?"

"Oh definitely. I think some police are dumber than crayfish. Some of them are even dumber than Nazis. Some of them even *are* Nazis and will look the other way."

"Well the *smart* ones are going to figure this out, and they're going to come after you, and they're going to come after Brunnig."

Jedediah glanced at his watch, which had a huge luminous dial and was easy to read, even in the pitch darkness. He stood up and bent down right in front of my face. "Then you've got to make sure they don't. You've got to be *some* good to me. I'm here risking my life to give you information. To help you. Well, it's time for you to help me. Keep them off our backs."

I shook my head. I knew this was coming. The real reason he'd dragged me out here. "Don't know if I can do that. They may not listen to us."

"They'll listen to you. Make it happen. Do your FBI shit. Get us our ticket to Germany."

"That's what I've been trying to tell you. I *have* your ticket to Germany!"

"What is it?"

"The Blood Flag."

He paused in the darkness. "*The* Blood Flag?"

"You know about it?"

"Everybody knows about it. You have it?"

"No. We're going to find it. Then authenticate it and take it to Germany."

"Do you know where it is?"

"I went to Germany and talked to the German FBI. They're going to help me find it."

Another pause in the darkness. "You didn't tell them about me, did you?"

"I told them we had someone on the inside, but not by name. No description, no nothing."

"I didn't authorize you to talk about me to anybody!" I could feel him breathing like a caged animal. "That's part of my deal with Karl. Shit, even him telling you was over the line. I can't trust any of you."

"I just said we had a guy. They have no idea who it is."

"So you'd be fine if they ID me, that I can take your government-issued handgun and shoot you in the chest with it, right? Because if you're that sure, then you're not taking any risk at all."

"Sounds fair to me."

Jedediah stood up. "You don't have a lead on the flag at all, do you?"

"No, I've only just come up with the plan. Give me a little time."

"Well, then we've got to go with our bird in the hand. And when you get a line on the Blood Flag, you let me know."

He walked to the wheel, started the boat, pulled in the anchor, and headed to where he had picked me up.

On the way home I called Karl from my car and told him what had happened. He was impressed both by the Southern Volk's industriousness and by the fact that they would all be in jail within a week. He too saw the threat to our plan, and agreed I had to go to Atlanta to stop it from blowing up in our faces. We couldn't let Jedediah get arrested.

First thing the next morning I called the Special Agent in charge of the Atlanta Division. I told her I needed a meeting with her, Atlanta Police, and the head of the Russian security. She said the Russian advance team was already in Atlanta and that the materials would arrive in about three days. I told her to set it up at the FBI office and I would be there by tomorrow. I called Alex and told her to clear her calendar. We were going to Atlanta.

CHAPTER SEVEN

The Atlanta office was well known as being independent minded. They didn't wait for direction from Washington. So the news that I was coming from D.C. uninvited and wanting to meet with them and the Russians (and make a big deal about something or other) was not going to sit well. If it was an Atlanta issue, they would believe they could handle it. And if it wasn't an Atlanta issue, then we should leave them alone. I wasn't looking forward to the meeting.

We took a cab to the downtown FBI office and were escorted to the top floor. When the elevator opened, we were met by the special agent in charge, Karen Brindle. We stepped out of the elevator with our roll-aboard suitcases. I greeted her, and she didn't respond. She just stared at my suitcase, pointed down the hall, and began walking. I had heard about Karen. She was well known as a hardass, both inside the agency and outside. She was all business, no nonsense, and no humor. I was a little surprised at her appearance. She was wearing a skirt. Not many FBI special agents wore skirts these days. In fact, when I looked more closely, she was wearing a suit. Even in these days of business casual passing for getting dressed up, most special agents dressed down as far as they could. She seemed to be going in the opposite direction. It was a nicely tailored suit and she wore medium high heels. She had shoulder-length dark brown hair and was actually quite attractive. After several seconds of silence, she said, "I have a conference room set up."

I walked next to her down the spotless hallway. "Thanks for helping. This is really important."

"It better be," she said as she opened the door to the conference room and pushed it away, indicating for us to go in before her. We put our rolling bags in the corner and stood by the table. Karen came in followed by two other men. The conference room was set up for ten people, and there were bag lunches stacked on a table at the end of the room.

She said, "I've ordered lunch. While we eat you can tell us what the hell is going on. The Russians will be here at one. Does that work for you?" she asked, seeming to hope that it didn't.

"Yes, thanks. Again, I apologize for this short notice and the intrusion. I will explain it all, and hope you can understand how significant this is."

She nodded, checked her BlackBerry, and looked at the lunches. "Tell us what you know."

I grabbed the first bag, opened it, and spread it in front of me. The others grabbed theirs and sat at the end of the table near me. I told them the whole story, starting with the ceremony at Normandy up to my conversation with Jedediah two days ago. I didn't tell them his identity, but they sure understood his significance.

After I was finished Karen asked, "We haven't had any issues with the neo-Nazis in our area. Aren't they just like a twisted Boy Scout troop?"

"Those days are over. They've decided to come out of the woodwork and be counted. The immigration thing has been a focal point, and they are gaining recruits faster than anybody expected. Some of it is because some actual leadership has risen to the top. Brunnig is charismatic. But the real threat is this guy in Germany trying to unify everybody, and he has the money to do it. That's what we've got to stop. But, right now we have to take care of what's going to happen here this week. Tell me about security for the exhibit."

One of the men spoke for the first time. "I have the federal side. We're pretty well organized already. The . . . " he hesitated, then went on, "The gist of it is the Russians have this display that they set up in a kind of labyrinth. At least according to the diagrams we've been given. You walk into the museum, it's dark, and you walk through a series of displays with photographs and writing and memorabilia that takes up roughly half the museum. It's quiet and subdued. This is the tenth and last stop for the tour. They have the setup down to a science. All they need is the space. But nobody cares about the items in the first half of the exhibit. Nothing there to really steal and no security really needed, although they have basic security. What really matters is the Hitler stuff. Once you get through the horrifying pictures and details of how hard Russia had to fight Germany—did you know that Russia lost twenty some million people in World War II?"

I nodded.

"Well, I sure didn't. It's unbelievable the carnage inflicted by this Nazi régime. Just evil. Anyway, once you get through all that, you get to a thing that looks sort of like a train car. It's not, it's actually an armored bunker. It's intended to be like Hitler's bunker, but you look into it from the outside, like through windows. So you don't really get that close to the stuff itself. Windows are pretty good sized, but bullet proof. And the bunker is reinforced and extremely secure. It's sealed. There's only one door, and it's a combination safe lock that is only known by the assistant chief of security for the Russian group. And notably, he's never actually near the display once it's open to the public. Once he closes and locks that door, he disappears where he cannot be found. So if somebody grabs the chief of security from Russia and threatens to kill him unless they're told the combination, it won't matter. They're not going to get the combination. Even if they killed the chief of security they still wouldn't have it. This guy goes out to zoos, movies, wherever he wants to go. He doesn't carry a cell phone and is completely out of touch. He only comes back once it's time to tear down the display."

I finished my sandwich. "Sounds like a hard target."

"It is. And if they try and get it during the load out, that's not going to work either. The whole display is set up separately from the Hitler materials. Including the bunker room. It's all finished and ready to go, and gets here by a series of trucks that are separate from the actual Hitler stuff. Neither one knows how the other is going, and they're required to take routes that are not obvious. The trucks are unmarked. Inside the truck is a container almost as secure as the one in the exhibits. There are Russian security officers with each truck and hitting one of the trucks would be as difficult as an armored car. You're just not going to get in there without an anti-tank weapon or a lot of time."

I asked, "So when are they vulnerable?"

"Only one time. When they transfer the materials from the truck to the exhibit. It's about a half hour set-up while the exhibit bunker is open. They have to go in and dust, clean everything up, set it all up, and then secure it. There are a dozen Russian security, fully armed. There are local police, state police, and FBI. I don't think anybody could get within a hundred yards of that transfer."

"Then they're going to hit it at the museum."

"It's pretty tough. It's impenetrable. It literally is an armored car. I don't know how they'd get through it. They'd never get through the key pad on the door and they'll never find the guy with the combination."

. I pondered how these amateur thieves were going to break into this vault. "When are the Russians coming?"

Karen glanced at her watch. "They should be here in a few minutes."

"Let's continue this when they get here."

We ate in something of an awkward silence for the next ten minutes until the conference room phone rang. One of the other agents answered the phone. The Russians were there. "I'll go down and get them," he said.

He returned in ten minutes with three Russian men, ranging in ages from thirty to fifty. They introduced themselves around, and it became clear that one of them was in charge. His name was Dmitri. He had a buzz haircut, was rather small, maybe five feet six inches, and had no sense of humor. His two colleagues were also from the FRB, the Federal Security Service of the Russian Federation, and were equally humorless. They looked uneasy being at the FBI station.

Karen offered them cookies from the leftover lunch, but they declined. Dmitri said, "You called us to this meeting in a great hurry. What is so important?"

Karen looked at me and then spoke before I could. "There's going to be an attempt on your exhibit."

Dmitri frowned. "An attempt? For what?"

I answered. "To steal the Hitler items."

"It's not possible. No one can do this."

"Maybe so, but they're going to try," I said.

Dmitri spoke rapidly in Russian to the other two men and then looked at me. "Who?"

I nodded. "A neo-Nazi group based in the Southern United States called the Southern Volk. They are determined to take the items from the bunker. They're going to do it this weekend while they're on display."

"How do they propose to do this?"

"I don't know. I don't think they know. They're amateurs. From what I've heard of the security so far, I don't think they have a prayer of pulling it off."

Dmitri nodded with some satisfaction. "That is my thinking too. Let them try. They will fail. They will not even get close."

There was a pause while everyone realized the truth of what he said. But that wasn't where I wanted this conversation to go. I said, "I want you to let them succeed."

"What? Let them succeed? Why would we do that?"

"Because it is to all our benefits if they do."

Dmitri looked puzzled. "How?"

"In a few weeks all of the leaders of the biggest neo-Nazi movements in the world will meet in Germany, including, I might add, from Russia. A very wealthy German has bought a castle to train neo-Nazi groups, and is going to provide them with uniforms, weapons, propaganda, and world-wide leadership."

"So?"

"The meeting is only for those who can persuade him, show him actually, that they're worthy of coming to Germany. We have someone inside the Southern Volk and we need to make sure they get invited. Their idea is to take these Hitler items from the bunker. From your bunker. We need to let them. I think that will almost guarantee that they get to Germany."

Dmitri looked dumbfounded. "You want us to give these neo-Nazis Hitler's last items? Are you insane?"

"No. And I don't mean for you to give them his items. I was talking to Alex on the way down," I indicated her next to me, "and we think we have a way to make this work. We can create near perfect forgeries of anything. Including clothing, shoes, desks, anything. I've looked at the photographs of the exhibit online. None of them are close up, and none of them are high quality."

"No. We want people to come see the exhibit."

"Exactly. But they don't really know what these items look like up close. They won't know the real from the fake. They won't have a high-resolution photo to compare them to. If we make copies, and if they're in the bunker, they won't even hesitate to think they're the originals."

Dmitri actually smiled.

"What?"

Dmitri inhaled sharply and then exhaled and shook his head. "We thought perhaps the biggest difficulties with neo-Nazism was in Russia. We guard these bunker items in Moscow as if they were all the gold Russia owns. There is a very determined neo-Nazi group in Russia: The Russian National Unity Group, or the RNE. They're in two hundred fifty cities. They publish a newsletter with a circulation of one hundred fifty thousand. They call each other *Soratnik*," he said, his tone dripping with anger and sarcasm. "Comrades in arms. They do military combat training near Moscow. They have openly declared their intention to overthrow the Russian government by force. We have long feared that they would try and use Hitler's items from the bunker as their icons. I thought in the United States we would be safe."

"Do you have anybody inside the RNE?"

Dmitri looked intently at me. "I am not free to discuss our internal intelligence matters. But you can remain confident that we are doing everything that we can." He continued, "I also need to know who will pay for the damage to our vault, our bunker."

I said quickly, "I will. We will—the American government—you have my word."

Alex and Karen both looked at me, obviously wondering how I could be so sure.

I said to Dmitri, "So how are we going to copy the items? Can we have access to the originals?"

Dmitri looked at the man next to him. "Sergei?"

He shook his head. "No. Not possible."

I said to Sergei, "The best copies would be made off the originals." Sergei shook his head. He wasn't having it. I didn't have time for this. "Then you must have good photos. And I'll need to see how they're displayed in the bunker."

"Fine," Sergei replied. "We have many good photographs."

"I need a CD of all the best photos you've got. I need to get my people working on these things. I'll head up to D.C., and I'll be back by Friday. I don't know when these guys are going to hit, but I think it will be near the end of the exhibit. They wanted to go through the display several times. When does this display open to the public?"

Sergei said, "Saturday morning at 10:00 a.m."

"Okay. We have to get you the substitutes by Friday."

Dmitri nodded. "Sooner would be better. We should probably discuss what needs to be replaced exactly. We can't replace the desk because they'd never get it out of there. I think we need to look at what can be taken out by hand."

Sergei agreed. "There are only four things anyone could carry out. His shoes, his walking stick, his hat, and his uniform."

I asked, "How are his shoes still in existence? I thought his body was burned."

"These were found in his closet."

I thought for a minute. "Was his skull ever found?"

Dmitri responded, "His body was found by Russian soldiers. They were told to crush his skull with their rifles and break it into bits so there would be nothing for anyone to ever see again."

"Which gave rise to the myths that Hitler lived on after the war."

"I suppose, but it also kept the Hitler worshipers at home."

I nodded. "I'll be back."

* * *

As we rode back to the airport Alex said, "You know that Russian was full of shit, right?"

"Which one?"

"About Hitler's skull?"

"What about it?"

"It wasn't crushed. They took it to Moscow. A lot of people think they still have it. I read all about it. I don't believe a word they say."

"Frankly neither do I." I pulled out my BlackBerry. "I've got to get on the phone."

I called Craig Phillips, the director of the OTD, the Operational Technology Division, a critically important office for the FBI. Our 'Q'. They come up with the technical gadgets, eavesdropping bugs, microphones, invisible ink, the James Bond stuff. They have access to things I don't even know about, and are unbelievably capable.

I told Phillips what I needed. He was intrigued until I told him when I needed it, and then he became annoyed. They were already working twenty-four hours a day, and didn't have the "bandwidth" to pull this off. He was unimpressed when I told him he had to, and he was even more unimpressed when I told him he needed to meet me at his office in the Hoover building that night. I told him this project had the attention of the highest levels of the agency. He told me he doubted it, but he'd see me at the office.

As we waited for our flight to take off from Ronald Reagan Airport, I called Karl and gave him an update. He was surprised by the developments and peeved when I told him what I had said to Phillips. He wondered who at the highest levels of the agency was so concerned about all this. I told him I didn't know yet, but I was going to try to generate the interest needed to get OTD to move this up on their list. Karl wished me good luck and hung up. Karl was distancing himself from me and whatever I was doing. He obviously thought it was all going to blow up.

When we landed, Alex and I drove directly to the Hoover Building and went to Phillips' office. He looked tired. He was looking at his computer through his bifocals and moving his head around to get the reading lens on whatever he was studying.

He peered over his glasses at me. The lab was behind the glass wall of his office. He said, "Pictures?"

No chitchat. I pulled out the two CDs Sergei had given me. He slipped the first one into his computer slot. I said, "I appreciate you meeting with me."

"You used the magic words. 'Highest levels of the Bureau.' So who exactly?"

I nodded as if that were a perfectly understandable request. What I didn't know was who I was going to say had any interest at all. Nobody even knew about it except Karl, who had no clout at all.

Phillips brought up the files with the photos in thumbnail, and double clicked on the first one, which brought it to full size. "Hmm," he grunted. "Interesting. This is the whole bunker. Take a look." He turned the screen so we could both see it. I had seen a photo of the bunker and its contents in an ad for the Russian display. But these photos were extremely high quality and very dense. The bunker was set up exactly as Hitler had it on the day he committed suicide. It had all the trappings of Nazism with wall hangings and maps, photos, and numerous smaller items with Swastikas. It was carpeted and in the middle was a heavy wooden desk.

He called up one photo after another and blew them up to their full size.

"These are good photos."

He looked at me.

"But we still need the items. We need to measure them."

"We can't get them. We just have to get close enough. The men who are going to take these things will have no idea what the exact measurements are. All they know is they were Hitler's."

He studied the last photographs with annoyance. "We can do it, but I don't have the time. You need to get somebody to order us to do this."

"Will do, but we don't have much time. We need you to get started tonight."

He looked at me sharply. "First you tell us what to do, and now you tell us *when* to do it. You know about everything we're working on? You ready to re-order all our priorities?"

"No, sorry. I'm just acutely aware of how important this is."

"And all the others are just shit projects."

"That's not what I'm saying at all."

He sat back. "I can get it by a couple amateur thieves. But if they take this anywhere to get it authenticated, we'll be in trouble."

"I don't think we have to worry about that."

"Get me the authority and we'll get started."

* * *

I went to my office, took off my tie, and put my jacket over the back of my chair. I was surprised when my phone rang as soon as I sat down. I figured it was probably Alex, but it wasn't. It was my unit chief. "Good evening. Surprised you're still here."

"And I'm glad you're back. Where the hell have you been?"

"Atlanta."

There was a pause. "You're supposed to be focused on al-Hadi."

"I'm working him."

"Remember I told you he was spotted in Europe?"

"Sure."

"Well, what has he been doing since? I haven't seen anything from you on this guy in days. If he disappears I'm going to be really pissed. I want to know where he is and what he's doing. You know he's a player."

"Financially. Yeah."

"I don't want you taking your eye off this guy *at all*."

"I'm on it."

"I want to talk to you at ten o'clock tomorrow morning. And I want to know *everything*. Where this guy's been, what he's been doing. He's your guy."

I turned on my computer. I'd seen a lot of emails on my BlackBerry about al-Hadi, but hadn't been able to open any of the attachments. Some of them were secret, which I could only view from my desktop. I grouped them all together and went through them one after the other. Before I knew it was past midnight. I had a cold feeling in the pit of my stomach. The only reason I even got a lot of these emails, mostly from the CIA, was because al-Hadi was tied to several Islamic "charities" in the United States. Most were fronts and were continually being investigated. We hadn't had much luck since the conviction of a Hamas-supporting charity in Charlotte. They had gotten much more clever. They had learned to filter the money and send it to reputable banks in the Middle East, where it was commingled with funds from other sources then redistributed to various terrorist organizations. But something was up. Al-Hadi was normally based in Yemen, the new wild west of the southern Arabian Peninsula. His trail led to numerous banks, shadowy organizations, arms dealers, and terrorist organizations.

One of the memos from the CIA said he might be the cleverest financial mind in the Middle Eastern terrorist network. The emails and the proof were interesting. He'd been tracked across the border three times in the last three weeks going into and out of Zurich and into Germany. They had no idea why. They couldn't connect him to any particular organization in any of those locations, and they saw nothing in the banking transactions—at least the ones we were aware of—that could tell us anything about his objectives. I saved the emails and attachments to my secure folder and then shut down my computer.

I stood in the elevator of the Hoover Building as it descended, wondering how I was going to get somebody with authority to make Phillips do what I needed him to do. I loved the government.

CHAPTER EIGHT

The next morning, I was awakened at 5:00 a.m. by my cell phone. "Kyle, it's Florian and Patrick. Did we wake you up?"

"You know it's only five o'clock here?"

"Sorry. We thought you would want to know this right away. Patrick thinks he has been able to track down the thing that you were interested in."

"Truly?"

"Maybe. He has a couple of possibilities."

"What are they?"

Patrick's voice came through loudly, "I have things I want to show you. There are several things you will find interesting, but I can't tell them to you over the phone. Why don't you come back over here."

"I can't. I've got something blowing up in my face right now. I'll tell you all about it. Any way you could come here? Don't you guys take like two hundred days of vacation a year anyway?"

"At least!" Patrick laughed. "Let us see what we can do."

Since I was up, I showered, dressed, and went into the office early.

I sat in the chair outside Murphy's office until he arrived looking intense and distracted. His secretary hadn't arrived yet. He looked at me confused, clearly not remembering who I was. He didn't greet me, he just said, "What do you want?" He was wearing a suit that fit four years ago.

"I'm the guy working with Karl."

He didn't respond.

"I need two things this morning; and if I could impose on you, I need them first thing."

"Perfect," he said as he opened his office door and put down his briefcase. "Love dealing with questionable shit before I can even get a cup of coffee.

How do I know it's questionable, you wonder? People don't show up at this hour unless they want to do something questionable."

"Not questionable, just important," I said, standing.

He looked at me with doubt. He went around to the other side of his desk, turned on his computer, and sat down, waiting for it to boot up. "Make it quick."

"You know the CI we're running inside the Southern Volk?"

He nodded.

"They're trying to get an invitation to a worldwide neo-Nazi meeting in Germany."

"You told me."

I went on. "There's a guy in Germany who is trying to unify all the leaders of the major Nazi groups from around the world. He has asked the leaders of each group to do something that would impress him and he'll decide who to invite based on whether he's impressed or not. Very vague. I have a plan that I think will get our CI to Germany, but his group has thought up a scheme on their own. They're going to break into a Russian display of World War II materials and steal Hitler's walking stick, shoes, hat, and uniform."

He looked at me frowning. "Where?"

"Atlanta."

"We've got to stop them."

"No. That's the whole point. I've set it up with the Russians so that we're going to let them do this. We have to let them think they've pulled it off. Otherwise the Georgia police will arrest them all and they won't be invited to go to Germany. We've got to make this happen."

"You can't let them have Hitler's things. That would be ridiculous."

"Exactly. I talked to OTD last night and they're prepared to build replicas. Phillips said he could do it, and he may be able to do it within time, but he's gotta get somebody—I was thinking you—to tell him to put it at the top of his priority list. He can't do that on his own. He said it's not up to him."

He nodded with understanding. "I'll think about it."

"Thanks. The other thing is, this whole thing is going to be a felony. I need to get OIA for our CI." I was talking about "otherwise illegal activity" status, an authorization for a confidential informant to commit a crime that we know about ahead of time.

He exhaled audibly and looked down at the floor. He wasn't happy I was there. "So first thing in the morning you ask me for an OIA? Seriously? What is your boy's role in this?"

"Well, I don't know what he's actually going to do. Not specifically. I just know he'll be involved."

"You in control of this? Maybe it's time to reel this guy back in."

"We need to close down the Southern Volk. And he's going to help us, but he can't yet because all we've got so far is talk."

"And soon, you'll have a brazen robbery of some items of infinite value, but they won't *actually* steal them because we're going to replace them with fakes. So it's actually not much of a robbery. And he'll be right in the middle of it, so your primary witness will be a co-participant which is, as you know, extremely problematic."

"I understand that. But that's not our long-term goal. Our long-term goal is to get us inside this international meeting, and try to shut down these groups worldwide."

He shook his head vigorously. "No. That's *your* goal. We don't give a shit about neo-Nazism in Russia, or Croatia. We deal with American issues. *Domestic* terrorism. Maybe you've forgotten."

"No, I haven't forgotten. But this is bigger than just domestic. This is international. They're all connected. What if those overseas strengthen domestic terrorists? You wouldn't care? Of course you would. Money and arms are starting to flow. It takes the internal threat to a whole different level. We need to shut it down."

He turned away, clearly done with the conversation. "I'll consider your request for Atlanta, and I'll talk to the director about the OIA. I sure hope you know what you're doing."

"And there's one other thing."

He looked back at me trying to control his frustration. "What?"

"The Russian display of Hitler's bunker is a metal container that is about the same as a train car. The items that are kept in there, as I said, will be switched out. But for the robbery, they're going to have to break into that container. My guess is they're going to do some damage. The Russians wanted to know who was going to pay to repair the damage. I told them that we would pay."

"What in the *hell* is wrong with you? Now we're an insurance company? How much?"

"No numbers were discussed."

He threw out his hands. "Perfect. No matter how much it costs, we'll fix it. That was how you left it?"

"I don't expect these guys to burn the place down. They're just going to have to cut into it or break into it somehow. So we'll have to repair whatever they use to get in there."

"Simple as that?" You don't have any idea do you?"

"No, but it's not like it will be hundreds of thousands of dollars. I would expect it'd be ten thousand dollars or less. But I don't know."

His voice was now rising and full of sarcasm. "Let's recap. You're going to allow this robbery to occur, your CI will be committing felonies, you're going to let them cut into a Russian display which you said is the equivalent of an armored train car, you're going to fund the immediate and emergency construction of Hitler's shoes and whatever the hell else, repair the train car, and we're paying for all of it. That about sum it up?"

"Yes. I think so."

"And what if I say no?"

"If you say no, I think the display will go on, and the Russians will make sure that there are enough Georgia and Atlanta police there that nothing happens. All the Southern Volk who are trying to commit the robbery will be stopped and arrested, and they will be put in jail, and that will be the end of our relationship with our CI inside the Southern Volk. It will be the loss of the only chance we have to get them to Germany to this meeting, and I'll go back to working my usual job and I'll find some other way to do damage to neo-Nazism."

He responded harshly, "Reminding me of course, again, that this is just really your *personal* vendetta."

"No," I said forcefully. "This is domestic terrorism. And if we don't stop this through the Southern Volk, we won't know which other U.S. group has found favor and financing. It is not a vendetta."

He shook his head. "I'm not promising anything."

The conversation was over. It could not have been more clear from the chill he sent across the room. I left his office and headed back to my cubicle.

* * *

It wasn't even 7:00 a.m. yet. I grabbed a cup of coffee and turned on my computer. The first email that came up was from Florian. He and Patrick were on their way. I did further research on al-Hadi, and looked at some additional CIA background information on him that I hadn't looked at in a while. All the message traffic indicated that no one could figure out why he was in Europe. He'd been there before, but not this broadly and not this extensively. I reviewed his most recent trip, from Tunis to Madrid to Marseilles to Frankfurt to Zurich, then to Geneva, and finally to Amman. He had never been to two-thirds of those cities before, and no one knew who he'd met with. European intelligence was too concerned about being seen to actually follow him. So the itinerary was based on passport scans and videos from airline and train terminals. The stop in Switzerland was of particular interest. He had stopped at a bank, but the bank wasn't talking.

I decided to pull out everything I knew about him from all of my old files and read it all again. I had to look for patterns, small pieces that might fit together. I stacked them up on the left of my desk and started reading, while wondering whether Murphy would give me the authorization I needed for Atlanta.

Shortly after lunch, I got a text from Florian. They had landed at Dulles and were on their way into the city. I alerted security and set up a conference room. I called over to Karl to see if he wanted to meet with them, but he said he was too busy.

Florian and Patrick arrived at 1:00 p.m. I waited for them to pass through security then escorted them upstairs. They were in good spirits and seemed excited to be in Washington. We went to the second floor where I'd reserved a conference room that was far too large for our needs, but comfortable. It was our "boardroom," our showy conference room where we would have meetings with dignitaries or whoever was injecting himself into the FBI's work at that moment. The wood paneling looked like it had been recently oiled or refreshed. The granite table and the leather chairs looked equally new.

Patrick carried a briefcase the size of a roll-aboard suitcase. I placed my notebook at the end of the table and pulled out the chair.

Florian asked, "Is it okay if I smoke?"

"No, definitely not okay. No smoking in this building at all."

Florian smiled. "I'm glad I asked. I'll take a break in a little while."

Patrick lifted his massive bag onto the table and began pulling out notebooks and papers. The briefcase was black and battered and looked as old as the copied documents coming out of it. The papers were copies of old Nazi documents that had been typed, not printed. Eagles sat on winged swastika crests on virtually every page. Patrick began arranging the documents and notebooks.

Patrick began. "So," his *s* was more like a *z*. "Here we have the best documents I have been able to find so far. They will help us find this flag, I think. Many of these documents we got back from the Russians only recently. As you know, the Russians took Berlin in 1945. As conquerors do, they took it upon themselves to capture all of the German documents they could get their hands on. Probably to identify people to hang. But we have recently gotten many of them, or copies, back. It is a very good thing for us, because I think it gives us a hint on where we should go."

I stood up then walked over to Patrick to look over his shoulder. He was excited and focused. Florian had his glasses off and was examining a particular document very closely. Patrick went over them all again carefully and then divided them into two piles. He nodded, as if he was finally ready. "Ok, I'm a little tired. I've been doing this round the clock for a few days now. But I think we have identified the two most likely possibilities for the current location of the flag. First, let me show you this."

I looked at it carefully, but it made no sense to me.

"It goes with a couple of other things," which he looked for and then found. He handed them to me as well. "These are the documents that talk about *die Blutfahne* during the time of the Third Reich. Early on, well before the war was started with Poland, Hitler had already identified the flag as special. It was displayed at rallies and marches. And he decided, hold on," as he looked for another document and found it, "to name an individual as the person who would be responsible for the flag. Who would carry it in public and keep it safe otherwise. He wanted one person to be in charge of the Blood Flag. That person is well known. We talked about him in Germany. Otto Hessler."

"Yes."

"This is the document that gave Hessler his commission as the one to tend to *die Blutfahne*. Full responsibility for it until it is revoked. See this here? This is the German word for 'until revoked.' And look at the signature."

"Adolf Hitler."

"Yes, exactly. His signature was very simplistic and readable. And it is authentic." He made a sweeping motion with his hand. "All these documents have been authenticated. And it was Hessler's job right up until the end of the war. We are sure."

"What happened to him?"

"He survived the war, and lived in Germany after. But, as far as we can tell, he was never asked about the flag. Quite remarkable, given the importance of the flag. In any case, he died in 1951. We found his grandson, though. He claimed to know nothing of the flag. He was of no help."

Florian said, "It's a little bit strange that his family claims to know nothing about it. This was something they were very proud of during the war. It was considered a job of highest honor. So we don't believe the grandson, which makes us look even harder at the family. We think the family does know, and the fact that they did not say long ago that the flag had been destroyed makes us believe even more that the flag does still exist and they know what happened to it. But they are clearly not telling us, so we have continued our research."

Patrick pulled some documents out of the middle pile, "Next is the possibility we consider the least likely. But it is a possibility. As we said, the Russians were the ones who took Berlin. The Americans could have, but you Americans think differently," he added nodding, looking at me to see if I approved. "The Americans knew the Nazis would fight vigorously to defend Berlin and the *Führer*. The Americans knew that Berlin would fall, but why expend the lives of tens of thousands of Americans to make that happen? Let the Russians do the dying."

I agreed. "That was the theory, at least in part. It might be argued that it resulted in millions of Germans in East Germany living under communism for almost fifty years."

Patrick nodded, "But again, it saved American lives."

"Without a doubt."

"Well the Russians grabbed everything in sight and took it back to Russia. We have found traces within the Russian archives that they took many Nazi flags back to Russia as souvenirs. It could be that the *Blutfahne* is among those flags. The Russians may not have identified that flag specifically. It may be in a Russian general's house, or Stalin's house. It's hard to say."

I thought for a minute, and then said, "I think I know the guy who would have just the answer to that. There is a Russian museum tour in the United States right now called *World War II through Russian Eyes*, and they have a lot of Hitler's materials. I'll tell you more about that later. But the

Russian in charge of that seems to know a lot about what the Russians ended up with. Maybe we should ask him."

"Yes, but as we said, we think that is the least likely location. And I wonder if they would tell us if we did ask them. If they know the true nature of the flag, I doubt it."

Florian spoke, "The last time it was seen in public was at the Induction Ceremony of the Volkssturm on October 18th, 1944. The creation of the folks' militia—really a draft of every man still standing, from sixteen to sixty. It was called the People's Army. But it never amounted to much.

Not enough weapons or training, and it reported to the Nazi party, not the Wehrmacht. Anyway, the induction ceremony was the last time the flag was ever seen."

"So one thing we wanted to check was where Hessler lived. We knew where he lived in Munich, near the Braunes Haus. But in 1945 he moved to Berlin, probably because Hitler wanted the flag near him as the noose closed around Berlin. He thought it had magical powers. So I looked on the street where Hessler lived in Berlin, and found something. Three senior members of the Nazi party. One lived right next door. Hessler's house, in fact, was a large one. Large even for the SS colonel that he was."

Florian continued, "So in the spring of 1945 the American Army is advancing from the West, the Russian Army is advancing from the East, they all knew that the end was near."

Patrick couldn't help himself. He interrupted, "It is our belief that Hitler told him to secure the flag so it could come back to life after the defeat and occupation of Germany."

"But how would they do that?"

"That's the question. How do you hide the flag so the Russians don't get it? How do you hide it so that nobody finds it? We think this is the most likely thing."

"What?"

"We think Hitler authorized one of these Nazi leaders to flee with the flag. He gave him documents for safe passage to leave the country. Anyone else trying to flee might be shot. But not with the right documents. We think he went north and took one of the ships out of Germany."

"Who?"

"We think one of the three people from Hessler's street in Berlin. One of them faked his own death and burned his own house down. We believe he found a body somewhere in Berlin—which wouldn't have been hard—put it in his house, and burned the house down while he fled."

"Can you trace these three?"

"Ah. Interestingly, they all fled to the same place. We think they all got papers to go. For whatever reason. "

I looked at Florian who was smiling slightly. They clearly thought this was the answer. "Where?"

"Argentina."

"Why there?"

"There has been a large German presence in Argentina for decades. All the way back to World War I. There are places in Argentina, even some villages, where they don't even speak Spanish, just German. Many people have family and friends there, and if you're German and you need to disappear, it's a good place to go. And as we now know, some of the most notorious Nazis fled there. Like Dr. Mengele, and others. It is well known that there are still some Nazis there."

"And that's where you think the Blood Flag is?"

"We don't think the Russians would have been able to keep quiet that they had captured the Blood Flag. And if they said they had it now, we don't think we would believe them. We think it left the country before Berlin fell. And it has been waiting for an opportunity just like this. The question, though, is who has it, and where are they?"

I sat back and rubbed my face. Argentina. How would we ever track a flag down in Argentina? "So how do we find it there?"

"We have to send someone down there to look for it."

"How? Just go and start asking every German-speaking person we can find, 'Where's the Blood Flag?'"

"Someone will have to go down there looking to buy it. Money will bring the flag to us."

"Who is going to go down there looking to buy the ultimate symbol of the Third Reich?"

Florian smiled, glanced at Patrick and then said, "You are."

As I contemplated what he had said the phone rang. I walked over to the phone and answered it. It was Murphy.

"I've considered your request." He was ice cold.

"Great. What do you think?"

"Denied. I'm not authorizing your OIA, and I'm not authorizing the United States Treasury to reimburse the Russians for damage done by a bunch of neo-Nazis. I don't really care if they get them, and I don't really care if they don't get them."

I took a deep breath and tried not to just react. "Why?"

"I don't like the whole thing. I'm not going to intervene and hang our asses out. I'm just not going to do it. So shut it down."

"We've already told the Russians the exhibit is going forward." I looked at my watch. It was Wednesday. "Russian security is in place and they're expecting our replacements. I told them we'd do it."

"Don't *ever* promise anything like this until you have authorization from me first."

"We're not going to have any credibility—"

"No, *you're* not going to have any credibility."

"I didn't see an alternative."

"Too bad. Take care of it. Shut it down."

I hung up and turned back to Florian and Patrick. "Let's finish up." I glanced at my watch, "I may have to go to Atlanta and pull some Russians down from the ceiling." I looked up at them both and a thought occurred to me. "Want to come?"

CHAPTER NINE

I got Alex and the four of us flew to Atlanta that night. I had emailed Karen Brindle telling her there had been some developments and I needed to meet with her and the Russians as soon as we arrived. If it's possible to transmit ice by email, she did. "As I expected. Come straight to the museum. They're setting up tonight."

The museum was fully lit and alive with security activity when we arrived. Brindle and the others were in the back conference room. We walked through the modern and attractive central entryway and down the hallway to the back office area. There were fifteen or so people around a large wooden table, some seated, some standing and talking on their cell phones. Most looked up as we entered the room. I saw Brindle and two of the three Russians I'd met on my last visit. They were pouring over diagrams with two Atlanta police officers. Brindle broke off and came over. "You're back."

"Yes."

Before I could say anything else, she asked, "Who are these two gentlemen?" It was a tone of accusation.

"Sorry, this is Florian Köhler and Patrick Sonnenstrahl."

"German?"

"They're with the Bundeskriminalamt."

She looked at Alex and asked her, "What are they doing here?"

Alex didn't miss a beat. "They're helping us," she said in a tone implying that Brindle wasn't.

She looked back at me. "I didn't authorize their coming here."

I said, "They're working with me on the 'project' from the German side."

"I don't care what they're working on."

I ignored her. I had no time for this. "I need to talk to the Russians right away. This is not going to go how I told them it would."

She stared at me and said loudly, "Dmitri!"

He looked up at me, "Ah. You're back. You have the items?" He came closer and we shook hands. He glanced at Alex while generally ignoring her, and then was suddenly aware of the Germans. "Who are they?"

I introduced Florian and Patrick again and told him they were with the BKA.

His eyes narrowed as he examined them carefully. "Germans? Were you both raised in Germany?"

They nodded their heads. "Educated in Germany?"

Patrick spoke, "We grew up in different cities, but yes."

Dmitri got an intense look on his face, which was colored with anger. "Did you study the war? World War II? Did you study it?"

"Yes, we did."

"Well then, tell me how many Russians were killed at the hands of Adolf Hitler and his troops?"

Patrick looked awkwardly at Florian. "Millions."

"*Twenty-three* million!" Dmitri growled. "At least! Some even say twenty-*six*! And why? Because you did not see this man for what he was. And then when you did, no one had the balls to stop him! How is this possible in Germany? The country of Beethoven and Kant?"

Patrick replied. "I believe twenty million Germans died in the war too."

"No! Maybe six or seven million! But so what? That makes it all the same? If Germans died too?"

"No, that's not what I was saying. It was a tragedy, a disaster."

"A tragedy? Ha! Like a flood, huh? No. Hitler was *evil*. You Germans were *murderers*. " He stared at Patrick for an awkwardly long time and then turned to me. " I need the items. We have already set up the bunker."

I sighed, "That's what I wanted to talk to you about. My proposal, well it wasn't accepted by Washington."

Dmitri was startled. "What?"

"They said no."

He stared at me. "You told me that you would do it. We relied on that in setting up this display. If we knew what you now tell us we would have canceled this show."

"I'm sorry. I thought I could get it approved."

He was disgusted. "Now what? We have confirmed the opening of the display on Saturday morning. That's a day and a half from now. We can't have the display without the items there, and you're telling me that a bunch of neo-Nazis are going to steal them and you have no plan. Is that what you're telling me now?"

I felt like a boy who'd been caught by the teacher. "I'd understand if you shut the display down and moved on."

"You don't understand! We have already taken the money!"

"Then we'd better make sure they don't take the items."

"Oh, and have a cowboy Western shootout? Have my men killed?"

"I'm sure there won't be a shootout."

"How? How do you know this?"

"I don't think they'd operate that way."

"You don't *think*? You can guarantee? Is the FBI going to provide perfect security? And the local state police?"

"Security will be fine."

Dmitri looked at me like he wanted to cut me open. "Your credibility is not high with me. We are in this position because we relied on you. Why would I rely on you now? We will handle this ourselves."

* * *

I didn't tell Florian or Patrick that I'd emailed Jedediah. That night I went to my hotel bar at exactly eleven. I was surprised to see how many people were in the dimly lit bar. It wasn't large, but it had an energy, mostly local office workers. I didn't think Jedediah would choose this kind of bar. I'd expect he'd want to meet at a biker bar or somewhere with pool tables.

I glanced at my watch. And how did he know where I was staying? Just then, I saw a man wearing a backwards baseball hat sitting in a booth in the corner behind the bar. I could only see the top of his head over the bar and through the people. I walked closer. It was him. He looked up at me without expression. He was wearing a long-sleeved, black, mock turtleneck T-shirt, which just covered the iron cross on his neck, and a Braves baseball cap. It was hard to see his face in the dark corner, but his massive form was unmistakable. I slid into the booth opposite him. "What are you drinking?"

"Sprite."

I leaned on the table. "You drink at all?"

"Quit."

"When?"

"While ago."

The cocktail waitress approached wearing tight black pants and a short white blouse. She glanced at Jedediah, wondering what he was, but was quite at ease with me. "What can I get you?"

"Beer. Whatever's on draft."

"Be right back."

"You used to drink?"

"Right."

"Why'd you quit?"

He acted as if he hadn't heard me.

I waited, then said, "Okay. Look, I've got to talk to you about your plans."

"Go ahead."

"You're in Atlanta for a specific reason."

"You know why I'm here."

"Yeah. And I thought I had it all taken care of. I thought everybody would get what they wanted and I could get behind it. But Washington didn't buy in. They shut me down. They don't want you anywhere near this place."

Jedediah stared at his glass, looked over my shoulder at the approaching cocktail waitress and waited. She placed the beer in front of me and a small basket of pretzels on the table, and then she left. He looked around and waited longer. The silence grew awkward. Finally he spoke, "We're way past that."

"You've got to stop it."

He stared at me. "How?"

"Tell him you've checked and they've doubled security. Everybody will get caught."

He shook his head. "He'd ask how I knew that. And then he'd ask me, 'Why would they double security?' And then he'd look at me with his narrow-eyed snakelike look."

I took a drink from my beer and pondered. "There's Russian security, there's FBI because you all crossed interstate lines, there will be Atlanta police, it's not going to happen. You'll be in jail for a long time."

He lowered his voice to a whisper. "You were supposed to help. You were to keep them off our backs. Now you're going to do nothing? Just tell us how tough the security is? What the hell good are you? Why am I even talking to you?"

"We should find the Blood Flag."

He sat back disgusted. "That's just your fantasy. You have no idea where it is."

"I have a couple of German FBI types here with me. They think they may know where it is."

He stared, then asked. "Where?"

"Argentina."

"Argentina. You've narrowed it down to a *country*. What bullshit. May as well just say we have no idea."

"We have an idea who may have it. We have to go down there."

"And then what? If someone took it to Argentina and has kept it hidden for decades they sure as hell aren't going to just hand it over to you."

"I haven't figured that out yet."

He shook his head and took a drink. "You don't have shit. You don't know if it even exists. You've got no location and you have no plan on how to get it back even if you do find it. This is a joke."

I leaned forward slightly. "I'm going to get the flag, Jedediah. I'm going to bring it back, and you're going to take it to Germany. And you're going to use it to set these guys up, and we're going to take them down. That's the plan. Are you with me or not?"

He leaned forward even more. "I don't think you *can* get the flag. You *clearly* don't even have influence in the FBI. If you think you're gonna go down there and *buy* it, the FBI won't give you the money. They wouldn't let you work this Atlanta thing out, what makes you think they're going to endorse a wild goose chase to Argentina?"

"I'm going to get it done."

"Maybe *I* should go down to Argentina and grab it. Tell me where it is and look the other way."

I couldn't tell if he was serious. "I don't think that's the way to go."

"Probably don't need to anyway. 'Cause in a couple days we're going to have all the Hitler stuff we need. We're going to get to Germany without your help."

"That's the point, I don't think you are. You're not gonna get through."

"Why don't you tell me the security setup and make it so we do."

"Can't do it."

He shrugged. "Then we'll take our chances."

"If you get caught, I can't help you."

"Who said I was going to be there?"

"I'm just telling you not to look to me to bail you out." I drank deeply from my beer. "Can I ask you one other thing?"

He nodded almost imperceptibly.

"I don't understand your motivation. Why are you doing this? Why are you turning on your Nazi friends?"

He looked out at the other people in the bar and back at me, clearly deciding whether to go into it. "I got saved."

"Meaning?"

"Saved. A church. I changed."

"Ah. That's why you don't drink?"

"I had a problem with alcohol. I can't really touch it anymore."

"When did that happen?"

"About a year ago."

"And that made you want to turn on your friends?"

"They claim to be Christians and that being Christian leads them to hating Jews and other races. It's complete bullshit."

His language surprised me. "So you go to church and all that?"

He wrinkled his nose slightly. "Did for a couple of weeks."

"So why only a couple of weeks?"

"I look like a freak to them. I can't be showing up at a normal church every Sunday. They think I'm going to eat their children." He looked at my watch. "I've got to get back."

I looked at the bill that the cocktail waitress had left and put a twenty on top of it. "So I can't stop this plan of going after Hitler's bunker?"

He shook his head.

"Well then, tell me when you're going to do it."

"Not a chance. I don't want any of our guys getting arrested because of what I told you. Not yet, not now. Not for this."

"I'll be in touch." I slid out of the booth and left.

* * *

Florian and Patrick walked next to me as we made our way through the Russian display. It was almost dark. Direct lighting illuminated the serpentine walk between two faux walls, with narrative text, photographs, and posters. The photos showed the massive destruction at the hands of the Germans in graphic detail. I stopped in front of the section on the Siege of Stalingrad. Eight hundred thousand Russians died, including hundreds of thousands of women and children. We moved on, to the cities destroyed, the buildings ruined, the crops stolen, and the viciousness of the killing squads—the Einsatzgruppen. The ones who sought out and murdered the Jews, the gypsies, and the political commissars. Shot like dogs, in ditches, in town squares, in front of their families, it didn't matter.

We paused in front of the panel that told the story of Babi Yar. I stared at the summary and the pictures. Patrick and Florian were silent. Alex caught up with us and was out of breath. "She's on the warpath. Using your name in vain," she said quietly.

"She can wait."

"What's this?" she asked.

"Babi Yar."

"What's that?"

"Never heard of it until five minutes ago. It was the bloodiest day in the entire Holocaust. The SS took," I leaned forward and read, "33,771 Jews out of Kiev, in the Ukraine. They told them they were going to be resettled.

Then they made them take off all their clothes, marched them into a ditch, and shot them in the neck."

"Shit. Seriously?"

"Look at the pictures."

She studied the panel and read about what had happened. In particular she studied the photographs of Kurt Eberhand and Dr. Otto Rasch, two of the SS officers responsible for the decision. She particularly studied Rasch's panel, which told how he studied philosophy and law, and received two doctorates, one in law and the other in political economy. He was called Dr. Rasch. He was the one who enforced the Babi Yar massacre. She looked at his eyes in the photo next to his panel. She spoke to me while staring at Rasch's face. "How did he get to the point in his head that murdering men, women, and children—because they were Jews—was justifiable?"

I studied Rasch's face as I had many other Nazis. They looked like local bankers or little league coaches. "That's why we're here. They bought into an evil philosophy. Really we should just say they bought into evil. Calling it a philosophy gives it more coherence than it deserves. And it's still alive."

"Shit," she said again. "And that was on September 29th and 30th." She looked at me. "In 1941, before Pearl Harbor. And what were we doing? The U.S.?"

"I don't think we knew about it."

"Shit," she repeated.

We walked on. Florian and Patrick were quiet. As we finished walking down the walled path to the central part of the museum, we paused before we entered the larger area. Florian finally said, "I have not seen these things before."

Patrick added, "We don't really seek them out, though. The period for our country from the thirties through the forties is painful. I think we don't want to know some of it. We are as puzzled as you how this could happen. My generation feels detached, we did not have anything to do with it, but we wish we could change it. We don't dwell on it. Maybe we should a little more."

I asked, "So this isn't taught in German schools?"

"We learn much about the war, but . . . not this. Not all this."

We stepped into the main display area, which held the bunker. In the low lighting the metal container looked like a train car. The four of us approached it, looking around for security and people loading the display. It was black with thick windows that looked bulletproof. I saw no door. I assumed the entrance was on the backside behind the curtains that touched the ends of the container. There were a couple of workers at one end and a few people standing near an exit. Otherwise, the main area was empty. We approached the bunker and looked into the window. It was broad enough for all four of us to see inside at the same time. The bunker was divided into two rooms. In front of us was Hitler's desk, with papers and combat maps, as if he had just stepped away. His uniform coat hung from a rack behind the desk, and directly in front of us, not three feet away, was a walking stick and his shoes. Hitler's uniform hung from a hook on the wall. I looked back at his shoes. They had to be a size twelve or even thirteen. I wondered if he wore oversized shoes to look more imposing. The walking stick looked heavy, like a weapon. The map closest to me was full of symbols of army units. It looked more like a city map than that of a country. It was probably Berlin. Hitler's last military objective—to keep the Russians at bay. But he was trapped in the bunker in Berlin as it fell. As the Russians leveled Berlin he took a cyanide pill and then shot himself—with Eva Braun, his wife of forty hours, also taking cyanide—to avoid being captured by the Russians.

I looked at Alex who was staring at Hitler's shoes. "Gives you kind of a creepy feeling, doesn't it."

She nodded and looked at Florian who was trying to read the map.

It's one thing to see a grainy black and white movie about Hitler, or read about him in history books, or even hear people talk about him who were involved in World War II. But it was another thing entirely to look into a room and see his desk, his chair, his hat, his shoes, and his maps, and think of the teetotaling vegetarian who had done more damage to the world than any other single human being.

I asked Florian and Patrick quietly, "You ever see anything of Hitler's before?"

Florian answered, "No. I don't know if anything like this even exists in Germany. It would be illegal to own it. Maybe a museum, somewhere. I don't know."

I looked around the large area. "Let's figure out how we'd penetrate the security if we were the Southern Volk." The display opened to the public the next afternoon.

CHAPTER TEN

The next morning I got up early. I showered and shaved, then ate breakfast with Alex at the hotel restaurant. Patrick and Florian had a conference call and said they'd catch up later, so Alex and I went ahead to the museum to be there by the 8:00 a.m. security brief. When we arrived in the conference room everyone was already there, including Atlanta police, FBI, Russian security, and Georgia State Patrol. Everyone talked excitedly and drank Starbucks coffee while picking through boxes of donuts and Danishes. I reached for a donut hole as the door to the conference room suddenly flew open and slammed against the wall. I turned to yell at whoever was making so much noise. An Atlanta police officer flew into the room with a terrified look on his face. A man with a black ski mask held a handgun to the policeman's head. Two other men with AK-47s were right behind them. All three wore black masks, black turtlenecks, black rubber gloves, and black pants and shoes.

The one holding the Atlanta policeman yelled, "Everyone shut up!"

I looked around the room for some solution. There were a lot of weapons in the room, but most, like mine, were in holsters under jackets or on belts. And none of us—even with our vests on—could handle an AK-47 round, a very fast 7.62 by 39 millimeter round that would penetrate any body armor in the room.

The man with the gun to the head of the officer yelled at him, "Kneel!"

The police officer tried to turn and look at his captor, but was pushed down to his knees. He knelt at the door, facing us, blocking the only exit.

"Hands on your heads! Everybody! Now!" he yelled.

We all complied.

"Don't even think about going for a weapon. Or a radio," he said. "Anyone does either of those things, and I'll put a bullet in Officer Malone's head."

Malone was furious. He had clearly been surprised, and now was at the center of a big problem. While Malone knelt, one of the other armed men kept his AK-47 on his shoulder aimed at us, as the third man put his rifle behind his back on its sling and went from one of us to the next, searching for weapons. He took the service weapon of the closest person to him, a female Atlanta police officer and examined it. He pulled a net bag out of his pocket and placed the weapon in the bag. He then pulled her Mace off her belt, and put that in the bag, then her radio, and finally her cell phone. He went to the next person, an FBI Special Agent, and took his weapon. He searched for a secondary weapon but found none. He took his BlackBerry and dropped it in his bag. "Turn around and put your hands on the wall! Feet three feet back from the wall! Lean!" he said to the first two. "You stop leaning, I'll shoot you in the back."

He went around the entire room disarming everyone in it, and put the mounting pile of handguns and cell phones into his net bag. He found a couple of secondary weapons and pepper sprays, but most of us, including the Russians, carried only one handgun and one phone.

He returned to stand next to Malone and trained his rifle on us, while the other man still held his handgun to Malone's head.

Malone said, "My knees are killing me. Can I stand?"

"Shut up," the man said.

We had no options. No weapons, no radios, no cell phones, not a chance of freeing Malone unless we all rushed them at the same time. But if we did that, half of us would die, and we still might not succeed.

I finally spoke, "What do you want? Why are you holding us?"

The one holding Malone said, "Shut up! No talking!"

No one spoke. We tried to memorize anything about them that was distinctive. Size, likely weight, any age criteria we could come up with. The voice of the one speaking was distinctive, and had no accent. I noticed that both of the men holding the AKs were the same size. Less than six feet, and less than two hundred pounds. Probably young. Their movements were fluid and easy. One of the men holding the AKs was left-handed. He held his rifle on his left shoulder, and he had taken weapons and radios with his left hand. Other than that, I couldn't tell you one other thing about them. And they just waited, saying nothing.

One of the Russians couldn't stand the tension. He pushed away from the wall and started walking toward them. "What is it—"

"Stop!" the leader said, holding Malone.

The Russian continued to close on him slowly.

The one holding Malone grabbed his hand, pulled his arm up next to his head and placed it flat on the wall. He put his handgun against Malone's hand and pulled the trigger. The shot was deafening and stunning. Malone cried out and crumpled to the ground grabbing his hand. His left hand bled profusely from the nine-millimeter wound that went completely through. "Go back or I'll put another bullet in him!"

The Russian retreated and leaned back against the wall.

Malone begged for help. He cradled his left hand in his right, trying to stop the bleeding. The blood ran out of his right hand and down to his elbow where it dripped to the floor. "Help me stop the bleeding!"

"Shut the hell up!" the gunman said gruffly.

They had trapped ninety percent of the security forces in the conference room right before the security meeting. Malone bled, and we all waited for something to happen.

Finally the phone of the lead gunman buzzed. He looked at what was probably a text message, and nodded to the other two. The one holding Malone let him go to the floor. He put his handgun in a holster on his belt and said, "We're leaving. If you come after us, Malone will die. We have placed a video camera outside in the hallway pointed to this door. If any of you come out of this door, he dies. You must stay in this room for thirty minutes, and contact no one. After thirty minutes, if no one has left this room, we will let him go. Do *not* move!" He looked at the left-handed gunman and nodded toward Malone.

They bent down and grabbed Malone under his arms and hauled him up on his feet. They opened the door quietly, looked out in the hallway, and led Malone out of the room. They closed the door behind them.

One of the Russians rushed the door, "Wait!" I said. "They may actually have a camera."

"They don't have a camera! That's a bluff! We must go after them!"

"No," I said. "Here." I ran to the other end of the room where there was a white board with various names and a security diagram. I reached up to the top of the board and pulled it as hard as I could. It pulled away from the wall. Others saw what I was doing and helped pull the board off the wall. I tapped on the wall to find the studs, then punched my fist into the wallboard between the studs. I stuck my hand into the hole and started breaking the wallboard away. "We need to get through this wall into the other conference room."

Others started smashing the wall and pulling wallboard away until we had exposed the studs. We then kicked the other wallboard out that led to the conference room next to ours and several of us crawled through. Karen Brindle in her skirt was right behind me. I stood up and ran to the conference room door. I opened it slowly and quickly stuck my head out and looked both ways. Nothing. I did it again, and looked toward the door of the other conference room. There was a camera on a tripod pointed right at the door. I hoped it didn't have sound.

The others came through the wall and out the conference room door behind me. We ran toward the main display area that had the bunker.

We entered the huge room slowly and carefully. Five security men were lying on the floor with zip-ties on their hands and tape over their mouths and eyes. I ran to the first one and pulled off the tape. "What happened?" I demanded.

He said, "Help me up."

I pulled him up to a sitting position and knelt down beside him. I had no way to undo his zip-tied hands. "What happened?"

"We were getting ready for the start, and about ten men rushed into the room. We started to draw our weapons, but they started shooting us with rubber bullets. Right in the chest, each one of us. Then they pepper sprayed us when we were down, tied us up, and taped us. Couldn't have taken more than a minute."

"Anybody hurt?"

"Don't think so. We heard them get into the bunker. Sounded like they had a torch."

I ran over to the display where Alex was inspecting the damage. The Russians had crawled through the hole cut in the window of the container and were looking at everything inside.

Alex was watching the Russians dart around inside the container. She finally turned to me with an ominous look. "They got everything."

"Meaning?"

"All Hitler's stuff. They got it all."

I was about to respond when I heard a loud commotion at the back of the building. Alex and I ran to the sound, and found the Atlanta police carefully opening the metal door that led to the street. Every time they tried to open it, someone on the outside screamed out. They finally were able to determine that it was Malone; his left hand was handcuffed to the outside handle.

Karen Brindle tapped me on the shoulder and said angrily, "Everybody to the conference room."

We made our way back to our original conference room. Most who had been there during the attack were back. We exchanged glances of anger and embarrassment.

Brindle got everyone's attention. "The police have helicopters airborne, and cars on the way. An ambulance is on the way for Malone. Here's where we are. Initial reports from the officers who were tied up are that there were at least ten of them, all in the same clothing as the men who were in this room. They came at them hard and fast, and the police didn't have a chance to do anything. They said there was one guy who was big, like a weightlifter, or football player. But the rest were unremarkable. We just looked at the security tape. After they broke in, they headed for the exits, different directions, and there were cars waiting for them at each exit. They had at least seven cars, all different makes and colors, probably a list of the most common cars in Atlanta. And they all headed off at normal traffic speeds and in different directions. They blended right into the Atlanta traffic. We're looking for them, but I don't hold out much hope."

The female Atlanta police officer said, "This was a professional job. The only reason anyone got hurt was because the Russians tried to make a play—"

Brindle responded, "Let's not worry about that right now. They're surveying the damage and seeing what was taken. But they are furious about how all this happened." She looked directly at me. "Did you know this was coming?"

"Of course not. And we don't even know if this was my guy."

"The hell we don't. Where is he?"

"I don't know. I met with him yesterday. I told him if they were planning anything they'd better call it off. But, he didn't really respond."

"And how is it they knew there'd be a security team meeting at eight this morning? Lucky guess?"

"I have no idea."

She asked, "Did *you* tell him?"

"Of course not. I didn't and I wouldn't."

"Then how did they know?"

I thought for a moment. "If I had to guess, I'd say that one of the members of the Southern Volk is on the Atlanta police force."

She looked at me skeptically. "And where are your German friends?"

I smiled, surprised at her boldness. "You think they were involved somehow? They're what, secret Nazis?"

She looked away, then back. "You'd better tell us who your CI is so we can arrest him."

I should have seen that coming. If one of our informants commits a felony that we know about that is not authorized, the relationship is over. She knew that. "We don't know he was involved. He might have tried to stop them."

"Right. Sure. What's his name?"

"I can't tell you that. He's a CI and you don't have a need to know."

"The *need* is that he just participated in one of the boldest heists in American history. You think the FBI is going to let this go because he is a CI?"

"No, but we don't know he was involved."

"You going to tell me his name?"

"No."

She paused. "I'm going to ask your boss. We need to get these guys. This is a disaster. And we both know the Russians will go public on our *inadequate* security."

"You mean Atlanta police's security."

"But we were here. If we're in the room, everything's our fault. You know that."

I nodded. "I'm gonna go look at the bunker."

Another special agent tapped Brindle on the shoulder and showed her a document. I turned and left. I walked straight back through the displays to the large room with the bunker. There were police and FBI everywhere. I walked straight up to the windows and examined them. The bulletproof Plexiglas was at least an inch thick. The main part of the window lay on the floor inside the bunker. I examined the edge where it had been cut. It was less a cut than a burn. It had a beaded edge like melted plastic. The torch used to cut through the Plexiglas and the two large tanks on a dolly were still there, right where they had been left. It looked like a common torch and I suspected tracing it would be futile, but I was sure we would try. I stood at the open window and looked into the bunker where I had stood the day before with Florian and Patrick. The room was in complete disarray. Everything on top of the desk was missing, and the coat rack behind the desk chair was lying on its side. The hook that held the uniform was bent down and the table on which the shoes and walking stick had been placed, right under the window so that you could look at them from eighteen inches away, had clearly been used to get in and out of the window. It was slightly askew. Alex had walked up and was standing next to me looking into the rooms inside the bunker.

I asked Alex, "They find anything? Any prints?"

I could see an FBI forensic team was already hard at work on the scene. "Not yet. They say it's pretty clean."

"Probably all wearing masks and gloves. What about their cars?"

"Found them all."

I turned. "What? Where?"

"Half hour ago a woman called the police station and said the cars matching the descriptions had pulled into a warehouse. The police went there, and found them all."

"And?"

"All intact, clean, undamaged. All stolen. And nothing there. None of the Hitler stuff. None of the people. No prints."

"Where'd they go?"

"It was a switch. They moved all the stuff to other cars or vans or whatever, and drove out the back door. She saw the cars go in, but she didn't see anybody go out. Different door on the other side of the block. It's a big warehouse. So now they're somewhere in Atlanta in cars or vans or pickups or whatever that we don't know anything about driving all over who knows where."

To South Carolina, I said to myself. "They pulled it off. They broke into the impregnable vault the Russians brought, made off with all of Hitler's mementos, and now the trail's cold. Fifty minutes later and we've lost them."

"In a nutshell," she said. "The press is going nuts. CNN has trucks on the way. Everybody's flying in. Commentators are standing outside the building with microphones, and the entire security force is standing around with their thumbs up their asses looking stupid. Including us. And by the way, just to make your day, since everyone loves a scapegoat, a lot of people think you started all this."

"If it had gone my way they'd have the fakes. But Washington was—as usual—unwilling to take any risk. Had to play tough. So here we are."

"I think we'd better get back to Washington."

CHAPTER ELEVEN

We got off the airplane in D.C. and pulled our roll-aboards hurriedly through Reagan airport. At the intersection of two major arms of the terminal we passed a bar where I could see Dmitri on the television behind the bar. I pointed him out to Alex, Florian, and Patrick, and we all stopped. I inched inside the bar until I could hear clearly. The bartender wondered how long I was going to stand there before ordering a drink. As long as I felt like it.

Dmitri looked sober standing in front of the bank of microphones. I put my bag next to me and put my hands on the back of a barstool.

I could hear what Dmitri was saying, " . . . surprised at the theft of these important items. We have had a very successful tour in the United States and never faced anything like this. I'm sure that the American investigators will find out who did this."

He was a lot more confident than I was. He also seemed calmer than I would have expected.

He continued, "The thieves had some important information. We had a security team meeting this morning at eight a.m. Almost all the security forces, including the FBI, were in one room. Three masked men broke into that room with Russian Army weapons, the AK-47. Such weapons, of course, would never be tolerated in Russia. It is a surprise to us that they can be obtained by average American citizens. They are very effective weapons, and would overcome any of the bulletproof vests that any of us were wearing. We were trapped while their accomplices broke into our display and stole the Hitler items placed in the bunker." He paused. "It is troubling that they knew of our security meeting. Someone told them."

My thinking exactly.

"This event is very disturbing, and it damaged our display by cutting through the Plexiglas window. But we also have good news."

I motioned to Alex, Patrick, and Florian to come closer. They stood next to me.

Dmitri continued, "The theft occurred two hours before the opening. What the thieves did not know—and that is because no one knew outside of the Russian crew—was that the items they took from the bunker were replicas. We had not yet put the authentic items into place. The items which were there at eight o'clock this morning were there to hold the place, to make sure the set-up was proper when our team went in. We only put in the real items exactly one hour before the opening of the display. That way we are able to keep complete control of the items. We do not allow them to be out of the presence of at least four Russian security individuals. We would never have allowed the real items to be in the vault with only American security police personnel nearby. It is because of exactly what happened that we have this policy. We've always had this policy. We were to place the authentic items at nine o'clock. So while the thieves accomplished their theft, what they got were worthless replicas. I am here to announce we have already replaced the windows in the display, and will be putting the authentic items into the vault in one hour. In two hours' time, the entire display will be open to the public with Hitler's authentic items. We apologize for all the difficulty, we hope that the Atlanta police are able to find the men who did this, but the good news is that other than the damage to the Plexiglas, we have not been hurt by this. That is all I have to say." Dmitri turned and walked away. The press core was stunned. So was I.

I turned to Florian and Patrick who were standing behind me and smiled, "Well, that's interesting. Wonder if it's true. I wonder if the thieves actually got the real items and they just put the replicas on display."

Alex said, "It does make sense that they wouldn't let the items out of the sight of Russian security. And there was no Russian security anywhere near the vault at the time. Makes me wonder if Russian security were the ones who told them about the eight o'clock meeting."

I frowned. "Why would they do that?"

"Because now everybody in the entire country knows about the tour, Hitler's items, and their clever security. You watch. I'll bet their tour—this was the last stop? I'll bet their tour suddenly gets new dates and makes a lot more money. They'll be on *Good Morning America* by Wednesday."

I thought about it for a minute but it made no sense. "And how would they know who to contact? How would they know how to get in touch with these . . ." I stopped myself, "thieves?"

"I don't know. Maybe the thieves were Russians—"

"Didn't sound like it. And shooting an Atlanta police officer in the hand?"

"We don't know who they were. It was a very professional job. The damage was so minimal they were able to fix it in an hour. Isn't it a little curious that they had replacement windows? You just happen to carry replacement bulletproof windows? Why? What could possibly damage a window like that? It's just hard to believe. You know how we're trained. Be suspicious of things that are too hard to believe."

I nodded as I reached for the handle of my roll-aboard suitcase. I held it and stood there pondering what Alex had said. It made no sense, but it was possible. It's possible the thieves had nothing to do with the Southern Volk. They had a big guy with them. So what? There are a lot of big Russian guys. Under black turtlenecks they all look alike. Especially when you're not the one looking and you've just heard a description of a guy who was big. I had formed the immediate conclusion that it was Jedediah, but I had no way of knowing. But one thing I did know. The Southern Volk would now want the Blood Flag.

Florian broke into my thoughts. "I know the Russians don't trust us." He glanced around, then up at Dmitri who was stepping away from the microphones after his press conference. "But I don't trust them either."

* * *

"What in the hell happened down there?" Murphy asked as soon as I walked into his office answering his summons.

He was always so subtle. "I'm wondering that myself. I met with our guy. He wouldn't tell me what they were planning on doing or when, and I couldn't get him to promise not to go forward. I told him they'd be waiting for him."

He yelled, "But they *did* pull it off! They made *everybody* look incompetent. It's all over the national news! We look stupid because we were there— even though we had nothing to do with security!"

"At least they didn't get anything. It's like stealing a fake Mona Lisa. You get to show the world what a clever thief you are, but in the end you just look like a dumbass. And the whole national news thing. That's really got me wondering. When I told Dmitri that I wanted to put replicas in there, he never said *they* had replicas. I had to come back here and beg Craig at the

OTA to make replicas, which you then vetoed. The Russians were *outraged* when I got back to Atlanta, like I'd left them out to dry. Why wouldn't they have told me then they had their own fakes? I don't get it. Plus, the whole way the theft occurred. Incredibly polished, very well thought out, and the more I think about it, the more I think maybe our Southern Volk never got anywhere near this museum. I don't even know how they would have known that there was going to be a meeting of the security team at eight o'clock. How would they know that? How would they know to come into a room armed and hold everybody hostage while they went and looted the bunker? That puzzled me. But then Alex, and Florian and Patrick—from the BKA— smelled Russian. They think the Russians set the whole thing up. They knew about the 8:00 a.m. meeting. They wanted to increase their visibility, get more tour dates, and get more money out of this. And they look smart as hell for putting replicas in place before the display opened. They're already on every national news show there is; the entire country knows about it and I bet they get dates in New York and Washington, which they didn't have before. Makes me wonder."

"It makes no sense. Why would they do that?" Murphy asked. "Money. *And* to penetrate the thick heads of Americans and tell the Russian story on a bigger stage. Americans think World War II was won by American GIs who went ashore at Normandy in 1944. The Russians know different. They want *everybody* to know that twenty some *million* Russians died in World War II. Only two hundred and fifty thousand Americans died in all of the war, Pacific and Europe combined. They want everybody to be aware that they suffered a hundred times more than America did, and they want everybody to know that they're the ones who captured Berlin and went into Hitler's bunker. I think they're defensive about not receiving credit by historians. What better way to make it known than to have all the artifacts? You can go to all the museums you want, and maybe a few hundred people, or a couple thousand, in each city are aware of it and go. But nothing like this kind of national notoriety. But two other things make me think it might have been the Russians. Can I sit?"

"No."

What an ass. "Couple of other things. One, a torch was used to cut through the Plexiglas. That makes sense. Maybe it was easier, melted at a lower temperature. Maybe. But the door to the car opened out and the hinges were exposed. Not a brilliant design. Could have cut the hinges off and walked in. But they went through the window, and sure enough, the Russians had a replacement window. And second, no one was seriously injured. One shot to a cop's hand, but nothing else. If it was a bunch of thugs, I think they'd have been much tougher on the guards in the main hall. They were unharmed. I don't know. Maybe they were concerned about what charges they'd get if they got caught. But it may also be that they didn't want to hurt any law enforcement. And then multiple cars and a pre-arranged warehouse switch to multiple other cars? Who does that? You ever heard of that happening? Ever? Very sophisticated."

"It still could have been your guys."

"I agree. But we don't know that. And I'm not sure they're smart or creative enough to have pulled it off."

"I don't believe in some Russian criminal conspiracy."

"Why?"

"You think they're going to break into an American museum and steal their own fake items to get more publicity and more money? And take the risk of killing somebody and getting some Russian arrested and the whole thing blown up?"

"They *weren't* going to kill anybody, and if one of them got caught, he'd just go quiet. They'd deny all knowledge. The fact that he's Russian would be irrelevant. They would probably claim it was the Russian mafia which is much bigger in this country than anybody acknowledges."

"Call your man, and find out if they did it. And if they did, we're going to arrest his ass and put them all in jail."

"You want me to call our CI without any *Miranda* warning, have him confess to a crime, and then arrest him for it?"

His irritation grew. "Call him."

I nodded, "But if he doesn't admit it we need to keep going with our plan to get them to Germany."

He was burning inside. "You created this shit stew and you should fix it."

"I didn't create *anything*. I had nothing to do with this. And I *told* you and the Russians that people were out to get the Hitler stuff. I was trying to stop it and you didn't let me!" He said nothing.

"I'm going to find the flag and we're going to take it to Germany. And when we get them all together in Germany, we'll arrest them all. Or rather the Bundeskriminalamt will arrest them all and put them in jail for using Nazi symbols."

"Where is this Blood Flag?"

"That's what my two friends from the BKA are helping me with. They think Argentina."

"So now I suppose you want time and a budget to go get it."

"Yes."

He wasn't about to commit. "Find out what your Southern Volk friend says first. Then we'll decide what we're going to do. Does Karl support this?"

I hesitated. "Not sure."

He replied, "See what you can find out."

I went back to my office and logged onto my Gmail account. I sent an email to Jedediah. "Was that you?" I waited for a response but there was none. I stared at the screen. Nothing. I minimized the email screen and opened the travel portal and began pricing flights to Buenos Aires.

As I studied the flights my cell phone rang. I looked at the screen to see who it was. It was Florian. "Morning, Florian. You ready to head back to Germany?"

"We have been talking. It was not clear whether you wanted us to go to Argentina. And we don't know if you're still going."

"Well, frankly I can't imagine how I'll find the flag without you. But I didn't want to impose. I assumed you'd at least help me narrow down where it was, but I'd love for you to come."

Florian said, "This is what we hoped. But you should know that the German community in Argentina is very closed. They are suspicious. They suspect every Jew they encounter as being from Israel and trying to put a rope around their neck to take them back to Israel for a war crimes trial. And anybody else who is outside of their circle is also suspect. Including Germans."

"Would they have more suspicion about Germans than Americans?"

"We're not sure. That's why we need a strong plan. We can't just find the person we think has it, and ask him for the flag."

"Agreed."

"So, if you have a plan, we would like to help. We have spoken with our superiors and the German government is behind you. They are concerned about what is happening and have given us permission to participate."

"I wish my government was as concerned. Where are you now?"

"At the hotel."

I looked at the clock. "Why don't you meet me at Hennigan's for lunch. It's one block west, on M street. I'll be there in about an hour."

"We will see you there. Bring Alex."

* * *

I beat Florian and Patrick to the restaurant and sat at the table fingering the menu. I wasn't hungry. In spite of my clever Russian theory, it probably was the Southern Volk. I wasn't really sure if the Russians were telling the truth about the replicas, but it wasn't a fine moment for the Bureau, the Atlanta police, or, frankly, for me.

Florian and Patrick came in and saw me toward the back. They sat down and we shook hands. "Long time."

"Hours."

I filled them in on what had happened since I returned. As we talked Alex joined us. I said, "I'm not sure I can get approval for Argentina."

Alex interjected. "Well, you've got to go, no matter what." I looked at her. "What's gotten into you?"

"You were determined and I was curious. But having seen Hitler's bunker, seeing all his stuff, now *I'm* determined. Absolutely determined. They have to be stopped. We're finding the flag."

"I don't think they'll let us go."

Florian looked eager to speak. "We've had the opposite reception at the BKA. The theft in Atlanta has awakened them. They were quite surprised—well some of them—that we were in Atlanta; they wanted to know everything that we knew. We had a conference call an hour ago, which is why we were a little late, where we told everybody what we were doing and your plan for the *Blutfahne*. They are eager to grab these neo-Nazis in Germany. They are very willing to help. In fact, if your FBI is unwilling to go forward, the BKA is prepared to take over the entire investigation. We will work together. And if you cannot do it, perhaps we will do it ourselves. This has become important."

I broke off a piece of bread and buttered it. "So, do you still want to work through the Southern Volk or did you want to take a completely different approach? I think that I'm coming to the end of my ability to get anything done with the FBI."

Patrick asked, "Can you still work with your contact? Or could we do that? No one in Germany would suspect German involvement in an American group. If we did it from a German perspective, and tried to infiltrate a German organization and do what you have already put in place, first, we don't have anyone there we can use, and second, they would suspect us. But they would never suspect us working with you."

"I can, but I don't think the FBI will be signing off on any big plan, let alone a budget. This Atlanta thing really spooked them."

Florian nodded excitedly, "Yes, while it may have scared your FBI, it has made the BKA realize that this issue is even bigger than they thought. German, but more international. And now that they know of this meeting, they've been tracking the goings on at Eidhalt's castle, and they have given us whatever budget we need. So we will take care of the budget."

I looked intently at him, "Seriously? How much?"

"It has to be based on a plan. We must tell them what we plan to do and how much it will cost, and they will then either approve it or not. But I think they will approve it if it has any chance of success."

"What about buying the Blood Flag? If we find it, we're going to have to buy it. That's going to cost a lot."

"I think if it is authentic, we can buy it."

I found myself reinvigorated. I might be able to pull this off after all. "How close are we to identifying the person who has it?"

"Working last night and this morning, we have been able to eliminate one of the three. And we were given permission to speak with those inside the BKA who stay in touch with others in other countries. We talked to some who know Argentina. They have gotten a good location for each of the remaining two."

"Where?"

"Buenos Aires."

"Let's go talk to them. And if one of them has the Blood Flag, we have to come home with it."

Florian nodded but hesitated, "Yes, but we can't just go down there."

"I agree. I have an idea. Let's go back to my office and set up in the conference room. Let me see if I can convince you to do it my way."

* * *

I hurried back and emailed Jedediah again. "We need to talk." I hit send and this time he replied immediately, but not on the computer. My Black-Berry rang. I picked it up and checked the number. It was a nine-one-nine area code. North Carolina. I answered it.

"Yes."

"What's up?"

"So you pulled it off."

"Pulled what off?"

"Atlanta."

"You said you needed to talk to me." He was being evasive.

"How did you know about the eight o'clock all-security meeting?"

"Who said I knew anything about a meeting?"

"Somebody did."

I could hear Jedediah breathing, but not answering. "Whoever did that job—they were pretty smart."

"Eye witnesses said there was a big guy—bulky guy—who pulled a torch into the museum and cut through the Plexiglas. I'm not sure who that might have been. I thought maybe somebody who, oh, I don't know, runs a body shop. You have any ideas?"

"Lots of bulky guys out there. Probably a fat guy."

"Said more like a bodybuilder."

"Probably hired the guy to haul that acetylene tank around."

"Who said anything about a tank?"

"You said a torch."

"You use torches."

"Lots of people use torches."

I dropped it. "Are we still in business? Your guy who wanted all these Hitler relics. He now knows they're all fakes."

"He knows what the Russians are saying, sure. But I'm not sure he believes them."

"He thinks maybe he has the real ones?"

"Don't know."

"What I care about—should we still be looking for the flag?"

"I'm planning on it."

"Why if he's satisfied?"

"Maybe it won't last. Maybe I have my own ideas."

"We've narrowed it down to two people. In Argentina. We're going to go get it."

"And?"

"We're going to meet to talk about it today. Do you have another phone?"

"I can get one. But this has to stop. Too much contact."

"I'll be in touch."

* * *

"How'd you narrow it to two?"

Florian looked around. He wanted a cigarette. He grabbed the coffee pitcher off the credenza and poured himself another cup instead. "It was a long process. We are not saying it *is* one of these two. We can't say with certainty, but we think they're the most likely."

Patrick added, "There are other possibilities, but since we don't know what happened we have to go based on those most likely to have it."

I grew more frustrated. "So we *don't* really know. We're just playing the odds."

"Like any investigation. Right?" Florian added. He then said, "But we think the odds are better than fifty percent."

"I need more."

Alex chimed in. "Fifty percent is pretty good considering we started at zero. I say we go for it."

Florian smiled. "Patrick, you explain."

Patrick nodded and opened the notebook again. It had new tabs and a diagram. "Yes, so we know that the man who was responsible for the *Blutfahne* from its earliest days was Hessler. Many Nazis, as we have discussed, went to Argentina. And as we said earlier, two of the senior officers who lived on Hessler's street fled to Argentina. It is very possible that Hessler gave the flag to one of them. We know Hessler didn't go to Argentina, and it is possible of course he kept the flag in Berlin or in Munich. But then why wouldn't it have surfaced? It is our belief he gave it to one of the men leaving the country. Those two officers, who were both very young for their rank, are in Argentina living under false names. But we have located them."

"They're both still alive?"

"Yes," Patrick said smiling.

"No doubt it's them?"

"No doubt."

"How old are they?"

"One's ninety and the other's eighty-nine."

I sat back and wondered how to go about this. We could go right up to them and demand the flag. Or we could threaten to disclose their past, but unless they were involved in war crimes no one would be very interested in old Nazis. I asked Florian, "What do you have in mind?"

"We have discussed this at length with the BKA." He glanced at Patrick who nodded. "And they believe it is best to go about it directly. To go right to the individuals, and confront them and tell them that we need to take possession of the Blood Flag, and if they give it to us without difficulty, we will leave them alone."

I thought about it for a second. "And they will of course, then just give us the Blood Flag and say thank you very much and that will be the end of it."

"Maybe not. But they thought that was the most effective way."

"What about using the actual threat more effectively. What about turning them over to the Israelis if they don't produce the flag?"

"The Israelis aren't interested in just any Nazi. They really only want war criminals. The ones who worked in the concentration camps. The ones who killed Jews. A regular Nazi officer is not of great interest to them."

"Do these two men know that?"

Patrick shrugged. "If they have looked into it at all they would know. I suspect they've looked into it from a computer at a coffee shop. I don't think they'd have a great fear of being sent to Israel, unless they are actually war criminals."

Alex asked, "Are they?"

"They were young and almost certainly had no role in the Holocaust. I don't think they have much risk of being put on trial anywhere."

"Then why flee to Argentina?"

"Would you have wanted to be a prisoner of the Russians?" Patrick asked.

I asked, "Why would they have taken the flag? Why would they still be holding onto it? And if we go down there and just demand it, they'll say they have never seen it, let alone possess it. And unless we're prepared to use force to search their houses, and their storage, and their safe deposit boxes, and their farm fields, we'll never find it." I sat forward. I leaned on my elbows and pushed my sleeves up. "They want to have this relic of Nazi Germany. But why? To sell it? To make money? No. To make a *difference*. Whoever this guy is, whoever has the flag, he wants it to be used." I considered. "I think the key is to give him the chance to do with it what he had hoped to do. We need to persuade him that this is the moment. This is the resurgence of Nazism. This is what he has been waiting for, and *we* will pass on that torch. We will take the flag back to Germany, and give it to the people who are going to take Nazism worldwide and challenge every government they can."

Patrick looked at Florian and back at me. "How could we do that?"

I considered. "We have to present him with a compelling face of Nazism."

Florian replied, "How?"

I stood up and looked out the window for a minute, thinking. "We take *him* to Germany *with the flag*. I had always thought when the time came, we'd buy it. We'd give this old man a million dollars and he'd gladly part with it. But, as I've been thinking about this, it's not about money.

"If he still believes in Nazism, he'll want to do this one last great thing for the cause. And he probably won't even care if he gets arrested. But the trick is how do we persuade him that we are the ones to take him to Germany? Unless we set it up perfectly, it will feel like a trap."

Florian stood up with me. He looked at all the materials on the table, and thought about the German implications. He said, "We look like we're from the FBI and the BKA. He will smell us."

I replied, "We have to take our CI. He can *persuade* him how important this gathering is, and that he's the one to take the flag back to Germany. They'll never suspect an American. He'll sell our story. And who else would have an iron cross tattooed on his throat?"

Florian and Patrick nodded. Patrick said, "Good. But we will still have to have a story. We have to explain it well when we surprise this old Nazi. And you have to have a story for you."

"I think it's time to build my background, Alex. Western rancher, rich guy. Airplane. Behind the scenes supporter of Nazi causes, but uncommitted."

Alex nodded. "I'm on it."

CHAPTER TWELVE

I had never been to Columbia, South Carolina, at least not for any length of time. I'd been to Fort Jackson a couple of times, and I'd driven through or by many times in my work. But I'd never spent any time there. I knew about it, though. It was a proud city. Proud of its heritage, proud of its Civil War role, proud of its state capital that still has stars on the marble exterior to mark where the cannonballs struck it during the Civil War. It is the place where the unanimous vote was taken to secede from the Union. It is the place where, until recently, the Confederate flag flew over the statehouse with the United States flag and the state flag, one over the other. Notably, with the Confederate flag above the state flag. That finally caused enough controversy that it resulted in the Confederate flag being moved to a flag pole near some statues, but still on the capitol grounds.

Columbia had a fairly modern look, unlike Charleston, which maintained its antebellum appearance, because most of Columbia was destroyed in fires during the occupation by the beloved William Tecumseh Sherman.

I sat down on a bench by the Edisto River, watching it meander across the countless rocks in the middle of the riverbed, and opened my computer. I logged onto my Gmail account and emailed Jedediah, telling him that I was in Columbia and needed to speak. I asked him to name the time and the place. I didn't think he would like it very much that I was there, but I really didn't care. This couldn't wait.

Once again, he responded immediately. I was curious how he did that. He must sit at his office at his body shop with his Gmail account opened and minimized. As soon as I would write, he would respond. It was also possible that he used that account to email other people. A thought that gave me pause. He said, "You shouldn't be here. Lake Murray. Midnight. End of Brady Porth Road."

I opened Google maps. I went to satellite view, then to street view and put the little man in the middle of the end of the street. I looked around three hundred and sixty degrees to see what was there. Nothing. It was a dead-end road that petered out at the water and Google street view didn't go all the way to the end. No houses, no cabins, no structures. No street-lights, no painted lines, nothing else to note. Just lots of pine trees, glimpses of the lake, and a sign that said "End of Maintenance" long before the end of the road. At midnight it would be darker than a witch's heart. I opened Weather Underground and checked moonrise for Columbia. 8:00 p.m., a waning crescent. We'd have a little light, but not much. I needed to get there before midnight.

I turned onto the road just before eleven thirty. The rusted sign for Brady Porth Road stuck up from the ground at a forty-five degree angle, a rem-nant of an accident years before. After a mile or so the road narrowed and the pavement disappeared. There was a slight berm on the side from where it had been bulldozed out of the woods. The berm went straight down to what I assumed was the lake, though I couldn't see any water from the road. The trees over the road formed a canopy that blocked the dim moonlight. I drove to the end of the road where the bulldozer had simply stopped and I was surrounded by trees. I looked in my rearview mirror and couldn't even see the road behind. I turned off my lights, then the engine, and sat in my locked car to let my eyes adjust. I finally got out, put my keys in my pocket, and felt the reassuring presence of my Glock under my arm. I wondered if Jedediah had decided to end his relationship with the FBI, and me with it. It wouldn't be smart. Karl knew who he was and would track him down if something happened to me, particularly in Columbia. But sometimes peo-ple like Jedediah weren't exactly the most logical.

I closed the door quietly and stood next to my car. There were no sounds other than insects. I looked at my watch, which had dots on the hour num-bers and small green stripes on the hands. It was ten minutes before mid-night. I listened for an approaching vehicle but heard nothing. Just stillness. I had no idea how far I was from the lake, or whether there was a path to the water. It occurred to me that he might take a different road and come through the woods by foot, so I wouldn't see his vehicle. I stared hard into the trees all around me. I looked up at the sky, and through the few holes in the pine canopy I could see the vivid stars. The crescent moon was some-where, unseen and not of much help.

"You gonna arrest me?"

The unexpected voice made the hair stand up on the back of my neck. It was spoken softly, but clearly. He couldn't have been more than ten feet away. He stepped out from behind a large tree in a black turtleneck.

"You scared the shit out of me."

"Needed to be sure you were alone."

"How long have you been there?"

He stepped across the slight berm that formed the road and stood next to my car. He looked around as I'm sure he had a hundred times before that. "You didn't answer my question."

"If I wanted to arrest you you'd already be in handcuffs."

"Thinking about it?"

"What? Arresting you? For Atlanta? No. They think you were involved, but they've got no evidence."

"So what's so important?"

I looked at the road and at him. "How did you get here? Where's your car?"

"Who said I drove?"

I nodded with new understanding. "A boat."

"So what's so important?"

"I told you, I think we found the Blood Flag."

"Yeah."

"We're going to go get it. And we've gotta sell to them that we're neo-Nazis and that they should come with us and bring the flag back to Germany, to the meeting."

Jedediah thought. He put his hands in his pockets. "And?"

"Whoever this guy is isn't going to believe a couple of Germans from the BKA and an American with an FBI haircut. But he'll believe you."

"You want me to go to Argentina?"

"Yes."

"And exactly what would the plan be? *Ask* this guy for the flag? Grab it?"

"Maybe. If you tell the German guy with the flag that you're bringing him to Germany for the big thing, he'll come."

"Why would he come?"

"He's been holding onto the flag for sixty-five years. Why? What better chance to put it back in play than to use it to unify all worldwide neo-Nazi groups?"

Jedediah shook his head slowly as he thought, clearly not impressed. "So, we all walk down there, knock on this guy's door, say hello, how about you take the Blood Flag back to Germany because we're a bunch of neo-Nazis and it's going to be great. That about it?"

"I'd hope for a little more nuance, but basically yeah."

"How will we say we happened to find him?"

"We did the research. Most of those are public documents. He won't know what's public and what's not. We'll tell him we did our homework. We expect that someone in his place will be surprised nobody had put it together before now."

"You guys just don't think like criminals."

"There's probably a reason for that."

"I can pull off going to Argentina. I can sell that. I can even tell him the real reason. But you've gotta give me some documents. I've gotta pretend like I've done all this homework myself. And I gotta have traces to U.S. sources. Preferably, on the Internet. I can get down there, but I'm not traveling with you, and I'm not associating with anything you guys are doing. I'll meet you there. You tell me where to be and when and I'll be there. If all you need is for me to look big and tough and glare at this guy, that's easy enough. But I'm here to tell you, that if you just walk in there, like three government guys, he's not going to give you shit. He'd rather die."

I thought he was probably right, but I didn't see any way around it.

"Then give us a better plan. Tell us how you would do it."

Jedediah asked, "These guys that you think may have the flag. Either of them SS? Any unique units or background?"

"No. Plain vanilla. Routine. That was one of the reasons they were hard to trace. My German friends did it by where the Blood Flag was kept and the men in the same neighborhood were traced to Argentina, and the time they left the country. We don't know if either of them has it, but they think these are the two most likely. If it still exists."

"Oh, it exists. I'm sure it exists," he said.

"How do you know?"

"It's the holy grail of the Nazi world. The magic flag that blessed everything else. So, maybe you should just tell me who these guys are and I should go down there and get it."

"How would you do that?"

"I'd have a chat with them."

"A friendly kind of chat?"

"Depends on how friendly they were to me, but I'd come away with the flag."

"Maybe I'm your financier. I need to be ready to write them a check for a million dollars for this flag."

"The FBI will let you have that kind of money?"

"Not a chance, but they don't know that and they'd have to let us see it."

"And then what?"

"And then my German friends will persuade them, or him, that he doesn't have to let it go at all. He can still keep it. That he should come to Germany with us to put it back into circulation in any way that he sees fit. With him or without him, selling it or not, we'll decide that in Germany, but he should come and raise it back up to where it belongs. At the top of the Nazi movement."

"Might work. When we going?"

"Next week. Can you get away?"

"Yeah. Send me the stuff to my post office box in Irmo."

I hesitated, wondering what else to tell him. Taking him to Argentina could be our smartest move; it could also be a disaster. Finally I said, "See you in Argentina."

"By the way. If you promise not to arrest anyone, or even pass anything on—do you?"

"Go on."

"I think you need to see Brunnig in action. You need to know what we're dealing with. We're having a meeting tonight. 2:00 a.m. At our headquarters."

"And?"

"And, I'm the one who set up the security for our place. Cameras, motion detectors, steel doors, everything. In the basement of a bar owned by one of our members. On the outskirts of town. Called The Traveller. We have an office, meeting room, all our weapons—*legal* of course—in safes, it's our place. I record every meeting on video, and keep all the digital files in a safe deposit box. Nobody knows they exist. I'm telling you because I set it up for Internet access. You can watch the meeting live. I'll give you the login info. Just you. No recording, and you can't use any of it against any of us. Deal?"

I wasn't supposed to make a deal where I listened to admissions of felonies and promised to do nothing about it. "Deal."

He reached into the back pocket of his black jeans and handed me a three-by-five card. Then he turned and walked into the woods. I got in my car, turned on the power, and rolled the windows down. I turned the power off, sat there in the dark, listening. I waited to see if he had come by boat or by car. I strained for the sound of any engine but heard nothing. I looked at my watch and continued to wait. Five minutes passed, then ten. Nothing. It's possible he'd walked so far that I couldn't hear the boat when it started up. But it was so silent and the air was so still, I thought I'd be able to hear an engine start three quarters of a mile away. I heard nothing. He could have come by rowboat or canoe or kayak, but that seemed unlikely. He was probably standing in the woods watching me. He wasn't leaving until I was gone.

I started my car, backed carefully into a multi-point turn, and headed back down the road.

* * *

I hurried to my hotel room and got on the Wi-Fi. The meeting was in a half hour. I went to the numbered website that Jedediah had given me and entered the login username and password, both of which were a nonsensical sequence of numbers and letters. The screen was dark and there was no sound. I wondered if I was in the right place. And then at exactly 2:00 a.m. the images went live. I leaned toward the screen of my laptop to see as well as I could.

Banners hung from the ceiling with the Confederate flag, but in the middle of the flag was a swastika; a combination of the Nazi flag and the Confederate flag. Off to another side were banners that had the classic Nazi insignia. Flags and banners were everywhere. A sea of red and black, and spot lighting. Music played in the background. Men stood shoulder to shoulder. I was shocked at the number of them. There was barely enough room in the large basement meeting room to hold them all. There had to be two hundred men. Many had shaved heads, in a classic skinhead look, but others had long hair like a biker gang. Many wore vests that said Southern Volk on the back, with their Confederate flag with a swastika in the middle. A few looked completely normal, like engineers or corporate IT workers.

There was a hum of conversation, of energy and expectation. Suddenly the lights dimmed and I could hear the beginning of "Dixie." It was slow and rhythmic. As it reached the chorus two men walked up onto the stage. Jedediah. And Brunnig. Then all the men started singing at exactly the same moment, "In Dixieland I'll take my stand, to live and die in Dixie, away! Away! Away down south in Dixie! Away, away, away down south in Dixie!"

Thunderous applause followed.

I saw that there were other views I could click on. I hit the next one, and it was a close up view of the stage and microphone where Brunnig approached. I could see his eager face clearly. He looked like he was on the verge of instability. But I could also tell he was charismatic. The men were clearly drawn to him. He was tall and thin, and wore his clothes well. He looked more like a lawyer than some thuggish neo-Nazi. He wore a black sport coat with a Nazi armband on his right sleeve. He wore a dark red tie over his crisp white shirt. His hair was very short on the sides, but longer on top, combed back with gel. He had very dark eyes and perfect teeth.

He stepped up to the microphone. "*Sieg*!" He thrust out his hand in the classic Nazi salute.

"*Heil*!" they all responded, extending their hands in response.

"*Sieg*!"

"*Heil*!"

"*Sieg*!"

"*Heil*!"

Applause. He basked in the energy, and waited. "The South shall rise again!"

"The South shall rise again!" they shouted.

"Men, in an amazing and bold daylight robbery in Atlanta, some very smart men stole Hitler's items from the communist Russians' display! Amazing! Courageous! Who could have done such a thing?"

His comments were met with laughter and nods.

"And somehow we came into possession of those items. Remarkable. But alas, it turns out that they are mere replicas." They booed. "I know, I know. I too thought maybe the Russians were lying to cover their asses, and that we had the originals, and they were claiming their replicas were not the originals. But just today I've met with some smart people who I trust, who know what they're doing, and they inspected these items. Turns out what we have are replicas. Not even old leather or material. Not even close to being sixty or seventy years old. So we 'received' things that will be of no help to us in getting to Germany."

The men shook their heads and looked around.

Brunnig's face darkened. "Nelson! Wylecki! Come forward!"

The room was instantly silent. Two men walked toward the stage and stood in front of it. They looked at each other but said nothing.

Brunnig hissed, "You were the men who were to scout this display. To make sure that the event would be successful. Yet you let them sneak *fakes* into the display without notifying us!" He stared at them. They said nothing.

"You *failed!*" They still said nothing. "Failure is *unacceptable!*" he yelled. They visibly recoiled from his anger. "Security!" Brunnig demanded.

Four enormous men ran from the back to the front and stood behind the two.

"Take these two *failures* into the back room. Show them how we handle failure!"

Two security men grabbed each of them and forced them down the hall to a room.

Brunnig waited until they were gone. He smiled. "But don't fret. Our man Jedediah," he indicated to Jedediah, who stepped from the back of the stage to be next to Brunnig at the microphone, "assures me he has something up his sleeve. Won't even tell me what it is. He doesn't want me to get my hopes up by overselling. Says he wants to under-promise and over-deliver. A good business man!"

The group cheered as Jedediah stood there nodding, unsmiling.

"So if Jedediah comes through, we will still get to Germany and be part of the leadership of the new worldwide Nazi movement! This is our moment! This is when we go from regional to national to international! The two greatest symbols in history, the swastika and the Confederate flag, will take their rightful place in human history! At the front of the most powerful movement ever!

"Now, we need to break into our operating groups. You all know what to do and where to go."

I sat back as the men dispersed into corners and other rooms to meet in their smaller groups. Jedediah and Brunnig spoke on the stage in a conversation too low for me to hear. I closed my laptop, sat back, and tried to catch my breath.

CHAPTER THIRTEEN

I had one other thing to do before we went to Argentina—visit the one person who would know the value of the flag. He'd know what a collector would pay for it, or what a neo-Nazi might pay for it, or, maybe even more important, what they might do to get it. I had asked around. Everybody led me to the same guy. A dealer of Nazi memorabilia. An odd loner, in Gatlinburg, Tennessee. I exchanged several emails with him and made an appointment to visit him. I didn't want to show up in a black government sedan, so I drove from D.C. to Tennessee in a borrowed pick-up. I wanted to spend some time with him, learn whatever he knew about the flag. Maybe he'd even heard some rumors about where the flag was.

I'd been to Gatlinburg once before and remembered it as a beautiful but touristy town in the Smoky Mountains. It was in a gorge through which the Gatlinburg River ran. This time, I spent the night outside Gatlinburg in a nondescript motel called Daisy's Inn. It was one of those white painted motels where you could pull your car up right in front of your door in the gravel parking lot. I was one of five cars in the lot when I got up in the morning and prepared the horrible coffee from the package in my room. I didn't shave, didn't take a shower, just pulled on my well-worn Leddy's cowboy boots and started up the Chevy 1500. I drove to Gatlinburg from the east. Even though I was focused on the visit, I couldn't help noticing how inviting and peaceful the drive was.

I passed through Gatlinburg before the tourist spots had opened, except for the pancake houses and coffee shops. I followed my handheld GPS, which showed my destination five miles on the other side of town. I drove past gift shops and rafting companies until I finally broke out into the countryside. I slowed as I approached the points where the GPS said his house was, but saw nothing. No structures, no farm houses, no numbers, nothing. The gorge was fairly narrow, but as I rounded a turn it flattened out to the left and the steep hillside was farther away from the roadside. The GPS said

I was a quarter of a mile away so I slowed almost to a crawl, straining to see anything that represented civilization off the road. I changed the scale on the GPS to eight hundred feet and waited until I was right on top of the destination. I saw a barely used dirt road to my left. I looked a little bit ahead and saw a wash bucket turned upside down with two stones holding a cardboard sign up that had his house number on it. This was it. I turned left onto the dirt road that had two tracks, one for each wheel, with grass in the middle. I followed it into what appeared to be an expanding valley. It was green and beautiful, and populated with trees that were far enough apart to allow grass to grow in between. The grass was low but not mowed; there were probably goats on the property. I followed the road around a curve and saw the house. It was set back from the road on the left and up the hill. It was a Craftsman-style house, white with olive accents, and was in perfect condition.

The only vehicle near the house was a van parked in front. I looked around for any other signs of life but saw none. I turned off the rough dirt road and drove right up to the house. I parked next to the van. I listened for a moment, then got out of the truck. I walked up the wooden steps and onto the porch. Before I knocked, I looked down across the rest of the valley. It was the only house in sight. The road continued for a little bit, but then got even less open and more overgrown. My guess was he owned this entire valley, and probably took care of it by himself. What a gorgeous spot. I could see retiring to a place like this. The air was heavy with humidity but full of the smells of trees and greenery.

As I approached the door I saw a dog lying on his bed on the porch. It was an old Australian Shepherd who was moderately interested in me, but not enough to get up. I knocked on the door and stepped back. After thirty seconds I heard someone walking inside the house. He opened the door behind the screen and then pushed the screen open. He stepped out onto the porch and extended his hand. "You must be Mr. Bradley."

"Yes. You must be Mr. Schuller."

"Absolutely correct. Nice to meet you. Call me Tom. And thanks for coming all the way out here." Schuller had a smile on his face that was cordial but reserved. He was shorter than me, maybe five feet eight inches, and was light, maybe one fifty. He wore tight Levis and gray Asics running shoes. He wore a black polo shirt that was untucked and had the yellow shield with the black horse-head silhouette that represented the Army's First Cavalry Division. He was tan and fit. He hadn't shaved, and had his dark hair combed straight back. He was maybe fifty years old, and had very dark brown eyes.

"Thanks for taking the time to meet with me. Your collection sounds amazing. I look forward to seeing it. You get many people out here?"

"Oh, I don't know. One a week or so. Like I said, most of my business is online these days. But every once in a while I'll get a serious collector who wants to come out and see things for himself. Seeing pictures is one thing, but seeing an item itself is a whole other thing. And if you're going to spend a lot of money—and some of them spend a lot of money—they want to see it. So yeah, sometimes people come here. I like meeting them. It's fun talking about what's rare and what's not. What's collectible and what's not."

He looked to his left where I looked for the first time. There was a door that was slightly oversized and led into a wall at the end of the porch on the opposite end from the Aussie. I had noticed when I pulled up to the house that there was a structure as big as a three-car garage to the right as you looked at the house. But what was noteworthy is that it sat on the same level as the porch, on steel supports, and was not accessible by cars. There were no windows and no garage doors. Now that we were on the porch, I could see that the door off the porch was the only thing that led into that structure. I nodded and looked at the door. "Is that where your collection is?"

"Most of it. I've got other pieces of it in other buildings around the property. But nothing that isn't at least represented here."

"This whole valley yours?"

"Yeah, a hundred and twenty acres. It was really my father's. He went off to World War II, and then came back and said he didn't want anything else to do with war or the army or working for somebody else. So, he moved to Tennessee, got a job as a diesel mechanic for trucks, and saved every penny he earned. In the late fifties, he bought this land, which was on sale for the first time by some family, and gave everything he had then mortgaged the rest. He built the house with his own hands. My mother died in 1990 and he passed in 1995. I got the house and the land and everything he owned, free and clear. So I quit my job and moved here. Lived here ever since. Never married, no family. I don't need much. Just enough to pay the electrical bill and help me keep my business going. But I make pretty good money from my business too, so I'm doing fine."

"Gorgeous place."

"Thanks. I take a lot of pride in it. I don't really have much else to do, except take care of my business and my property." He said, "You want to see what I have?"

"Can't wait."

"Great. One thing. Can you stand right there for a second?" He took his iPhone out of his back pocket and took a picture of me. He checked it to see if it was okay, then texted it. "Won't be a minute."

I felt my mouth going slightly dry. If he found out I was an FBI Special Agent this was going to be a short meeting and could have very bad implications.

We stood there silently, awkwardly for one minute. Two. Three. "What's going on?" I finally asked.

"There we go," he said smiling again. "You're fine."

"Meaning?"

"Well, I have some things in here that some people, mostly the ATF, don't think are okay. So they might send someone out here to take a look, and shut me down. Let alone put me away. And I don't want that, so I have a friend who knows if you're that kind of someone."

"Inside the ATF?"

"Maybe."

"Good source," I said chuckling. "And I got the thumbs up."

"Yes sir, you did. Come right over here." He turned and walked to the end of the porch opposite the dog. Over his shoulder he said, "So, I didn't really understand what your interest is in all of this."

"Sort of a collector, but only recently. I don't really know much."

"You in it for the money?"

"Not really, no. I'll explain in a bit."

"Alright. 'Cause if you're in it for the money, there's some good money here, but it's not walk-away kind of money. I make a good living and it's getting better, but it's not the kind of money you can take to Wall Street to go own something."

He took keys out of his pocket and opened the door in front of him, which swung toward him. That surprised me until I saw the bars right behind that door. It was like a jail cell door. He took another key out and undid a bolt, and then a third key to open the lock on the jail door. The barred door swung in and he stepped into the room. As soon as he moved the barred door an alarm started its countdown. I heard him enter a long code—probably sixteen numbers—and the alarm stopped. He yelled out to me, "Come on in."

I stepped into the room and was shocked by the size. I could tell from the outside that it was a large building or room, but what I hadn't appreciated was the depth. It went back into the hill three times as far as it went across. The room was immense and immaculate. The other thing I noticed immediately was the lighting. I had expected fluorescent lighting, but this was more like what you'd see in an art museum or high-end retail store. Small spots had up-lighting on the walls. It gave it a very classy feel and look.

He said, "Want me to show you around?"

"Absolutely."

He closed and locked the jail door behind us, which gave me pause. "Let's start over here," he said pointing to the right. There were display cases that stood on wooden legs and had glass covers like in a museum. Under the glass were numerous Nazi insignia and patches. "I think at some point or other I've had the insignia and patch of every German unit that ever existed, including Navy. Right now I'm kind of low on them, because people buy them so quickly. Probably because people like Nazi memorabilia but don't want to buy the expensive stuff. These I usually sell for twenty to fifty bucks."

I leaned down toward the display cases and looked at the patches. There were SS badges, shoulder patches, collar insignia, and even a few iron crosses. "Are those hard to find?"

"Legitimate iron crosses that were actually awarded to someone are kind of hard to find. There are a lot of fakes out there. But authentic ones are worth a lot of money. Authentic ones from World War II, that is."

He led me down the rows and showed me helmets and boots, uniforms and canteens; all authentic, and most in pristine condition. He then said, "Come over here."

We went around to another aisle and there were rows and rows of Mauser rifles and display cases full of Luger pistols. "These the real thing?" I asked.

"Oh yeah. And, one thing I haven't told you, my other part-time profession is as a gunsmith. Mostly on German weapons. I know these things like the back of my hand. I've personally checked every one of them and they are in perfect working order. I don't sell them unless they are shootable. I let other dealers take care of the junk and the broken ones."

"Are these rare?"

He shrugged. "Not rare exactly, but they're not easy to find. Especially in good condition. They command a good price. People love German weapons."

"You ever shoot 'em?"

"Sure. All the time. I even set up a firing range on the back side of my property. I bench test every one of these and zero in the sites on the rifles. These things are ready to go. I could arm an entire company with what I've got stored in my warehouse. I've also got hundreds of boxes of ammo. I even have some boxes right here in this room. You never know when somebody is going to try and get in here and take some of this stuff. And if I'm in here, I can pick up a weapon and shoot back. Hey, check this out."

He went to another case and opened it. He pulled out a weapon that looked like a submachine gun with an ammunition clip that extended below the face of it. "People often talk about the AK-47 as the first so-called assault rifle. Not the case. The AK-47 took its design from this right here, the Sturmgewehr. The StG 44. This was the first machine gun fielded by a single infantryman with unlimited fire and detachable clips that came in through the bottom of the stock. Absolutely revolutionary. See the basic idea of the AK-47? Even this top part here. Looks identical."

"Completely does."

"Yep. The first true assault rifle."

"Does it work?"

"Of course. Maybe if we have time later, I'll show you."

"That'd be great. I've always wanted one of those."

"You know this weapon?"

"Yeah. I'm sort of a gun nut. Especially automatic weapons. Supposed to have a permit to own one, but on my ranch I don't really care much about permits. I just shoot whatever I want."

He smiled. "That's what I like."

I looked at the next table, which was uncovered, and saw several German hand grenades. 'Potato mashers,' as they were usually called. "These live?"

"Oh yeah. Live as hell."

"Think they'd still work?"

"I wondered the same thing myself. Walked to my front porch, pulled the pin and heaved it at a maple tree. Not the smartest thing I've ever done. Blew the tree to hell, and sent shrapnel all over the front of the house. Took me weeks to pull pieces of metal and wood out of the front of the house and the porch. Thankfully, I didn't have to pull any out of myself."

We walked around the rest of the displays and looked at fully intact officer uniforms, SS knee-length leather coats, knee-high SS boots, and a whole corner devoted to SS materials.

"Here, I've got a present for you." He picked up a pin off a table and handed it to me. It was the death skull worn on the hat of an SS officer. Just holding it almost made me angry, and sick.

"That's unbelievable. Is it authentic?"

"Yes. I can even tell you where it came from, if you want to know."

"I do."

He went to a table and opened a reference book. He looked at the back of the skull at a number that he had etched on it, and read through the pages. He finally found it. "Here. It's from the Sturmgruppe 675 based in Poland. You know them?"

"Of course. They're one of the death squads. The ones that went through Poland looking for Jews and gypsies."

"Baddest of the bad."

"Yeah, tough guys. Shooting unarmed people."

He looked at me with a pulse of scrutiny, "I'm not about judging people in World War II, I'm about collecting memorabilia."

"I'm about both. Nazis lost their way. Even if they believed in what they said, they didn't have to murder people to do it. Nazism would have been a much more powerful force without that. That's why it's still alive and well today."

He seemed to relax. "There you go. You want that?" he asked, indicating the pin in my hand.

"Absolutely. This is priceless."

"It is actually a pretty high value. Hundreds of dollars. But you came all the way out here and I wanted you to have it."

"I appreciate it." I slipped it into my pocket.

We worked our way through the rest of the material he had displayed all the way to the back of the building, deep inside the hill. There was a bar set up with stools and belly tables and a sixty-inch high-definition television that was running Nazi war footage. "What's the movie?"

"These are actually very rare. These are Nazi movies that I bought from a movie collector. In the actual cans. Most of this footage has never been seen since the war. There are only a couple of remaining copies, and I have most of them. I also bought a machine from California," he indicated by nodding toward the side, "that converts the film into digital. High definition DVDs. You may not know this—most people don't—that film is far more dense than the highest definition digital picture. So it's actually easy to convert film to high-def. images. Sometimes the formatting has to be messed with, but the density is there, so you just stick your film in one end of this machine, rewind it at the other end, and in between it gets converted to a Blu-ray DVD. It's unbelievable. These things have been selling like crazy, and I charge ridiculous prices for them."

"Like how much?"

"I only sell them in a ten-DVD set. They are training videos, combat footage, some German units' inspections and parades, random assortment of things. But very high quality, and very well done. So I sell the ten-DVD set for a thousand dollars."

"Who buys it?"

"Beats me, all over the place."

"Germany?"

"I think people are a little hesitant to own it in Germany, but I do mail these to German addresses. They just insist that I do it in plain brown wrappings and call it 'movie classics.'"

"That's just unbelievable. I have to get copies of those."

"Sure, of course. It's amazing. Old movies. There is a market for *everything* Nazi. It never goes away. Part of it is because the Swastika is the most intriguing symbol ever used by anybody. It's just captivating. The other is a lot of people secretly agree with Nazism and some of its pieces."

I nodded. "Well, I told you I had something I wanted to talk to you about."

He nodded and turned to the bar. "Did you want to buy anything?"

I hadn't expected the hard sell. "Absolutely. Several things. I'd love one of those Sturmgewehrs, if you are willing to sell one. How much would you let one go for? Assuming it works and you have some ammo for it."

"It's illegal to own in the U.S., you know. Well you can, but you have to get a permit, which are pretty much impossible."

"How much?"

"Can I get you a beer? German, of course. You can have Paulaner or Spaten? Both on draft. Where else can you find that?"

"Spaten."

He went around behind the bar, drew two glasses of beer out of the Spaten tab, walked back around the bar, and set them on the bar table where we had been sitting.

"So how much?"

"These things are in great demand. And unless you got it through the '68 amnesty with BATF, you're in the shit for owning one. But let's talk about the . . . not quite public market for this. I can get forty grand for it from the right collector. If it's a beater it can be as low as fifteen grand. If it's not in working condition or has been smashed and reassembled, maybe five grand. But this one, the one I showed you, is in good shape. It's worth probably twenty grand. But for you, today, I'll let you have it for ten."

"That's pretty generous. Let me give that some thought."

"Sure. But after today, it goes back to twenty grand."

"Okay. I may very well do that."

He chuckled. "Definitely don't put it in your carry-on luggage accidentally." He drank deeply from his beer. "But on the phone you said you had a question you wanted to ask."

"Yeah, thanks. I have a lead on something. I don't have it yet, but let's assume my lead is good, and that I'll actually get it. What I'd like to know from you is how valuable it would be and how sought after it would be and if you can put a price tag on it. And then if all that comes to fruition, whether you could sell it. I don't know if I want to sell it, but if I did, you seem like the right guy to do it. For a piece of it, of course."

His eyes grew bigger. "What is it?"

"I'll say it in German. Do you speak German?"

"Little."

"*Die Blutfahne.*"

His mouth opened slightly. He said, "The Blood Flag?"

I nodded.

He sat back, his mind racing, "Seriously?"

"Seriously."

"That thing has been missing since late '44."

"Exactly."

"How did you get a lead on it? How legit is it?"

"Well, I hope it's real legit. I think it's the real thing, but I won't know till I go get it."

"Where is it?"

I shook my head.

"Okay, let's assume it's the real thing. Wait, how can you prove it's the real thing?"

"Don't worry about that. Let's assume it's the real thing and that I have irrefutable proof it's real."

"I don't know how you would do that."

"DNA."

"Alright. So you've got the real Blood Flag. First of all, don't let anybody near it. That's the most coveted and sought-after Nazi item *ever*. That was Hitler's magic flag. It's just hard to describe how significant that is in Nazi lore."

"I know. That's why I want it."

He paused. "If you're this big a collector, how come I've never heard of you before?"

"I've been in the background. But now, here I am. So what's the answer?"

He breathed quickly. "So, the value. There are some wealthy collectors who might pay a huge amount of money for something like that. Huge. But how much? The most expensive piece of Nazi memorabilia I remember was fairly recent. Hitler's Mercedes sold a couple of months ago to a Russian billionaire for eight million dollars."

"There have been a few other things in the millions. Some of this stuff is sort of like dealing with stolen art. You don't want it publicized. Not that it's illegal, it's just thought to be in bad taste. You familiar with Hitler's original paintings?"

I nodded.

"Those can fetch a pretty good penny. They go for several hundred thousand each. There aren't many of them, and they are pretty easy to authenticate. I've got pictures of all of them. I've bought and sold many of them. But the flag . . . shit. I don't know. I'd have to think about it. This kind of a setting where there is no market that's been previously identified, where it's never been on the market before, it's almost like you have to have an auction and let the rich guys bid against each other. That's the only way you'll find the market. But I would guess it would sell for somewhere between ten and twenty million."

"That's about what I thought, actually."

"Let me warn you, though. With the flag, trust me, it's not about the money. It's about what it stands for. Every neo-Nazi, pseudo-Nazi, proto-Nazi, former Nazi, and maybe-Nazi will come out of the woodwork to get it. And," he hesitated. "I'd bet some would even kill for it." He thought about that, then got up quickly. "Come on. Let's go shoot that Sturmgewehr. Maybe I can even convince you to buy it!"

"Maybe I will."

"I've even got extra magazines and boxes of ammo. You know Hitler gave it its name? Sturmgewehr? It means the 'storm rifle.' There were over four hundred fifty thousand of them made. Used mostly in the eastern front. Shoots a 7.92 by 33 millimeter round. Very effective."

"Let's go shoot."

"By the way, if you're from Montana, how did you drive your pick-up all the way to my house?"

"I am from Montana. But I have a ranch in Virginia too. Not too far from Roanoke. And my own airplane to go back and forth, and to my other ranches in Texas and the Central Valley of California. That's why I don't have to worry about putting my new Sturmgewehr in my roll-aboard. I own the airplane."

"Nice!"

"Let's try it. Where's your shooting range?"

"It's a couple of miles back into the valley. But if you just want to test it out, let's just go out on the porch!"

We walked out of the room and he closed the door and gate behind us. He took out a metal ammo can, opened it, and put the bullets in the Sturmgewehr magazine. "Here," he said. "You take it. Put the magazine in there . . . put a round in . . . good, just right. Now make sure to aim over your truck, and fire away into the woods."

I pulled the trigger and the Sturmgewehr kicked into my shoulder in automatic fire. I fought the slight tendency to climb and found it to be very accurate. I could hold the fire onto a tree fifty yards away. I finished the ammo and pulled the barrel up. A slow curl of smoke climbed out of the barrel as it cooled. "Very sweet," I said, smiling. "I'll take it, if you take American Express. I want the points."

"No problem!"

* * *

I tossed my umbrella into my roll-aboard and looked at Michelle, who was sitting on the bed frowning. "What's the matter?"

"So you were where?"

"Tennessee."

"Why?"

"To visit a collector, to see how much the Blood Flag might be worth."

"And?"

"And what?"

"What did he say?"

"He said ten to twenty million probably. But since it's never been on the market it's hard to say. But some would do almost anything to get it."

She pulled her foot up across the bed and leaned forward, alerted. "Like what?"

"He said it's hard to predict, but they might try very hard to get it, even by violence."

She looked at the ceiling, trying to decide whether to say what she was thinking. "So if you have this flag you'd be the one they'd be violent against."

"That's not going to happen. No one would know."

"But if they did, or suspected, you'd be the target."

"There is some risk, I suppose," I said as I put my fleece into the suitcase. "Could you stop packing for a minute and talk to me?"

I put down the shirt I was folding and sat at the end of the bed.

She continued, "I think you ought to really re-think this. Argentina? Really? Why? This has become an obsession with you. You've put your FBI career at risk, you've offended people above you, you've been blamed for that mess in Atlanta, and now you're going to run off to Argentina with German FBI and a nutcase neo-Nazi you don't know very well? For what? Why is this your fight?"

"These are bad people, Michelle. They need to be stopped."

"By *you*? There are a *lot* of bad people out there. That's why the FBI has people who focus on certain things. Your focus is international terrorism and finance, last I checked. I think you're obsessed because of your father. You are doing this to honor him, or to echo him or be like him. I don't know. But you're putting our family in danger, Kyle. It scares me. Taking on all of neo-Nazism at once around the world, and now off to Argentina, and then if everything goes well to Germany? For what?"

"I don't expect people to under—"

"*People*? What about me? I'm not just people. Make *me* understand."

"This is really important, Michelle. It can be stopped and should be stopped. I think I can do it if what we're planning works."

"And if it doesn't?"

"Then we won't succeed and that will be that."

"Or someone will kill you for that stupid flag."

"Not going to happen."

She had heard enough. She fought back tears, got off the bed, and walked out of the bedroom.

CHAPTER FOURTEEN

The Paris of South America. That's what everyone says about Buenos Aires. Actually, that's what Argentina says about Buenos Aires. The people I had asked about it, who had actually been to Buenos Aires and to Paris, shook their heads. Just marketing that drew tourists but led many to feel disappointed. I had never been to Buenos Aires and looked forward to going. I wouldn't be there long, but I still looked forward to seeing it. What really intrigued me was the German ex-pat population, which included many Nazis. Some who admitted it, and many who didn't. If the American veterans of World War II were the greatest generation, what were the Germans?

When I arrived and checked into the Panamericano Hotel the front desk clerk handed me an envelope with my name on it. When I got to my room and closed the door behind me, I crossed over to the window and pulled back the drapes. My room looked over Carlos Pelligrini Street, and I could see the famed obelisk, which looked like the Washington monument, only smaller. The street was full of traffic and energy.

I opened the envelope and pulled out the single sheet of paper. "Welcome to Buenos Aires! We have met someone who will be of interest. Be in the lobby at 8:00 p.m." It was signed by Florian. It was already seven thirty. I quickly unpacked, shaved, and put on my sport coat. I checked outside again to see if it was raining. I went down to the lobby and spotted Florian and Patrick as I stepped out of the elevator. They saw me at the same time and crossed the lobby. I shook their hands and evaluated their beaming faces.

"Welcome!" Florian said, echoing his note. "We must go to dinner. You must meet someone."

I nodded and shook Patrick's hand. "Good. Who?"

Florian smiled, "You will see. Come on."

We went outside to the curb and the bellman hailed a cab for us. We squeezed in and Florian gave him the name of a restaurant.

I asked, "It's not Blick, or Schullman is it?"

Patrick said, "No, no. Absolutely not. But this is someone who knows of both of them."

"How did you find somebody who knows them both?"

Patrick said, "The German community here is close. And closed. That is good and bad for them. They know each other, but anybody who knows the community either knows the ones you're looking for or can find out about them quite easily. Some try to stay out of sight and out of touch. But all those that came here right after the war know each other and talk. Some hate the Nazis who came here; they say the Nazis ruined Germany. Others sympathize with the Nazis. All the tension that was there in 1945 is still here."

"Should be interesting. Does this person speak English?"

"Everybody speaks English. German is a dying language. I'm surprised *we* still speak German!" Patrick laughed. "Spanish is not dying, but even they all speak English."

The cab pulled over and we climbed out. Florian paid him and we turned and walked into the restaurant, La Cabrera. The décor was rich and engaging. Florian checked in with the woman at the maître d's desk.

As we waited, Patrick brightened as he looked over my shoulder. I turned and saw a beautiful woman walk through the door from the street. He walked around me to approach her. I followed. She smiled. She held out her hand and they kissed on both cheeks. Patrick turned to me and said, "This is Kyle Morrissey, the American I told you about." She faced me directly and extended her hand. I shook it. As I shook it, Patrick said to me, "This is Manuela Gabrielli."

I'm not sure who I expected to meet us at the restaurant, but Manuela was not on the list. She was in her mid thirties, and had beautiful long black hair. She had deep brown eyes and olive skin. She couldn't have been more than five three or five four, but was wearing three-or four-inch heals. She wore a navy blue skirt and pink silk blouse with a French scarf around her neck.

Our table was ready. We followed the hostess who took us to a corner table in the crowded main room. As I placed my napkin in my lap, I said to Manuela, "You said your name was Manuela Gabrielli?"

"Yes."

"I take it that's Italian."

"Very good," she said with a faint smile. "Most Americans think it's Spanish, but of course it is Italian."

"How did an Italian family end up in Argentina?"

"There are more Italian people in Argentina than Spanish. By a good measure. Probably sixty percent Italian."

We all ordered steak based on Manuela's recommendation of Argentinean beef as the best in the world, and she ordered a local wine to go with our steaks. As we ate our appetizers, Florian said, "Manuela is with the Argentine Federal Police. She is very familiar with the German ex-pat community as well as the Italians."

I looked at her and decided to ask. "Did the Italians who came here come when the Germans did?"

She nodded as if she had heard the questions a hundred times. "It is a mix. Some fled when Mussolini took over, and others came after he fell. Some were for him, some against him. It has made for an interesting community. But Germans are the same, though it seems there is a larger percentage of Germans who were Nazis than Italians who were fascists, but it's difficult to say with certainty."

"What about your family?"

"They came much earlier. In the twenties. From Roma."

Our steaks came and we started eating. A minute passed in silence. I occasionally glanced at Manuela who looked back at me. She was intriguing. Beautiful and intriguing. She ate thin slivers of steak that she cut off, European style; she had no intention of eating the whole thing. After a few minutes of silence, Florian said, "We've talked to Manuela about *die Blutfahne*. She had never heard of it. The thought that it could be here is very interesting to her. And she has current addresses for both of the men we're looking for. And one of them, Blick, is living under a different name."

I looked at her and frowned. "How do you happen to know that?"

"Israelis."

"Meaning?"

She leaned forward. "The Israelis have been chasing war criminals ever since the end of World War II. They track down every evil Nazi in the world that they can, and put them on trial. Remember when they came down here and got Eichmann? There he was, living in the German community in Argentina. San Fernando. About twenty kilometers from here. We hadn't really thought much about Nazi war criminals hiding out in Argentina. We knew that there were a lot of Germans, and many came after World War II, but we didn't think people who had been in charge of exterminating Jews were hiding in Argentina. We were horrified.

"The Israelis, though, didn't go through official channels. They just came down here and kidnapped him. Pretended they had a flat tire and nabbed him when he got off a bus returning from a Mercedes factory. Maybe they thought that we would not extradite him to Israel. But they kidnapped him, put him on an airplane, and took him back to Israel. Then he was hanged." She paused. "Ever since then we have quietly cooperated with the Israelis in knowing which German immigrants could be from World War II. They're not looking for people who fought as soldiers in the Abwehr; they're looking for war criminals. These two men were 'cataloged.' They share the list with us, and we help them by tracking whoever is on it."

"You know where the two men are that we are focused on?"

"Yes. We have known where they live for a long time. What I did not know was about this Blood Flag."

"Do you suspect these men of anything in particular? Have they done anything illegal that you are aware of?"

She took a small bite and shook her head. "No, they are quiet. The people who know them think they're just quiet old men."

"I assume they are retired?"

"Actually no. Most of the German war veterans are in their late eighties or nineties. A very few are still working. The two you are interested in are both self-employed. One is a watch repairman who has his own little store and the other translates German novels into Spanish and Spanish novels into German."

I asked to no one in particular, "So which one has the Blood Flag?"

Florian shrugged. "One of them. We will talk to both of them. Pick one. And is your man here?"

I nodded.

Manuela looked at me. "What man?"

I wondered how much I should really tell her, "We had to have someone who is authentic. A true neo-Nazi. But working with us."

She frowned. "And what will he be doing?"

"Lending an air of authenticity to our search. He'll explain why we're looking for the Blood Flag, which will in fact be true."

"Then what will you do with him, the one who has the flag?"

"Florian and Patrick will be the connection with the neo-Nazis in Germany and I am the American financier. We originally thought about buying it. But the more we thought about it, the less we liked it. So we're going to play to his ego and tell him *this* is what he's always waited for. This is the reason he's saved the flag. He can bring out the most important symbol in all of Nazi history to reunite world organizations under the banner. If he has any lingering Nazi beliefs, we think he'll jump at the chance."

She nodded, thinking. Florian got the waiter's attention and asked him to pour us more wine. After he left, Manuela said, "Then you don't need us. You know where they are, and you can go talk to them."

I replied, "Yes. Tomorrow."

Florian raised his eyebrows in surprise. "He is here?"

I nodded. "He's here. We're going to meet tonight."

"Shall we come?"

"Yes. I think it's time you met him."

* * *

The meeting did not go well. Jedediah was in Argentina all right. He'd been there for some unspecified period before we arrived. He seemed to know his way about Buenos Aires like he'd been there before; but he said he hadn't. We met him in a dark bar at a hotel where none of us were staying. Jedediah wore a white V-neck T-shirt. Just enough to see the major tattoos, and in particular, the iron cross on his throat. Florian and Patrick were stunned. They weren't accustomed to seeing anything like it in Germany. When we told Jedediah how we saw it playing out with these two Nazis, he balked. He said, "Makes me sound like a prop. I don't think that's how this would really play out. If this was real, I'd be the one in the lead; I'd have my German contacts, and my American financier. I'd do most of the talking. I don't think your way will work at all. You need to let me run it."

The idea of Jedediah running anything was scary enough, but at this critical moment when we might actually have the chance to get the flag in our hands, to let him be in charge could result in one or both of these Nazis denying any knowledge of the flag at all. It could be sitting in the other room.

But unless they *wanted* to give it to us, or sell it to us, or go to Germany and play the role that we had in mind for them, they might just let it pass and not even hint that they had it. To get this close and go home without it was unacceptable.

I could tell Patrick and Florian were considering backing out. The assurances that they had to give the BKA were endless, and caused them extreme anxiety. Their bosses talked about the impact of "releasing" the *Blutfahne* like it was a virus. Jedediah scared them, but we had no other choice. We decided to visit the two men the next night. We'd visit the first one right after he was likely to have had a drink, or a glass of wine, just before he was ready to go to bed. When he was tired and dull.

Jedediah left the bar first, and the rest of us stayed. I ordered another scotch.

Florian asked me, "How do you know you can trust him?"

"He's here, obviously to do what we have in mind to do."

"How well do you know him?"

"I've only been working with him for the past couple of months. Before that, he was working with another special agent. He was very reliable."

Patrick shook his head slightly, and said, "Those tattoos. They are just shocking. Someone must feel something very deeply to get those tattoos."

I nodded. "No doubt."

Patrick pressed, "So how do you feel so strongly about Nazism that you get an iron cross tattooed on your throat, and then turn on your friends? How does that happen?"

I understood his concern. "I asked the same question. He was converted. He became a Christian, and rejected his old ways."

"He became a Christian?" Florian asked doubtfully.

"Yeah. Probably more common in the U.S. than in Germany."

Florian peered at me through his small glasses. "You believe him?"

"Why would somebody make something like that up? It's not something that most people just say in ordinary conversation, let alone brag about. Why would he lie about it?"

"So you believe what he's telling you."

"You think he's making this up?"

"I don't know. I'm simply evaluating."

"Well, I don't know why he'd be turning his fellow neo-Nazis in, giving us their banking and meeting information, bugging their headquarters, and telling us about this international meeting if he's not who he appears to be."

Florian and Patrick glanced at each other. They looked like they were still skeptical. Florian said, "I hope you're right."

* * *

The next evening I met Florian and Patrick in the lobby. We picked up Jedediah in front of a bookstore several blocks away. He had walked there from his hotel to make sure no one was following him. He wore a navy blue turtleneck and a cap. He squeezed into the front seat of the Fiat. It was for a man half his size, but he didn't complain. Patrick pulled away from the curb. I was in the back with Jedediah.

"How are you doing?" I asked him.

He nodded.

"You ready?"

"Which guy is first?"

Florian responded, "Blick."

"Why him?"

Patrick said, "I reviewed the documents again, and he lived closest to the house in Berlin where Kessler lived with the flag. Right next door, in fact. And I was able to find his date of departure. It was earlier."

"You think these guys know each other? You think they both know about the flag?"

I replied, "Almost certainly. Two guys left Berlin about the same time. Might have even gotten here on the same ship. We don't know. We just know they got here, and have been quiet ever since. No trouble. No rallies, no secret Nazi blogs, nothing. Just going about their business. Hiding."

Jedediah asked quietly, "What are they hiding from?"

I replied, "Their past. Or others who would want to dig into their past."

"Like us."

"Here we are."

We pulled over to the curb and turned off the engine. Florian turned around and looked at Jedediah. "His apartment is around the corner. It's on the second floor."

Jedediah began getting out of the car and said, "I know."

I looked at him quizzically. "How do you know?"

"You mentioned the address last night."

"And?"

He stood on the sidewalk as he peeled off his turtleneck. All he was wearing underneath was a white sleeveless T-shirt, what these days is called a 'wife-beater.' It was stretched tight across his massive chest and his tattoos were ominous even in the dark. He threw the turtleneck into the backseat of the car and closed the door. He answered, "I never go anywhere to do something if I haven't been there before. I took a look around this neighborhood this morning. I know exactly where his apartment is. I can also tell you exactly how many other apartments are here. Where the exits are, where the service doors are, and where his car is parked. It's the same shit you ought'a know. You guys are lazy."

I felt stupid. I knew I should have done that myself. We closed the other doors to the car, locked them, and looked at each other wondering whether Jedediah had something in mind other than what we were planning. As we walked down the sidewalk toward the apartment, I walked next to Jedediah. "You ready to take the lead?"

"Yes."

"You got anything in mind other than what we've planned?"

He glanced at me with that look I first saw in the café in Virginia. The look that told me he was just tolerating me and that at any moment he might not talk to me, or worse. "Like what?"

"Like anything. I get the impression you've got an agenda other than what we've agreed to. If you do, I want to know about it."

The black, high paratrooper boots he was wearing were imposing enough, but they had leather heals. Every step he took was like a rifle shot on the sidewalk. It echoed against the stone façade of the building we walked in front of. I looked around to see if there were any other pedestrians who had noticed his walk, or him. But there was no one else on the street. It still made me feel uneasy. I felt exposed. He answered, "My agenda is simple. Get the flag."

We stopped in front of the apartment building and looked up. The lights were on in the second-floor apartment. It was a four-story building, with two apartments on each floor. One to the left and one to the right. They all had windows facing the street and were accessed by a single stairway up the middle of the building. A set of concrete steps led up from the sidewalk to the lowest floor. I looked up and down the street then at the other buildings to see if anyone was watching.

Jedediah was tired of waiting. He said to Florian and Patrick, "You ready?"

They nodded. Jedediah marched up the steps to the door and swung it open. The stairs were marble and his boots echoed as he walked up. The four of us stopped in front of Blick's door. We looked at each other, nodded, and Patrick knocked on the door. His knock was not intimidating, but not gentle. We could hear Spanish-language television from behind the door and heard someone call out in a muffled voice. His wife had died years before, so we thought it was unlikely that he was calling out to anyone other than whoever was at the door. But we couldn't make out the words. I could smell food being prepared somewhere else in the apartment building, and listened for unusual activity. I could hear voices in the apartment above speaking loudly in Spanish. Suddenly, the door opened and an old man with a stooped posture looked at us, blinking his eyes.

"Si?" he said.

Much of the conversation after that was in German, but Florian told me every word. He said to the old man in German, "There is something that we would like to talk about."

The old man looked surprised to hear German. "What is it about? Who are you?"

"May we come in?"

"I don't think so." He stood there with one hand on the door handle inside and the other on the door jam. Jedediah pushed the door hard enough that the old man either had to let go or fall over. Jedediah walked in, followed by Florian, Patrick, and me. Jedediah closed the door behind him and stood in front of it. The old man was suddenly aware of Jedediah's presence and his tattooed muscular frame. He breathed with his mouth open and looked around the room nervously.

"Who are you? Are you Israelis?"

Florian responded, "No we are Germans. Germans and Americans." The man pleaded, "What do you want with me? Why are you here?"

"May we sit down? We want to ask you about something."

He looked at each of us again, with grave concern. His hair was somewhat unkempt, especially in the back. His shirt had stains on it, and his pants were wrinkled. He finally realized he didn't have much choice and pointed to the couches in front of the television. He turned off the television and we sat down. Florian turned the television back on and sat with Patrick on the couch. I sat in the chair across the coffee table from Blick and he sat in the other chair. Jedediah stood ominously between us and the door. Florian asked Blick if he spoke English. He did. They switched.

Florian began the conversation. "In 1945, just before Berlin came under attack by the Russian Army, you lived on a street near Hitler's bunker."

Blick listened, his mouth slightly open. He said nothing.

Florian continued. "And sir, of course you know about the Braunes Haus in Munich, and what was kept there?"

He continued to stare without agreeing or acknowledging anything. He watched Florian, still not understanding where he was going.

"There was a certain item that was kept there. It was in the place of honor. And it was kept there by a certain individual. Do you know what we're talking about?"

He nodded his head and spoke, "I know the house you mean. I know there were many things kept there. I think probably you mean the *Blutfahne*." Florian and Patrick nodded. Patrick said, "Exactly. And that flag, and Otto Hessler who controlled it, was moved to Berlin in late 1944, to your street. And two of the people who lived on that street left before Berlin fell. You are one of them. We think you have the flag."

Jedediah crossed from where he stood by the door and said firmly, "It is time for the flag to take its rightful place. The Nazis are about to return to the international stage that they should have taken sixty years ago. Nazi groups from all over the world are going to gather in Germany to promote Nazi ideology throughout the world. To reestablish the supremacy of the Aryan race. We believe that the *Blutfahne* should be the centerpiece of this new movement. And we believe that flag is in your possession."

Blick looked shocked and disgusted. He looked down at the coffee table and adjusted his glasses, and then looked up at each of us. "You're Nazis." He shook his head as if encountering something that just kept coming back. "I was a Nazi. I was a member of the party. But it wasn't anything that I believed in. In my position, you joined or you were sent to the front lines or worse. And for the right war, to defend Germany, I would gladly go to the front lines. But for *him*? No. So I was a member of the Nazi party and served in the army staff. I was smart and was promoted rapidly. I was twenty-four in 1945. My goal was to survive the war."

His hands shook as he removed a pack of French cigarettes from his shirt pocket and lit one. He did it quickly with the memorized movements of thousands of previous cigarettes. "So I don't care about Nazism. I'm not waiting for it to rise again or start some new worldwide movement of hatred and murder." The more emotional he got, the thicker his accent became. "And I don't have your flag. I never saw it, except in a parade. So you've got the wrong person, and you can leave now."

We looked at each other and all formed the same conclusion. He was not our guy. Florian bent down and looked at him closely in an intimidating way. "If it is as you say, that you don't have the flag, someone else from that street has it. Probably someone else who came to Argentina. Who else is here?"

"I don't know anyone from my street who came to Argentina. I am a lonely old man with no friends. I don't know any other Germans who were on that street—there are other Germans here—but no one from my street." His tone changed to one of contempt. "You will have to look elsewhere for your flag."

Florian stood up, looked at the rest of us and said, "Let's go."

Jedediah held the door for us as we walked out. I stood outside the door as Jedediah stood there with the door open, holding it with his hand, looking back at the man with that intimidating stare, as if he was deciding whether to tear him apart or leave him alone. The German wouldn't look at him. Jedediah stepped out and closed the door loudly behind us. He moved by us and rushed down the stairs. Florian, Patrick, and I looked at each other and started down the stairs wondering what Jedediah was up to.

When we got out to the street and closed the door behind us, we looked around the dark, silent neighborhood and saw no one. Including Jedediah. As I was about to speak, Jedediah came out of the door behind us and down to the street. I said to him, "Where have you been?"

"The basement."

"What were you doing down there?"

"Phone line."

I thought for a second. "You cut the old man's phone line?"

Jedediah stared at me and said, "You think anybody's going to really believe the three of you are Nazis? You look like cops. They'll believe me. He did believe me. But he didn't believe you. That's why he had to give you his speech about how he wasn't really a Nazi. How he didn't really believe. That's bullshit. He probably thinks we are Israelis, and we're going in there to find out what he knows, and if he knows about the flag. He probably doesn't even think we're looking for it, but on the off chance he does, he probably knows who has it. And it's probably the guy we're going to see right now. The last thing we want is him calling that guy and warning him. So yeah, I cut his phone line."

"How did you know where it was?"

"I told you I came here before. I told you I don't walk into a situation without knowing everything. That's probably the same thing you've been taught. But you don't think like a criminal. You don't think of cutting someone's phone line on the way out so he doesn't call somebody else. I do. And I did. And he won't be calling our other friend."

"How do you know he doesn't have a cell phone?"

"I don't know many eighty-nine-year-olds who operate cell phones. They don't want the added expense. Probably doesn't go out much, so he figures he can call whoever he wants from his home phone. Not tonight."

Florian looked distressed. "If it's so obvious that we aren't Nazis, how are we going to persuade anybody to give us the flag?"

I looked at Jedediah and then answered Florian, "We just have to find the person who has it. Doesn't matter if he believes us."

* * *

The drive to Schullman's house was less than ten minutes. Jedediah had been there too, and he showed us where to park so the car wouldn't be heard. We started walking and noticed a few pedestrians returning from a late dinner. The neighborhood was nicer than Blick's, and had trees on the sidewalk between the walking area and the streets. The streetlights cast long shadows.

Schullman lived in the basement apartment of a three-story building. Lights were on behind the curtains, which were lined with old beige linen. There were lights on in the other apartments. It was approaching ten o'clock at night.

I put out my hand for everyone to stop. I said softly, "Maybe we should approach this guy differently."

Florian replied quietly, "I think it's a little late to change our approach. We have to go in now."

Jedediah, who had been looking at the neighborhood over our shoulders, said, "Like you said. Doesn't matter what we say, we just have to get in there, 'cause either he has the flag or he doesn't. And if he does, we'll know it."

"Let's go," I said. We walked down the stairs to Schullman's apartment. Florian knocked loudly. Once again, we could hear a television playing.

The door opened and a tall, elegant man with white hair combed straight back stood staring at us.

Florian said boldly, "*Guten Abend.*"

The old man looked at Florian and repeated the word back to him slowly, "*Guten Abend. Was wollen Sie?*"

Florian continued, "*Wir möchten ein Wort mit Ihnen reden und wir möchten Ihnen etwas anbieten.*"

The man looked at me, at Patrick, and then at Jedediah. He was startled by Jedediah, who had been standing behind Patrick. But once he had a clear view of Jedediah, his eyes widened.

He said, "*Habe ich eine Wahl?*"

Jedediah said in German, "*Ja. Wir wollen Sie um einen Gefallen bitten, und wir haben einen Vorschlag, von dem wir denken, dass er für Sie von Interesse sein könnte.*" Florian and Patrick were surprised. The old man looked at Jedediah, looked at his tattoos, and stepped back into his apartment to allow us in.

There was an open book face down on the coffee table in front of an easy chair, which was facing the television. The lamp was on next to the chair. There was a faint lingering smell of spicy food.

Jedediah asked him, "*Sprechen Sie Englisch?*"

The man responded, "A little."

Jedediah switched to English. "I'd like my financier," he said pointing to me, "to understand. He's American."

The man looked at me and back at Jedediah. "As are you."

"Yes. And these gentlemen are my comrades from Germany."

He frowned. "We don't use the word comrade. That was the Bolsheviks."

"Friends."

Schullman looked at me. "What about him, who's he?"

Jedediah said, "I have the dedication, but not the money. He has money."

"For what?"

"For training, weapons, explosives, whatever we need."

I thought I saw a small smile break out on the old man's face. He tried to look disinterested, but he was clearly intrigued. "And what is it you plan on blowing up?"

"The things that need to be blown up," Jedediah replied.

"Who are you people and what are you doing here? And you, with all these tattoos," he said gesturing with his hand to point at all of Jedediah's ink at once.

"We're the ones carrying the Nazi torch. It was almost extinguished but we're blowing on the coals. And you can help us."

"And what would make you say that?"

Jedediah stepped closer to him, about an arm's length away, and said, "Because you have the *Blutfahne*."

He recoiled slightly and looked at all of us quickly. "What makes you say that?"

He'd given himself away. He started looking around the room. Florian jumped in. "We know that you lived near Otto Hessler's house in Berlin. You left in the spring of 1945, before Berlin fell, and took the *Blutfahne* with you. We have come to ask you to come back to Germany, and to bring the flag with you."

Patrick said, "Come back with us to Germany. There is to be a meeting where the leaders of all the neo-Nazi groups around the world will come to unite in one great movement. There will never be a better time to use the *Blutfahne* than now. We'd like you to bring it back to restore it to Germany, to *rejuvenate* the movement."

Jedediah leaned closer to him. "I know you've kept it for a reason. Not for money, or you would have sold it a long time ago. You kept it for a purpose. *We* are that purpose."

The man looked at Jedediah with skepticism and a glimmer of something. Maybe hope. He considered, thinking of what all this meant. He said quietly, "If I did have it, what would you do with it?"

"Either you could let us have it, or you can come with us," Jedediah said. "We'd rather you come with us to Germany. There's going to be a meeting, in a castle. All the leaders of all the neo-Nazi groups around the world will finally unite under a common creed, a common uniform, and common goals. We will share financing, intelligence, and weapons. And there's no better way to unite that group than to bring the flag that started it all."

I added, "The world is changing. People are identifying with their own groups. Their own people. They've had enough of diversity and multi-culturalism."

The old man seemed comfortable. He smiled. "If I did have this flag and I wanted to go to Germany, who would pay for that?"

"I would," I said. "We would put you up in the best hotel, provide you with a car and driver, and you would be one of the featured people at the meeting. Will you come?"

The man stood up tall, regaining lost pride. "I will show you what I have."

He was clearly intrigued by going to Germany as a returning hero. Then a cloud formed over his face. "Would the public know? If I brought the flag back to Germany, would we get past the police? Through customs?"

I said quickly, "We have people everywhere. We will take you to Germany on a private jet, to a private airport in Munich. We will make sure you arrive at a certain time, and the men who will check your passport and your luggage will be sympathizers. You will have no problems."

He snapped his head to look around at me. "You can guarantee this?"

"We can guarantee this."

Florian and Patrick nodded, probably wondering where this would all lead.

He contemplated as he ran his hands through his hair, pushing it back.

His watery blue eyes brightened. "Okay. I will get it."

He crossed over to the far corner of the room and knelt down beside the bookcase, which reached to the ceiling. The bottom section had sliding panels, and he slid the panels open. Inside were games, chessboards, and children's toys. At the bottom of the stack was a large Tupperware container. He moved the games and toys off the Tupperware and slid it out from the cabinet. We all started moving toward the container sitting on the carpet, but he said, "Please stay back. I will pull it out and open it up for you."

He reached across the Tupperware container and began running his fingers around the lid. I could hear him pop the lid off and break the airtight seal. We all watched expectantly as he pulled the lid back. All I could see was a cloth of some kind, like a heavy towel made of linen, and folded on top. He put it aside.

"What's that?" I asked.

"To help absorb the moisture and keep the flag in place."

I could see the solid red flag in the bottom of the container. I felt my heart skip as I gazed on the flag that I had hoped existed. I couldn't take my eyes off it.

He pulled the container over toward the corner, and used the built-in bookshelf to steady himself. He reached underneath the flag and pulled his hand back, holding a Luger. He pointed it at each of us in turn. I stared at the handgun. It was rust free, freshly oiled, and in good condition. We all looked at each other wondering what his play was. His hand was steady. His face was red with energy, anger, and fear. He said in a hiss, "Take everything out of your pockets and put it on the coffee table. Everything!"

I said to him quietly, "What are you doing? Why are you doing this?"

"I have no idea who you are. You come down here looking for the flag, claiming to be some neo-Nazis; I don't know you from anybody. You could be the Bundeskriminalamt. I don't know. And you bring this muscle with you," he said, pointing his pistol at Jedediah. "To intimidate me. Well, I don't scare. And you can't have the flag."

He looked at the items on the coffee table. "Wallets too!" He picked up my wallet and looked through it. He pulled out the driver's license. "Virginia?"

"Yes. I told you I was American."

"What do you do?"

"I'm an investor. I make a lot of money."

He tossed the wallet back onto the table. "Weapons? Are you armed?"

I shook my head. "Why would we be armed to come and see you? We thought we were coming to see a friend."

"I don't care what you thought, or what you tell me." He continued going through the wallets when suddenly Jedediah moved faster than I've ever seen any person move, especially someone his size. In less than a second, he was on top of the old man and his huge right forearm slammed down on the man's gun hand. I heard a crack, like a plate dropped onto a tile floor, as he dropped the gun and grabbed his arm.

"You broke my wrist!"

"You're lucky I haven't broken your neck. *Nobody* points a gun at me." Jedediah bent over and picked up the Luger. He pulled the slide back to eject the cartridge, released the slide and looked at the bullets. They were new, clean brass. He stared at the old man angrily as he put the magazine in his pocket and tucked the Luger into his belt. He put his left hand back in his pocket, where it lingered for just a moment. Jedediah looked at the rest of us, and said, "I'm not taking him to Germany. And we're sure as hell not paying him for the flag now; we're just going to take it." He reached down, put the lid back onto the container and picked it up, as the old man leaned against the bookcase holding his fractured wrist.

Suddenly, I heard breaking glass in the back of the apartment and the *whoosh* of an explosive flame. I could see a reflection of a large flame in the glass of a picture in the hallway. Before I could do anything the window behind me broke and another Molotov cocktail flew into the apartment, smashing into the corner of the room where we stood. The gasoline splashed all over the bookcase while it was in the process of igniting. The room was filled with smoke and flames, and the back exit was cut off by the already burning kitchen.

Jedediah screamed at Schullman, "We've got to get out of here!" The old man started to flee, holding his wrist. Suddenly he stopped and looked back. I watched him carefully as he went to the corner of the bookcase, still holding his broken wrist, and pushed on the edge of the bookcase with his good hand. It gave a little bit and then popped out. He swung it out, revealing a large wall safe. It looked like a sophisticated safe with a digital keypad for the combination. He quickly typed in six numbers, and the door popped open. It wasn't a thick door, and would not withstand the fire that was about to consume the building. He grabbed cash and what appeared to be a passport folder out of the safe and stuffed them in his shirt. He reached in and grabbed a compressed plastic packing sleeve that had all the air pressed out of it and was sealed tight. It had two handles on it, like a stadium cushion. He grabbed it and began running out of the room. Jedediah put his hand on Schullman's chest to stop him and took the item from him. He said loudly, "The real flag?" The man nodded as he began to panic. He pushed Jedediah's arm aside and rushed for the door. Jedediah rushed right behind him as we all fled the room that was now nearly consumed in flames. We stumbled onto the street to avoid the flames.

Schullman bent over gasping and coughing. "Why did you do this to me? Everything I own is in there!"

Jedediah pulled him up and looked him in the eye. "Maybe you should have thought of that when you pulled a gun on us."

I walked over to Jedediah, as the fire grew behind us. We had to get out of there. "Give me the flag," I said to him.

He turned and looked at me with deep hostility. "If I'd left it up to you, we'd have left with the fake. Now we've got the real one."

"Let me have it."

He held the two flags close to him, looked at each of us individually, and turned and walked down the street. "Jedediah!" I yelled. He didn't ever respond. He took two more steps, then broke into a trot, and ducked around the corner.

We could hear sirens of fire trucks, and people were coming out of their apartments to look at the fire. I said, "Let's get out of here."

CHAPTER FIFTEEN

As soon as my airplane touched down at Dulles, I emailed Jedediah. Unlike so many other times there was no instant response. I stared at my BlackBerry waiting for his reply. Nothing. I checked it every ten seconds as I worked my way down the aisle and into the terminal and while waiting to pass through immigration and customs.

Either he was still with me and didn't trust me to carry the flag, or he had turned on me, and was now on his own. With the flag. And he'd brought at least two people to Argentina I hadn't known about or approved. They had to know the arrangement and that Jedediah was working with us.

I drove straight to FBI headquarters and went to see Karl. He looked at me with surprise as I sat down on the edge of the chair in his office waiting for him to get off the phone. He could see the annoyance and frustration on my face. He said to the person he was talking to, "Let me call you back." He hung up the phone and said, "So, how was Argentina?"

"We found the flag."

He looked stunned. "Seriously? That's unbelievable."

"BKA came up with a short list. We cross checked with the Argentine Federal Police—a woman named Manuela Gabrielli—know her?"

"No. Never worked with them."

"She knows the Germans living in Argentina. We found the two guys, and the second one said he had it. Manuela said to leave our weapons behind and just talk to these guys. So he tried to give us a fake, then pulls out a Luger and holds us at gunpoint. Then, *curiously*, our boy Jedediah breaks his wrist, takes the gun, puts his hand in his pocket for a second, and the next thing I know two firebombs come in through the windows. The old man panics and opens a secret panel in the wall to save the real flag. Jedediah grabbed the real flag and I haven't seen him since."

He shook his head and adjusted his glasses. "You're making this up."

"Nope. Definitely not making it up."

"So, Jedediah took somebody with him and signaled him to firebomb the place? Pretty clever, thinking the old man might hand you a fake but he wouldn't let the real one burn."

"Have to admit that. Maybe I could have just looked the other way if he had called me in Buenos Aires and given me the flag. We might not have had a conversation about the coincidental firebombing. Not in our jurisdiction. But he didn't call. Haven't heard a thing. Now I'm wondering if he was just using us. Pisses me off."

"And the old man?"

"He's fine. Broken wrist, but nothing else, and he just lost his beloved fascist flag and everything else he owns."

"Yeah, too bad." Karl paused and waited for me to respond, but I didn't. "So, you want to know about Jedediah. Anything else I haven't told you."

I nodded. "Is he with us? Or is he using us?"

He thought for a moment. "He can't be using us to get the Blood Flag, because we had never thought of it till you came along."

"Maybe he was using us to maneuver himself. Find out what we knew about the Volk."

"Doesn't work that way. You and I both know we don't tell them what we know. Maybe he got this idea when you started talking about the Blood Flag. He saw this as his big chance."

"That's what I'm afraid of. He delivers this Blood Flag to his superior in the Southern Volk and they have their absolute guaranteed ticket to go to Germany. He doesn't need us."

"And you think that's what happened?"

"Like I said, he's gone silent. And the way he conducted himself in Argentina, assuming—which I think is certain—that he had somebody throw firebombs into this guy's apartment, that was not our plan."

He smiled ironically. "*Your* plan was to walk into an old man's apartment unarmed and have him turn a Luger on you. *That* was your plan."

"Who said I was unarmed?"

"I thought you said you left your weapon at the apartment."

"No, I said that's what Manuela told us to do. I didn't think she'd agree to an American cowboy running around Argentina armed. That old man didn't have a chance if he was really going to try something. But before I could do anything, Jedediah smashed his arm, firebombed the place, and took the flag."

Karl drummed his fingers. I waited. He finally said, "I guess there is one thing I should tell you."

I waited.

"Jedediah had a brother."

"Had?"

"Yeah. Jonah. One of the two founders of the Southern Volk, with Brunnig. Jedediah joined them after he got out of the army."

"And?"

"Jonah was thought to be the brains of the Thom family. Jedediah was always thought to be the muscle."

"But you think differently?"

"I think Jonah was probably smarter, but Jedediah is underestimated by most people. He's very smart, but more . . . clever. He sees ways through problems that others don't see. Probably can't do calculus, but if he wants to get something done? Look out."

"So what about Jonah?"

"That's the thing. Jonah Thom didn't make it to the first anniversary of the founding of the Southern Volk."

"Why not?"

"We're not sure. He disappeared. No trace, no body, no nothing. Jedediah put out a missing person's report. Said he didn't have any idea where his brother had gone. Hadn't seen him in days. Shortly after that, Brunnig took over as the undisputed leader. Been there ever since."

"How long ago did this happen?"

He thought for a minute. "About two years. Maybe more."

"And what does Jedediah think happened?"

"He thinks Brunnig made him disappear. Buried him in some swamp somewhere, or mountain ravine."

I felt a little heat building. "Why didn't you tell me this earlier?"

"Don't know. Didn't occur to me."

What bullshit. "So Jedediah has a big motivation to overthrow Brunnig. He may be using the flag for that. He may have no intention of helping us. This changes everything." I stared at him. "How the hell could you not tell me about it?"

"Just did. I didn't think anything would come of this. I thought you'd babysit Jedediah for a while then go on your way. I never thought you'd find that silly . . . that flag."

I fought back my inclination to yell at him. "You think it's *silly*?"

"I didn't mean it like that."

I stood up. I'd heard enough. "Anything else you should have told me?"

"I don't trust Jedediah. I guess I implied I did. I do in minor respects, but in terms of whether he's with us or not? I don't know. You know the old saying, never trust a traitor."

What an ass. "Yeah. I know the saying. Another saying I know is FBI special agents should share information with each other. Do you know that saying? Especially information on a case they are working on together? Do you know that one?"

He was feeling the heat. "I didn't know what we were dealing with. I didn't really have any idea whether Jedediah was involved in his brother's disappearance. Almost certainly not. But the head guy probably was."

"So that's what you thought the motivation *really* was for Jedediah coming to us. Yet you never told me that. He tried to sell me on this thing about him being 'saved.' Is that what he told you?"

"He mentioned it. May even be some truth in it. Did he land in the U.S.?" I nodded. "And hasn't been seen since."

"They gonna charge him in Argentina?"

"If we want them to."

Karl had been playing with his computer and looking at the screen intermittently while we were talking. He squinted at the screen, sat up, and said, "Well, here's our answer. Check this out." He turned the flat screen around so that I could see it. It was the home page of the Southern Volk's website.

I looked at the banner. "Southern Volk appoints new president— Jedediah Thom."

* * *

When I got back to my office, Alex was waiting for me. She was looking at the Southern Volk website. She looked up at me. "So where's the former president?"

"Why don't *you* tell me."

"I think he's a goner. I think our boy Jedediah . . . pushed him aside."

"And now I know why. Karl just gave me one of those critical pieces of information I should have had weeks ago." She waited.

"Jedediah's brother was one of the founders of the Volk. He 'disappeared' a year later. Jedediah blames the current president. Well he *was* the president." I contemplated the implications. "Does it say what he's doing?"

"No."

"Check local news sites to see if he has disappeared." She typed his name into Google.

I went to the Southern Volk website and looked at it carefully. There was no mention of Brunnig. "It's like he doesn't exist. He's not even in the article about Jedediah taking over."

"What do you make of it?"

"I think this was Jedediah's plan the whole time. As soon as he heard about this German thing—about the chance to be on the world stage—he decided it was time to make his move. He's hated Brunnig ever since he took over. Jedediah thought he should be in charge, now he is. The question is, who are we dealing with? Is he still talking to us? But if he's still talking to us, and he's killed Brunnig, we're done with him."

Alex wondered what the next step was. I wondered that myself. This thing could go wrong in so many different directions. It already had. Finally, I said, "How would you like to go to Columbia? Can you crash a car?"

* * *

We flew to Columbia, South Carolina, the next morning and went straight to a shady used car dealer near Five Points. It looked like it used to be a doughnut shop. The owner had about twenty used cars, most of which had probably been stolen, submerged, or totaled at some point. We bought an iffy green Accord for a thousand dollars. It had two hundred thousand miles on it. I didn't care though, as I only needed it to go about five more.

Alex got in the driver's seat and we drove off the lot. It was a blistering hot day with humidity that made you want to stop breathing; unusual for October. The engine sounded fine and the car drove well. I turned on the air conditioning, which blew hot air in our faces. We drove through a couple of neighborhoods.

"We need to find a steel pole somewhere. Let's go down by the stadium."

She drove the short distance to the football stadium and into a parking lot that had light poles with cement bases. "What's the plan?"

"Back it into a light pole. About five or ten miles an hour."

"*You* back it into a light pole."

"Fine. Get out."

She stopped, put the car in park, and got out. I walked around, got in, and put it in reverse. I looked over the seat with my right hand on the passenger seat and backed it toward a pole. I glanced up and saw Alex standing there with her hands on her hips and her teeth clenched. I looked back and saw the pole. I was going maybe five miles per hour. So I hit the accelerator to ten. I slammed into the light pole and the impact was much harder than I expected. I felt my head go back sideways, which surprised me, but I was confident I'd inflicted enough damage.

Alex walked over and looked at the damage. "Holy shit! I'm glad I wasn't in the car! You must have been going twenty-five miles an hour! You're going to have a sore neck."

I got out to look at the damage myself. It was a serious impact. More than I had intended. I was worried it wouldn't drive. I climbed back in the driver's seat, Alex got in, and we drove away. I could hear a strange sound coming from the rear end, but the car drove.

I drove straight toward Jedediah's auto body shop. We stopped two blocks short and pulled up to a Starbucks. I took out my pocket notebook and tore out a sheet of paper. I put it in the center of the steering wheel as I wrote "Same place as last, 11:00 p.m." I handed it to her. "You sure you can pull this off?"

"Just stay here."

"I'll be waiting." I got out and stood on the curb as she pulled away. The Accord looked like it had been in a demolition derby. I'd overdone it a little bit. I was lucky I hadn't punctured the gas tank.

I walked into the Starbucks and ordered a cappuccino and a Danish. I sat in the corner and pulled out my iPad. It had been a couple weeks since I had looked at the neo-Nazi websites and news stories on Nazism.

I checked out the American neo-Nazi websites to see if anyone was talking about the meeting in Germany. Or the change of command at the Southern Volk. Not much new. I started wondering how we'd prove this flag—assuming we got it from Jedediah—was *the one* that was bled on in the twenties and carried in the thirties and forties. We had already been shown one fake, and we now knew that the Russians had a whole trailer full of fake Hitler memorabilia.

I googled "Otto Hessler" again to see if I could find out anything about his family. We had to get DNA. The Blood Flag was called the Blood Flag because it had blood on it. Those stains were still there. But could they be used? Were they too old? And tested against what? Who?

I'd been in a lot of cases where DNA testing was used. It was now so common that it was done almost as a matter of course. It had changed forensics forever, and frankly, made it far better. DNA testing has been so much more accurate than all the other types of forensic evidence put together that it has made the odds of a wrongful conviction significantly lower. We, of course, always deny that there is any chance of a wrongful conviction. That's what law enforcement always says. But wrongful convictions are well known. By the hundreds.

But I had never had a case where the DNA I wanted tested was from 1923. DNA testing was really about cell biology. I got on my BlackBerry and sent an email to the head of our forensics lab near Quantico. "Assume a blood stain on a cloth from 1923. How can I prove it's a certain person (I know whose blood it is)?" I hit send.

I knew the names of all the men who had bled on the flag. Of course none of that mattered if we couldn't persuade Eidhalt. He'd have to be involved in the testing to really believe it.

I sent an email to Florian asking him to start thinking about the best DNA lab to use in Germany. After getting sidetracked by checking sports scores and political blogs and losing track of the time, I was brought back to the present when the door flew open and Alex came in looking like she'd seen a ghost. She looked around desperately then saw me. She came over to me and dropped her purse on the small table in front of me like it contained all her burdens. She sat down and tried to catch her breath. She was nearly unable to speak. I waited. She shook her head subtly, got up, went to the counter, and ordered a cup of green tea. She returned to the table and played with the tea bag in the hot water. Finally, she looked up at me.

"Never in my life have I ever met or even seen anyone so completely . . . intimidating."

"You're FBI. You're not supposed to be intimidated by anybody," I said half joking. "He was there?"

She nodded.

"What happened?"

She took a sip from her tea. She was holding her cup with two hands, probably so her hand wouldn't shake. Finally, she spoke. "I found the shop, and pulled in. I haven't been to a body shop in a long time. It feels strange, especially for a woman. This isn't one of those fancy shiny body shops that your insurance company sends you to if you get hit. This is one of those dirty, greasy, body shops where sketchy men hang out and probably chop stolen cars and fix cars involved in hit and runs. The kind that never wants any insurance company to pay them for anything, because they don't want the scrutiny. Once I pulled in it was much bigger on the inside than it looked from the outside. The door is kind of small to drive through, but once you get through, it's like you're in a warehouse."

"Go on."

"I got out of the car and stood there waiting for somebody to approach me. I was looking for Jedediah the whole time, but didn't see him. You know those offices that have a glass window and they can see the whole shop floor? They have one. And a guy was staring at me from there and not moving. I stood looking around with some of the men working on cars glancing at me now and then, but nobody moved. It was damn awkward. Finally, the guy in the office gets up and comes out. Looks like he's doing me a huge favor just by getting his ass out of his chair."

"What did he look like?"

"Skinny guy, tall, maybe six two, not muscular. Wearing jeans and a white T-shirt. Blonde hair. Spiked. He had earrings in each ear, sort of pointed earrings where they go through and then they're open at the bottom but they point down to the floor. He came up to me. 'What can I do for you?' "I was trying hard to look sheepish. Not something I'm good at. Anyway, I said 'I backed into a pole. I need you to fix it.' I led him around to the back of the Accord and pointed to the damage. He looked at it, put his hands on his hips, and said, 'Shit lady. What were you doing? You musta been going backwards at thirty miles an hour. Not that easy to do.'"

She looked at me intensely. "I *told* you you overdid it. Anyway, I assured him that I was not, and that I was simply backing out of a parking space and hit a pole. He just looked at me and shook his head. He didn't believe me. But it didn't matter. He probably deals with liars all the time, and I was just the latest. 'You want an estimate?' he asked. I told him I didn't want the insurance company involved. I'd submitted two claims already this year and if they got a third one, they'd cancel me. I told him I'd pay cash."

"Go on," I said.

She nodded, relaxing slightly. "So I told him, yeah, I need an estimate. He went into his office, brought out a clipboard with a blank piece of paper—I kid you not—a blank piece of paper. He looked at the damage, crawled under the back of the car, tried to open the trunk—which wouldn't open—and wrote a number on the piece of paper. Twelve hundred sixty-four dollars. I told him that was ridiculous. I told him, 'You're out of your mind. This should be about six hundred dollars.' And he looked at me with complete apathy. He clearly didn't care if I had my car fixed there or not. So he said, 'Have you done a lot of estimates?' I, of course, had to say no and he said, 'You need a new bumper, a new trunk lid, there's damage underneath, a lot of work.' I said, 'Well can you do any better than that number?' He shook his head. 'Nope.' So I began my little charade. He just shook his head. He didn't even bother to respond. So, I asked him, 'Are you the owner?' He said, 'Nope.' So, I told him I wanted to see the owner. He simply told me I didn't need to see the owner, that he was the estimator, and that was the number. I told him I insisted on seeing the owner. He insisted I didn't need to. I then told him, I wasn't leaving until I saw the owner and he started to look at me a little funny, evaluating me. He asked me, 'Where do you live?' I said, 'What do you mean, where do I live?' 'Where do you live in Columbia?' I was a little bit taken aback. I said that I lived near Lake Murray. He looked at me again, and then started checking me out. Not like sexually, but evaluating my clothes. I think he was starting to suspect something. He then asked to see my driver's license. I didn't know what to do. I panicked. Why would they need to see my driver's license? We hadn't talked about that at all."

"We should have anticipated that. We should have gotten you a fake ID."

"It didn't matter. I told him it had been revoked and I didn't have one."

"You told him your driver's license had been revoked?"

"What else was I going to tell him? I was going to show him what, my Virginia driver's license? My FBI ID? What the *hell* would you have had me show him?"

"So what happened?"

"I told him it had been revoked because I'd had too many points. So he frowns and tells me I must be a really shitty driver because I've had two insurance claims and enough points to get my license revoked and backed into a light pole at sixty miles an hour. I got pissy and told him he didn't need to worry about it, he just needed to fix my damned car for less than twelve hundred sixty-four dollars and that I wanted to see the owner if he wasn't willing to lower it. He told me he absolutely wasn't willing to lower it, that was the price, and I didn't need to see the owner. I told him I needed to deal with the person who had the authority, as he was clearly a *lackey* and I needed to talk to the person in charge. Well that got his back up, he got pissed. If I didn't like his estimate, I could go elsewhere. I told him I might very well do that, but first wanted to see the owner. I crossed my arms and stood there making it clear to him that I wasn't going anywhere until he got the owner. And I had left my car just inside the entrance so that nobody was going in or out until my car was moved. The keys were in my purse so they couldn't just move the car easily. So he goes into his little office, throws his clipboard onto the desk and picks up the phone and was gesturing—but I couldn't hear what he was saying—and then put the phone down. He sat down at his desk and then didn't say another word. I stood there waiting, looked around the shop at the activity and nobody was making any move toward me. It got awkward. I started looking at the ceiling and the walls and then realized for the first time there were security cameras everywhere. He was probably studying me on the camera. I just waited, and still nothing happened. I walked over to the lackey's office and talked to him from out-side his doorway. I asked him if the owner was coming and he didn't even respond. He didn't look up; he didn't say anything.

"Then, from no more than twelve inches behind me, 'You looking for me?' It's bad enough to get surprised. But when the surprise is so close you can almost feel his breath and then it's a gruff voice and then you whip around and the person looks like a serial killer? I swear I thought I was go-ing to wet my pants. Literally. You just don't even understand. I'm not afraid of many people. I've taken Kung Fu, I can defend myself reasonably. Well probably not, but I *think* I can, which is good enough, and, if I feel like I'm really in danger, I'll just get out my weapon, and if some man is truly going to attack me, I'll shoot him. Deader than a doornail. With a clear conscience. But when you're face to face with somebody who could clearly pinch your head off, and might in fact do that? Whole different deal. And close enough to do it faster than you could even object. It's just something about the intimidating presence of a guy this big and this strong. Not that he's that tall . . . he's just massive. I could literally hit him as hard as I could with just about anything and it wouldn't even phase him. I haven't felt that exposed and vulnerable in a long time. Well, ever. I really wanted to know why I had left my handgun with you and why you weren't a quarter of a block away, and why I wasn't wearing a wire so you could come rescue me.

It made me realize how stupidly we had gone about this. Those were the thoughts that went through my mind in the first tenth of a second. In the second tenth of a second, I tried to gather myself and face him squarely. Even though he was twelve inches away and he was way inside my personal space and the only option I had was to step into Mr. Lackey's office, I had to push back. I told him that his estimator's number was ridiculous; it was on a blank piece of paper, he didn't seem to know what he was doing, and that I wanted him to give me a discount from that estimate.

"He stared at me with these cold eyes and told me that he wouldn't change anything. This guy was the best estimator in the city. So I looked right back at him and asked him if he would take a look at the car himself. He looked over my shoulder at his estimator, then back at me. Then he said, 'Sure. Why not.' He sort of pushed me aside as he went into the office and picked up the guy's clipboard with the estimate on it. He walked out to the Accord, went around to the back of it, did nothing but glance at it, circled the estimate on the clipboard, and put a big check mark by it. He handed the clipboard to me. 'That's our estimate.' So, I asked him if that was it. If that was the best they could possibly do. He stared right back at me, again getting too close, maybe a foot. I could smell the sweat on his body. 'No, it's not the best we can possibly do. But it's the best we're going to do.' So I told him I didn't think that was very helpful. He stares at me, then he looks me up and down. He asked me what I did. I told him that I was a secretary at the University and worked in the Department of Education. And he asked me why there wasn't a USC parking sticker anywhere on my car. I told him I lost my parking privileges when I lost my license. He didn't buy it. 'So you went out and scraped off your sticker? Where's the residue? Where's the outline of where it was? I think you're a cop. I don't know why you're here, but I think you probably oughta get going.' I laughed. 'A cop. That's a good one.' But he was right. I needed to get out of there. So I put out my hand, where I'd hidden the piece of paper between two fingers. He paused, then shook my hand and felt the paper. He curled his hand into a fist and put it into his pocket. He turned his back to me, and walked back in the direction he'd come from. I shook my head, got in the car, backed out, and drove straight here."

I sat back and considered what she had said. "Do you think he knows who you are?"

She shook her head. "Probably. He knows something's up, that my story wasn't holding together, but I don't think he really cared what the real story was. He just knew he didn't want anything to do with me. Do you trust him?"

I took the lid off my Starbucks cup and scraped the remaining foam from inside with the stirring stick and ate it. "I'm not sure. As of right now? No."

"So you set up a meeting with him for you and me in the middle of nowhere in the middle of the night."

"Yes, tonight."

She finished her tea. "You've been such a comfort to me, thank you so much."

* * *

We drove to the dead end at Lake Murray at ten o'clock. We turned at the same bent road sign and drove to the end of the road, right by the water. I stopped in the same place I had stopped before, turned out the lights and shut off the engine. We were an hour early. I wanted to see where Jedediah came from this time. No surprises. If Jedediah Thom had in fact gone out on his own and had killed the head of the Southern Volk, he might feel free to do whatever he thinks will make him more secure in his position. "Let's check the area and wait outside the car in the woods. I want our eyes to adjust to the dark before he gets here."

We opened our doors at the same time and just as I was closing mine, I saw a rush of motion on the other side of the car. I heard a shocked cry from Alex and a rustle of activity, which then went silent. I unholstered my Glock and ran around the car. Jedediah was standing at the edge of the trees holding Alex with his forearm around her neck. He was barely visible in black jeans, a black turtleneck, and black rubber gloves. His other hand was over her mouth. I could hear her panic, but he had obviously threatened her as she was not fighting his grip. I raised my gun and pointed it at his head, twenty feet away. "Let her go."

Jedediah began moving slightly in unpredictable ways. I could and absolutely would shoot him in the head from twenty feet away with Alex right next to him. I could hit a head-sized target from twenty feet away ten out of ten times, swaying or not. He said softly, "Put your gun down."

"Not a chance. Let her go."

"You have to answer a question for me first."

"Here's one answer. If you kill her I'll either shoot you right now, or I'll make it my life's mission to get you a special injection that will put you to sleep forever."

He shook his head. "You here to arrest me?"

"No."

He said to Alex, "How dare you come to my shop with that bullshit story. Everyone in the shop wanted to know why the cops were after me. Worst thing you could have done."

I said, "You steal the flag, come to the U.S., and then go silent! What the hell was I supposed to do? I thought you'd turned on us!"

He twisted Alex's head sideways until she was wincing in pain while he looked at me. "Give me your word you won't arrest me. That you're here to have a civil conversation and I'll let her go."

"Of course I give you my word! Get your hands off of her!"

He released her and pushed her away slightly. She turned around, looked at him in the face, and said, "You asshole!" She balled her hand into a fist and slugged him in the gut as hard as she could.

It had no effect on him at all. She ran over to where I was as I re-holstered my handgun. I said, "Shit, Jed. What the *hell* was that?"

"What the hell was that? What the hell was it when you sent her into my shop? Right into my freaking shop! She backs into a pole going sixty miles an hour and then makes up some bullshit story about a parking lot. Everybody there knew it was a lie. Everybody there knew she was a cop. They could smell it. They didn't know why, but they knew she was a cop. Do you think we usually do estimates on a blank piece of paper where we just write a number? Then she gets into a huff, where the estimate he gives her is about seventy percent of what it ought to be, and she demands a lower number? She may as well have worn a sign on her chest that said, 'FBI agent with an agenda.'"

"You weren't returning my emails. I needed to talk to you after that stunt in Argentina. Why the hell did you go cold on me?" I tried to read his face. I wasn't getting good feelings.

"Too much going on. The whole Russian thing, then the Southern Volk president disappears while we're in Argentina—"

"By you?"

"Hell no. I have no idea where he is. All I know is that I'm in charge and I'm hyper sensitive. I'm not talking to anybody about anything except going to Germany."

"So you're still planning on going?"

"Of course I am. I've got the Blood Flag."

"Yeah, you do, and I'm supposed to. Where is it?"

"You're not supposed to have it. I am. I'm the one taking it to Germany. I'm the one selling this story."

"I need to know right out, Jedediah, are you still with me or not? You and I still on the same page?"

"Yeah. We're still on the same page. But you need to give me a lot of room. I don't want to have any more phony collisions brought into my shop."

"You have to communicate with me. If you're working with me, you've got to communicate. And if you made Brunnig 'disappear,' we're done. I need to know you didn't do that."

"I didn't do anything."

"So you're still planning on taking the Blood Flag to Germany? We're down to twenty days."

"I know. I've already told Eidhalt I've got the biggest surprise ever. And I'm going to be one of his people coming to Germany."

"How does it work? I thought he had to pre-filter it—determine the value of what people had done—and then he would invite them."

"He insisted on knowing, but I said I wasn't going to tell him. He *demanded* to know."

"So now what?" I asked.

"I told him I'm coming to Germany to show him. So I'm going to Germany. He finally gave me a secret phone number."

I looked at the stars through the trees overhead. I looked back at Jedediah. "You've got one problem."

"Really? What's that?"

"Authentication. You've seen how good the Russian fakes were. What do you think is going to make him believe that your flag—our flag—isn't a fake?"

I could see the shock on Jedediah's face. "What are you going to do when he tells you you have to prove this was the original Blood Flag? How you going to prove it?"

"It is the original. We got it from the Nazi in Argentina. He tried to unload a fake on us, but we got the real one."

"How do you know that? He might have a whole pile of fakes for just this kind of thing. He may have the original in a safe deposit box somewhere."

He hadn't thought of that possibility. "So now what?"

"I think I know what needs to be done, but what I don't know is whether I should tell you. I'm not sure I trust you anymore. I thought we had an understanding in Argentina. But you took it upon yourself to fire bomb an apartment—that I'm *standing* in—and take off with the Blood Flag. You could have gotten somebody killed."

"I didn't care about some old Nazi getting killed. Hell with him."

"You could have gotten Florian or Patrick killed. Or me. Or you. It was stupid. If you had something like that in mind, you should have told us. And the fact that you didn't makes me wonder what else you have in mind. I just don't know if I trust you."

"I've got nothing else in mind. You can walk away if you want. But if you do, I'm gonna keep going. And you can't stop me."

"If you keep going without us, and you don't authenticate that flag, you don't have anything. It's just a matter of time until he figures it out and calls you before the meeting."

"So what do you suggest?"

I looked at Alex and back again. "We've got to get the DNA out of the flag and match it with one of the people who died. We know all the names."

"Can you do that?"

"I'm asking the people at the FBI forensics lab. But what I think we're going to have to do is go to Germany and dig up some graves."

"And then the meeting."

"Right."

"So you're coming with me?"

"Right."

"What's our story? Who are you?"

"I'm probably your financier. I've already put myself out as a rancher when I was in Tennessee. Probably need to stick with that."

He thought for a moment. "We don't know who is connected to who. You need to come to one of our meetings."

"In person?"

"Yes."

"Will Brunnig be there?"

"Probably not."

Alex said, "Yeah, because he's dead."

Jedediah looked at her. "What makes you say that?"

"Because he's gone and now you're in charge. Where is he if he's not dead?"

"No idea. He just vanished. Guess he had something to run from."

"Like your brother?" she asked.

Uh oh, I thought. Jedediah turned to face her. "What the *hell* do you know about my brother?"

"Did Brunnig kill him? Make him disappear? You returning the favor?"

He breathed heavily. "You don't know what you're talking about."

I intervened. "I've seen how these meetings go. It's a lions' den."

"It'll be fine. I'll be running it."

"Yeah, but some of your people are crazy."

"Most of them."

"So I'm supposed to walk in there and be the great financier and you'll introduce me and all will be well?"

"You want to come to Germany? We need to really nail your background. You need to be part of us."

"I don't know." The mental images I had of the meeting I'd watched were vivid.

Jedediah continued to stare at Alex. After an awkward interval he said to me, "Wednesday. Be there. The Traveller. And let's make sure your story on the Internet is even better. Fully developed, so anyone who reads it will believe it."

I held up my hand. "So before now you wouldn't even return my calls, and now you want to introduce me to the Volk."

"Brunnig and his suspicion are gone. It's my organization now. They'll do what I say."

CHAPTER SIXTEEN

Wednesday came quickly. I flew to Columbia in the morning, then waited until midnight passed. At one thirty I drove to the Traveller and parked by the dozens of cars already there. I sat in my car, pretending to work on something as I watched the members of the Southern Volk arrive for the meeting. Most of them came two or three to a car. Although I'd seen them in the video, seeing them in person was even more disturbing. Many of them were young, early twenties, and full of piss and vinegar, as my Marine friends used to say. They were looking for a fight, at least when they outnumbered the opposition.

Alex had worked tirelessly to create my Internet existence. Enough to convince even a diligent researcher of my authenticity. Jedediah hadn't told them I was coming, so no one would have done any research. But I was sure they'd look after I'd gone. And if they found any holes, it could mean the end of Jedediah.

I opened my car door and stepped out. I was wearing my jeans and cowboy boots with a black windbreaker. I fell in behind two young men headed for the basement headquarters. They glanced at me, then stopped and turned.

"Who are you?" one of them said.

"Friend of Jedediah's."

"Really."

"Yes, really."

"You coming to the meeting?"

"Yeah."

"We'll follow you," the other said as they walked around behind me, waiting for me to move.

I walked toward the basement following others, and down the stairs, which were steep and dark, with a railing built out of steel pipe. Several men descended in front of me and my two escorts followed behind me. At the bottom of the stairs was a flat area and an open steel door. Two large men stood at the door like bouncers. They waved the men in front of me into the basement, but stepped in front of the door opening when they saw me. One of them put his hand on my chest. "May we help you?"

"I'm here for the meeting."

"What's your name?"

"Jack Bradley."

"And who invited you?"

"Jedediah."

One looked at the other. "Go get him."

The second one left while others poured in around me getting nods from the remaining bouncer who had to be at least six feet four inches and had long stringy hair. The second man returned and gave a nod to the first, who stepped aside and let me pass.

I walked into the room, which was filling fast. It looked smaller than it had on the video. Aggressive rock music played loudly as the men milled around laughing and pushing each other. Some drank beer, others smoked. All waited for the beginning of the meeting. The meetings all started in exactly the same way, Jedediah had told me, like any good club. At some signal I didn't see, the two bouncers slammed the steel door closed and threw the bolt home. They ran a massive padlock through the bolt, slotted it home, and the one with stringy hair put the key in his pocket.

But this was already different than the meeting I had observed under the direction of Brunnig. The lights went down, and the music changed to restrained martial tunes. John Philips Sousa. "The Washington Post March," then, louder, "Stars and Stripes Forever." The effect was surreal. The stately, historic, patriotic music rolled over the mob of neo-Nazis who were taken aback by the change in theme from Brunnig. Jedediah was merging their neo-Nazi inclinations with their childhood patriotism. American songs instead of German. As "Stars and Stripes Forever" approached its climax the volume rose and rose again, until the rhythm thumped through the high-quality sound system. Some marched and stomped their feet while others looked around, wondering how to respond to the new way.

The music stopped, and the lights went out. I stood to the side. As the music began again I immediately recognized it. The march that started with

"Auld Lang Syne." George M. Cohan. A spotlight pierced the darkness and illuminated the back of the stage, where the flag of the Southern Volk was proudly displayed, the Battle Flag of the Army of Tennessee, the flag commonly called the Confederate Flag, with its red background and crossed blue bars with stars. But unlike the Confederate flag, it had a white circle with a Swastika in the middle. Up came the music, louder and louder as it finished the "Auld Lang Syne" introduction and rolled into a booming deafening version of "You're a Grand Old Flag," one of the greatest patriotic songs in American history.

It was a twisted, disturbing development. Jedediah had melded neo-Nazism with American patriotism. I had always loved the music and even had an old record album with nothing but martial marches on it that my father had given to me. When I was a boy he had taken me to see the United States Marine Corps silent drill team perform at Headquarters Marine Corps at 8th and I in D.C., where their stirring finale featured "You're a Grand Old Flag." I tried to look enthusiastic instead of how I felt.

Finally the introduction was over and the lights came up, but only slightly. Jedediah stepped to the microphone and into the spotlight. He extended his arm in a Nazi salute and began a pledge of allegiance. No one knew it was coming or what he was saying. They extended their arms and listened carefully as Jedediah yelled the pledge into the microphone.

"I pledge allegiance! To the flag! Of the Southern Volk of America! And to the future, for which it stands! One people, pure and right, with Liberty and Justice above all!"

He started it again and they all joined enthusiastically. He led it again and they all yelled out the pledge with eagerness.

He spoke. "Men, tonight we take a new course. Brunnig has gone his own way for reasons we don't know. But the Southern Volk live on!" Clapping. "We will continue to grow, and continue to thrive. And we will get to Germany to join the other Nazi groups who will change the world! Tonight, as you know, we have numerous things to plan, and will break into our planning groups shortly. But before we do, I want to introduce someone to you. Someone who is going to make a very big difference in our future, in our finances, and in getting us to Germany. Once in a while someone comes along who really can affect things. And that person is here. I have been talking to him for over a year to persuade him to join us. He is one of us already in ideas and beliefs. But he's one of those people who are usually behind the scenes. Tonight, I persuaded him to come meet you, to hear you. And I wanted you to hear him.

"Why do we need him? We don't really. But sometimes people on the same path can help each other. He has things we don't have—like money—and we have what he'd never have. An army!" They erupted in cheers and screams. Several of the men tore off their shirts revealing their Nazi tattoos as they flexed and yelled.

"Let me invite him up. Jack!" He motioned for me to join him on the stage. I stepped up and the room lights came up a little more. I stood next to him. "This is Jack Bradley, a rancher from the west—although he has ranches elsewhere too. He has been on the fringes of the movement for years, but has never come out of the shadows until now. He has picked us as the group most likely to succeed, to achieve some real progress, and has thrown his lot in to back us. Not the Aryans, not the Supremes, us. He has agreed to finance us, and, I can now tell you, gave us the idea that will get us to Germany. Not only did he come up with the idea, he helped us execute it. And I can now tell you what we have."

"As you know, someone tried to take Hitler's things from Atlanta." They hooted and screamed.

"And while whoever it was got what they were after, the Russians out-smarted them and had fakes in place. So those people—whoever they were—accomplished nothing." They hissed and booed. He held up his hand.

"But we had another plan. Jack and I planned it, and two of you who had been sworn to secrecy helped. We went and got the most coveted thing in all of Nazi history. Any guesses?" He waited. They looked around confused, wondering.

"The Blood Flag! We found the flag that holds the blood of the first Nazi martyrs! We have it! And we will take it to Germany, where we will take leadership of the international Nazi movement! The Southern Volk will be the World Volk and we will be in charge! And Jack financed it, and planned it. And we have it."

They roared approval. So I wanted you to meet him. Please give a Southern Volk welcome to Jack Bradley."

They clapped, studying me. One man directly in front of me wasn't buying it. He took off his shirt to reveal a tattoo across his chest in English script that said, "Dirty White Boy." He was cut, and looked like an MMA fighter. And his eyes bore holes in me. I returned his look, but he wasn't the kind of man who would be intimidated by anyone's look. He either fought for a living or should.

Jedediah interrupted my thoughts. "Why don't you say a few words, Jack?"

I looked at him and hesitated. I moved toward the microphone, and said, "Thank you for having me here tonight. Jedediah was right. I've been watching all the groups in the U.S. for years. Yours is the only one that's creative, that has the greatest potential. What are your roles now, Jedediah? Twelve hundred?"

"Officially fifteen hundred."

"Fifteen hundred. There you go. Others claim more, but most of them are in prison. We need people on the outside, people who can move out tomorrow, or the next day, and do what needs to be done. If Germany is what I think it's going to be, we're going to need to be able to move fast and effectively. You're the ones to do it, and I have the funds to make it work. And we have the flag! I can get us arms, transportation, airplanes, whatever we need, let's do it together!" I tried to finish with enthusiasm I didn't feel. They screamed and clapped, except for Dirty White Boy who saw right through me. I then noticed he was wearing a watch on his right wrist. I suddenly wondered if he was one of the men in the conference room in Atlanta. Jedediah looked at him and knew he needed to get me out of there before something happened. He yelled into the microphone, "Let's take five for a drink, and break into our operational groups!"

He shook my hand and led me backstage. When we were alone I asked, "Was that guy in Atlanta? He's left handed. He may have recognized me."

"Don't worry about it. I've got it covered."

"Meaning what? This could blow us up!"

"He's one of my boys. He does what I tell him. And he knows if he doesn't he'll end up in a landfill. He won't cross me. Just don't worry about it."

"I'm going to worry about it. Keep your eye on him. I don't trust him."

* * *

If you dig up a skeleton buried ninety years ago, can you get DNA out of his bones? And if not, can you get DNA from his family? If I found a grandson, would his DNA help me identify a likely match on the flag? I had no idea. I knew the manager of our DNA lab arrived at seven so I got there when he opened. I pushed open the glass door and was immediately assaulted by the smell of formaldehyde and other unidentifiable chemicals. The FBI forensic lab is massive and the best in the world. It's a chemistry major's dream. It was always updated with the newest technology and equipment. It was where they learned to identify bomb traces and triggering devices and chemical contents of explosives. It's where they first came up with the ability to identify a murder weapon by the unique marks left on a bullet by a specific gun—the gun's fingerprint. Their reputation was well earned, and they went to great lengths to maintain it.

I went to Dr. Ray Wilson's office in the back of the lab. I knocked on the door gently and he looked around from the Excel spreadsheet he was studying on his computer screen. He said, "Enter."

"Hi, I'm Kyle Morrissey. I wondered if you could give me some help." He looked at his watch and frowned. He had a tan face and closely cropped white hair. He was probably sixty-two or sixty-three and appeared to be in very good shape. He wasn't wearing glasses, which surprised me. I'd only encountered him a few times, yet he appeared to remember me. "What brings you in so early?"

"I need to pick your brain."

He glanced at the clock over my shoulder. "I've got fifteen minutes or so, what's up?"

He was not the typical bureaucrat with a lab. He wasn't the kind of guy who had turf, and protected it; he was more like the smart kid in science class who knew everyone wanted his study notes. Everything was a mystery to him; everything was a puzzle to be solved. And he was given the biggest and best lab in the world to do it. He loved what he did, and he was the best.

"DNA."

"What about it?"

I didn't know whether to tell him the whole story or just part of it. "I'm trying to take down neo-Nazis worldwide."

He was surprised. "Curious role for the FBI . . . "

"I have a flag. A Nazi flag from 1923. The very *first* Nazi flag. Used by Hitler and his henchmen in their march in Munich."

"I've heard of it. And you have it?"

"Yes. We went to Argentina to track down an old Nazi hiding there who had the flag. He tried to give us a fake, but—well, we think we got the real one. But we need to authenticate it."

"Okay."

"It's called the Blood Flag; *die Blutfahne* in German. The blood is from the Nazi martyrs killed during the beer hall *putsch*. They died and bled on the flag. I need to know if I can pull their DNA and prove this is actually the flag from 1923."

"You need blood cells. It's unlikely there's any biological material left. May be able to find some mitochondrial DNA."

"Could you tell by looking at it? Could you examine it and know whether there was enough of—whatever—to do a test? Without disturbing it?"

"We can throw it under a microscope, see if there's enough to do a test."

Well that was something. "Let's say there is enough left on the flag to authenticate it. What do we compare it to? How can we prove it was the blood of one of the men killed in 1923?"

"Do you know where they are?"

"Who?"

"The men who were killed. The ones who bled on the flag."

"Well, obviously, they are dead."

He rolled his eyes. "Obviously. I mean, do you know where they are buried?"

"My recollection is that they were buried under or near a monument during Hitler's reign, but after the fall of Germany, the families were told that they were either going to destroy the bodies or that they would give them back to the families but they had to bury them in unmarked graves. So, I think they are still around, at least the skeletons—and they're in some unmarked graves."

"How many of them bled on the flag?"

"Sixteen were killed, probably three or four bled on the flag. The main guy who died on the flag is well known."

"You have to find the one who left blood that's testable. We have to match it to that guy."

"Let's assume we can find the grave of the right guy. Will there be DNA in somebody's skeleton after having died ninety years ago?"

"Sometimes we can identify really old skeletal remains. We'll have to see. How well-preserved is the flag?"

"I think in its early years it was probably kept in a chest, folded. Then in the thirties it was brought out as the magic flag of the Nazi regime. It was probably kept on a flag staff in a protected room when it wasn't being used.

And it was used sparingly. After that, it was flown to Argentina and kept in sealed container—probably never displayed at all—or rarely."

"There's a chance. I can't tell you how good a chance without seeing it. But if we find something on the flag, maybe we can dig up the bones of the ones who died and get some DNA out of the skull. If that fails we can try and use mitochondrial DNA, probably from the teeth if they're still there.

When can I get my hands on this thing?"

"I don't actually have it. Our informant has it. . . . I don't think he's going to let go of it."

"So, what's your plan?"

"Do you think other labs would be able to do the testing?"

"What lab do you have in mind?"

"The Bundeskriminalamt."

"The Germans? Of course. No problem at all. But you're going to take the most important Nazi flag in history to Germany to have it tested by the Germans?"

"Maybe. We've got a couple of guys there who are helping me."

"You do know the history of the BKA, right?"

"That it was started by Nazis?"

"Yes."

"Yeah. I saw they finally admitted that a couple of years ago. They said it was because no one else in Germany had the investigative skills."

Wilson chuckled. "Yeah, that's it. They *had* to use elements of the SS and the Gestapo. That's the only choice they had."

"Right."

"I'm just saying that an outfit that started that way may have some roots, some sympathies. Be careful who you trust in the BKA."

"I hadn't really thought that through."

"Talk to your guys in Germany and see what they think. I would just have some real hesitation. But yeah, they could do it. They're competent. There are also probably several commercial labs in Germany that could do it." Wilson sat forward suddenly. "You hear about that testing of what they thought was Hitler's skull?"

"No. I thought he was burned outside the bunker after he shot himself."

"He was. But the Russians were there the next day. Or in a couple of days. I don't remember. They said they destroyed the ashes, but secretly they took the skull back to Russia."

"What happened?"

"Discovery Channel, or somebody, got ahold of the couch Hitler shot himself on, and pulled DNA off the blood on the couch. So that was in 1945, and they got good samples. Then they went to Russia—got them to let them take samples from the skull, amazingly—and compared it against the couch blood.

"The skull had a bullet hole in it and everything. Great show. Of course, the Russians only gave them thirty minutes access when they got there. Why would they do that? Anyway, you should check it out. It was on TV last month."

"So what happened?"

"They used some forensic scientists from Connecticut. I watched it over and over. I checked all their procedures—what they told us about anyway—and it looked correct. They knew what they were doing. So they compared the blood, and it wasn't a match."

"How did I never hear about this?"

"Probably because it wasn't a match. If it had been Hitler's, it would have been front-page headlines."

"So whose was it?"

"Well, the scientists said the skull was more likely to be a woman, and I think they're right. So what woman had a bullet hole in her head that was close to Hitler?"

"Eva Braun."

"Well supposedly she just took the poison. But who knows."

"How do they know they got Hitler's blood off the couch?"

"Never authenticated it. All they did was try to match it against the skull."

"Why didn't they get more blood from the couch?"

"Not sure. But for your problem, I can recommend some labs in Germany where you can get it tested. But what are you going to do once you get it tested?"

"We have to get it done quickly. In a couple of weeks. Our guy has to meet with this new Nazi who is trying to put together the leaders of all the Nazi movements around the world. One uniform, one leader, one structure, worldwide Nazism."

He frowned. "That's gotta be stopped."

"That's what I'm trying to do."

*　*　*

I went to my office and called Florian.

"Ah," he said. "Good to hear from you. Have you found your missing friend?"

I wasn't sure Florian would still work with me after Buenos Aires. "Yeah. He's back on board. He says he was never not on board. I'm still skeptical. And the leader of the Southern Volk—the former leader—has now gone missing. I think there's an even chance that our friend did away with him."

"Well, he has the flag. If we want to do anything with it, we need him."

"Exactly. But I'm going to need your help."

"Sure, anything."

"How do we prove to Eidhalt that this is the actual Blood Flag? We have to authenticate it."

"We could do some kind of carbon dating. Although, I don't know if that works for something this young."

"No, anybody could get ninety-year-old cloth. All that would do is date the flag. That doesn't get us there. We have to prove it's *the* flag. I think we have to get the blood sample off the flag and test the DNA of the men who were shot. How can we find them?"

"The ones who fell on the flag?"

"Right. Where are they buried?"

There was a period of silence. "I think Patrick may know. I know that there was something that happened with them. I don't recall what it was. How much time do we have now?"

"Ten days. Then we have to be ready to go to the meeting."

"Has your friend told them what he has?"

"Not yet. He's supposed to meet Eidhalt in Germany. Then we'll have to find someplace—a commercial lab—that can do this kind of testing that we can sell to Eidhalt."

"I'm sure we can find such a lab. How do we go about this?"

I looked at the clock. "Assume we can get a blood sample from the flag. We've got to find either the remains of one of the men who bled on it, or one of their descendants. I think we've got to find where these guys were buried."

Florian hesitated. "You can do DNA testing from someone who's been dead for ninety years?"

"Depends. I know you can do testing on skeletons that have been around for hundreds of years. I'm trying to figure it all out. But for now, see if you can find the guys who were killed. Concentrate on the ones that would be the most likely. One guy apparently fell directly on the flag and bled to death there. Most of the blood's probably his."

"Let me talk to a guy who has suddenly become interested in what we're doing."

My antenna went up. "What guy?"

"The Verfassungsschutz. You know who they are?"

"Yeah, sort of closer to the CIA," I responded, not liking what I was hearing.

"We got a visit yesterday from one of them. About this."

"About what?"

"He heard we were asking around. Involving neo-Nazis."

"Why was he interested?"

"Said he was working on a similar project. Wanted to make sure we didn't bang into each other."

I wasn't sure whether to say what I was thinking or not. "Did you know him before yesterday?"

"No. We had never heard of him."

"Did you tell him about the *Blutfahne*?"

"Yes, we mentioned it."

"How did he react?"

"I'm not sure how to describe it. I'm not sure of the best English word. Enthusiastic."

"Eager?"

"Perfect. Yes. Eager and enthusiastic about our project."

"Did you say much else?"

"No. He said he wanted to meet soon."

"I wish you'd talked to me first. I don't like it. I'm coming over there. I'll see you tomorrow."

I picked up the phone and told Alex we were going to Germany that night.

* * *

On my way to the airport, I texted Florian and asked him to meet us in Munich. Alex and I checked in at the Sofitel, a beautiful old building that had been completely modernized. We dropped off our bags and went to the restaurant in the lobby for a late breakfast. Florian and Patrick arrived as we were finishing. I waved. Florian looked a little disheveled with his hair in something of a mess. He was wearing a high-collared zip sweater. Patrick was wearing a sport coat and a blue shirt open at the collar. They ordered coffee and we got refills.

I said to both of them, "I checked the notes you gave me. The guy who seems to be the one who bled right on the flag the most is Jens Friedl. Any idea how to track where he was buried?"

Patrick looked around. He pulled some papers out of his coat pocket and laid them in front of him. "The men who died were buried in graves here in Munich. All marked. After Hitler went to prison, most people thought the movement was dead. Well, after Hitler got out of prison—after writing *Mein Kampf*—he rebuilt Nazism with new energy. The same people who were in the *putsch* were right there with him. Luddendorff, Hess, Röhm, Göring, all of them. They picked up right where they left off. The conditions in Germany were terrible and getting worse. After Hitler maneuvered himself into the position of chancellor, he then made it so that he could never be removed. This was all well known. He dug up the bodies, how do you say it?"

"Exhumed."

"Yes. He had the bodies of the men who died in the beer hall *putsch* exhumed, and re-buried them under a monument to honor them. In 1934. I have found a picture of it." He handed me a Xeroxed copy of a photograph that showed an ornate marble monument in honor of the martyrs of National Socialism. I couldn't read the inscription, but the message being conveyed was clear. I handed the picture back to him.

"Then what?"

"Then the Blood Flag became the centerpiece of Nazism. The one magical thing. It, of course, was nothing of the sort, but Hitler made it into that. And the men who died—and bled on it—were the first martyrs of Nazism. So the monument was almost worshipped."

"What happened to them?"

Patrick nodded. "At the end of the war the Russians were going to tear down the monument and destroy the remains of the 'martyrs.' They were going to dig them up and burn their bones."

Patrick continued. "But the families heard about it. They begged for the remains so they could re-bury them. The Russians agreed, but only if they were buried in unmarked graves and never identified."

Alex frowned. "We have to find unmarked graves?"

Patrick nodded. "Yes."

"That will be impossible."

Patrick shook his head, "No it won't. We Germans keep track of everything. The families will know, or someone else will know. We'll find out."

I nodded as I drank my last bit of cool coffee. "If we find Friedl's, which is the one we have to look for first, you do understand we're going to have to dig it up?"

"Of course!" Patrick said enthusiastically, like it would be the most fun he'd had in years.

"And we have to do this in a way that our buddy, Jedediah Thom, can persuade Eidhalt. I need to get him on the phone, but let's locate that grave first."

Patrick and Florian prepared to leave. Then I added, "And then I want to hear about your contact with the Verfassungsschutz. But don't talk to them directly. Not yet."

Florian nodded.

I paid the bill then said to Florian and Patrick. "You guys find that grave this afternoon. Think you can do that?"

"We can try."

"After you do, let's get together tonight and go look at it. Then you can tell me about this visit that you had. I had an idea on how we might use that to our benefit."

* * *

As the sun set, Alex and I walked out of the hotel and down the street to see the center of Munich. We had spent the entire afternoon researching the flag. I needed fresh air. I sent an email, high priority, to Jedediah's account, telling him we needed to talk.

"Where are we going?" Alex asked as we walked briskly in the cold evening air.

"I want to retrace the route."

"What route?"

"From the beer hall to the City Hall. The *putsch*."

"Is the beer hall still there?"

"No. It was called the Bürgerbräukeller, but that building was torn down in the seventies. The Hilton sits on that property now. Tonight we'll go eat in another huge beer hall, Hofbräuhaus, but before we do that we're going to walk the same route Hitler led his Nazis on when the Blood Flag was created."

We walked along the pristine sidewalk and looked at the old buildings. I looked at the map where I had outlined the course and turned to go down toward where the old Bürgerbräukeller was. "To think of Hitler walking in there—do you know how he did it?"

"Did what?"

"Started this whole march. This *putsch*."

"No, no idea."

"They met in that massive beer hall often, giving speeches, inciting people, getting his brown shirts to intimidate people. All the stuff we've heard about. It wasn't a huge deal, but it was noted. So on November 8th, 1923, he decided to make his play. He had his brown shirts bar or chain the doors closed. Three thousand people in the Bürgerbräukeller. He had it ringed inside by six hundred of his storm troopers. He fired a pistol into the air and jumped onto a table to announce the time for the revolution had come. I don't know if you've ever seen any of his speeches, but he was mesmerizing. Almost didn't matter what he was saying. He got people worked up. *He* got worked up. He told them it was time to stop putting up with what had happened to them! They had been stabbed in the back! The German people had been betrayed by the immigrants, and Jews, Bolsheviks, and traitors! The conditions were because of them! And the weak government surrendered their honor in the war! He told them it was time to take action. To take things into their own hands. And within that group of three thousand people, each had something against somebody that they wrote into his speech in their own minds.

"They weren't sure what to do. They had the energy, the anger, but nowhere to go. So Ludendorff, this old timer from WWI yells, 'We march!' And they headed for the Bavarian Defense Ministry. Two thousand men, some armed, some in Nazi uniforms, the about-to-be famous Blood Flag, and off they went."

"Okay, here we are." I stopped and pointed at the buildings around. "Bürgerbräukeller would have been behind us. They came down this street, two thousand strong, many armed, yelling, screaming for the overthrow of the corrupt government of Bavaria, and the beginning of a German-wide revolt.

"But one man wasn't going to have it—a German state police officer, senior lieutenant Baron Michael von Godin. He blocked the Odeonsplatz— the city square—with a hundred soldiers. The Nazis kept coming, threatening. Finally someone opened fire."

We stopped. "Right about here."

We surveyed the beautiful Odeonsplatz, imagining the confusion and anger that filled it ninety years ago.

"Then?" she asked, imagining the whole story. I pulled up pictures of the people involved on my iPad.

"Four state police and sixteen Nazis were killed. And several Nazis fell on the flag. Right here," I said pointing down. "The one who bled the most on the flag was Jens Friedl. Hitler and Göring were both injured. Göring was shot in the groin. Most fled after people started falling. Pandemonium."

We walked on another eight hundred yards and stopped. "Check this out," I said, studying a map I'd called up on my iPad. After Hitler came to power, he made the walk from the Bürgerbräukeller to the Odeonsplatz, a holy walk. To 'honor' the Nazi martyrs and the *putsch*. He even posted guards here, like honor guards, for years, to honor the walk where they were shot. Check this out."

I pointed to the Feldherrenhalle, the ornate, Italian-style building at the end of the Odeonsplatz. "That building was the background for the fight. It was where Hitler put up the monument to the dead Nazi martyrs of the *putsch*. Right there at the base of the building. And posted SS guards in front of it, who had to be saluted by everyone who passed.

"But not all Germans were so deferential. Thousands walked around to the back of the building, through a small street, rather than pass in front and do the Nazi salute. Come over here. There's supposed to be a bronzed brick path."

We turned the corner and found Viscardigasse. We stopped and looked at the stones of the narrow street. "Here," she pointed. There was an eighteen-inch path of bronzed stones in the middle of the street representing the path people took to avoid honoring the memorial.

"They called this Drückeberger Gaßl. Shirker's Alley. Like they were shirking their duty to the Nazis."

Alex looked around and studied it all. "This is amazing. It seems so long ago. Munich looks so normal, so beautiful." She knelt down and felt the bronzed stones and contemplated. "But why not more? Why not most? If most had refused, resisted, walked around the Nazis, Hitler never would have succeeded."

I nodded. "One of the great questions of history. I think we're wrong though if we assume it couldn't happen anywhere else."

My phone buzzed. It was a text from Patrick.

"What is it?" she asked, standing.

"They found the grave."

* * *

We agreed to meet Patrick and Florian at the graveyard at 10:00 p.m. The streets were quiet. It was a cool evening and the stars were hidden by a thin overcast. They were waiting for us when we got there. Both were wearing dark clothing; an intuitive decision by amateur grave robbers.

Florian spoke quietly, "This way." He headed down a sidewalk then turned down an alley. The buildings came right up to the streets and some overhung the pavement. We walked in silence. I resisted the temptation to look behind us.

We went a quarter of a mile and Florian stopped when there was an area to our right with no buildings. There was no light. Florian said, "This is it. Very old graveyard."

From the edge of the cemetery I could make out some large gravestones with crosses, casting ominous shadows from the minimal moonlight penetrating the wispy clouds. I turned on my small LED flashlight. I was ready to go look. "It's unmarked?"

Florian indicated for me to come closer and put my flashlight on a piece of paper he unfolded. It was a map of the cemetery. "Patrick thinks he knows where it is."

Patrick leaned in and touched the paper. "There are several unmarked graves in this graveyard. They are numbered though, of course!" he said smiling.

"And you have the list?"

"Of course. We have access."

"Let's go."

Florian folded the paper and turned toward the graveyard. There was an iron fence with a sidewalk passing through an opening in the fence, but no gate. The fence was black iron, probably eight feet high with freshly painted ornate curved tops. The sidewalk was well maintained. As we followed Florian, I said quietly, "Is there a caretaker, a night guard?"

"No. They have weekly maintenance, mostly gardeners, but this cemetery is full. There are no open spaces. Nothing happens here; no need for security." Alex touched my arm and pointed. There was one large gravestone that had a top that was shaped like a World War I helmet with a spike on it. I nodded and looked for other distinctive markings. There was no pattern, but there was a notable lack of religious symbols. There were a few crosses, but not many, and no Stars of David. The trees were old and thick and contributed to the darkness and the spookiness. It was probably five acres that got deeper and wider the farther in we went. I had assumed another street would be on the other side in a hundred feet or so, but that was not the case. There were no buildings at the far end of the cemetery, but rather a field or meadow.

Florian and Patrick walked on, glancing at headstones for orientation. It was hard to see in the dark, but Florian used his own flashlight to compare what he was finding to the diagram he'd brought. There were actually two cemeteries with the same name. One old, one new. Friedl's grave was supposed to be in the "new" one; new meaning less than two hundred years old. We crossed other sidewalks that led to different areas of the cemetery, which were divided into numbered sections.

Florian looked around, and shined his flashlight onto the large headstone in front of us, just on the other side of a fork in the sidewalk. We approached slowly. The headstone appeared even larger as we got closer. I put my flashlight beam on it and walked directly up to it. Patrick and I started rubbing dust and dirt off the stone, to see if there was anything readable. It was very readable. You could see four-inch tall letters that had been chiseled into the mahogany colored marble. FRIEDL. There were four names, including Jens. I stared at the lettering. I said to Patrick quietly, "I thought you said it was supposed to be unmarked."

"It *was*. Looks like the family had a different idea." He studied the stone. "They're all buried here," he said. "The father, the mother, Friedl himself, and it looks like his . . . probably his sister."

Alex came up behind me. "How will we know which skeleton is Jens's?"

Florian heard her question. "Maybe we can tell from the caskets. If not," he said staring at the names on the marble, "we'll have to take all of them."

"That sure complicates things," I added.

I examined the surroundings. It was as remote as you could be in a city cemetery. There were no buildings or apartments that overlooked this area of the cemetery. We could work here at night without being seen. Whether we'd be heard was a different question. I looked at Patrick. "Any chance a police officer might walk through here at night?"

"Not likely," he replied.

I walked around behind the large stone, then to the sides. I knelt down and felt the dirt. Not too hard. I stood. "Let's go find somewhere to talk about how we're going to get this done."

We started walking out of the cemetery. Alex walked beside me and said quietly, "I still don't understand what exactly you have in mind."

"You'll see."

* * *

The four of us sat at a table in a busy restaurant with red-checkered tablecloths. Patrick ordered a pitcher of beer and some French fries. The restaurant was full and loud with people laughing and drinking all around us. No one was paying any attention to us.

Alex asked, "Okay. Let's hear it. How do we do this?"

I drank my beer deeply. "If we can get blood off the flag, and dig up Friedl, we can compare the DNA. But the trick is to make this all look like Jedediah's idea. Because the person we're trying to persuade is Eidhalt. If we bring Jedediah over here with the flag, we can get the testing done. But how do we get Jedediah to dig up Friedl so Eidhalt knows what is happening? If he just gives him DNA samples, Eidhalt will think the whole thing is fake. Anybody can phony up DNA test results. Anybody can make it look real, but it has to *be* real. The funny thing is, we're not even *trying* to fake it. We have the real stuff."

I looked up at Florian. A thought had just occurred to me. "You said that somebody from the Verfassungsschutz was asking around." I said softly, "Any chance we can make him believe *we're* on the other side? His side?"

Alex said, "That would mean that Jedediah would have to tell this guy what he has right now."

I nodded. "We're there already. Jedediah has to dig up this grave. It's time to make our play. We just have to make sure our plan is thought through. We have more moving parts than I had expected." I looked at the others. "I think we have Jedediah tell Eidhalt he has the flag, and he's going to authenticate it. And he wants Eidhalt involved in the entire thing, so he *knows*. So he *sees*."

Alex got it. "We can get Jedediah to say whatever we want him to say. Give him a good backstory. I'm still adding background to your new existence, and by now I don't think anyone could find any flaws."

"Good."

Alex said, "You'll have to get an iron cross tattooed on your throat though."

"Very funny. I don't think so. I just don't know if we'll be able to sell it." I said to Florian, "What do you think? If your Verfassungsschutz guy is with them, can you make him believe you're sympathetic? That you're ready to help the neos penetrate the BKA?"

Florian looked at Patrick and frowned. "I doubt it. I don't have any history like that. He wouldn't believe me. I've done my own checking on him. It will be quite a game of what I think you call cat and mouse. He will wonder where my sympathies are, and I will try to feel him out. I don't know if he's actually involved with them. I just know some in his organization are. He may be where we are, trying to root them out. And if he thinks we're sympathetic, he may do what he can to have us arrested. I'm not sure how to go about this."

"Refer him to me," I said. "He can't have me arrested. I'll tell him what I'm thinking, and feel him out."

Patrick, who had been mostly quiet, looked at Florian and then said, "Not too sure about that. I think we should leave him out of it."

I could feel his hesitancy. I said, "What if we assume he is with them, but that he's interested in us from an official position? We pretend like his interest is appropriate and we then proceed to tell him what we want him to know."

"Which is what? What do we tell him about you? What about Jedediah?" Florian asked.

I said, "You tell him that you've been following Jedediah, that you've heard about this meeting with Eidhalt, and that Jedediah not only has the Blood Flag but has money. That he's being funded by a reclusive American rancher who has picked the Southern Volk as the neo-Nazi group to back. That he's giving them millions of dollars and is building their following all over the country. That he's thinking big, and they now have the Blood Flag. That he's ready to pay to have the best DNA testing in the world done to prove this flag is authentic, and is ready to unite their energy with other groups from around the world, and Germany is their first public step."

Florian smiled, "And you are the rancher?"

I nodded and smiled back. "That's me."

Patrick put up his hand. "Wait, if we don't know you, if you're his financier, how do we know what we know. What is our role?"

"You know *of* me. You know Karl. And he doesn't tell you his sources, but he tells you about me, and what the Southern Volk is up to: that we have the flag, that we got it in Argentina, and that we're coming over here to show it to Eidhalt. And we're going to get it authenticated."

Patrick understood, but he had another question, "I understand all this, but what is the point of all this? Why do we care about him?"

"Because he may give that final bit of authenticity to Eidhalt we need for Eidhalt to take the bait."

Patrick nodded, understanding. "So if we get Jedediah into this meeting, then what?"

I said, "We take advantage of the German laws against Nazism and arrest them all. Put them in prison for the maximum punishment available."

Florian interjected, "Yes, we could do that, but that assumes they'll display Nazi—"

"They'll have to show the Blood Flag. That's good enough, right?"

He nodded, "Yes, but it's not a huge crime. After minimal jail time they'll be out doing it again, calling themselves something else."

"That's it?" I pondered that for a moment. "Well then I don't know." I sat back. "Shit. That's it? A few months of jail time?"

"What would you have us do? Execute them? We don't even lock away mass murderers for life."

"So that's all we have? A few months of jail time?"

"I'm afraid so."

"That's not how this is going to end. I'm telling you that right now," I said.

CHAPTER SEVENTEEN

I woke up the next morning before dawn to someone banging on my door with his fist. I picked up my Glock, kept the lights out, and went to the door. I peered through the peephole but couldn't see anything. I checked my watch. It was five thirty in the morning. "Who is it?"

"It's me."

"Jedediah?"

"Yeah."

"Step to the middle of the door so I can see you." He put his face in front of the peephole so I could see him. He looked peeved. I undid the chain and opened the door. I had told him to come right away, but hadn't expected him to fly overnight.

"Any trouble getting the flag into Germany?"

"Nope. They didn't even look at it."

"Good."

"Not an issue. But if I'd worn a T-shirt I'd still be there."

"How are you supposed to contact Eidhalt?"

"A one-time-only number to use when I arrive in Germany. I got a pre-paid cell at the airport."

I told him to get some rest. He agreed and went to his room. I went downstairs to meet Alex.

Alex got on the wireless in the lobby on her computer and checked my identity on the Internet to see whether anyone had been looking at the pages she'd set up. They had. But the story looked seamless to me. Very well done. She looked up and saw Jedediah. "Over here."

He came to where we were then pointed to the bar. We followed him in as he ordered a beer, never asking us if we wanted anything.

I said, "We're going to the graveyard. I want you to call Eidhalt while we're standing there looking at the grave. He will almost certainly come directly to meet us."

He nodded, understanding. "How long before we leave?"

I checked my watch. "Three hours."

"I'm going to get some shuteye. Meet in the lobby?"

* * *

It was barely light when we walked into the graveyard. We took Jedediah to Friedl's grave. He looked at the stone. "I thought you said it was unmarked."

"That's what we thought. That's what the BKA thought. But here it is, the whole damned family."

"I'm surprised people haven't made it into a shrine."

"Probably not too many people even know it's here."

I looked around to make sure we were alone and said, "So this is it. The Reveal, as the magician's call it. Call Eidhalt. Tell him you have the *Blutfahne*. Tell him I'm with you. We'll see what he says, but tell him where you got it, and that you're sure it's real, but you figure he'll want to get it authenticated."

He paused, looked at me, looked at the grave, looked at Alex, and dialed the phone. He had it on speakerphone, even though he held it up to his ear. A voice answered, "*Ja?*"

Jedediah looked at me and then answered, "Southern Volk."

"Ah. The American. I was wondering when I would hear from you. What do you have?"

Jedediah paused, "*Die Blutfahne.*"

There was silence on the other end of the phone. "This is not possible."

"I'm holding it."

"Where are you?"

"In Munich."

"Why are you here?"

"Because I knew if I brought this flag, you'd think it was a fake, just like the Russians faked out my predecessor in Atlanta."

"I saw that. But a failure."

"Yes. He is gone."

"What happened to him?"

"He has disappeared. No one knows."

"Yes. So what do you have in mind?"

"I want you to know that this is the real flag. I want to prove it to you."

"How do you propose to do that?"

"DNA."

"Get blood off the flag. And compare it to what?"

"The blood of the man who fell on the flag and died. Friedl."

"He's been dead for ninety years."

"We can get DNA from his skull."

"No one knows where he's buried. It's unmarked."

"No it's not. It's clearly marked."

"How do you know that?"

"Because I'm standing in front of his grave. He's buried with his parents and his sister."

"That is not possible."

"I'll send you a picture of the stone."

"No. This number can only be used once. Where are you?"

I held out a piece of paper that had the name of the graveyard. He read it as best he could.

"Yes, I know that place. The old section or the new?"

"The new."

"I'll be right there."

"No. I don't know you yet. I'll meet you, but you can only bring one other person. No weapons. I'll have the Blood Flag nearby, but if anything goes wrong, you'll never see it. If all goes well, I'll show you the flag. Then I'll show you the grave."

"I will be there at 10:00 p.m. Meet me at the entrance on the east side."

"No. Come in that entrance, and keep walking. If you go about three hundred yards, there is another path. I'll meet you where those paths come together. I have someone with me too. I want you to meet him."

"Who is it?"

"You'll see." He hung up the phone.

I looked over at Florian and Patrick who were showing their technical people where to put the hidden microphones. I said to Florian, "He's on his way. We need someone at every entrance."

I looked around the graveyard. "And we've got to find a place to hide the flag, not too far from here. We'll need to set up Alex so she can give us a signal. We can't be wired. We've got to be clean."

Jedediah said, "What happens when they get here?"

"We show them the headstone, we tell them the plan to dig up the skull, then we show them the flag."

* * *

Florian had his men in place by eight o'clock, and Alex was in her place by eight fifteen. Jedediah and I walked through the still graveyard. It was cool with no breeze. After the clock in the city center struck ten, Jedediah and I moved to the intersection of the two paths. Alex was on the radio with Florian and watched as Eidhalt and one other man walked into the cemetery. We could see their silhouettes maybe two hundred yards away at the entrance. They were looking around. They couldn't see us.

They walked cautiously down the path, pausing every twenty feet or so to listen. As Eidhalt approached, almost to within speaking distance, I saw three faint flashes of light from Alex's flashlight over his shoulder. They were alone.

They stopped. Eidhalt examined Jedediah, and said, "*Guten Abend.*" Jedediah and I both responded in English. "Evening."

He asked in faintly accented English, "Which of you is Jedediah Thom?"

"I am."

"My colleague is going to check, to make sure you are not carrying weapons."

Jedediah said, "Not until I check him. When he gets over here, I'll check him and then he can check me. Then he can check my friend, and then I'll check you."

Eidhalt hesitated then said, "Fine."

The man approached Jedediah and stood there with his arms out. Jedediah frisked him, and then placed his own arms out for the same treatment. When the man felt Jedediah's massive shoulders underneath his dark high-neck sweater, he looked at Jedediah's face in surprise. Jedediah looked back at him in the darkness, conveying that unspoken message that he could crush him like a cockroach if he chose to. The man frisked me, then Eidhalt came over to where we were and Jedediah frisked him.

Eidhalt asked, "Do you have anybody else around? Anyone else in the cemetery?"

"No," I replied.

He looked at me, "And who are you?"

Jedediah replied, "He is the money behind the Southern Volk."

"What is your name?"

"Jack Bradley."

Eidhalt looked at Jedediah. "How do I know that he's not really someone other than who you say?"

Jedediah said, "Check him out yourself. I don't know anything about you either."

"Yes you do."

He looked around, overhead, and then back at Jedediah. He couldn't see the microphones that had been planted at the gravesite by Florian's men. He said to Jedediah, "Where is *die Blutfahne?*"

Jedediah didn't even flinch. "Nearby."

"I want to see it."

"In due time. First, let's talk about what we're going to do after you've seen it. If we're in agreement, I'll show it."

"If it is what you say it is, it will be at the very center of what we're doing." You could hear the enthusiasm in his voice. "It will be the rallying cry to restore the Aryan race to its rightful place, to rid Western Europe and North America of the scourge of Jews and mongrel Arab immigrants, to awaken our sedated cultures from the drug of multiculturalism, to stop the corrosion of society, to restore pride and duty and the inevitable supremacy of the white race."

He looked directly at me and crossed over from where he was standing. "You agree?"

I nodded and stared back at him. "I agree. You have the Turks; we have everybody else, Mexicans, Arabs, Jews, running everything, and a society addicted to every bad thing you can imagine. It's exactly like what Hitler saw in Vienna."

His eyebrows went up. "Ah. You know about Vienna."

"It's what he saw. It's what made him react like he did. It's what made him write *Mein Kampf*."

He stared at me without speaking. Finally, he said, "You have read this?"

"Of course."

"Really? When did he write it?"

"When he was in prison, after the beer hall *putsch*."

"And how did he write it?"

"Mostly dictated it to Hess."

"Excellent. But I still don't know you." He studied me. "I have been aware of Mr. Thom for a long time, but not you."

"When you invited him, you invited me. He is the face of the organization. I'm behind the scenes. The one with the money, giving orders and direction. If he's going to come here and commit the Southern Volk to anything, then I'll be there."

Eidhalt was troubled. "He never mentioned this before."

"I hadn't authorized him to. There's no need for me to be known publicly. I only show myself when it's absolutely necessary. And if you think you're going to be telling the Southern Volk what to do, even indirectly, then you'll have to deal with me."

He drew closer. I could smell his breath. He said almost in a whisper in his German accent, "But we investigated the Southern Volk. I've been investigating them for months. Your name has never been mentioned."

"That is how I like it. Your name was not known until recently. You and I, we know when it is time to take the stage. I will never be on the stage, just in the background. And you think Mr. Thom," I said looking at Jedediah, "you think he could have come up with the idea of *die Blutfahne* on his own and then found it in Argentina?"

"That is why I expect that it's a fake."

"It's not a fake. I went with him to Argentina."

"And what is the name of the man who had the *Blutfahne* in Argentina?"

"Schullman. He lived in a basement apartment in Buenos Aires. He tried to give us a fake, but we fire bombed his apartment with all of us in it expecting that he would not let the true flag go up in flames. When the fire started, he went to a hidden drawer in his bookcase and extracted the real flag."

"Did you kill him?"

"No. He escaped the fire, but everything in his apartment was destroyed."

"But you got the flag?"

"Yes. And it's within a hundred meters of us now."

"Where?"

"Nearby here. If we go forward, we will show it to you."

He stepped back, looked around the cemetery, and put his hands in the pockets of his black leather jacket. He looked at the gravestone, and then back at us. "How did you learn that Herr Schullman might have the flag?"

"You Germans are very good record keepers. I found the names of everyone who lived on Hessler's street in the fall of 1944 and spring of 1945. It was last seen in October of 1944, of course, but where did it go? My theory was one of the Nazis who knew Hessler took it out of the country to preserve it. Turned out I was right. We traced him to Argentina. We weren't sure he had it, but we had it narrowed down to two or three names. He was the second one we visited."

"Let's see it."

I couldn't tell if he believed what I was saying or if he was going to simply reserve judgment. It didn't matter. "First let's make sure we understand each other. If it is the true Blood Flag, this will be what brings the Southern Volk to your meeting. Yes?"

"Yes, absolutely."

"And we will get it authenticated by DNA."

"Yes, but how?"

"You will see. If it goes as planned, are we in agreement?"

"Yes."

"Jedediah, show him where it is."

Jedediah turned without saying anything, and walked down the path. Jedediah turned off the path and walked on the grass over to an elaborate gravesite that was surrounded by an iron fence that was six feet high and had intricate scrolls and ornamentation. It had a gothic feel to it and stood by itself, with no other gravesite closer than fifteen feet from the fence. Jedediah swung open the gate and stepped inside. I did likewise and Eidhalt and his man followed. I looked to see if there was a visible microphone, but saw nothing. No signs of any disturbance. Jedediah asked, "See anybody else?"

We all shook our heads. Jedediah hesitated then looked up toward the top of the elaborate stone structure, over the grave of Franz von Lossow. The enclosure was large enough to be a family burial site, but it was only for one man. Lived from 1895 to 1917. Died in The Great War. While some of the gravestones had some religious indication, a cross or inscription or an occasional angel, von Lossow's had none. The three of us watched as Jedediah walked under the lichgate and climbed up onto the first level of the altar tomb. He reached up into the black night as high as he could and pulled the worn suitcase off the top of the marble structure. He held it in his right hand and stepped down.

Eidhalt couldn't take his eyes off the suitcase. Jedediah looked at me, "You got your flashlight?"

I pulled it out of my pocket and directed it at the suitcase. Jedediah opened the two over-center clasps and pushed the lid up and back. My light illuminated the dark red cloth of the Blood Flag. It was folded, but still had a lot of bulk. It was made of very high-quality cotton that had maintained most of its bright red color for the past ninety years. This wasn't just one of the millions of Nazi flags that had been made during the thirties and forties, this was *the* Nazi flag.

Eidhalt said, "Take it out."

Jedediah looked up at him from his kneeling position over the flag. "I don't want to damage it."

"Take it out!" Eidhalt yelled.

Jedediah reached in and gently lifted the entire flag. He unfolded it carefully and held it up above his head with his arms spread wide so that the flag fell down in front of him. Even with his arms fully extended, the flag was too large to not bend gently and touch the ground. I had to admit that just looking at it gave me the chills. The dark red contrast against the black swastika angled aggressively inside the white circle in the middle of the flag. The flag looked like it was suspended from a cross-beam pole on this massive gravestone. Eidhalt approached it and knelt down by the foot of the flag. I approached with him. He looked at me and took the flashlight out of my hand. "I have looked at every photograph that exists of this flag. I know where the stains should be. You see here, and here," he said pointing, "it's hard to see the color because of the red flag, but as you can see, it's darker. Almost brown. These stains are in exactly the right place."

He stood up and shined the flashlight on the entire flag again. He looked at the edges and felt the cloth. "Either this is *die Blutfahne* or it's an amazing fake." He glanced at his man, who nodded in agreement.

I replied, "Schullman tried to give us a fake, but we think we have the real one. I suppose he could have had two fakes, but why would he care enough to almost die in a fire to recover a fake?"

He smiled with an animal-like smile. "Nicely done. Did he resist?"

"Let's just say we have the flag and he doesn't."

I looked up at Jedediah. "You can come down."

Jedediah folded the flag in half and jumped down to the bottom of the stone. He began refolding the flag like a map, honoring its pre-existing creases.

I said, "We have to be absolutely sure it's the right one so you can use it for the meeting. As the rallying point. But we also want to know, because the Southern Volk now owns it."

Eidhalt was suddenly furious. "You're going to keep it?"

"*We* went to Argentina to get it. We *own* it. We brought it here because you invited us to your meeting. We want to come, and you asked us to do something to impress you. You asked everybody to do something you'd hear about. Not to give you anything. So it's here, and you can use it at the meeting. Rally the entire Nazi movement around the world. But it's ours, always will be."

He turned and faced me directly. He said in a low whisper. "If you do not give me this flag, you will not come to the meeting. You will not be part of the future of National Socialism. You will be a memory. A relic. A bunch of southern rednecks who can do *nothing* without *me*."

I stepped forward slightly. "We have the flag. We will get Friedl's DNA and we don't give a shit whether you're involved. We'll tell the whole world we have it and that history is now on the side of the Southern Volk, the new worldwide leader of Nazism. We'll set up our *own* meeting. We'll invite everybody in the world to the United States. We'll have all the freedom we need to operate. We don't have the laws you have in Germany. In the United States we can wear swastikas all day long. We have the *First Amendment*. Something you'll never have. We can do anything we want and we can say anything we want. We can scream all the racist and anti-Semitic things we want. We can rally everybody to the international cause with complete impunity. And we will tell them that they can come and do what Hitler did at the party convention in Nuremberg in 1936. They can bring their flags, their banners, and *touch* them to the Blood Flag!" I watched his face as he tried to contain his anger. "I can buy a new thousand-acre ranch in Idaho or

Wyoming *tomorrow*, and give it to the cause. We can build a massive compound, with buildings, dormitories, gunnery ranges, a chow hall, a *movie theater*—whatever we want—for anyone we invite. They can stay for weeks. We can train. We can train with weapons. Real weapons. Fifty-caliber sniper rifles, M4s, AK-47s, bulletproof vehicles, and a driving track to learn evasive driving. We can have night scopes, night vision goggles, GPS tracking devices, whatever our military has, we can have—as long as it's not fully automatic. And it's all legal in America, unlike Germany. We'll teach them urban combat tactics and the use of explosives. Molotov cocktails, dynamite, and fertilizer. In fact, that is our plan. You were part of that plan, because you're going to do the first thing—unify the international movement. But we plan to train them, and lead the armed side of this struggle. Something that you can't possibly do here because *everything* is illegal in Germany. But everything is *legal* in America. Isn't it a beautiful country?

"So you decide. Tell me how you're going to play it. If you try to cut us out, it's the last time you'll see us or the flag. And I'll make sure you're no part of the rise of the Nazi Army that is about to occur." I paused. "So, if you think we need you, we don't. We can do everything alone that you plan on doing, and probably better. You have money, so do I. Maybe more than you. And I don't have the notoriety that you do. I'm not in the *papers* like you have been. I haven't bought a come-and-get-me castle. And people will come to the United States. They'll come to my new ranch. So don't push me. I'll work with you. We'll work together if we can. But if we can't," I shrugged, "I don't really give a shit."

Eidhalt watched Jedediah finish folding the flag and put it back in the suitcase. He said, "You have the flag, and it should be at the meeting. Maybe our next meeting will be in the United States, and we can organize it together. But for now, we need to know if we have—if you have—the actual flag. We must get it tested." Eidhalt hesitated, nearly choking on his words. "We want to work with you."

I said, "The best DNA lab in the world is in the United States. But I don't want to go back there right now. And I don't want to send the flag back there. So tell us whether you know if there is a place we can do it here. Right away. Because we have to get this done before the meeting."

"The German laboratories here in Munich are among the best. Everyone knows that. If you're confident they can get a sample off the flag, we can get it identified. But are you sure about getting a DNA sample from an old skeleton?"

I nodded. "I'm sure. We're going to take the skulls and get them all tested, to make sure we get Friedl's."

"Take what skulls?"

"From Friedl's family. I pointed back to the grave. "There are four names on the gravestone. We're going to take them all."

"When?"

Jedediah closed the suitcase and picked it up. He turned and walked toward me and said, "Right now."

CHAPTER EIGHTEEN

We walked directly to the gravesite. Eidhalt and his man stared at the enormous stone with the large letters FRIEDL on it. "His grave was to be unmarked," he said. "Leave it to ignorant Americans to look anyway," he said.

Jedediah walked behind the gravestone and pulled out shovels and a pick ax. He tossed one of the shovels to the other German, looked around, and slammed his shovel into the dirt. He smashed it with his foot, then dug up a foot of dirt and threw it over his shoulder. He stopped, took off his turtleneck, and was wearing just his tanktop T-shirt.

Eidhalt frowned as he saw the tattoos in the dim light.

Jedediah looked at him and didn't respond. He looked at the other German and said, "*Dig*."

Eidhalt said, "Do we have time to do this?"

Things were out of his control and he didn't like it.

"One hour." Jedediah responded as he smashed his shovel into the ground again and tossed another pile of dirt. The ground was soft and moist and turned over easily. The other German tried to keep up, but was contributing a quarter of the total effort. Jedediah was like a human steam shovel. His massive muscles were visible in the moonlight. They glistened with sweat as he grunted and tore through the dirt.

A little over an hour later Jedediah and the other German were deep enough that only their heads showed above the hole. The German was exhausted. Jedediah kept digging. His shovel hit something hard. His muffled voice called out from below, "We're there."

He scraped his shovel on top of a casket. He said, "Two caskets side by side. The other two must be underneath. Let me get these two first . . . let me see if I can . . . open it from the side. Otherwise I'll need the pick ax."

I pointed my flashlight on the caskets as the German climbed out. Jedediah knelt on one casket with his hands in between the two. The latches faced each other and were in the middle of the grave. He tried to pull up the lid of the opposite casket without luck. He looked up at me and squinted in the light. "Hand me the crowbar."

I handed down the three-foot-long crowbar. He placed it under the edge of the lid and stomped on it with his booted foot. The lid popped open, revealing the deteriorated white satin lining and a skeleton. Pieces of clothing and hair lay around, remnants of what had been there more than ninety years before. Jedediah looked up at us, grabbed the shovel, and slammed it into the skeleton at the base of the skull, severing the spine. He took the burlap bag hanging out of the back of his jeans and tossed the skull into the bag. He slammed the lid closed on that casket, went to the end, then grabbed under the lip and pulled it until it was standing upright. He then leveraged it over until it was standing on top of the other one. I knew he was strong, but to watch him exercise his nearly superhuman strength with such ease and fluidity was remarkable. He handled the casket—which had to weigh two hundred pounds—like it was a bushel of corn. He took his crowbar out, and pried the lid open on the next one underneath the one he'd already opened. I illuminated the inside of the casket with my flashlight while standing on the edge of the gaping hole.

The inside of this casket was much less luxurious. It was wood-lined, probably with spruce, as it showed no evidence of bugs. The skeleton looked a little shorter than the previous one. Probably one of the females, but we weren't taking any chances. Jedediah lifted the skeleton out of the casket, grabbed the spine with one hand and the skull with the other, and tore it off. He dropped the skeleton back into the casket and put the skull into the sack.

I glanced at Eidhalt who was nearly falling into the hole with fascination and amazement. Jedediah moved the first two caskets back to where they started, handling them like they were empty boxes, and pried open the lid of the third. He didn't even hesitate. He slammed the shovel into the spine again. The skull flew forward and hit the front of the casket. Jedediah tossed it into the sack with the other two skulls, slammed the lid shut, wrestled the casket up, and opened the fourth. This was the largest skeleton of all. Probably the father, or Friedl himself. He smashed his shovel down, severing the spine of the fourth buried Friedl. The skull came free but the shovel continued through the bottom of the casket. The metal blade was completely out of sight. Jedediah looked surprised. He removed the skull and tossed it into the bag where it clicked audibly into the other three, then pulled his shovel back out. He closed the lid on the casket, and pulled it until it stood upright. He maneuvered around it and moved it to the other end of the hole, and looked down to where his shovel had gone through. We could see what appeared to be metal underneath the dirt. He got on his knees and began moving the dirt aside to reveal what appeared to be an aluminum floor for the grave plot. He could see the hole his shovel had made, but could not see what was on the other side of the aluminum. He looked up at us. We stared at him and the aluminum with puzzlement.

I asked the obvious question, "What is that?"

"Looks like a floor."

I looked at Eidhalt. "Graves have floors in Germany?" He shrugged. "Not that I know of."

Jedediah slammed his shovel into the aluminum again and again until he'd outlined a square with one side still attached. He bent the aluminum up and then back so the square was exposed as a hole. He looked up at me. "Toss me your flashlight."

He caught it and plunged the light into the hole. It wasn't just a floor. There was empty space on the other side of the aluminum. Jedediah got down on his knees and put the light into the hole. He turned and looked up at us. "It's an aluminum box the size of the whole grave area. And it's full of ammo."

I asked, "Ammo? Bullets?"

"Well ammo boxes, steel ammo boxes."

"Can you get one?"

He nodded and turned back toward the hole. He lay down on the dirt and reached his arm in and pulled out one of his ammo boxes. It was nine inches tall, twelve inches long, and four inches wide, with a lid that opened lengthwise. He put the small flashlight into his mouth, pointed it at the ammo box, undid the clasp and opened it. He pointed the light into the box and we all saw it at once. Gold. Jedediah let the lid fall back away from the opening, put the flashlight into his left hand and reached into the box. He pulled out what appeared to be a solid gold coin, one of hundreds shining in the intense LED light.

I said, "Is that box full of those coins?"

Jedediah examined the coin, and nodded. "Nazi coins. Gold Nazi coins. Minted in," he turned the coin over to the other side, "1944."

I asked, "Are they real?"

Jedediah was apparently wondering the same thing himself. He felt the coin, pressed a fingernail into it, bit it, and said, "I don't really know what a gold coin feels like. Feels a tiny bit softer than a U.S. silver dollar would, but I don't know for sure. I don't know why somebody would bury a bunch of fake coins."

The other German said, "How many boxes are down there?"

Jedediah put his head into the hole and shown the flashlight around again and counted. He came back out of the hole. "Hard to say for sure, but looks like maybe ten."

"Is there a floor underneath this aluminum that you just cut through?"

Jedediah nodded, "Looks like a box. A big aluminum box. Nothing else in it except these ten ammo cans. My guess is they're all full of these gold coins. But I can check them."

I nodded. "Open them all."

He did. Each box was full of the same gold coins. All apparently minted at the same time, never used for anything and stored away for sixty-five years.

Jedediah stood up, took his shovel and slammed it down through the hole all the way through to the bottom of the aluminum box he had identified. The shovel tip penetrated the bottom layer of aluminum and then stopped. Thom looked up and said, "Looks like that's it. Nothing but dirt on the other side of this aluminum bottom."

I said, "Hand the ammo boxes up to us." Eidhalt's man asked, "Why store them here?"

Eidhalt said what I was thinking. "Because they knew the name of the first Nazi martyr. They knew somebody would come back some day."

Jedediah asked from inside the grave, "Why not a bank account?"

I answered. "Bank accounts are traceable, and safe deposit boxes have keys. Whoever had the Blood Flag, had the future of the Nazi movement. And whoever buried this gold wanted to finance it."

Jedediah was skeptical. "How would they have known about DNA in the forties?"

I said, "How do we know the gold was buried in the forties? We don't. But whoever had the gold didn't have the flag. He wanted them to go together. And maybe there is gold buried under every one of the martyrs' graves that Hitler honored."

I looked around the graveyard then said to Eidhalt, "Since it was our idea to dig up Mr. Friedl, the gold is ours."

Eidhalt was instantly angry. "*We* are the future of the Nazi movement. *I* am the future. This entire unification movement is *mine*. The gold stays with the movement."

I looked at him intensely. "*I* am the movement in the United States. This is our gold."

He bristled. "This is on German soil, put here by Germans, for the future rise of the Nazi party. It was put there for *me*."

I knew this was the moment. I looked at him and said, "We both have important roles. I say we split it."

He was surprised by my sudden change of heart.

I said, "Five boxes each. But we need to get it out of here tonight. We can't leave anything here for somebody else to come and get. Once somebody sees this fresh dirt, they're going to start digging."

His face lit up. "I accept. But these are heavy. How do we get them out of here?"

"We'll drive right into the cemetery and load the boxes into our cars. We're going to have to move fast. Call me in the morning and let me know where you want us to bring the flag for the testing."

"I think we should keep the skulls, you have the flag."

I shook my head vigorously. "No way. We're not letting these out of our sight."

He looked at me suspiciously. "How do I know that you haven't brought a phony flag with you and skeletons that you know will match? No. You keep the flag, we'll keep the skulls, and we'll meet at the lab and give them both things at the same time."

His position was actually smart. "I agree. Call Jedediah tomorrow and tell us where to meet."

He nodded. "If this is the Blood Flag, and if this matches, you will have invigorated Nazism like nothing else could have. This will be the very thing that we needed to unite all movements around the world." He looked at me directly, "And I will need you as part of the international movement."

Jedediah jumped out of the grave. "I'll get the car."

* * *

As soon as we cleared the curb at the edge of the cemetery, I started driving around Munich randomly. After an hour, when I was sure we weren't being followed I pulled off the road under some overhanging trees.

We opened the trunk and took out the suitcase holding the Blood Flag. I gently removed it and laid it on the seat, and folded back the false bottom to the suitcase. I took out one of my two handguns that I'd placed there in its holster, and put it on my belt. I handed Jedediah the other one. He checked it and put it inside his waistband in the small of his back. As we drove on, randomly watching the traffic, I started calculating. Each ammo box weighed about fifty pounds. Assuming the gold was relatively pure, with sixteen ounces to a pound, that was eight hundred ounces of gold. At twelve hundred dollars per ounce that made nine hundred and sixty thousand per box. About a million dollars. Five million dollars for our five boxes.

We headed out of Munich. Jedediah asked where we were going. I told him I wanted to end up in a random German town and stay in a nondescript hotel no one would ever think of. When we learned where we had to be later that morning, we'd be there. But no one was going to know where we had come from. I wasn't even going to tell Alex or the BKA.

Michelle's voice was echoing in my head. This was where it started getting dangerous. Five million in gold and a flag people would kill for. Danger I'd brought on myself. All to prove a point, or prove something to myself, as she saw it. Unnecessarily.

I stayed on two-lane German roads. After driving through the dark countryside for a half hour, we entered a town. By the time we pulled in it was two in the morning. All I needed was a light. I didn't mind waking somebody up. It wasn't a big town, maybe five or six thousand people. It was near the mountains so I hoped it had a tourist base, and at least a couple hotels. We looked for any signs of life and then I saw a hotel sign. It was lighted, although the building was dark. As we pulled up in front, I could see the glimmer of a light in the lobby. I walked in and went to the reception desk, which had a bell on top. I rang it a couple of times and waited. I heard someone stirring in the back. A woman in her sixties came out through the door in her house slippers. The back of her hair was flat. She regarded me with skepticism. She said nothing.

I said, "Do you speak English?"

"A little."

"I'm here with five other colleagues. We are a geological team studying the mountains. I apologize for arriving so late, but we didn't finish our work until recently. So if possible, I'd like six rooms. Do you have six rooms available?"

She looked at me quizzically. "Six? I see only you."

"One is out in the car with me, the other four are on their way."

"It's one hundred euro per room. How many nights?"

"One night. Then we're back on the road."

"How are you paying?"

"In cash, if that is alright."

She nodded. She turned and prepared six electronic keys. She put each of them in small envelopes and put the room numbers on them. She stopped. "Do the rooms need to be together?"

I shook my head. "No."

She nodded and finished preparing the keys. She handed them all to me and I handed her six hundred euros. I then took another one hundred euro bill and put it on top. "That's for disturbing you. I'm sorry, again, for the late arrival."

She waved me off. "Check out time is eleven."

"We'll be on the road long before then. I'll leave the keys on the desk. We also have some boxes with valuable equipment that I'll be taking up to our room; nothing too large but we need to have them with us. I can't leave them in the car. So, we'll be making a couple trips in the elevator, but we'll try not to disturb you."

I went back out to the car and got Jedediah. I said, "I got six rooms." He looked at me confused. "That oughta do it."

"If somebody finds out we're here they'll have a one in six chance of finding us. And if we hear a lot of ruckus, we'll be ready."

"We're staying in the same room?" He said as he opened the trunk and surveyed the ammo boxes.

"Absolutely. Now that we've shown the flag we've set all kinds of forces in motion. Let's get this stuff up to the room. From now on one of us will always be awake."

It took us several trips. The room I picked was on a middle floor. It was close to the elevator so we could hear if it opened on our floor.

We closed and bolted the door. We put the ammo cans on the far side of the bed and the suitcase with the Blood Flag on top of the bed. Jedediah glanced at the door. "Think they'll try anything tonight?"

I sat down and started unlacing my boots. "They don't know where we are. Alex and Florian will know where *they* are because of the GPS tracker we put in the skull bag. She'll call us if she thinks they're up to something. And while they may want us dead, they're just now getting their feet under them. They may fear that we have duplicate flags, and maybe the one we showed them was a duplicate. Even if we have the real one, it doesn't mean we'd show it to them first thing. What they know is that we'll have to bring the real one to the DNA lab. That's when he'd make a move."

"Think he will?"

"Maybe. But even if we authenticate the real one, we could switch it any time with a fake."

Jedediah pondered the problem for a while. Then he asked, "How can he prevent it?"

"Oh, he could try to attach something or mark it somehow. It's hard to imagine anything that we couldn't either remove or duplicate given enough time. So, I don't know what he'll propose. He may propose taking it with him. Which isn't going to happen."

Jedediah lay down on the bed and put his arms up over his head on the pillow.

I nodded. "I'll wake you in two hours."

* * *

Early in the morning, before the sun was up, I walked out of the hotel through a side door to buy some pastries and coffee and brought them back to the room. Jedediah looked as intense as I felt. Neither of us spoke. He wasn't used to having the feeling that people were after him. I wasn't either. I couldn't really tell him it was all in his mind because it wasn't.

As we ate our pastries in silence Jedediah's phone rang. I looked at the number. It was Eidhalt. I answered. "Yes?"

"We have the lab. They can do it all today. We . . . encouraged them."

"Where and what time?"

The address was in the center of Munich. "Nine o'clock. Can you be there?"

I looked at my watch. It was 7:00 a.m. "Yes. See you there." The line went dead.

I gave Jedediah his phone. "Let's go. I want to get there before they do."

"We taking the gold with us? 'Cause if we go into the lab someone will break into the car. You know that."

"You drive. I'll call Florian on the way."

"We keeping these rooms?"

"No, we're out of here. Nothing traceable."

I pulled the car around to the front, while Jedediah carried the gold and the flag down to the car. As we headed toward Munich, I dialed Florian. He answered on the first ring. I told him the name of the lab. "We're meeting at nine o'clock."

"It's a good lab. They can do it."

"We need to give you the items we found for safe keeping. Tell us where to meet."

Florian gave us an address and we typed it into our nav system. We headed directly there and arrived fifteen minutes before eight. Alex was with Florian and Patrick and three other men. I said to Florian, "You have to give me your word that no one else will touch these. You have to keep them, and keep them safe. But I have to have your word that no one will even look at them. Otherwise, I'll have to come up with another plan."

Florian nodded his head knowingly. "This is not a problem, we will take care of them and return them. The gold was quite unexpected."

We moved the ammo cans to his trunk and closed it. Alex tried to read my face. I gave her a knowing look that everything was fine. Patrick asked, "Can I take one piece of gold to have it checked out? See if it's real gold and truly Nazi minted?"

"No," I said. "I don't want anyone's attention on any of this other than what we have already. Especially tied to the BKA." I turned to Alex. "I'm beginning to think we should have let him have all the gold," I said. "We don't need to give him another reason to do something stupid." I looked at my watch. "We've got to get to the lab."

Florian asked, "How will this happen? You will give the flag to the lab?"

I nodded. "And I think we will wait there until they're done with it."

"It's a reputable lab. Unless they have somebody on the inside—a couple of people—I don't think they could do anything with it. We'll see if it matches." We arrived at the lab intentionally late. I wanted them all there. Jedediah and I got out of the car with our weathered brown suitcase and walked in.

Eidhalt was waiting. "All set?" I asked.

"Yes. They are waiting for us."

Jedediah asked, "What did you tell them they were doing?"

"I told them it was a family issue. That we represented some grandchildren who wanted to determine whether the flag you have is from their grandfather's unit and the one on which he died. It's simply a historic curiosity, and that he was buried in a family grave so we had to bring all four of the family members for testing."

I nodded, "Did they buy it?"

A slight smile formed on his hard face. "They think it's odd, but they say they can do the test. And we offered them five times the cost of the test to put us in the front of the line."

"Hope they're quick. We're not leaving the flag here."

It caught him by surprise. "They have a safe."

I shook my head. "Whatever can be put into a safe can be taken out. They can get whatever DNA they need off the flag, then we'll be on our way."

"What if they need more?"

"Then they don't know what they're doing and we're at the wrong lab. If they can't do it here, we'll take it back to the States and get it authenticated."

"These skulls aren't going anywhere," he said firmly.

"Then let's do it. Do you know the people here?"

"Just by reputation. I spoke with the head of the lab last night. I tracked him down to his house. They're expecting us."

Eidhalt went to the receptionist desk and asked for Herr Bloch.

While we waited for Bloch there were awkward periods of silence. I was imagining how many ways they could try and separate us from the flag.

Eidhalt finally said to me, "Are you armed?"

"What difference does that make?"

"Curious. In case someone tries to take the flag."

"No one knows about the flag except you. Who would take it?"

He shrugged and tried to look disinterested. "There are thieves all around. Crime has been increasing."

"Probably true. But if I were armed it would be illegal in Germany, right?"

"That is true."

I saw the door open and a gentleman who was almost certainly Bloch walked toward us. He was of medium build with a shaved head and glasses. He wore a white lab coat and black soft-soled shoes.

I said in a low voice to Eidhalt, "I may be armed, and my good friend may also be armed, and I may have several friends here with me from the United States who have an ability to look very German. Or maybe I *should* have friends with me. If the crime problem is so bad, I should have *lots* of friends with me who could help me in a time of crisis. Maybe I do, maybe I don't."

He looked at me with some alarm then turned to Bloch. They greeted each other in German and then he introduced us to Bloch as the one who had the flag Eidhalt wanted to buy for his clients, assuming it could be authenticated as having come from their grandfather's unit. Bloch looked at Jedediah who stared at him with that serial killer stare that he had mastered. It gave people a cold chill.

Bloch said in English to all of us, "So you have some blood to have tested?"

"Yes. There is blood from a few different people, but we're sure blood from one of the people whose skulls we have is on the flag."

He waved his hand and said, "Come into the lab and let's sit down at our conference table and discuss this."

We walked through the first door and into the lab area, which was large and impressive. He took us to a conference room that had a long white table and ten leather chairs. The lighting was intense and direct from numerous small halogen lights in the ceiling. Jedediah and I sat on one side of the room while Eidhalt and his men sat on the other side, with Bloch at the end. Bloch started, "Let's understand exactly what we're doing." He looked at me. "Since you have the flag, tell me what your objective is."

"They," I said, indicating Eidhalt, "believe their family member's blood is on this flag, and if so, they would like to purchase it."

Bloch nodded and looked at Eidhalt. "What is it that you are going to use to prove this?"

Eidhalt lowered the satchel gently onto the table. The skulls clicked together.

"You have a skeleton?"

"There was some question of which skeleton it was. There were four in the grave so we have all four."

Bloch indicated the bag with his chin. "What pieces?"

"The skulls."

Bloch nodded. "Let's see them."

Eidhalt opened the bag and pulled out the four skulls and set them in front of him. It looked like four people sitting under the table with their heads projecting through.

Bloch nodded again. "They are in good condition. You do understand that we will have to bore into the skulls and take out the inside of the bone to extract the DNA. It is a process."

"We understand. That's no problem."

"So these are your relatives and you're okay with us drilling holes in their heads?"

"Yes. My clients' need to know."

"Why?" he asked with some skepticism.

Eidhalt looked at Bloch intensely. "It's important to the family."

Bloch shrugged. "Let's see the flag."

Jedediah opened the suitcase gently and lifted out the flag. He unfolded it onto the table next to the skulls. With the intense halogen lighting you could see the dark blood stains on the still bright red background. Bloch was taken aback. No one had told him it was a Nazi flag. He looked around the room then took out what looked like a jeweler's eye and examined the flag closely. He went to several areas that were clearly stained and looked at them closely. He picked up the flag gently. He folded the corner up and looked at the flag on the other side. He laid it back down. "I believe I can get enough material off of this flag for DNA testing. I will take samples from several different locations without cutting the flag, and prepare each of those samples separately for testing. I will then take bored sections from the skulls to extract the DNA and keep those four sections separate. You understand that will give us many different possibilities."

I nodded, "But that means that at least thirty of those will be non-matches because we don't expect three of them to match. Only one of them bled onto the flag."

"Yes, but they are related. What is their relationship?"

"Father, mother, and sister."

"Well, it is possible then that they will have some match. It won't be as likely or as good as the gentleman himself, but you could get some matches."

"Well, any match would confirm what we're here to find out. Because no one else would match. Right?" I asked.

"Well, it is theoretically possible. But it's close to a one in a billion chance that any given person will match another. So you're right. If there are any matches in any of these sets, then that confirms that the family member died on this flag. But if all goes well, we should get one perfect match. If he bled sufficiently, and as you said most of this blood is his, we should be able to match it perfectly. It will take some time."

All of us immediately thought of the meeting. Eidhalt asked, "How much time?"

Bloch considered, "Well, we have to culture the DNA and grow it in the lab. Then the matching testing itself shouldn't take more than a day, so I would say that we can have an answer for you by Wednesday."

Eidhalt immediately turned to me and said, "So you will leave the flag here until Wednesday."

"You've forgotten what we just said," I said harshly. "I'm not leaving it *anywhere* for *any* period of time. If they need to take samples, they can take as many samples as they want. From any part of the flag they want."

I looked at the owner of the lab. "You can take the samples right now, can't you? It can't take that long."

He looked at his watch. "The people that will do that are involved in another extremely important matter."

I raised my voice, "I don't give a *shit* how important their other matter is. We're paying you a lot of money. Get them over here now and take the samples. We will all watch and then I'll take my flag and go. Then we'll come back and you can tell us what the results are. Get them now."

Bloch looked a little concerned and quite peeved, and said, "Let me see." He left the conference room and left us alone with the flag.

Eidhalt said, "I don't think you trust me."

I responded, "You are correct."

"We're on the same team. We are trying to get things together for our meeting. We are supposed to be working together."

"You're the one putting the meeting together. You haven't even told me where it's going to be or what will happen. This is all about you. Not about the movement. You're trying to put yourself at the top of the movement. I get that. But don't expect me to trust you because of it."

* * *

Two men and a woman came into the conference room where the flag was spread out on the table. It was too large for the table, and was bunched at the two ends; but the black and white striping and the red color made clear what kind of flag it was. They tried not to look startled. They bent and examined the flag with a magnifying glass. We all stood around wondering whether there would be any problem.

Bloch said, "We will begin. I have informed Franz, our lead laboratory technician. He understands what we're doing." He asked Franz, "Do you have your locations selected?"

Franz answered, "Yes. We will take numerous samples because of the number of people."

One of his colleagues handed him a small case, which he opened. It contained glass test tubes with screw-top lids. When he unscrewed one of the lids, it came out with a Q-tip-like swab attached to the lid. He dipped it in some liquid that was in a small container also in the kit, and leaned down to examine the first place in the flag he wanted to lift a blood sample from. He rolled over the same spot with the moistened swab in an area about one inch by two inches several times, like he was painting the spot with an invisible liquid. I expected the swab to turn pink with blood remains, but it didn't. It remained pure white and moist. After fifteen or twenty seconds, he was satisfied and put that swab back into the tube and screwed the top on. He spoke in German to his colleague who wrote on the tube. He took out another test tube with the swab cap and began working on another spot. His two colleagues did likewise. Before long, they had twenty or thirty different swabs that had extracted whatever they could from the flag and they had placed them back into the tubes with markings showing the location of the sample on the flag. Why the location would matter, I didn't understand. But, I also didn't care. Franz was done. He placed the last vial into the box.

He closed it and locked it, and nodded to the head of the laboratory. He said, "We have all the samples we need."

I asked, "Do you think you got enough?"

"It's impossible to say at this point, but the flag is in such good condition that I am hopeful. I have pulled DNA from much rougher pieces of cloth that were much older."

I turned to Bloch. "How long before you'll have the results?" The clear implication of my question was that his answer the last time we asked was inadequate.

Everyone in the room looked at him in expectation. He pondered.

"We have to take the skull samples . . . we must have the DNA replicate itself, we have to put it in a machine overnight. I would say by this time tomorrow, we should have an answer."

I nodded and took the corner of the flag into my hands. "I'll give you my phone number." As I began folding up the flag, I said to him, "You do understand how important it is that this be kept confidential. Right?"

He nodded. "All our work is confidential."

"Not all your work involves something of this magnitude. The bigger the magnitude, the bigger the public interest might be, the more important it is to keep it confidential. You understand?"

He frowned. "I thought this was a simple family issue." He paused. "But of course, nothing will be said to anyone. I will make sure."

I took the folded flag and handed it to Jedediah who put it back into the leather suitcase and closed it. I said to everyone in the room, "Then we will be going." I looked at Eidhalt. "Call me if you hear first so I can meet you here to get the results."

He looked enthusiastic. "Of course. I look forward to it."

I nodded, and Jedediah and I walked out of the room quickly.

CHAPTER NINETEEN

Jedediah put the leather suitcase into the trunk of our rental car. He climbed into the passenger seat and I drove off. He asked, "Where are you headed?"

"Into the country." I glanced at the car's GPS for directions to the road that I'd chosen the previous night while studying a map. I wanted a road that was lightly traveled, where I could pick out someone who might be following us.

We drove through the city and onto a road that led out of town. I looked in my rearview mirror for cars that were following us but didn't see anything. This was our point of greatest vulnerability. They had to suspect that we could switch the flag with a fake once out of their sight. But they knew we had the real one in the car as we left the lab. I drove below the speed of the traffic so everyone passed us. After we'd driven ten miles to where there was only an occasional intersection or country house, I noticed a black seven series BMW a half-mile behind us. I continued on another ten miles and all the other cars passed. But the BMW stayed back.

"They're on us," I said. Jedediah turned and looked back.

"The Beemer?"

"Yeah."

My cell phone rang and I pulled it out of my pocket and looked at the number. "Yeah?"

It was Alex. "You know you're being followed, right?"

"Yeah. Black BMW."

"There's a second car about a mile behind him. You want me to get our German friends to intervene?"

"Where are you?"

"In a helicopter a couple of miles behind you, with Florian."

"If you guys jump in they'll know we aren't what we appear to be. Let me take care of this."

Florian who was also on the line responded, "I don't know if that's so smart."

"Hold on," I said as I looked in my rearview mirror and saw that the BMW had accelerated. "Shit." He was closing in on us at over a hundred miles per hour. I put the phone on the seat, still connected to Alex and Florian. I said to Jedediah, "Here they come."

He glanced back. "What are you going to do?"

"Nothing, until they get here." I looked ahead and there was no traffic in either direction. The terrain was perfect for an ambush. Grass and trees on both sides, no houses or buildings. No witnesses. The BMW flew up toward us and grew larger and larger in the rearview mirror. By this time, I could see two faces in the two front seats, but I couldn't tell if there was anybody in the back. They closed on us fast, then pulled over into the other lane, to go around us. "Here they come." I changed nothing, driving as I would if it were just another car passing us. "See if you can tell how many men are in that car."

The BMW was on top of us. He swung into the oncoming lane to pass. Jedediah called out, "Four men in the car." Just as he said that, the BMW braked hard and swerved over to hit us. I anticipated his move and slammed on my brakes and swerved to the right. The BMW kept slowing and cutting me off, which forced me over onto the shoulder. Before I knew it, I was across the shoulder and on the grass. The BMW kept coming, driving me completely off the road. The brakes pulsed as the anti-lock brakes fought our speed in the slippery grass. But it wasn't enough and it wasn't quick enough. I steered hard left to avoid one tree, but smashed into another head on. Our airbags fired out and punched us in the face as our car came to an immediate stop. As the airbag deflated, I asked Jedediah, "You okay?"

"Yeah. You?"

I reached for the door handle and my handgun. "Get your weapon and get out! You see one guy with a gun, you start firing. Go right at them! Don't let them out of their car. They won't expect it. No hesitation! Go!"

We jumped out of the car, put our guns up and ran at the BMW. They had just come to a stop as they had much more speed than we did and didn't have a tree to help. They were a good thirty yards ahead of us. We ran up from behind them as they got out of their doors. The first man I saw got out of the rear door on the right side. He was carrying a handgun in his right hand. That was enough for me. I aimed and fired and hit him in the head. He dropped straight down onto the ground. The others had now heard the gunshot and hurried to get out and turn toward us in a firing position. But we had the advantage. The man in the right passenger door jumped out in a crouch and tried to run away from the car so he could turn toward us. Jedediah saw him and fired three shots. The man went down in a heap. We ran to the left side of the BMW and the third man got out of the left rear door. He had a submachine gun and aimed it toward us to fire. Jedediah and I fired at the same time, both hitting him in the chest. He was knocked back, but not harmed. He was wearing a vest.

"Vest. Close on him! Aim for his legs!" We continued to fire, hitting him in the groin and legs. He cried out in pain as Jedediah shot him in the head from fifteen feet away. The only one left was the driver. He got out with his arms up. Jedediah shot him in the chest and the man collapsed next to the car.

I said, "Get their weapons, clear out our trunk, and put them in it." Jedediah went to the driver, checked to see if he was alive. He was.

Jedediah shot him again. He took his weapon out of his hand, and pressed the lever to release the trunk. The trunk popped open. As he collected the weapons and checked the BMW I retrieved the flag and my cell phone from our rental. I put the suitcase in the rear seat of the BMW and looked at their weapons. "They had a lot of ammo. It's all over the trunk. They were loaded for bear."

"Anything else in the car?"

"No, we got the keys."

Just then, I looked over Jedediah's shoulder as a black Mercedes S class slowed and looked at us. I looked back at the car, unable to see who was in it. They could see us standing there with guns in our hands, and bodies around us. They sped away. Jedediah dragged the four dead men to our car and threw two of them into the trunk, and the other two into the back seat. My phone rang. They must have hung up and called me to make it ring.

"Yeah."

"Shit, Kyle! What are you doing? Are you okay?" Alex sounded frantic. "Yeah. We were driving along here through the grass and noticed a car in front of us that was stopped. I quit paying attention unfortunately, and I hit a tree. When we got up there, it looks like there are four guys that have been shot by somebody. We're going to have to go, so you might want to send some people out here to clean this up."

Florian interrupted. "You shot four of them?"

"Somebody did."

"We'll have to talk about this. This is not how this was supposed to go."

"Whenever you like. But we've got to get out of here. That other car may be coming back."

I hung up my phone, and said to Jedediah, "Let's go. You drive."

"Where to?" He said as he raced around and climbed into the driver's seat of the BMW 750i.

"The airport."

* * *

Jedediah floored the BMW. The wheels spun as we went from the grass back to the pavement and back toward the city on the two-lane highway. There was no sign of the Mercedes, but a couple of other cars went by. Before long we were a good distance away from the scene and Jedediah slowed down to normal highway speeds. After a few minutes, Jedediah asked, "Why the airport?"

"I'm going to rent another car. I don't think I'll tell Hertz that their car is piled against a tree for a while yet. I think I'll go to Avis or whatever else is out there. Then we'll drive around to this car and transfer their weapons— now ours—to my trunk, and take the BMW key with us. It will be all nicely locked and left in long-term parking like somebody's gone on a flight. Then I'll drive you around and you can rent another car. That way we'll have two. We need to keep making random decisions so nobody knows where we are."

Jedediah nodded. "Except the BKA knew where we were. They were following us with a helicopter."

I looked at him driving, and thought about what had just happened. "I may need to ditch my phone . . . You handled yourself well back there. You know how to shoot."

"I wasn't in the army for nothing."

"There are a lot of army guys who don't know how to shoot."

"Not in the Rangers."

"You were in the Rangers? I didn't know that."

"Whatever file you have on me is incomplete. I guarantee it. There's a lot about me you don't know."

"Like what?"

"Don't worry about it."

I thought to myself that I needed to go through his file again. I didn't like not knowing things. I thought again about the men in the forest. "You didn't have to shoot that guy in the head."

Jedediah glanced at me. "The one who just tried to kill us?"

"Yeah. That one. The one who was wounded. The one who had no chance of doing us any further harm."

"Really? No chance? Like making a phone call or living through that and telling someone about us?"

"Telling who what? That we took the BMW? That was pretty damned obvious. That what? We had the flag? They already knew that. He was no threat to us."

"He's one of them. He's bad."

"We're not executioners."

Jedediah grunted. "If you came face to face with Satan himself, wouldn't you shoot him in the freaking head, even if he was unarmed?"

"Never thought about it."

"Some people are just like that. They *are* Satan. They need to be destroyed. And if *you* can't do it, don't worry about it. I can."

I looked up and saw the large Lufthansa hangar at the Munich Airport. "You see the sign for the rental cars?"

"Yeah."

"Drop me off, then go to long-term parking. I'll come pick you up and we'll transfer the guns. Then I'll take you back to the rental counter."

Jedediah nodded and pulled up to the rental agency site. I climbed out and he headed for the long-term parking. "Give me your cell." He did. I broke his and mine open, took out the SIM cards, and smashed the various pieces and dropped them down the storm drain. "Follow me at all costs. Do *not* lose me. We're going to drive a long way. Nothing close. Just somewhere where they won't think to look at all. We're going to go rent an apartment.

I got a feeling that they know all the hotels around here. We've got to find something a lot less predictable."

"What're you thinking?"

"Austria."

* * *

With Jedediah right behind me in his rental car I drove through Salzburg for forty minutes. It was a beautiful city surrounded by mountains. The idyllic setting conflicted with my heightened state of alertness that caused my hands to sweat on the steering wheel. When I thought about the four men intent on stealing the flag and taking us out with it, I started wondering what the hell I was doing. Michelle wouldn't need to learn about that little event.

I had started this whole thing with a burning anger toward neo-Nazism, any strain of the virus out there. And now I was starting to come face to face with it. But this fight was bigger than me. I couldn't take on all of international Nazism by myself, but that was the corner I'd backed myself into. Even though I had help within the Bundeskriminalamt, I was starting to wonder if I could trust them. They had been started by Nazis. And Alex was with them, which made me reluctant to rely on her. I couldn't tell her everything I was thinking because she wouldn't know not to tell them about it.

As we pulled away for the third time from the center of Salzburg I noticed an apartment building about four stories tall that had a sign in the window on the ground floor. It was in German; I assumed it said there were apartments available. We stopped at the next block and parked our cars. I told Jedediah to wait at a local café and watch the cars and me while I walked back to the apartment building. I walked into the ground floor and into a narrow hallway to a door that had a sign on it. I knocked on the door and walked in. It was a cramped and cluttered office with a man in his sixties sitting behind the desk. He greeted me in German and I responded, "Do you speak English?"

He nodded and said, "A little."

"Do you have any apartments, any flats, for rent?"

"For how long?"

"I don't know maybe a month?"

He frowned and threw up his hands. "A month? Why a month? Why not six months? We like one-year leases. Do a one-year lease."

"I don't need to. I'm just here for a month."

"You're American. Why are you here?"

"I'm writing a book about the Sound—"

"Ach. The world has too many books about it. Go do something else."

"No. I have a whole different angle on it."

He looked at me in disgust. "One month. How much can you pay?"

"How much is the rent?"

"Fifteen hundred euros."

I looked shocked. "That's ridiculous. I will give you a thousand."

"Twelve hundred."

"Eleven hundred."

"Paid in advance, cash."

"Two bedrooms?"

"No. Three."

"Good enough." I reached into my pocket, took out my wallet, and handed him eleven hundred euros.

He looked at me with suspicion. "Most people don't have that kind of cash. And you're a writer? Writers don't have money. Why do you have so much cash?"

"Because I expected to rent a place for a month, and I thought they'd give me a discount if I paid in cash in advance. This is my rent money. I've been carrying it with me until I found the right place."

"You've been to other places?"

"A few."

He took the money. "Here's the key." He tossed me two keys on a ring. "Third floor. No elevator. 315."

I nodded, took the keys and walked out of the office. I walked up the stairs to apartment 315 and opened it up. It was actually quite nice and fairly large. The building was built in the sixties and suffered from the ignominy of 1960s architecture, but was airy with clean windows and had three bedrooms and a small kitchen. I forgot to ask if it was furnished; it wasn't. He hadn't seen Jedediah, so if anybody came asking for two men, one of whom was built like a weight lifter, he wouldn't have seen him. Nor did he have our names. Just cash, which was all he was interested in.

I got Jedediah and brought him up to the apartment. We went out and bought a couple of pillows and some blankets. We took the blankets to the cars and wrapped our newly captured firearms in them and brought them up to the apartment with the leather suitcase. We put the suitcase in the back corner of one of the bedrooms and checked the weapons. We left them loaded. I went back to the suitcase and carefully removed the flag. I put it into a backpack to take with us.

"Let's go get some dinner."

"Wiener schnitzel."

"You got it. And tonight, I don't think there's a prayer that they're going to find us here. But in any case, we're going to have a watch scheduled."

Jedediah smiled. "Two on, two off."

"Exactly. And no sitting at all. Ever. Not even any leaning. Your only contact with anything is your feet on the floor. Then tomorrow we'll get up at the crack of dawn and head back to the lab. Tomorrow we find out if this is the real Blood Flag."

"It is," he said.

I nodded. "I think so too. And when that's confirmed, this is going to get real interesting."

The dinner and evening passed without problem. The Wiener schnitzel was excellent and the beer was perfect. We had no communication with anybody. Our cell phones were gone, and I wasn't going to replace them until we got back to Munich. No one had any idea where we were or how to contact us. Exactly how I wanted it.

* * *

We got up at 4:00 a.m., grabbed the backpack, put our weapons in the empty suitcase, and headed to our cars. We found a café that was open early and grabbed some Americano coffee and headed to Munich. We arrived in the heart of the city by six thirty. We parked our cars away from each other in spots near the city center. We found an open restaurant and ordered some eggs. We sat quietly until our third cup of coffee.

Jedediah asked, "So, what's the plan?"

"They said they'd know this morning. I'm sure the answer is going to be yes, let's assume so. We've seen what they'll do when they think it *may* be real. Imagine how the stakes will go when they know it is. They're going to try and get it. So we have to make it real clear that it's literally not possible. Our only safety is in them not being able to get the flag."

"And?"

"And last night when I went out during your watch, I went to the internet café across the street. I was looking at banks in Munich. I don't want a German bank, and I don't want a Swiss bank. But surprisingly, there is a Scottish bank in the heart of Munich that has safe deposit boxes. We'll have a signature card on file with your signature and mine. Either one of us can get in. But even if Eidhalt were to get the key from us, he'd never get the box open because he can't match the signature card. And we're not going to tell them where it is anyway. They can go ransack wherever they want.

"We'll put the flag in there, put the case in one of the cars, and then go to the lab. I'll also get us a couple of new prepaid cell phones. If we want to call somebody we will, but nobody is going to call us."

Jedediah surveyed the city street for any signs of interest. He looked back at me. "You think these guys are able to eavesdrop on cell phones?"

"Sure. It's not hard. Just illegal. And I don't know who they're working with. If you can explain to me how they knew where we were driving yesterday, I'll have some comfort in what their limitations are. Right now I'd rather over-estimate than underestimate."

"Fair enough."

As soon as the bank opened I signed an agreement for one of the largest boxes. Jedediah and I went into the carrel and transferred the flag from the backpack to the steel box. We put it back on the lower section of the column and with the banker's back turned, slid it into the wall. The banker turned back around, pulled out his key, and with my key and his we locked the box. I put my key in my pocket, and we walked out. I told Jedediah to put the backpack back in the trunk of his car and meet me in front of the lab. I walked straight to the lab. Eidhalt was already there. Along with two other men I'd not seen before.

He said good morning to me in German with a smile on his face, but as before, although he smiled with his mouth, his eyes remained cold. I returned the greeting in my best German, which was bad, and asked if the lab was open. He said it was and asked where Jedediah was. I said he was coming and I'd wait for him on the sidewalk. He said he would too. We stood there silently for a moment, then Eidhalt said, "Where are you staying?"

"At a place."

"What place?"

"In Berlin. Here he comes," I said as Jedediah quickly walked around the corner and saw us standing there waiting for him. He slowed slightly and walked up to us. He had a hard look on his face, which was appropriate given that he was staring into the eyes of the man that almost certainly had sent others to try and kill us.

Eidhalt asked, "Did you have any trouble getting back to your place yesterday?"

I shook my head. "No, no problem."

He smiled again slightly. "Let's go find out what the results are." He turned and all of us followed him into the waiting area. He asked the receptionist to summon the head of the laboratory, who came out about fifteen minutes later.

The head of the lab had a stoic look on his face that revealed nothing about what the results might be. He invited us into the lab and we went straight into the conference room where we had taken the samples from the flag the day before. We all fit in again, and the technicians who had drawn the samples came in. But the room was set up differently. No flag, but a computer with a projector attached by cable was pointing toward a screen. The head of the lab sat where the computer was, and the rest of us filled in around the table. He dimmed the lights, and projected the computer onto the screen. "Let me explain what it is we have done." He went through the procedures of the DNA testing in great detail. Far more detail than I had ever seen, even in a courtroom. He clearly knew what he was doing. But his face was completely blank. He wasn't projecting any hint of whether there was a match or not. Whatever the answer was, he was letting us know that he had done his homework, and that their testing had been done properly and within scientific standards. Because of all the preliminaries, I found myself becoming more concerned than calmed.

Finally, he projected some images on the screen of a type that I had seen before. They were the actual DNA test results themselves. It was mostly white with blotches of dark in something of a pattern. They were microscopic slides of the DNA itself. When he brought parallel images up the similarities were obvious even to me. In some respects it was like a fingerprint. It had a physical similarity, where one gene or a piece of a gene looked like another. It was like columns of numbers. Where one four looks like another four and a seven looks like another seven. They're not just random shapes. The director of the lab paused on one slide. "This is the most significant slide I will show you. As you can see, the result on the left is the DNA that we were able to extract from the flag. On the right is the DNA of one of the skulls you gave us. Although it is perhaps not completely obvious, they are a perfect match. There is *no doubt* it is his blood on the flag."

The room went into a stunned silence. We had all theorized that there might be a match, but probably internally each of us had reserved a lot of space for the possibility that the match would be ambiguous, or the DNA that they could extract would be incomplete, or they wouldn't be able to extract anything that would give us complete confirmation. We were all wrong.

"No doubt?" I asked.

The lab director shook his head. "None. Other than the general rule that it is possible to have very very similar DNA in two people out of a billion. But based on how you represented this DNA was collected and the probability that that person in fact bled onto this flag, I would say the identification is absolute."

I stole a glance at Jedediah. He was clearly impressed. He tried to control his expression. We had the Blood Flag. The most important remnant of Nazism in the world. And people had already shown themselves ready to kill to get it.

Eidhalt looked at me from across the table. "Where is the flag now? Perhaps you should give it to me for safekeeping for our . . . " he looked around the room, "meeting."

I looked into his eyes and could see the mischief. "I assume I'm still invited. I'll bring it. It's in a safe place. But if you don't want me to come to the meeting, just let me know. Jedediah and I will just return to the United States now."

Eidhalt looked at the lab directors and others and said, "Thank you for your work. We have your pay with us, plus an additional amount for putting us at the front of the line and your quick work. You have done excellent work." They could tell they were being dismissed and quietly left the room.

They left the presentation up on the screen.

Eidhalt looked at me. "Would you be willing to sell it to me, for the cause?"

I could feel something coming. "I have no intention of selling it."

"You did."

I frowned. "Really. When might that have been?"

"In Tennessee." He pulled an iPhone out of his pocket, touched an icon on the screen, turned it sideways, and showed it to me. It was a video of me asking Schuller how much the Blood Flag would be worth. I wasn't surprised that Schuller had videotaped our conversation. What surprised me is that he was connected to the head of the German neo-Nazi movement.

"So what?"

"So you wanted to sell it."

"I wanted to know what it was worth. If you know the value of something, you know how much you need to protect it. And it's actually worth millions."

He smiled.

I stood, and Jedediah stood next to me. I lowered my voice. "But since you've taken to spying on me and sending men to try and kill us, I really don't see any point in going forward with you. You're just another lying piece of shit who is not ever going to be a leader of any meaningful organization. I think I'll take that role on myself." I paused, "We don't need you. And whatever you start, we'll bury you, because we have the flag, and you never will. I can even leave without the flag if I want to, then I can come back and get it whenever I feel like it. You'd never even know I was here."

Jedediah stared at the two men next to Eidhalt who were twitching agitatedly.

"So have a good meeting. Let's go, Jedediah."

We walked out the conference room door, and slammed it behind us. We walked out the glass door to the lobby, and Eidhalt followed right behind us. "Wait!"

We turned around and he was alone. "What?"

"I have not handled this well. I am inherently suspicious. I've known about Mr. Thom for a long time. I've watched the Southern Volk. It's you I didn't know. And I didn't trust you. I'm still not sure I completely trust you. You don't fit the usual mold. So when I started inquiring about you, I learned a lot of information that was out there, but that I had not been aware of, okay? And then I talked to my friend in Tennessee, who had recently met you. I thought that was an odd coincidence. Then I inquired of my friend inside the Southern Volk. He too was suspicious of you, and sent me a video of you at one of their recent meetings. Nicely done.

"But now you have the flag, and we've proved it. And I want you to bring it to the meeting. This is the most important meeting in the history of Nazism since the destruction of Germany in 1945. We're going to change things. And the *Blutfahne* is just what we need to do that. I still want you to be a part of this."

Jedediah said in a near whisper, "You got a video of one of our meetings? From who?"

"A friend," Eidhalt said smiling, clearly pleased at the ugly surprise he had just sprung.

"Who?" Jedediah demanded.

"No need to say," he said.

"Yes, there is, or we're not going forward. Who?"

"Dirty White Boy."

I stole a look at Jedediah who was making mental notes.

I said to Eidhalt, "How do I know you're not just luring us into a trap to be killed? Like earlier."

"I don't know what you're talking about. The German authorities monitor everything I do. The last thing I want to do is give them an excuse to put me in prison. This is the beginning of the rise of the Nazi movement worldwide. I'm not going to jeopardize that by being stupid."

I didn't believe a word of it. "We'll see. The meeting is still on as scheduled, right?"

"Day after tomorrow."

"And where are we to go?" I asked.

He indicated to go outside, so we stepped outside the glass door onto the sidewalk. He looked around. "I need to give you a new number." He looked at Jedediah who nodded. He wrote it on a piece of paper and handed it to Jedediah.

"Call it at one o'clock in the afternoon, day after tomorrow. You'll be given instructions. But one thing that might not have been clear, is this may be more than just a few hours. I have quite a surprise in store. You'll be amazed."

"Where?"

"You'll be told. Stay near Munich, call, and I'll tell you what the plan is. Everything is in place. It's going to be the biggest event in Nazism since 1945."

CHAPTER TWENTY

After the meeting, Jedediah and I walked around the downtown section of Munich for an hour or so until we were sure no one was following us. We stopped into a cell phone store and bought two prepaid cell phones. We wrote each other's numbers on pieces of paper and put them in our pockets. We got into my car and I called Alex.

"Hello?"

"It's me."

"Where the hell have you *been*? I've been trying your phone but you don't answer."

"Tossed it. Didn't want to be tracked. People out there with a lot of equipment and influence. And I still don't know exactly who tried to kill us. Maybe in the BKA. What about Florian and Patrick. Are they with us?"

"I've been with them all day every day since the cemetery. I don't see anything that gives me any concern at all. Maybe somebody else inside of the organization is tracking things, but not them. They want to meet. They want to figure out what the plan is from here on out. What *your* plan is."

"Okay, in the cemetery. Where we hid the flag. One hour. Just the three of you. And park a long way away. Walk from three different directions. Have them post guards at the corners. See you then."

* * *

The thing about an ambush is you have to know where your target is going to be. Since I had just set the location, anybody who was inclined to ambush us had to be there before I got there. Jedediah and I drove directly to the cemetery and parked two blocks away. We entered the cemetery from different angles. We checked the area and were confident no one was waiting for us. We took two different spots and stood in silence among the trees, watching the approaches. We saw nothing out of order.

Right on time, I saw Florian, Patrick, and Alex. They converged on the ornate grave, which had held the flag when we first met with Eidhalt. They looked around for us and didn't see us even though we were fifty yards away standing in the trees looking directly at them. Humans are like other animals. Our visual cues are tied to motion. Even without camouflage it's much more difficult to see somebody standing still in a complex background than if that person moves.

We finally walked down to them and greeted them. Florian looked surprised. "Where were you hiding?"

"We weren't hiding, we were standing right up there in those trees."

"How long have you been here?"

"Awhile. We're fine. There's no one here."

Florian nodded. "Did you really have to kill those four men? Do you know how difficult this makes it?"

"What did you see as my options exactly?" I said, peeved that he'd be more worried about "difficulties" than me. "I guess we could have made it so you'd only have two dead men to worry about. That would have been much easier. Two foreigners."

"I didn't mean it like that. I meant there's an investigation, and they want answers. We don't have massacres along the roads in Munich. People want answers and who the other people are who were involved."

"Well, it shouldn't be too hard. I rented the car as Jack Bradley and if they ask Hertz, they'll tell them. So that would give them a good clue as to who was involved. And you watched the entire thing from a helicopter, so tell them what happened. That we were ambushed and responded. Simple as that."

He frowned, knowing I didn't quite understand how things worked in the BKA. "I told them to lay off the investigation for now. They want to come arrest you and ask questions."

"They're welcome to do that, but after this is over."

"And him?" He said pointing to Jedediah. "How did he get armed? We don't have Americans carrying guns around Munich."

"Yeah. I had two guns, and I asked for his help when we were under Siege. I hope you allow for self-defense when four armed men—one with a machine gun—come after you."

"We'll figure something out. They have given us a little bit of time. But we have to know what your plan is. What is going to happen?"

"We don't know what Eidhalt's plan is. All we know is that we're supposed to make a phone call. Until then, we will have nothing."

Alex asked, "So how do we put a fence around this group and put them in prison?"

I looked at Jedediah who stared back at me wondering the same thing. I had finally come to the point where I had achieved what I had set out to do. All the leading neo-Nazis in the world were coming to a meeting, and I would be there. But I didn't have an end game. All that passion, all that outrage, all that determination. For what? To get rid of an idea? To cripple the movement? How? What was I going to do in Germany? I turned to Florian. "So if they use the Blood Flag and fly it over a meeting in his castle and scream out *Sieg Heil!* they go to jail for a year at the most. Right?"

"Yes."

"That's not enough."

Alex said, "We should have them for attempted murder."

I looked at Florian. "You're never going to track those four to Eidhalt. They're like the mafia. Unless you've got a wire on them or someone in the room, you'll never hear the order. You'll never tie it. Plus, if you do, we take out the one guy. That leaves all the rest of these people to return to their countries and keep right on going."

Patrick said, "Well, this was your idea, what did you have in mind to finish this?"

"Maybe the smell of jail for a year will get them to start thinking about what they're doing. And maybe if I play it right, I can get them to discuss a plan to overthrow the government of Germany and a few other governments to boot. I assume there is some German law that would make that illegal for more than a misdemeanor."

"Yes, of course. But it is hard to prove."

"Well, before we go, I'll make sure I understand and we'll make sure we entrap them—in a legal way."

Alex said, "Call us when you know what's going on."

I nodded. "And I promise that I will break out the Blood Flag, and I will display it. Everybody will give it the deference it deserves, and I think it will be enough for you to arrest a whole lot of them. So you better have an army of men ready to come into his castle, and arrest anybody for Nazism. And my guess is when you get there, you're going to find a lot of illegal weapons and other violations that will put these guys away for a few years."

Florian nodded enthusiastically, "See you tomorrow."

"And Alex," I said. "I need that other stuff we brought. I'll let you know how to get it to me."

"What other stuff?" Florian asked.

"Don't worry about it. A little extra self-defense."

* * *

I had the last watch of the early morning. I woke Jededian before the sun had peeked into Salzburg. He sat up quickly as if he were ready for a fight.

"No attackers. Just time to get up."

He arose like a good solider and washed. He asked, "What's the plan?"

"We'll bug out before the city wakes up and get to Munich early. I want to park, eat, and be at the bank the second it opens. We'll put the flag in the case, put it in my car with both of us in it, then we'll drive around, armed to the teeth, until it's time to make the call."

I put one pistol in my shoulder holster, and another in my belt, and the others in pillows. He asked, "We're going to drive around all day?"

"We'll make some stops. Maybe take in a museum, who knows. But we're going to stay on the move. They won't know where we're going because we won't know where we're going. And then when the call comes, it's game on."

"Do you know what the game's going to be?"

"I do. I'll brief you when we get to Munich."

When the bank opened Jedediah stood guard at the door while I retrieved the flag from the safe deposit box. I put it in the leather suitcase and dropped an envelope into the now empty box before replacing it. I had written down everything that happened since I first became involved in the operation, including the attempt on our lives and our current plan for the meeting. After locking the box, I went to the small carrel room with the Blood Flag and pulled down my pants. I took my key from the safe deposit box, stuck it to a large piece of duct tape with a business card from the bank, and taped them to my inner thigh.

I dressed, grabbed the leather case, and walked out of the bank. Jedediah said nothing. We put the case in the trunk and drove around Munich. We stopped at a couple of cafés, had some coffee, drove to the countryside and back, the airport and back, and waited for noon. It was finally time.

I pulled out my cell phone and called Eidhalt's new number. A man asked, "Where are you from?"

"States."

"What group?" It was not Eidhalt.

"Southern Volk."

"Tonight at 8:00 p.m. at his castle. Just the two of you."

"Understood." I hung up, rolled down the window, and threw the cell phone out into traffic.

"What's the word?"

"Eight o'clock at his castle."

"And until then?"

"It's time to tell you what I have in mind, and to prepare. And we've got to meet up with Alex."

We met in a Starbucks, where she gave me a heavy shopping bag. The rest of the afternoon seemed to take three days but finally darkness enveloped us. We pulled off the main road and on to the road to the castle. We turned the car around so we were facing outward. We turned off the lights and waited. There was no one around. No one had followed us and there were no other cars on the road. "You ready for this?" I asked. "I'm ready for anything. I wish I knew what we were doing though. We're going in there with no plan, which isn't a good idea. Just my opinion."

"It's like I told you. We do have a plan. Just depends on how things play out. If all we can do is get them for Nazi flags and salutes, then that's what we'll do. But if we can find a way to get them for anything else, we will. And Alex, Florian, and Patrick are standing by. They and a force of a hundred can be here in five minutes."

"I don't know," Jedediah said. "I think this guy is more clever than that."

"So do I. Which is why we have to stay flexible. We'll respond to whatever happens."

He pondered.

We turned on the lights, turned left, and headed toward the castle. It was a dirt road but perfectly maintained, like tightly packed dust. We couldn't see the castle initially, but as we drove around a large grove of trees on our left it came into view in the distance. It was spectacular. It was illuminated by floodlights pointing to the sky whose beams rubbed the light colored stone on their way by. The castle was made of thick limestone, with parapets and towers at the corners. It was much bigger than I had expected, and sat on property that had to be a hundred acres of forests and lawns.

We pulled up to where there were large spotlights trained on the approaching traffic. Ours was the twentieth or thirtieth car outside the castle. We got out, gathered the heavier leather suitcase, and walked directly to the castle entrance. Two men stepped out as we approached. They were next to lights so bright we could barely make them out. They spoke loudly. "Halt!"

We stopped and waited. They examined us, and in a German accent said, "Are you the Americans?"

"Yes."

"They said to look for a man who was built like the old Arnold Schwarzenegger. The one on steroids. Please step forward."

We did. They stepped out from the lights and we could see them. They were dressed in khaki uniforms with riding boots. They wore armbands, red with a white circle and a black swastika in the middle, just like Hitler had worn in the twenties, and illegal as hell in Germany. They were clearly not afraid of being arrested. They walked up to us. "Put out your arms."

Neither of us did. "We're not going to be searched. We're armed, and we're not turning over our weapons. If that's not agreeable, you'd better contact Herr Eidhalt right away."

"No one is to be armed."

"*You* are."

They looked at each other unsure what to do. Everyone had been searched and everyone knew that they were not to be armed. It was one of the preconditions. "Everyone is searched, no exceptions."

"We are the exception. Call him."

One of them retreated to the guardhouse and picked up the phone. He spoke in a tone low enough that we couldn't hear, looked at us, nodded, and hung the phone back up. He came out of the shack, came over to us, and said, "He will discuss it with you himself. Follow me."

He turned and walked as the other guard remained in position. We followed him, with Jedediah carrying the leather case. He opened a huge wooden door in an arched entrance to the lower level of the castle. When we stepped inside two more guards joined the escort, walking behind Jedediah. We followed the first guard down a long hallway that was damp and cold. We went up some stairs in the middle of the castle to a large receiving area, where a wooden door led to another room. The guard opened the door. We entered, and he closed the door loudly behind us. It was an ornate den with leather furniture, tall bookshelves, and a massive desk in the middle of the room.

Rolf Eidhalt was sitting at the desk. He rose, came around, and shook our hands. "Welcome! I'm glad you came. Many of the others are here, but we still have many more to arrive. I'm letting them gather in one of the ballrooms where there are hors d'oeuvres and alcohol, as well as innumerable pieces of Nazi memorabilia and photographs. In the room next to that ballroom, however, is a room full of uniforms. Tonight, as a symbol of our international unity, and the resurrection of Nazism as a worldwide movement, we will all don the new uniforms that I have designed based on the old Nazi traditions. Mostly, those of the SS, of course," he said smiling. "I have uniforms for the two of you as well. But first, we must discuss your insistence on remaining armed. I don't allow anyone to be armed."

I looked at him intently. "Except you and your men."

"Exactly. Except me and my men. I'm putting this on, I'm paying for everything. It is my thing. I will not have anybody disrupt it by a coup of some kind."

"There cannot be a coup because you don't *lead* anything. This is a volunteer gathering. Anybody can leave anytime they want."

"I agree. But I will *not* have any violence." He sounded like he was trying to be in charge but at the same time was afraid he wasn't.

"Nor will I. But the only way I can prevent it is by making it known that anyone who might try it, will end up dead. See, we stupid Americans believe that the best way to avoid violence is to be ready to defend yourself. Just a bunch of *Second Amendment* bullshit, you understand, but there you are."

He fought back a smile. "Yes, I have heard that you handle a weapon very well. How is it that you have that skill?"

"Where'd you hear that?"

"Just around."

"Former military."

"What military?"

"Navy."

"You were a former SEAL?"

"No. Aviation."

"And you know how to handle weapons like that?"

"Like what? What exactly have you heard?"

"It doesn't matter. But you may not be armed here."

"Then we will leave. We are carrying the most important symbol here. The thing *some* people have already tried to kill us for. Maybe that's what you heard about. We found it, we have it, and we've tested it—"

"We all tested it."

"We all tested it, and know it is of literally infinite value. If you think we're going to walk unarmed into a room of men who would like nothing more than to have it for themselves, you're mistaken. We'll keep our weapons or we will leave. You tell me which."

"If you try anything, I have hundreds of armed men around and you will not succeed."

I said nothing.

"So now, if you would go to the uniform room and select a uniform for tonight."

The thought of wearing a Nazi SS uniform almost made me throw up. "I don't wear uniforms."

"It is for unity. Everyone will wear it."

"Everyone except me. If you push it we'll take our flag and go home."

He smiled and paced around the room. "Your trump card, yah? You'll take your flag and go home. Well, maybe I wouldn't care."

"That's fine, we just have to do this in a way in which we both agree. You're setting up the meeting, and I'm deferring to you. But I am not going to be your boy. I'm not going to dress up in a uniform just because you said so." He considered me, looked at the flag, said, "At least you wore black. That's enough for tonight." He looked at Jedediah then back. "What about him?"

"He can speak for himself."

Jedediah volunteered, "I'd be happy to wear an SS uniform. Best damn uniform ever designed in the history of the world. Sign of strength and dedication. And intimidation. I assume yours isn't like the old uniforms, but if it's close, I'm in."

I asked, "Tell us how you're going to conduct all of this. What's the plan?"

"You'll see in due time, but now we have to get you dressed," he said to Jedediah. "But I will tell you this; the center piece of this entire production will be the flag. I'm going to have both of you behind stage. We're going to put the flag on a pole, and I want you to carry it." He said, staring at Jedediah who stared back.

"I want you to carry it with one hand on the pole, like a leader of an Olympic procession. And I want you to bring it out at just the right time. No one knows it's here except the three of us, and a couple of my friends. But I will tell you, once we do this, it will be the thing around which everybody rallies. It will be the greatest thing in the movement."

"Okay, what else is going to happen?" I asked

"You'll see. But it's going to be a long, long night."

He checked his watch and walked to the door. "It is time for you both to go. One of my men will show you where to go behind the stage, I will be preparing the rest, and you'll know when it's time to start."

One of his men escorted us down to the stage area. We could see it from behind the curtain. It opened up onto a huge courtyard. The courtyard was surrounded on three sides by the castle, whose ornate stone walls rose to a height of four or five stories. It was beautiful and in immaculate condition. The courtyard was a deep cobblestone that looked to be hundreds of years old. At the end of the cobblestone was a huge grassy area, like a football field or a parade ground, the size of five or six football fields together. It was where there might normally be an ornate garden in a medieval castle. But here it was just grass, extending perhaps four hundred yards to the end. It was completely surrounded and enclosed by a fifteen-foot-high stone wall made of the same stone as the castle itself. On top of the wall was broken glass embedded in the concrete capping. At the end of the grass area, right by the wall, were two huge barns made out of wood. They appeared to be new and unweathered. Their construction and design were out of character with the rest of the castle.

Jedediah looked around for the flagpole as I stood waiting. "You gonna wear the uniform?" I asked him.

"Might just go with my own uniform." He removed his fleece and underneath I saw a skin-tight, short-sleeved black V-neck shirt that had a large bold SS on it. The Schutzstaffel.

"Where did you get that?" I asked.

"Had it for a long time. Always waited for the right time to wear it."

"Now's the time. You look pretty menacing with that shirt on. I think Eidhalt will approve."

Jedediah stopped what he was doing and looked at me. "I look menacing all the time."

I couldn't disagree. "Is that how you like it?"

"Makes life easier. I usually get what I want."

Eidhalt came out wearing a black uniform in the form of the World War II SS uniforms with knee-high shiny leather boots. He wore a cap with a skull on it, but noticeably absent from his uniform was any insignia. No SS or Nazi insignia. I asked, "Is that the new uniform? There's no insignia."

"You'll see."

Jedediah asked, "Where's the pole? How am I supposed to display the flag?"

Eidhalt shook his head. "Again, you will see. You must be patient." He checked his watch. "But now, everyone is here. It's time." He looked at me, "You keep the case with the flag. I want them to see Jedediah and make a hint to them that something important and special will occur later. Come with me."

We walked onto what I thought was a patio but turned out to be a long deck that went halfway around the castle two stories above the courtyard. We walked around to the middle of the deck overlooking the courtyard, which was completely dark. There were no lights anywhere but you could see dark forms of people seated below. They could probably see the silhouettes of the three of us standing on the balcony from some ambient light from the castle. I stepped back out of sight, still carrying the case. I set it down beside me and ensured I was out of the line of sight against the wall of the castle. Eidhalt turned around and looked at me and gave me a slight nod, understanding, and then turned and took a step forward to a microphone that was awaiting him. Jedediah was one step behind him and to his right. Eidhalt stepped up to the microphone, and yelled in German, "*Steht auf!*"

I moved around to the right so I could see across the balcony down to the courtyard. I could barely make out fifty or sixty dark figures now standing rigidly at attention. Suddenly, I heard soft music, growing louder. It was a men's choir, building; then the music was turned up so loud conversation would have been impossible. "*Deutschland über alles.*" The German National Anthem, a recording of a male chorale with a hundred-piece band. It was spectacular. I could hear many of the men in the courtyard singing in the dark. And they were all singing the now prohibited first stanza, the one with the famous lyrics, "Germany, above all." Only the third stanza was the official National Anthem now, about unity and justice and freedom. Not tonight. Tonight it was Germany, Germany—Nazism—above everything, *über alles.*

At the climax of the song, suddenly flood lights illuminated everything. The castle was lit by up lighting and the people in the courtyard were bathed in direct white light. There were poles extending fifty feet into the air with draped Nazi flags hanging vertically, held in place by cross bars above and below. They were brand new and their blood red colors were vibrant. The white was perfect and the black swastikas in the middle were crisp, symmetrical, and stunning. I looked behind Eidhalt and saw that a massive crest, the Nazi Eagle with the eagle's talons wrapped around arrows and the swastika—just like the one pulled down from the Reichstag at the end of the war—was suspended from the top of the castle behind him. It must have been ten feet high and forty feet across. It shimmered in the light. As the German national anthem ended, a door opened to my right and a line of men emerged and marched in front of me around the balcony. The line kept coming and coming. When they were done there must have been a hundred men lining the balcony overlooking the courtyard. They all wore black uniforms, and insignia of the SS. But on the other collar, instead of another SS insignia there was a silver W. They all wore the same knee-high leather boots and riding pants that Rolf Eidhalt was wearing. They wore uniform blouses with choker collars and a leather holster with a leather strap that hung across their chests in black patent leather. They stood there silently at attention as Eidhalt approached the microphone again.

Eidhalt spoke. "*Willkommen*! I began in German, but I will continue in English because I know each of you speaks English. It will be our language of choice since we come from so many countries. You have come here from twenty different countries. I have picked each one of you for distinguishing himself within your own country in the Nazi movement. A movement which is the Third Reich emerging from the shadows, from silence, from its underground ways for the past sixty-five years. We have chosen the moment. We emerge now to change the world! To take over the parts of the world that we can subdue, and to rally the people to our cause! Many important and significant things will happen tonight. Give me your time and your attention! It will not be wasted. You all know me, I am Rolf Eidhalt. I am the chancellor of the Third Reich in Germany, or the Fourth Reich as we will call it. My vice chancellor is Konrad Krupp. And you can see some of my men, of which these are simply a few of thousands, have their insignia. I will now receive my insignia from Herr Krupp. Please stand at attention as I receive my insignia. He turned to his right and Krupp moved up and extended his arms and pinned the insignia to his two collars. He turned back to the microphone as Krupp stood behind him. And now each of you will receive the same insignia from another member of our corps."

A large number of men emerged from under the balcony. I couldn't see them but could now hear them. They must have come out at the same time as the ones on the balcony and lined up underneath us. Each went to one of the men in the courtyard and pinned the SS insignia on the left collars and a new insignia on their right collars. They then went back to their positions underneath the balcony.

Rolf spoke, "You will see that while we have insignia and we have membership badges, we do not have rank. None of us have rank. None of us is above or better than any of the others. How do you propose that we establish a hierarchy, a structure? I called myself chancellor, the chancellor of the German Nazi Party, but it is my objective to form a single, unified world party. But I will not do that on my own. I will provide the ability, but we will all agree on the structure. We will do it the same way Hitler first came to power, democratically. But thereafter it will be a dictatorship. Just like Hitler. I ask you all to please remain standing. Assume a position of parade rest. On my command, "*Rührt Euch!*"

The men assumed a position of parade rest in a slightly relaxed formation. Many of them looked a little awkward, never having been in the military or marched in formation of any kind.

Eidhalt continued, "I have many surprises tonight. Many that will inspire you, motivate you, and thrill you. But first, let me direct your attention to the eagle behind me."

A motorized screen came down from just under the eagle. It had to be twenty feet by thirty feet. The floodlights were dimmed except for those trained on the Nazi flags draped around the courtyard and the eagle above the screen. Suddenly the crystal clear image of Adolf Hitler came on the screen. Hitler waited for his audience to give him their undivided attention. He stood solemnly in his Nazi uniform, with his armband and his hair perfectly combed, staring at the adoring crowd, waiting, waiting longer inside the cramped and jammed building. Everyone waited for him to begin. And he let the tension build.

I knew the speech. I had watched all of Hitler's speeches. It was from the Bundestag, in 1933. It was famous. People who were there were interviewed years later; they said the speech electrified them and energized them for the rest of their lives. Even fifty years later they spoke in glowing terms. Hitler's unmistakable voice came through the loud speakers. The recording had clearly been re-mastered and digitized. The clarity of the recording was stunning. He spoke with passion and power. His unmistakable gestures were present throughout. And for those who did not speak German the film had subtitles. Many of the men standing in the courtyard began applauding with the live crowd in the film, a marriage of the old and the new.

But soon we could see that the speech was not the full speech. It was a medley of Hitler's greatest moments. From Munich to Nuremberg to Berlin, from the Olympics to German Army units, building and building in its drive and determination. And then there were images clearly taken from *Triumph of the Will*. The adoring crowds, the crying women, the people reaching out to touch Hitler and then the scene that I really should have expected but didn't. Hitler walked slowly in front of several German units, stopping at each one, and then reaching beside him, where Otto Hessler held the Blood Flag. Hitler took the Blood Flag in his hand and touched it to the banner of each unit and then Hitler glanced up at the Blood Flag in admiration, a moment I had never noticed before. The image froze and stayed on the screen above the eagle.

Eidhalt stepped up to the microphone. "I told you I had a surprise. The surprise is far greater than anything you could have imagined. I knew when I issued my challenge that one of you would distinguish himself in a way that would set the direction of this movement for the remainder of a thousand years that began with the *Führer*. As you can see in the image behind me, the most treasured item in Nazi lore was the *Blutfahne*. The Blood Flag. And many of you, who know our history, know that it disappeared in 1944 and has never been seen since. Until tonight."

I could hear the men in the courtyard murmuring and looking around. Eidhalt continued, "I would like to introduce to you Mr. Jedediah Thom, from the United States. It was he who tracked down the *Blutfahne*." He paused and lowered his voice. "How do we know it's the real one? Because we have now authenticated it with the DNA of one of the men who died on it during the beer hall *putsch* in 1923! We dug up his grave! We have the Blood Flag! It is authentic and we have it here *tonight!*"

Spontaneous applause thundered through the courtyard, with cheers pushing the clapping ever higher. Even Eidhalt's men who lined the balcony above and below burst into applause. They were unaware of the flag's presence. The energy generated from Hitler's speeches had just been ignited. The applause built to a roar. I had to hand it to Eidhalt. He had watched enough of Hitler's ways to know how to motivate people, and how to stimulate them. Eidhalt raised his hand to quiet the men. They stopped. He said, "The Blood Flag is with me on the balcony. Right now, as we speak. I know you want to see it. And I want to show it to you. It will be the focus of what we do." He held up his hand. "But not yet. You'll see it tonight, I promise, but not yet, and—not here. This, this is simply our first stop tonight. I suspect that we're being watched. It may even be that some of you have alerted the authorities to what is happening tonight. I don't think so, and I hope not, but I prepare for everything. We all need to take security precautions. There are those who hate our movement and will hate us. The government of Germany hates its own past and history, even if the people might rise in favor of it. But that will not stop us. Because tonight the Fourth Reich begins! So we will bring the *Blutfahne* with us. *Achtung!*"

The men all came to attention immediately, as another song came over the loud speakers. I recognized it. It was the "Horst Wessel Song." The rallying song for the Nazis in the forties. As the music grew louder, I noticed a sound that I'd not heard before. Turbine engines. Flood lights flashed on and illuminated the buildings and the grassy area far from the courtyard. As I looked at the barns and the light I could see that the buildings were artificial. Men in black uniforms ran to the sides of the barns, pulled on levers or chords and the walls of the barns fell to the ground. Behind the fake walls were three large black helicopters. They were starting their engines and the rotors were starting to turn.

Eidhalt yelled through the microphone, "Men of the Fourth Reich! Join me in my helicopters for a journey. A journey to the past and the future!"

The assembly broke up and was directed to the helicopters by Eidhalt's men. We followed. Jedediah and I headed for the first helicopter, a large Super Puma. It held about twenty and it filled up quickly. Jedediah and I sat in the front row on the outside by one of the portholes. Jedediah looked at me with a little bit of concern in his eyes. He spoke loud enough to be heard over the whining jet engines. "Where the hell are we going?"

"No idea."

"So what's the plan?"

"Well, my former plan is now out the window. Sort of like war, as soon as the fighting starts the plans go to shit."

"How are our friends going to track us?"

"I still have another cell. Only Alex has the number, and it's on, in my sock. They'll be able to track us for a while, and know we've left."

"Hope it works," Jedediah said.

Our helicopter was the first to go to full power. I felt the blades take the weight of the helicopter and lift us off the ground into the night. We leveled off quickly at a very low altitude, climbed over the wall and turned away from the castle, flying fast. I was disoriented and couldn't tell which direction we were headed. I could make out the lighted castle through the small window. We might be heading south to Berchtesgaden, Hitler's old headquarters. I was sure we were off to some historic Nazi location.

We settled in for the ride, which was aggressive and rough. We turned frequently but I couldn't tell if it was to avoid things or simply to be unpredictable in our flight path. We flew fast along the ground, maybe at a hundred feet. I was sure all their transponder radar gear was off and the Germans would have to find them by raw radar hits, which was unlikely at this altitude. Jedediah and I settled in for the journey, however long it was going to be. It turned out to be two and a half hours, always low, always fast, always in complete darkness. And flying in formation with two other helicopters that we could see next to us. There were no anti-collision lights—another violation of aviation rules—but enough exterior lighting that the other helicopters could be seen by the pilots. Finally we slowed, then came to a hover. The helicopters spread out, and we all descended slowly. I strained to see below us and could see the glow of lighting, but couldn't see the ground. We went into a circling pattern and I could see there were three illuminated targets on the ground. A large white center with a second large white ring on the outside.

We settled and the weight came off the blades. The engines began to quiet, and slowly the blades stopped turning. The doors opened and we were ushered out. We stood and stretched. We stood in an empty field apparently in the middle of nowhere.

There were circles painted in the grass under each helicopter illuminated by a circle of small spotlights that were outside the rotor arc of each helicopter. I could see that they were buried and anchored into the ground. The pilot got out of the helicopter and came over to the group of men we were standing with. "Won't be long. We are only here to refuel."

"Where exactly are we?" one asked.

The pilot just smiled and walked toward one of the three fuel trucks that drove slowly out of the woods and directly to each helicopter. The driver jumped out near our helicopter. He hooked a grounding clip to a steel point on the nose wheel of the aircraft then attached the single-point refueling hose. He rushed back to the truck and turned on the pump. We could hear the jet fuel rushing through the hose. Each of the other helicopters was being refueled equally quickly.

As the driver of the truck detached the hose, the pilot said, "Everybody back into the helicopter. Off we go."

The same one as before asked, "Where are we going?"

"It's just for me to get you there."

"Well, what direction are we heading?"

"We're heading in the direction I've been told to take you. Now please, get back into the helicopter. Although I suppose if you don't want to, we can leave you here. But with you or without you, we're leaving. So please, get on board."

Most complied quickly and lined up to get back to the seats they had just departed. I took one last glance around the field and saw nothing other than the people who were with us or who had come to refuel us. It was an extremely remote spot and the lights for the landing areas had already been turned out. There were just dark helicopters sitting in a dark field, with the engines now starting to turn.

CHAPTER TWENTY-ONE

We flew for another long stretch and landed in another field and refueled. I tried to remember the range of this helicopter. It was probably two to three hundred miles. We were going a long way, but since all our flying was in the complete darkness and there was no moon, I couldn't get my bearings with the stars. I had no idea what direction we were flying. It wasn't getting warmer, and we hadn't hit an ocean. So my guess was we were going east. Why we would be going east was beyond me. I, like the others, was along for the ride, hoping I'd have the wits to make all this come out right. But now I had no backup at all. No army of BKA to storm the meeting and arrest everyone. The last thing I wanted was to create the perfect meeting for all the world's Nazis and let them go back to their countries with the new weaponized version of the Nazi virus.

Finally, at what must have been two o'clock in the morning, the helicopter slowed and began descending. We settled to the ground, the engines spooled down, and the blades came to a stop. We were ushered out. I looked around quickly. A field surrounded by woods with nothing else visible except for three waiting buses. This entire thing had been planned with remarkable attention to detail.

We boarded the buses, which drove slowly over the uneven field until we reached a smooth dirt road. After a few hundred yards we rounded a corner and turned onto a paved road. We drove for about a mile. I could make out lights and vague shapes in the darkness. I was sitting in the front seat with Jedediah, with the driver slightly below us and to our left.

I could make out fences and dark, thick shapes. But the shapes were in odd formations that looked overgrown or disassembled or built into the sides of hills. As we got closer I could see the lights more clearly. There were spotlights and floodlights with other general lighting. The spotlights were illuminating something I could not yet make out. We drove through a fence and a gate into what appeared to be a compound.

It suddenly struck me where we were. The Wolfsschanze. The Wolf's Lair. Hitler's eastern headquarters in the forests of eastern Prussia, present-day Poland, where he conducted the war against Russia that he launched in 1941. Operation Barbarossa. Hitler often referred to himself as Wolf, or The Wolf. He saw it as a reflection of his destined greatness, based on the old High German combination of words Adal and Wolf, that led to the name Adolph. Noble Wolf.

The Wolf's Lair was mythical. It was where Hitler spent hundreds of days from the summer of 1941 until it was overrun by the Russians. It's where Hitler spent most of his time at the height of his power. It was where he planned the destruction of Russia that would give Germany access to the natural resources necessary to feed the German economy and arsenal, and where he would resettle German soldiers after the war and achieve the *lebensraum*, the living room, that Germany needed.

As our buses pulled up, men dressed in the now recognizable Eidhalt Nazi uniforms opened the large gates to the fence surrounding the Wolf's Lair and directed us into the compound. I could see massive chunks of stone and concrete as big as houses that used to make up the impressive bunkers of the Wolf's Lair. As we made our way deeper into the compound, I saw more men dressed in Nazi uniforms. It was like a flashback to the forties, except all of the vehicles were modern, as were the weapons. Mostly AK-47s, and some I didn't recognize. It was a heavily armed compound. How did these men even get here? How did they take over the Wolf's Lair? I didn't even know it was still standing. I had assumed, like most of Hitler's places, it had been torn down and ripped apart to avoid this very kind of thing. The Wolf's Lair was probably so well constructed that it didn't justify the amount of dynamite necessary to destroy it. It looked like most of the buildings had been destroyed, but not the massive bunkers. The forest had grown right up to the edge of the Wolf's Lair and it gave it a concealed feeling. Even at the peak of it's use, the Wolf's Lair was considered to be in the middle of nowhere, even by Hitler. He said of all the places for the generals to pick to place his headquarters, they had picked the most out of the way, near nothing, mosquito-infested swamp they could find.

And what better place to start a new war? And of course, it was here that Hitler had shown his immortality. It was here in 1944 that Operation Valkyrie came to a head and colonel Von Stauffenberg placed a bomb under the table where Hitler stood during a meeting in one of the non-concrete bunkers. The bomb blew up, killing four and injuring Hitler, but not killing him.

The buses stopped and we were escorted to a central area. Eidhalt welcomed us and directed us toward a low-lying building. It was part of a small hotel that was run on site by a Polish couple. We filed into the building. The couple sat bound and gagged in the corner with their eyes wide open. The room was a small café. The sixty of us crowded in, standing around not quite sure what to do. There were sandwiches and coffee waiting, and small pastries. We'd been traveling for hours and were famished, so most made for the tables with the trays of food. Some went straight to the coffee in an attempt to load up on caffeine.

The room was smartly decorated with modern tables and chairs that you might see in a new European café, with industrial carpet all over the concrete floor. The walls were painted a pale yellow and there were several inexpensive photograph replicas framed on the walls with recognizable European scenes.

I stole another glance at the couple in the corner. The contrast between the laughing men fresh out of the helicopters in their SS uniforms, the common Nazi soldiers with their Nazi helmets, and the couple bound and gagged in the corner was stark. Some sat at the tables and some stood eating sandwiches and conversing. Eidhalt walked over to Jedediah and me. "I trust your travels were comfortable."

"I didn't expect to be here tonight," I replied.

Eidhalt smiled, proud of himself. "I doubt anyone did. I bet most didn't even know this place was still accessible. They tried to destroy most of Hitler's places, but this one was indestructible. Surprisingly it is a minor tourist spot, but it is out of the way. Nobody comes here. Which makes it perfect for our purposes. I think you will enjoy tonight's festivities, and I look forward to unveiling *die Blutfahne*." He looked at his watch. "We begin in twenty minutes. I will want you with me at the back of the stage."

"Stage?"

"Yes. I have had a platform erected on top of the highest bunker. We will be flooded with light and speak through the most powerful PA system in Poland. The power of the Reich will begin again tonight."

Jedediah and I sipped coffee as Eidhalt walked to others and conversed briefly with them, making sure he knew each person by name and their country now that each was in an SS officer's uniform. I had to note that the uniforms, just like in World War II, were incredibly impressive. They were probably the best looking and most intimidating uniforms ever designed. I realized I was wearing Hugo Boss shoes; the same designer who made many of the SS uniforms in the thirties and forties.

A man approached us in one of the SS uniforms and said quietly, "He would like you to come with me now, to the back of the stage."

We followed him around to the back. As we walked toward one end of the compound, I saw the stage. It was a large wooden structure erected on top of one of the intact bunkers, an arc of impenetrable concrete overgrown with vines. Massive speaker stands stood beside it, both at the level of the stage and at the ground where we now walked. There was a large screen at the back of the stage and lower down on both sides of the bunker. There were long red Nazi banners hanging next to the screens. Lights illuminated the banners, the bunkers, and the people.

We walked around beside the bunker to the stairs that had been built up to the top. We headed up the stairs. Eidhalt was waiting for us at the top, as were several other men I didn't recall seeing before. Eidhalt turned to me, "So what do you think? Good setting?"

"Stunning," I said. "Well done. No better place to reveal *die Blutfahne*."

He grinned. "*Danke*. And we have some other surprises in store for tonight. This is the beginning!" He looked at his watch. "Five minutes. Prepare the flag. Take it out. I have prepared the perfect standard for it. It is identical to the one used by Hessler the last time the flag was seen."

Jedediah opened the case and pulled out the Blood Flag. Jedediah went to push the case aside, and realized it was still heavy. He looked up at me with a knowing glance, which I returned without expression. He moved the case carefully aside where it wouldn't be kicked or moved. We carefully unfolded the flag and put it on the standard with a Nazi Eagle on top of the wooden pole. Jedediah leaned the flag over on the pole to me while he adjusted his tight SS tank top. His tattoos and the iron cross on his throat made him the perfect Aryan.

We followed Eidhalt up the stairs to a platform that was elevated above the main platform and out of sight. In the center, directly underneath the screen, was a wide series of steps with railings that led down onto the stage. It was made for a dramatic entrance as everyone emerged below the screen into the spotlights. You could also see through the screen to the crowd beyond. Others had assembled for the ceremonies. In the darkness the spotlights cast eerie moving shadows on the trees.

Suddenly, the lights on the stage went up to full bright and music blared over the massive PA system. The German National Anthem again, then the "Horst Wessel Song." Then silence. Finally Eidhalt, with two of his men on either side, marched down the stairs and out into the center of the stage in front of the microphone. There were high-definition cameras on stage and in front of the stage taping everything.

He stood at the microphone looking out over the group of newly dressed SS officers and his numerous Nazi soldiers that surrounded all of them. There had to be two hundred men, maybe three hundred. All dressed in black. All illuminated indirectly by the spotlights that highlighted the banners climbing to the sky and the Nazi emblems everywhere. Eidhalt spoke, "Fall in!"

No one knew what to do, but the Nazi soldiers guided them. Each line on the right was designated and one man was told to stand there at attention. Others fell into each person's left, forming eight or so lines deep. They were all at attention.

Eidhalt yelled, "Dress right, dress!"

Some who had been in the service knew what was meant and extended their left arms out while looking to their right to make sure they were lined up to the person to their right. The others copied and the lines quickly formed in perfect symmetry.

"Ready front!"

They dropped their left hands and turned their heads toward the front, toward him.

Eidhalt paused, looked around, and yelled, "*Sieg*—"

They all got it. "*Heil!*"

As soon as he said *Sieg* he raised his hand to the middle of his chest and when they said *Heil*, he extended his arm fully with his hand out flat in front of him in the traditional Nazi salute.

"*Sieg.*"

"*Heil!*"

"*Sieg.*"

"*Heil!*"

It was a chilling sight. The international leaders of the neo-Nazis were relishing their chance to play Nazi. The soldiers behind them and around them and behind the stage and in the woods all matched the Nazi salute.

Eidhalt spoke, "The Fourth Reich begins tonight! We have waited for this moment. The whole world waits for this moment. Those who now follow us wait, and those who live in fear and frustration and anger, wait. Those who can't identify the source of their discomfort, wait. Those who have fought against oppression their whole lives, wait. And they all wait for *us*. They wait for vision, leadership, energy, determination, and justice! The things we bring!" The world Nazi leaders burst into thunderous applause. There had been hesitation on whether they were bound to stand silently like soldiers at a lecture, but that was gone. They could not contain their enthusiasm and energy. I could see him looking toward us. He had a strong powerful voice. He had watched enough Hitler videos. He knew how to pause. He knew how to raise his voice in anger and yet subside in humility. He was powerful, and would be a powerful adversary.

"Why now? Why us? Because the time has come and we have waited long enough. Events have come together. What events? Many of us are from Europe, and Europe is on the verge of collapse. They made the foolhardy decision to make one currency! They allowed the drunkards from Greece and Spain and Italy to have the same borrowing power as the great Germany. They will pull us all down and we will all drown in the miscreated 'European Union.' The currency will collapse, and it will be like Germany in the thirties! Money will have no value, governments will be in a panic, and people will look for answers. That time is nearly upon us. One year, maybe two. We will be prepared.

"But more importantly, people have now understood what we have understood. The only way forward is *security*. The curse of progress is mongrel immigration.

"But what about the Jews? The scourge of the thirties, the scourge of history. The Jews are easy, we need not concentrate on the Jews. They will always be there. We always go after the Jews. People are not focused on them like they were at one point. Today's Jew? Today's Jew? Today's Jew is the *Muslim*!

"It is Islam that is Satan's hand, ruining the world. It is Islam that has tried in the past to take over Europe militarily, and is now taking over all of our countries and most of yours by immigration, forced imposition of sharia law, and terrorism! Our governments do nothing! They cower and cry 'multiculturalism!' They quiver and shake under the pointed finger of the Imams, who stand behind political correctness to keep us from even *criticizing* Islam. It makes Jewish Bolshevism child's play. Islam demands spiritual allegiance. Islam demands obedience at the point of a sword. Islam takes over countries and eliminates all other religions and ways of thinking. Islam determines what is right and wrong for itself. Lying for Islam is acceptable.

"They hate everything that we stand for. They hate everything about us and yet they continue to immigrate like rats to our countries. Muslims make up over twenty percent of France. Turkish Muslims make up fifteen percent of Germany, and the number is increasing every day. Pakistani Muslims are taking over England! Mohammad is the most common baby name in England today! This is a disgrace!

"This is our rallying cry. *We* will do what our governments are afraid to do! We will take on Islam. We will fight these rag-head terrorists! We will throw them out! We will push them back to where they came from. We will establish the Fourth Reich and the dominance of white rule!"

The crowd burst into screams of "*Sieg Heil! Sieg Heil!*"

Eidhalt raised his hand again. "But we and those who are with us are men of *action*. We will not stand by and watch the Western world collapse under financial irresponsibility. We will no longer allow our governments to borrow away our future and our children's futures and welcome a take-over from Islam. We will not allow our countries to degenerate morally and spiritually under pressure from the Jews and Muslims. We will no longer prostrate ourselves in front of the oil-rich Arabs who use oil to choke us to death. Once we take over our countries' governments, we will establish an international oil cartel whose prices will be determined by *us*. That will allow for thriving economies without extortion from Islamic rats who never created or did anything! They own the oil wells through no effort of their own! They were all developed and run by Western companies!

"To all of those who know we are coming, the wait is over. It is time to rise up! To take on the forces arrayed against us. To throw out the immigrants from the Middle East. To reestablish the sovereignty of our countries. To reestablish financial stability, and racial purity. Mongrel nations fail. Pure nations thrive! *Sieg!*"

"*Heil!*"

"So where do we go from here? We will have elections. But inside our party I have made temporary assignments of authority. It will be by region. I will be the *Führer*. I take that only because of my experience and, frankly, my finances. I'm able to do this, and I'm able to finance all of you. Each of the rest of you will be the head of your country's Nazi Party. We will all wear the same uniforms, we will all swear allegiance to the same constitution. We will all begin our efforts to rally the people in our countries who agree with us. And we will do it with action.

"You will see action tonight. In just a few minutes, you will see something that will shock you and will inspire you. We strike in every country at the same time in the same way. We will strike the mosques, we will strike the markets, and we will strike television stations. In particular, we will strike everything owned by Muslims. You remember *Kristallnacht*? It was on *this very day* seventy-one years ago! November 9th and 10th, 1938! People rose up against the Jews in Germany. Thousands were arrested. A thousand synagogues were burned! Jewish shops were destroyed! Glass from the shops covered the streets! Crystal everywhere! Crystal Night! November 9th! But for us, today? The same thing? No. Not the Jews. Not yet. For us it is the Muslims! I want *ten* thousand Mosques burned all around the world! I want fire bombs, Molotov cocktails, assassinations, looting! Mayhem and pandemonium on the Muslims! And every day thereafter until the revolution is over."

He waited while the applause died. He continued, "Tonight, I have another surprise. Perhaps one of the greatest moments in all of Nazi history will be before you tonight."

Eidhalt turned to us and gestured. Jedediah lifted up the flag and we walked to the front of our platform and prepared to go down the stairs. He continued, "Tonight, as I promised, we have with us the most important piece of Nazi history in existence. I challenged each of you to do something to prove your worthiness to be here tonight. And each of you did. But one group rose above the rest. The American Southern Volk achieved what I thought was unachievable! And they have brought here something that I did not know existed any longer.

"Gentlemen, what holds the blood of the first Nazi martyrs? What accompanied Hitler on his beer hall *putsch* ninety-six years ago today?" He paused and waited. "*Die Blutfahne*! The Blood Flag!" He turned and gestured for us to come down.

Jedediah began walking down the stairs with the flag out in front of him, low enough to get under the screen. The "Horst Wessel Song" began again, but at a lower volume. As soon as Jedediah cleared the screen he raised the flag straight up, and it swayed in the light breeze.

Eidhalt spoke over the song as Jedediah walked. "We dug up the bodies of the first Nazi martyrs and matched their DNA to this flag. This is it! Rally to it, men! Rally to it!"

Jedediah stood just to his right with the spotlight focused on him. The flag now lowered slightly so that it draped down and could be seen. The men below started screaming and yelling. "*Sieg Heil!* The *Blutfahne!* Long live Nazism!"

They were nearly in a frenzy. He waited, encouraging them to continue their outpouring of shock and joy. He said, "*Die Blutfahne!* Our rallying point! We will keep it safe! We will display it! Each of you will touch it tonight and take the blessings of this talisman with you back to your countries! Begin your own flag tradition based on this night! And one week from Monday, show your flags! Put them on your cars! Put them in your windows! Leave them at the scenes of the fires! Tell people who we are!"

Eidhalt waited as the men cheered and roared. He spread out his arms, waiting for more. Encouraging them, yet more still.

"*Sieg!*"

"*Heil!*"

He raised his hand to quiet them down, but they would not, they carried on and on, screaming their support for the Blood Flag. Expressing their energy, their anger, and their enthusiasm.

He raised both hands and they quieted. "The Blood Flag. We have built the bridge from the founding of the Nazi party to today. We have retrieved the first and most important symbol of Nazism and are prepared to carry it forward into the future. Tonight it begins. But we must show the world we are serious. Dead serious. This is not some club. This is not a debating society." He looked around with his arms out to his sides. "What is the threat?"

He waited. There was no immediate response. He yelled, "*What is the threat?*"

Finally, a few yelled out. "Islam!"

He yelled back, "Islam! They hate everything we stand for! They have invaded our countries, they have crippled and intimidated our governments, they have killed our people, and they will never rest." He paused. "Neither will we!"

Suddenly, I felt a rustle of people to my right as three or four men's boots clattered up the stairs past me. They were four Nazi-uniformed soldiers dragging a man whose hands were handcuffed behind him and who had a hood pulled completely over his head so he couldn't see. He was struggling and fighting. The men holding him were too big and strong to give him any room. They forced him down the steps and out onto the stage.

Eidhalt looked at them and motioned for them to stand to his left out on the front of the stage. "And here, here is our first message. This is where it starts. Men, I bring you a terrorist. A man who has sworn the destruction of the Western world. A man who was sent to infiltrate anti-German groups and finance them, to create even more difficulty in our country.

"This is Mohammed al-Hadi! This virus, this Muslim pile of shit, is from al Qaeda, the bacteria that infects everything and ruins everything. Just like the Jewish bacteria did in the twenties and thirties, it must be stopped. And the stopping begins here. And it starts here tonight! Why him? Because he is the one who killed Germans in Munich and Berlin! He is the one who is responsible for the bombings of the subways! And what have our security forces done about it? Nothing! How is it we have him and they don't? Because we have better intelligence than they do! We are better informed! And we are more effective!

"Answer this: How many Westerners, how many Europeans, how many of your people have been killed by al Qaeda? How many have been murdered and beheaded on the Internet? Well, we can access the Internet too. Let's see how they like it."

He stepped back and nodded to one of the guards holding Mohammed. The guard undid the rope around his neck and ripped off the hood. Mohammad shook his head and blinked at the bright spotlights that shown on him from multiple angles. Two cameramen approached closely. One from below the stage. The other climbed up on the stage and stood three or four feet away, focusing the camera directly on his face.

Eidhalt yelled, "They want beheadings on the Internet? They shall have one. One of their own! And if this angers them? All the better! We are coming after them. They will never know where to find us. They will never know who we are! This man's death will be posted on the Internet in hours. And we will disperse from here and make our way out of Poland and disappear. They will never find us. I will operate from an undisclosed location, but I will be easy to communicate with. I will tell you what to do next. Let it begin!"

He stepped back as two of the guards forced Mohammad down onto his knees. The other two removed large hook-shaped knives from sheaths in their belts and pulled Mohammad's head back. One took his right hand and dug the point of the knife into Mohammed's neck. Mohammed began screaming and fighting, which caused the point of the knife to go deeper into the neck. Blood ran down the knife point and dripped onto the stage. Mohammed screamed and fought. The guard dug the knife deeper.

I couldn't believe my eyes. They were going to cut this man's head off right on the stage in front of us as he screamed through his death. The very man I had been tracking. It seemed suicidal to pick a fight with al Qaeda, but I also noted its brilliance. If Eidhalt and others could operate in an area outside of the ability of al Qaeda to find them, al Qaeda would attack the countries where these men came from. They would attack Germany and England and America. And if the attacks had any degree of success, they would cause panic and anger at al Qaeda. If the attacks were even marginally effective, they could shut down entire sections of cities for days at a time. One bomb in one pizza parlor in New York City would create havoc for days. They were begging al Qaeda to attack, to cause the very panic that they wanted to take advantage of. To impose "security and discipline" they were going to take on Islam directly.

And if Eidhalt was even half right, that Europe was on the brink of financial disaster and economic decline, if depression was around the corner and the populations felt insecure because of al Qaeda attacks, he might very well have success in creating the fertile soil necessary for Nazism to rise again. It was completely rational and frightening.

Mohammed screamed as the knife plunged deeper as his head tilted slightly to the left. I didn't see any arterial blood yet, but I was sick from what I was seeing. Jedediah stole a glance at me.

Suddenly from behind me, I heard an outburst of gunfire. I couldn't see clearly but I saw lights from vehicles. Then I saw the flashes of police lights on top of the vehicles. The Polish police. They were at the gate demanding entrance. But the Nazi guards were having none of it. They fired their automatic weapons directly at the police through the fence as other Nazi guards raced toward the gate, assault rifles ready. Hundreds of rounds flew back and forth. Eidhalt told the guards on the stage to stop as he walked up the stairs underneath the screen and looked back toward the gate. He yelled some commands in German and several men ran toward the gate. Three of them had RPGs. At least fifty more Nazi's unflung their automatic weapons and ran toward the fight. In seconds dozens of automatic weapons were unloading on the Polish police as others opened the gate. Those with the RPGs knelt and fired on what I could now see were Polish SWAT vehicles. They exploded in seconds and fireballs illuminated the area. I could see at least ten policemen dead on the ground. The Nazis opened the gate and rushed through. In less than a minute, the entire fight was over. The Polish police lay dead and their vehicles burned in the darkness. One Nazi guard was dead leaning against the fence, but I saw no other casualties. Eidhalt saw what I saw and returned to the microphone.

"Our time has now come. We have been discovered and now go into our operational plan. We will finish this video elsewhere and put it on the Internet tonight. For those of you who came with me in the helicopters, it is time to go!"

The men looked around.

"We will not be heading back to Munich." He could see the look of surprise on the faces of those in front of him. He held up his hand to pacify their concerns. "But you may trust me. Our plan all along, has been to go back a different way than we came. He yelled into the microphone, "To the helicopters!"

The crowd headed toward the buses.

Jedediah lowered the flag and headed to the back of the platform. He quickly removed the Blood Flag from the pole and folded it. I knelt down and opened the case. He knelt down next to it and began placing the flag inside. He looked back over his shoulder and then looked at me with concern. "So what's the freaking plan? We're going to let them all just fly out of here on helicopters?"

I also looked around. "I thought we'd be in Munich, and we'd have the BKA to help. We're on our own now. At least we can get the leaders for murder in a Polish court."

He looked at me in amazement. "They're not going to be found. You heard him. He's got some place set up where no one will find them. And the other people, what did they do? They just came here and listened to a speech. They didn't do anything. We can't even get them arrested."

"I know. We've got to stop them."

Jedediah snapped the case shut. "Right. How?"

I stood up and held the case. "Depends on where we end up. Let's wait and see what all this brings."

"Well, what was your plan in Munich? Even if we had help."

"I have some things with me that could take care of a lot of issues."

"What the hell does that mean?"

"I replaced the lead in this case with C4. Enough to blow up a lot of things."

"And what did you plan on doing with it?"

"You know how to disable a helicopter?"

"You want to shut them down here?" He looked around. "In Poland?"

"Where better than where they murdered a bunch of Polish police? These guys will be in jail forever."

"Maybe. But by the time we get to the helicopters the blades will be turning. I know how to disable them, but I'm not getting up there with spinning blades. That would disable me."

"I'm not letting them just fly off into anonymity and hiding."

"Then you better think of something else fast."

"We've got to end this."

We went down the stairs of the platform to the bus that waited to take us to the helicopters. "If your plan is to just get them arrested and slapped on the wrist in Germany, then I don't know what I'm doing here. That's not my objective. I'm here to end it. Are you not?"

"I am. But I'm not a murderer."

"Killing in war is not murder."

"There's no war."

"Really? What do you think those Polish police think of that? Soldiers in Nazi uniforms with automatic rifles? Shooting the police force and blowing up their van with RPGs? That's not an act of war?"

I nodded. "It is. But it doesn't mean we can do whatever we want. We have to see how this plays out," I said.

"Cut it as thin as you want, but we're going to have to take drastic action. Are you ready to do that? 'Cause if you're not, give me what you have and I'll do it myself."

We climbed on to the bus and I stopped talking. Jedediah looked at me with blazing eyes. He saw the intensity of my own look and wasn't quite sure what to make of it.

* * *

As Jedediah predicted, by the time we got near the helicopters the engines were racing and the blades were turning. The three helicopters took off quickly when the last person hurried aboard. As we flew over the compound, we could see everything being dismantled. We saw Nazi soldiers removing their uniforms and leaving them on the ground. We saw others pulling motorcycles and bicycles out of hiding behind trees and riding off. The lights went out as the dark helicopters stayed low and flew north.

After fifteen minutes we passed over a small town and into a patch of vast blackness. I suddenly realized we had headed north, to the Baltic Sea, the sea north of Poland that extended past Germany to Denmark.

We stayed low. I couldn't estimate the altitude. The Polish military would certainly have radars to detect airplanes but at our altitude we were likely to evade detection. I was sure we were also EMCON, no electronic emissions at all. They couldn't be traced by the Polish Air Force or any other air defense network by their electronic signature. They'd have to find us by raw radar hits, which is nearly impossible so low over the water.

We'd been flying for an hour when I felt the nose of the helicopter come up and our forward speed slow. I tried to look out the small window next to our seat but saw nothing but darkness. The rotor grabbed more air as the slowing helicopter began to hover and descend gently. I couldn't imagine that we'd made it across the entire Baltic, to Russia or Finland. And I was quite sure we hadn't gone far enough to get back into Germany. My guess was we were still at sea.

We settled down gently, went into a short hover, and then dropped the last three or four feet. I still couldn't see what we were landing on. The weight came off the rotors, and the helicopter settled. The engine RPM decreased as the engines were shut down. Red cabin lights came on and the door to the helicopter opened into darkness. A man climbed up the steps with a flashlight and motioned for all of us to get out of the helicopter. We unbuckled, stood up, and moved to the door then down the steps. When we emerged, I saw that we were standing on the deck of a substantial ship. I looked behind us and saw the other two helicopters on their own spots, with their blades just feet apart. It was a magnificent demonstration of flying capabilities by the pilots who landed these helicopters on the ship. The ship was completely dark except for the landing area.

The landing lights went off and the regular ship's lights came on. The man with the flashlight indicated for us to follow him. He stepped inside the ship's superstructure and led us down several ladders to the main deck. We followed him down the passageway and into the ship crew's dining area. It was cramped, but all of us ultimately fit. Jedediah was right next to me and clung tightly to the case.

Eidhalt entered the room. He stood with his hands behind his back like a general waiting for his troops to be quiet. Finally everyone was quiet. He said, "I am quite sure that none of you expected to be on a ship in the Baltic when you came to my castle in Munich yesterday evening." He smiled.

He continued, "Sometimes the unexpected is pleasant. I hope you find your stay on this ship exactly that. We have staterooms for each of you, sleeping in groups of two. If you would like to change out of the uniforms, we have provided additional clothing for you to use. In fact, you may discard those uniforms for now, as new ones have been sent to your home addresses. It could be somewhat inconvenient for you to be seen ashore today or tomorrow with an SS uniform on." He chuckled and others joined in, many happy to relieve the tension.

He continued, "So what happens next? I will tell you. We are heading west in the Baltic, as an ordinary merchant ship. We look like a container ship, and we have erected large structures over the helicopters which will look from any distance of more than twenty feet like stacked containers. It will not be possible to tell that they are not, even with a very high-powered camera lens. If they have infrared, it might be more difficult, but we do not anticipate that there will be any military out here looking for us. Perhaps the police are looking for us. But that's about all. And I really doubt they're looking for a ship. We believe we are completely safe and will remain undetected. After sunrise, and the next daytime passes, you will all be taken to different locations in small but powerful boats that will meet us at a rendezvous point. Each destination will be different. Each of you will travel differently, and none of it will be traceable back to us. Some will go to Germany, some to Denmark, some all the way to Norway and even Sweden. As I told you, I have now nearly unlimited resources and want to share much of it with you in the building of the next Nazi empire. This is a small first step as we will be providing each of you with first-class tickets back to your homes when you debark from your boats.

"And now, I have a special treat." He nodded to one of his men in the back who dimmed the lights on the mess decks. Suddenly a screen was lowered behind Eidhalt, and a video began. It was of the ceremony just completed in Poland, but from a distance. You couldn't recognize anyone in the video. The picture changed, and instead of pageantry was filled with a man fighting for his life.

I tried not to gasp. It was al-Hadi. Before anyone could say anything the room was filled with al-Hadi's screams as men off-screen dug knives into his neck and blood began to run. I watched horrified as they continued to cut. I looked away, trying to appear disinterested and trying not to throw up. I looked around the room at the faces illuminated by the light reflected off the screen.

Al-Hadi continued to scream. Several of the neo-Nazi leaders in the room smiled as they watched, a couple even cheered. Others like me looked away. I glanced at Jedediah who was watching every second of it. Al-Hadi stopped screaming and all I could hear was a gurgling and cutting. I looked at Jedediah again as I heard what sounded like a head falling to the ground. He nodded. My heart raced as I fought the impulse to imagine what it looked like on the screen.

In the dim light Eidhalt spoke again. His voice sounded different. Gruffer. Meaner. "Will anyone in the world think we are something to be trifled with after this? Will anyone dare challenge us? This is just the beginning! This man, Mohammed al-Hadi, was an al Qaeda financier! He came to Germany, to fund those who agreed with their objectives. He came to me! Because he said we shared the same objective of havoc! Of wrecking the country! He didn't know who he was dealing with. I played along. I took his money—lots of it. Millions of dollars. And told him we would create havoc like he had never seen. But it won't be what he hoped for. We hate him and everything he and al Qaeda stand for! And we've shown it tonight!"

There was a splattering of applause.

Eidhalt was dark and swollen. His eyes were barely perceptible in the shadows, but his teeth glistened as he contorted his face. "The world will never be the same," he whispered. "This video will spread throughout the world like wildfire within forty-eight hours. It is our declaration. We throw down the gauntlet to al Qaeda and all of Islam who intend to destroy our countries. We will destroy them. We will destroy all of Islam. This is the beginning. Our war begins in earnest on Monday! On Monday, before midnight, as I said at the *Wolfsschanze*, I want ten thousand mosques burning. I want twenty thousand Muslim shops burned to the ground! I want the world to wake up on Tuesday to a different world!"

Many of the men nodded, although the horror of seeing the man who had been in front of them beheaded on videotape caused one or two to pause.

Eidhalt finished, "We have commissioned each of you with the *Blutfahne*, we have shown you who we are, and what we are made of, and that we are not to be trifled with or taken lightly. Return to your countries, strengthen your organizations, and begin the attacks as scheduled. You may retire to your staterooms, and each of you will be contacted and told your route, and where you will go after the rendezvous approximately eighteen hours from now. Thank you. *Sieg Heil!*"

"*Sieg Heil!*" Everyone said back.

One of the crew approached Jedediah and me and handed us keys to our stateroom, which had the number on them. He also handed us a map of the ship so that we could find it. He said, "You should be able to find it without any difficulty. If you can't, let one of us know, and we will help you."

I nodded.

I looked at Jedediah and said, "Let's go."

* * *

I knew how ships were put together and how to find a stateroom. I walked right to it, used my key to open the door, and stepped inside.

Jedediah asked quietly, "So what's the plan?"

I shook my head, put my finger to my lips to show him what I expected from him, and said, "I'm too tired for much of anything; let's just get some sleep." I shook my head indicating that's not what I had in mind at all. I looked around and he watched me as I held my hand to my ear and indicated that almost certainly this cabin was bugged and our conversation would be recorded. We stepped out through the door silently, and I closed it behind me. Anyone listening to the tape would assume that we had walked in, had a two-sentence conversation, and then closed the door behind us and gone to bed. If they listened carefully, they'd hear silence rather than the sounds of men undressing, but I'd hoped they wouldn't be listening for some time. We walked down the passageway. I carried the case in my hand. We turned a corner and headed outboard. We walked to the bulkhead and I stopped. I nodded to him.

"When I have a chance, I'm going to go up on deck and pull out my cell phone. I'll alert the BKA to where we are."

"May not have the range."

"I agree but it's worth a shot. Plus I have something else in mind."

"What?"

"I want you to get topside and disable those helicopters. Think you can do that?"

"Don't you think they'll be guarded?"

"I doubt it. He thinks they're among friends. I think everybody is going to go to bed, get up, eat breakfast, and wait for the big rendezvous."

"If there are any guards I can disable them in fifteen minutes."

I nodded as I contemplated what I had in mind. I didn't know if it would work, but if it did, it would be the end of the beginning of neo-Nazism, as Churchill might have said. "Here's what we're going to do."

CHAPTER TWENTY-TWO

By this time I knew I could count on Jedediah. They had tried to steal his soul and he was holding it against them forever. I didn't know if he had truly been "saved" as he claimed, but he sure was a different person than the one who got all those tattoos and spouted the slogans. He wanted revenge. He undoubtedly knew that the Scriptures said vengeance was God's, but he clearly thought he was the one God would use to exact that retribution.

While he headed toward the helicopters I took the suitcase and headed down the hallway. The suitcase had the Blood Flag, and in the lining underneath were fourteen bars of C4, each one inch by two inches by eleven inches wrapped tightly in thick green cellophane. This wasn't what I had thought I'd be using them for. I had thought in my super-hero mind that when the BKA closed in on the castle in Munich I could destroy some of the weapons and vehicles; but even that hadn't been all that well thought out. The BKA would almost certainly want to confiscate anything they found. Everything would be evidence. But now I was all about destruction. I couldn't even explain my expectations to myself.

I looked both ways then turned down the passageway that ran athwart ships. It would almost certainly lead to a ladder that if followed down would lead to the bilge.

I walked aimlessly like I was unable to sleep and wandering around the ship. I turned down the passageway and still saw no one. I could feel the movement of the ship under my feet. It took me back to my days in the Navy. For some reason I felt reassured by the vibrations and movement.

I found a ladder and as I turned to go down it I heard a voice behind me.

"Where are you going?" I recognized the leader of the Russian neo-Nazi group. He spoke perfect English. Kobarov was his name, as I recalled.

"For a walk. I'm like a caged animal. I need to get around some."

"By going below?"

"I'll head up on deck in just a minute."

"What's in the suitcase?"

"The flag."

"Yes," he said smiling in a way I didn't like. "I'd like to see it close up."

"No, sorry. Not for showing any more tonight."

"Why are you carrying it around?"

"It never leaves my sight."

"What about your strong friend? Why couldn't you leave it with him?"

"He's snoring away in our stateroom. One of us has to stay up. I had to get away. Goodnight," I said and turned quickly and descended the ladder, then another after that, and the one after that. I stopped, and listened, to see if he was following me. I heard nothing.

I could feel sweat forming in the small of my back. I turned away from the ladder and saw that to descend further I had to get through a closed hatch. It had a handle, like a steering wheel. It wasn't locked. I tried to turn the handle but it was frozen. Maybe dogged too tight. I put all my force into it and it finally turned. I pulled the hatch cover up, and went down into the bilge, the lowest part of the ship, separated from the ocean only by the hull. I didn't have a flashlight, but with the hatch open I could see just enough to move. A rat scurried away from me as I invaded his space. Some bilge water splashed underneath my feet. I could tell it was a single-hull ship. A double-hull ship would have presented different problems. This was an older, midsized container ship, and not well constructed.

I knelt down, pulled one of the bars of C4 out of my suitcase and jammed it against the hull in the corner with the crossbeam. I inserted the detonator and attached the timer to the detonator. I turned the dial to ten minutes, and hit start. I checked my watch and noted the time. I moved over as far as I could in that compartment to the far bulkhead and did the same thing. A rat ran across my hand as I jammed the C4 into the dark corner, inserted the detonator and set the timer for nine minutes forty-five seconds. I went to the other far bulkhead in that same compartment and did the same thing, and set that timer for nine and a half minutes. I hurried up the ladder, closed the hatch, and walked down the passageway outboard looking for another hatch. I couldn't find one.

I finally found another hatch on the port side and tried to open it. It was impossible to open. It was stuck. I saw no lock, but the handle wouldn't turn. I looked around for a tool but couldn't find one. I ran back down the passageway and turned the corner and found the fire hose on the bulkhead. In the glass window was an ax. I opened the door, pulled out the ax, and ran back to the hatch. I stuck the ax head through the handles and out the other side so that it would catch the spoke of the wheeled handle, then I pulled on the ax handle. Still nothing. I sat on the floor and braced my feet against the wall and pushed with my legs as I pulled hard, and finally the wheel gave. I turned it again with the ax handle, then pulled the handle out and turned the wheel by hand. I pulled the hatch up. A horrible stench struck my nose. The smell was violent. I descended into the dark room, and slipped off the ladder, stepping onto something soft that gave way. I knelt down and reached out with my hand to feel what it was. I felt a hand and an arm. A rotting body. I wretched, and threw up. In the near complete darkness, I could barely make out six or seven bodies in varying stages of decay. Eidhalt hadn't hired a ship, he'd stolen it and killed the crew and thrown them into the bilge. I held my breath as I planted the C4 under three of the bodies. I quickly took my cell phone out of my sock and took pictures in the darkness, hoping some would turn out. The flash of the phone camera told me I'd at least get an image. I quickly set the timer on the blast. I hurried back up to the ladder and closed the hatch. I ran to the other side of the ship and found another hatch; it opened quickly. I hurried down the ladder, set three more charges, and closed the hatch. I had three charges left, and less than seven minutes. I dashed up one ladder after another until I reached the open deck inside the simulated cargo containers. I walked to the structure that held the bridge, the electronics equipment, and all the radio equipment operating the ship. I opened my cell phone and searched for coverage. No service. Had to try. I texted the photo to Alex.

I heard a voice behind me, "What are you doing?"

I turned around to see Eidhalt as I slipped the phone into my pocket. He was smoking a cigar. "What are *you* doing?" I asked back.

"Getting fresh air and smoking a fine Cuban cigar. It was quite a day." He took a deep pull on the cigar and inhaled the smoke. He said through the smoke, "But what are you doing up here?"

"Couldn't sleep. Too much excitement."

"What were you looking at by the bridge?"

"I thought I saw something leaking."

"Really. A leak? Did you find anything?"

"No, it was just a stain on the deck."

"A stain?"

"I'm sure it's fine." He continued to stare at me, clearly not believing what I was telling him.

"I'd like you to come with me to my stateroom to discuss some things."

"Nah, thanks. I just need to get some air."

"No. Come to my stateroom now."

"Actually, I'm not feeling very well. I'm a little bit seasick. And I've heard that if you stay up on deck, you are much less likely to get sick."

"Perhaps. But you're coming to my stateroom now." He reached into his shirt and pulled out a gun and pointed it at me. "And I think it's time that you gave me the Blood Flag."

"So this is how it is, huh?" I kept my hands at my side, but was very conscious of the .45 in his hand. "We do everything you ask; we come over here and help you with your meeting. You feature our flag as your centerpiece and then you take it from us at gunpoint?"

"That flag is the last piece of the puzzle I have been putting together. I would offer to buy it from you, but I don't believe you'd sell it to me."

"You're right. I wouldn't."

"You have nowhere to go. You were never going to leave this ship with the flag. We'll just have this conversation now, earlier than I had originally planned. Come with me."

"Who are you anyway?" I said closing the distance slightly, almost within arm's reach. "Rolf Eidhalt isn't your name. You think I wouldn't know it's an anagram used by Hitler when he was in exile? It's the letters of "Adolph Hitler" rearranged. You didn't think I'd know that?"

He smiled. "I actually hoped someone would. I chose it carefully and with pride. I knew you were smarter than the others."

"You can't have the flag." I could almost feel the time ticking away. I had placed one of the C4 sticks against the superstructure right behind him. If it went off we'd both be vaporized.

"Yes I can. You have nowhere to go."

He raised his handgun, which gave me the one second I needed. I grabbed his right wrist with my right hand and pushed his arm away from me. I leaned back and stomped on the outside of his right knee, smashing it to the deck and ripping tendons. He cried out in pain as I took both hands and twisted the weapon in his hand. He had to let go or his hand would break. I took his weapon and put it in my belt.

"Your time is over." I brought my right foot up sharply and kicked him in the face. He fell over on the deck as I sprinted toward the back of the ship. The best I could tell the large tent-like covering that made the ship look like a container ship had only two openings, one forward near where we'd been standing and one in the stern. I ran to the stern, found the flap in the heavy fabric, pulled them apart, and dove off the ship into the black sea below. The deck was fairly high off the water and I would have preferred to have jumped feet first, but didn't want to take the additional time.

I wished it even more when I hit the water. I had over rotated and landed nearly flat on my back. It knocked the breath out of me as I sank into the water. I held my breath and tried to maintain my consciousness while evaluating whether I had broken my back. I didn't go too deep because of the flatness of my entry, and I was soon back on the surface. I gasped for breath and began treading water. I took my shoes off and let them drop into the Baltic. I was in the process of removing my pants when I heard a voice.

"You okay?" It was Jedediah rowing one of the lifeboats from the ship.

"Yeah," I said, breathing hard. "I thought I broke my back."

"That was some exit. I thought you'd be a little more cautious."

"Eidhalt found me planting C4 by the superstructure. He was holding me at gunpoint."

"Shit. What happened?"

"I grabbed his gun and smashed his knee and ran for the back. Here I am. Thanks for picking me up."

"You get the charges set?"

"Yeah." I looked at my watch. "One minute."

Jedediah rowed away from the ship as the ship steamed away at eight or nine knots. I waited. I thought of everything that had transpired, everything I had done, every place I had been. Everything since the summer in France, which now seemed so long ago.

I stared at the ship as it got smaller. I was beginning to wonder if I had set the charges right, when I heard the first one go off. I expected a sound like a crack or a loud bang, but instead it was a muffled whoompf followed in rapid succession by several other explosions. Some loud, some muffled, but now cascading over each other as the shockwaves rolled over us. Suddenly, more lights came on and the ship stopped dead in the water. I thought I saw the bow come up, and then I saw the frame that held the tent-like super-structure painted to resemble containers collapse. The bow of the ship was pointing upward in a sick broken way. The ship's back had broken. The stern now pointed upwards and raced the bow to the sky. Jedediah continued to row slowly as we watched the ship sink. From the first explosion until the ship vanished was less than four minutes.

Jedediah said, "Nice job setting those charges. Are you a secret ordnance guy or something?"

"Just went low and stayed by the waterline. You get a big enough rupture the ship just can't stay afloat. All the damage control in the world won't help you."

"I've never seen a ship sink before," Jedediah said.

I listened to the lifeboat cut through the flat Baltic and stared in the direction of the ship. "I found a bunch of rotting bodies. Ship's crew I'd bet. I got a couple of photos, but my phone is now soaked. I tried to text one to Alex. I think Eidhalt stole the ship and murdered the crew in cold blood."

"Guess he got what was coming to him."

"We'll need to keep rowing to make sure we don't run into any of their lifeboats."

"Nothing to worry about there."

I turned and looked at Jedediah behind me. "Meaning?"

"I disabled some of their lifeboats, and locked the others to the deck with steel cables."

I stared at him in the dark and he stared back at me. I saw no remorse. "They don't have lifeboats?"

He shook his head slowly with satisfaction.

"We've got to go get the survivors!" I moved toward Jedediah who held tight to the oars. I knew I couldn't wrest them out of his hands.

"Not a chance. They are a bunch of murderers."

"Yeah but we're not. I didn't come here to kill anybody. I just wanted them floating out there, so the German Navy or Polish Navy or whoever could pick them up and put them in prison. We have them for even more murders with the ship's crew. Turn around!" I stood in the bobbing lifeboat.

Jedediah continued to row slowly. I heard the slap of the oars against the water. He said, "This is *exactly* what you wanted since the day we met. You just needed me around so you could tell yourself it was all my doing."

I scoured the water for survivors. I listened for cries. Nothing. I sat down.

He kept rowing, then asked, "What happened to the flag?"

"I wrapped it around one of the bricks of C4."

"Gone forever," he said with satisfaction. He rowed in silence, then said, "Your father will be proud."

After contemplating I finally answered him. "I'm not so sure."

ACKNOWLEDGEMENTS

Many have helped immensely in the creation of this book. I would like to thank especially my good friends from Germany, Florian Köhler and Patrick Sonnenstrahl, who not only encouraged me and helped me with innumerable details about Germany, German law, and German history but also were gracious enough to allow me to use their very authentic names as characters in the book. I would also like to thank Nita Woodruff for her research assistance into DNA. My thanks also go out to my good friend inside the FBI, who gave me great insight into the inner workings of the agency and details that are difficult to come by. He asked that he remain anonymous, and I am happy to honor that request.